Showdown!

"Come across with my money, McCall!" Texas Jack demanded.

"I don't owe you a damn thing," the rancher snarled.

"The hell you don't. I played your dirty game rustlin' calves for you....And all fer nothin'?"

"You're a liar, Texas. I'll blow your laig off!" McCall roared, his right hand going for his hip.

But the cowboy's brown hand flashed down and out—and there was a deafening roar.

McCall's gun clattered to the ground, and his hands clasped his stomach. "My—Gawd!" he gasped. "You've bored me!"

WYOMING
was originally published by Harper & Row, Publishers, Inc.

*Are there paperbound books you want
but cannot find in your retail stores?*

ZANE GREY

Wyoming

PUBLISHED BY POCKET BOOKS NEW YORK

WYOMING

Harper & Row edition published July, 1953

POCKET BOOK edition published November, 1962

8th printing.........March, 1972

This POCKET BOOK edition includes every word
contained in the original, higher-priced edition. It is printed
from brand-new plates made from completely reset, clear, easy-to-read
type. POCKET BOOK editions are published by POCKET BOOKS, a division
of Simon & Schuster, Inc., 630 Fifth Avenue, New York, N.Y. 10020.
Trademarks registered in the United States and other countries.

L

1

WHEN MARTHA ANN DIXON found herself on the open Nebraska road she realized with a shock that at last her innate propensity for running away from home had definitely materialized. She pinched herself. . . . It was true. She was here, and her face was turned to the West!

Her first yielding to this strange wanderlust had occurred at the age of five when she ran off from her aunt's home on the shore of Lake Michigan and was found strolling about in the woods as naked and unashamed as any little savage. The second excursion, a flight from school, had come somewhat later; and then there had followed other occasions not so vividly remembered.

But this one, in the last year of her teens, was vastly different. This adventure was the result of long planning and deliberation to make a dream come true, a dream of lovely roads and bright-colored hills, of dim horizons and purple ranges, and at last the longed-for goal—the West.

The rattle of a slowing Ford swerved Martha Ann off the road.

"Hello, kid. Want a lift?" called out a cheery voice. A redheaded, freckle-faced youth accommodated the speed of his car to her brisk stop.

"No, thanks," she replied, "I'd rather walk."

"Cripes! If youse ain't a girl! 'Scuse *me*," the driver ejaculated with a grin. "Come on. It ain't every day a dame gets a chance to ride with me."

"I'll leave that golden opportunity for someone more appreciative."

"Aw—awright. I jest thought mebbe you was tired. What you doin'?"

"Hitchhiking."

"Say, you ain't hitchin' on very well this mornin'."

1

"I'll hike every day till I'm tired."

"Where you goin'?"

"Wyoming!" exclaimed Martha Ann, belligerently. It was the first time she had spoken that magic word aloud.

"Whew! . . . Well, I'll be dogged!" the redhead exclaimed. Then with an incredulous glance at the diminutive figure on the highway he started up his ancient car and was soon lost in the clouds of dust.

Martha Ann giggled softly to herself. So she finally had nerve enough to speak it! "Wyoming!" How sweet it sounded! What untold promise the word held! What did it matter that her destination was some unknown town in Wyoming—what difference did it make that she had only fifty dollars in her pocket which would have to last indefinitely?

She walked on happily. Spring was in the air. The fields were golden and the trees and fence rows showed freshly green; swamp blackbirds and meadowlarks sang melodiously from the roadside; a fragrance of burning leaves was carried on the soft breeze. From beyond where the white road disappeared over the horizon something beckoned imperiously.

To the girl it still seemed like a miracle that she should be here. Again she reviewed the events that had led her to this open road which she hoped would take her to Wyoming.

There had been sufficient money to put Martha Ann through high school. That had satisfied her mother, but Martha wanted to go on. Mrs. Dixon was making too many references to Martha Ann's chances of marriage. She argued that Martha at eighteen had grown into an attractive girl who could marry well. But Martha Ann had ideas of her own which had nothing at all to do with marriage.

She wanted to go to the university for a while, and then work, and above all to see something of the world. The world to her meant the West. A twofold reason accounted for Martha's obsession. As a child she had heard all about her grandmother's only brother, who had run away from home to seek his fortune in the West. And it had helped to make her a rabid reader of Western romances.

For thirty years Uncle Nick Bligh had not been heard from. But when Martha Ann was seventeen, her grandmother had received a letter from the missing brother, explaining that as he had failed to make his fortune he had never troubled himself to write. But age and poor health, together with a realization of the false pride that had motivated his silence, had prompted him at last to write for news of his family. The letter bore a postmark of Randall, Wyoming.

This communication from the long-lost uncle had fixed in Martha Ann's mind a secret and daring idea. She would go west to find Uncle Nick. That was incentive and excuse enough to crystallize what had been only a vague purpose.

Ways and means to attend the university and at the same time save money enough to start her trip kept Martha Ann wide-eyed for many long hours at night, as well as pensive by day. But she had solved the problem. She obtained work as an assistant in a dentist's office, and in addition to after classes she worked on Saturdays, Sunday mornings, and during all vacations.

More than a year and a half of this intensive strain had told upon Martha Ann's mental and physical well-being. But nothing daunted her. As time went on her secret purpose grew more and more alluring. It satisfied her longing for happiness. But strange to discover, the busier she became the greater grew the masculine demands upon her leisure. To their persistent requests for dates she remained indifferent.

Martha Ann had long wondered about her attitude toward men. Perhaps, as her mother and some of her friends claimed, she was abnormal. But she could not willingly admit this charge, and from distress she passed to impatience and finally to disgust. Yet she liked boys. She admired young men who were making good in life. She could at times have great fun with them—in the earlier stages of friendship—and could by intense inward pressure wring some sort of romantic emotion out of her heart for them. But to her dismay, almost every friendship led to one of two sad conclusions—a proposal of marriage or a fumbling pass which disgusted her. Why couldn't they just be friends? As for those few bolder young men who attempted to be too free with their hands—Martha Ann despised them.

The time came when the strain of study and outside work, the importunities of her admirers and the constant nagging of her mother had changed Martha Ann, even in her own eyes. She wanted to get far away from the dirty, noisy, crowded city. Open spaces beckoned her. Into her dreams came more and more lovely green places, where flowers and birds abounded. From feeling stifled and weary she gradually sank into a state of real melancholy. The terrific burden on the slender shoulders had at last become too heavy; her flesh was not the equal of her spirit. Also, her mother, anxiously regarding Martha's future, was now urging her to marry young Bob Wirth; "who can take care of you nicely, so you won't have to worry about a little money or a new dress." But worry had become part of Martha's very existence—worry about school credits, about making her little earnings go a long way, about the dissatisfaction and nagging at home, about the pressing fact of the increasing demands of the young men. The proms, the formals, the movies, all had become stale and unprofitable to her. She longed for something to happen—something unforeseen and tremendous.

Finally the pressure had become too great. Even though she had not finished her semester at college she realized with the coming of spring that the time to leave had come. Martha Ann caught her breath as she recalled the day of her decision.

Deceiving her father had not hurt her conscience. He had never appeared to care whether Martha came or went, and outwardly at least he had evinced little interest in her pursuit of happiness. But to deceive her mother! That had hurt. Suddenly faced with the enormity of what she was about to do, she was filled with remorse. Never in all her life had she told her mother a deliberate lie. She now thought to excuse herself on the basis that the glorious end justified almost any means. But a still, accusing voice kept calling at the gate of her consciousness. Lie to mother—who had always been so good, so faithful, so forgiving! It gave Martha Ann a painful twinge. But she had launched her canoe on the current of this great adventure. She could not turn back.

And yet, how simple and easy it all had been to accomplish! Martha Ann had calmly announced at dinner one evening that a girl friend at the university had asked her to drive with her to Omaha, and she wanted to go. Her father and brother made the usual perfunctory murmurs. Her mother, however, had anxiously asked how long she would be gone. Martha could give only a vague answer.

"Dear, you're sure you are going to Omaha?" asked Mrs. Dixon.

"Mother! . . . Yes, of course," she had replied hastily. At least that was no out-and-out falsehood!

"I was afraid you might be remembering your old madness to go out West," concluded Mrs. Dixon.

But Martha had been impatient, too, even with her mother.

4

Why could she not understand how wonderful it would be to go out West? If Mrs. Dixon had ever had any adventurous desires of her own they had long ago become atrophied.

Every moment that Martha had had to herself in the apartment, she had spent getting her belongings into readiness. What to take and what to leave? How impossible to remember that she had to *carry* everything, and therefore the less she took the easier would be her burden! Finally she had decided on her brother's packsack! She was agreeably surprised to find that it held so much. Still she wondered how she could ever manage with anything so small.

As the day of departure had drawn nearer, her feeling of anticipation had become mixed with other emotions. What might not happen to her on the way! She elevated her chin and smiled oftener to reassure herself. Nevertheless there lurked the shadow of panic in her consciousness. Once while kneeling in the middle of her bedroom, trying to find place in her pack for a precious book, she had found herself murmuring aloud: "Oh dear Lord—I want to go so terribly. I must go . . . please don't let anything happen!" and the very next moment her hoydenish nature had asserted itself, and she had cried with Topsy-like simplicity: "Can't you heah me, God?"

At length Martha Ann had her packsack ready. It could hold no more. Besides a few infinitesimal underthings, it contained one pair of pajamas, two toothbrushes, soap, towel and wash cloth, comb and brush, two pairs of heavy woolen hose, three pairs of cotton socks, an emergency kit containing tape, Mercurochrome, bandages, cotton, a bottle of disinfectant, a few threaded needles, a tiny pair of scissors, a fountain pen and some sheets of paper and stamped envelopes, and three clean shirts. She had pondered a long while on the possibility of ever having an occasion to dress up, and at last had put in her navy blue crepe with the flat pleats. This would fold easily and flat. In the end she had found room for her patent leather slippers and two pairs of silk stockings. Her short suede jacket, her hiking boots, and corduroy breeches she would carry in a box, ready to don when she started on the road.

Then had come, finally, the day of parting, the tears, the incoherent farewell, the precipitate flight to meet the mythical girl friend, the station and the train. She could scarcely clamber to the Pullman platform. Her eyes were so dim that she could not see the steps. A voice had whispered: "Running away! . . . Leaving home, mother, brother, Bob—all of them—

forever!" It was the "forever" that had appalled Martha Ann.

And now, after a night on the sleeper, Martha Ann was on the road outside of Omaha, hitchhiking toward the next town.

She still felt self-conscious and queer in the soft corduroy riding breeches and high-topped boots that she had donned in the dressing room of the station. She had rolled her heavy woolen socks down over her hiking boots; and the sleeves of her white shirt over slim round arms that she hoped would soon get tanned.

As Martha Ann swung along the road her mind seemed both busy and absent. How good it was just to be alive and free on a morning like this! She had a heavenly sense of having been newly born. Would it not be wonderful to walk on like this forever? There was no need of hurry. Even the goal of Wyoming failed to seem so far away and unattainable.

For a while Martha Ann strode rhythmically along, her feet light, her heart dancing, her thoughts at peace. She stopped at the first gas station she came to on the road, where she was favored with amused glances and deluged with maps. A few cars passed her, and as one of them seemed about to stop, she waved it on. Martha wanted to prolong the enchantment of these first hours of freedom.

The sun rose high in the sky. It was beginning to get hot. After a time the road began to slope uphill, necessitating a change in her gait. Near the summit, a Ford coupé came puffing up behind her and stopped. A sandy-haired young man put his head out of the window.

"Hey, pigeon, where do you think you're flyin'?" he called, in a good-natured voice.

Long had Martha Ann schooled herself in the replies that would have to be made. Always it would be diplomatic to name the nearest town as her destination, which subterfuge would enable her to take her leave of any undesirable who might offer her a lift. Accordingly she named the first village she had read on the road map.

"Hop in. I'm going within half a mile of there."

Martha slid off the packsack, the weight of which she had not fully appreciated until relieved of it, and climbed into the car.

"Got relatives there?" inquired the driver, as he put the Ford into motion.

"Yes," replied Martha, warily.

"Where you from?"

"Chicago."

He whistled his surprise. "Hike all the way from there?"

"No. I came as far as Omaha by train," she replied, feeling that she liked this not overly curious driver. He glanced at her packsack.

"Nice army pack. That leather bottom keeps your stuff dry."

"Yes, Colonel Brinkerhoff gave it to my brother."

"That so," he said, and flashed a keen glance at her. Then he attended to the road ahead. The car was speeding between fields of winter grain and pastureland. Farmhouses stood among groves of trees rapidly turning green.

Suddenly he launched a query: "Do your folks know you're out here alone like this?"

"No," rejoined Martha Ann, caught unawares.

"Ahuh. Well, why don't they?"

"Why? . . . I—I suppose—because if I'd told them—I wouldn't be here," she replied, haltingly. It annoyed her to be quizzed but his directness had momentarily confused her.

"Does anyone know you're hitchhiking?"

"Yes, our family lawyer. I bound him to secrecy. He promised, provided I'd keep in touch with him. If I didn't he threatened to have the police on my trail."

"Not a bad idea. How old are you?"

"Nineteen."

"Humph! You look more like fifteen."

Martha Ann glared at him.

"Listen, kid," he said, ignoring her look of disdain, "you can't lie worth a hoot! Some girls are like that. Just where are you headed for?"

"I'm going to Randall, Wyoming, but I can't see where it's any concern of yours," retorted Martha.

"Good Lord! . . . Say, do you know how far that is? To hitchhike?"

"I've a pretty good idea."

"And do you know you'll have to go through the Black Hills?"

"N—no-o, I didn't. . . . Are they as awful as they sound?"

"You'll never come out alive. A few tourists motor through the Hills. But for the most part they're darned lonely and deserted. A refuge for fugitives and criminals. Believe me, kid, you'll get yours!"

7

"Gracious! . . . Oh, you're just trying to scare me."

"Not a chance! Look here. I belong to the armory. I know Colonel Brinkerhoff, whose packsack you're carrying. I'm going to take you to the armory with me while I wire the Colonel to find out if he really approves of this crazy hike you're on."

Martha Ann sat back stunned. What if this assertive young man were to make good his threat? What would her mother say? And do! Martha could see what a disgrace it would be to be sent home just when she had such a fine start. But she simply must not let this terrible thing happen.

"Wiring Colonel Brinkerhoff won't be any use now," she spoke up, her wit reasserting itself.

"Why won't it?"

"Because he isn't in Chicago now."

"Where is he?"

"Fishing in northern Canada."

"How do you know that?"

"Because he went with a friend of my uncle."

Plainly the sandy-haired young man was at a loss as far as proceeding along the line he had adopted was concerned.

"I'll bet you haven't any money?"

"Indeed I have."

"Enough to get home to Chicago?" he queried doubtfully.

"Yes. And then some."

"What on earth put this crazy idea in your head?"

That for Martha was waving a red flag of battle.

"Crazy! Sure I'm crazy. But it's to see the West. Why, I've never been away from home in my life. I've never seen any places but Chicago and Lake Michigan. This is my chance. I *must* go on. . . . Besides, I've never seen my uncle. I wrote him. . . . He—he's expecting me."

This last was far from the truth, but Martha Ann had become desperate.

"Uncle, uh? That's different. Still my duty to Brinkerhoff is to hold you till some of your people are communicated with."

"Hold me! How?" burst out Martha. If she ever got away from this armory person she would never accept another ride.

"Well, you can't jump out while we're doing forty-five," he declared, grimly. "I'll drive straight to the armory and hold you till Captain Stevens can be notified."

"Hold me—by force?" faltered Martha. She realized that he was in the right and it gave her a sense of guilt. What

8

could she do? She must fall back upon feminine wiles, a procedure she usually scorned. Whereupon she made a frantic pretense of escaping from the car.

"Hold you? I should smile I will," he said, suiting his action to the word. "If necessary, I'll hold on to you with one arm. But, heck, I'll bet you wouldn't make too much fuss."

Martha Ann resorted to tears, which were so near the surface that weeping was hardly any dissimulation.

"Say, I give up, young lady. I can't stand for bawling," he said irritably. "I'll let you go if you promise to watch your step. Don't get in cars where there's more than one man, and be sure you're never in *any* car after dark."

Martha promised eagerly.

"And look each driver over before you accept a ride?"

"Yes, sir," replied Martha, demurely.

"I've got a kid sister. And I'd have a fit if I caught her hitchhiking alone. But she has queer ideas, too. Girls are sure beyond understanding these days. . . . Well, here's where I turn off. And there's the village."

Martha got out and thanked him.

"Would you mind dropping me a post card—if you get by the Black Hills? I'll be sort of worried. My name's Arthur Anderson. And I live here."

"Mine's Martha Ann Dixon. I'll send you a card. Thank you—and good-by!"

She started down the road, and after a little turned to look back. The car was still there at the turn-off. And the young man was waving his cap. Martha went on, a considerably sobered and thoughtful girl.

In the village she stopped at a little hot-dog stand to rest and eat lunch. From there a farmer and two small boys gave her a lift that took her thirty-five miles to another crossroad settlement, where she decided to call it a day. And upon being directed to a tourist home, she found pleasant accommodations for the night.

The twittering and fluttering of birds in the vines outside Martha's window aroused her at five-thirty. She bounded up, eager and refreshed. Another day—the second! What would the day bring forth? How beautiful the rosy sunrise over the rolling eastern Nebraska hills! At breakfast she was informed that if she did not mind riding in a truck, she could accompany her host as far as the next town.

"Oh, fine! That will be fun," she exclaimed.

But that anticipated lift turned out to be all too short, and therefore not such fun after all. Halfway up a steep hill the engine stalled. The driver had to begin tinkering with obstinate machinery. Martha got out and began to walk.

The truck never caught up with her. After several cars had passed she accepted a ride with a merry family of five, who cheerfully made room for her, and welcomed her without curiosity. Martha liked this plain man and his fat spouse, and the dirty, bright-eyed children. It was noon when their village was reached. Martha had lunch and once more went on her way.

It occurred to her that she was now traveling through the Nebraska plains and that towns would be few and far between. Farms seemed to spread out. Anyway, there were fewer farmhouses. Cars passed her. She had learned by now that her solitary, unusual, little figure would not escape notice on the road. The afternoon sun grew hot. She rested, and hoped an acceptable lift soon would happen along. Then she started hiking again. She walked on and on, and in two hours' time not a single automobile passed in her direction. Then came a string of cars, so close together that Martha could not get a good look at their occupants. She found, presently, that when she was tired and impatient, as she grew to be by late afternoon, she was likely to forget the good advice she had been given, and to accept any ride that was offered. She began to wonder—was she being erratic, irresponsible? Was this unheard-of adventure for a girl of nineteen who looked fifteen a proof of an unstable character? She defended herself stoutly, but somehow the buoyant spirit of the morning had vanished.

A lengthy hill invited a long rest. When she resumed her hike and had surmounted the grade the sun was setting red and glorious in the west. The rolling plains began to disappear in the purple haze of the horizon. In this scene, still dominated by the habitations of man, Martha imagined she saw a semblance to the western range. And this thought so thrilled and delighted her that she forgot her hot tired feet and aching limbs, and trudged on, almost her old self once more.

From the height she looked down upon lonelier country, which the road bisected to the next town, now visible in the clear evening light some few miles ahead. Martha thought that she could still make it before it became pitch dark. Downhill was easy and the air had cooled. At the foot of the incline the road turned abruptly. A brook gleamed under a dark patch of woods that shaded the road and there was a bridge to cross. Below the bridge Martha saw a little fire and two rough-looking men, sitting beside it. Could they be tramps?

Martha realized that she had to pass them. With bated breath she quickened her steps. Twilight was stealing out of the woods. She might get by without attracting notice. But when one of the men called out, her heart leaped wildly.

"Bill, stop thet boy, an' see what he's got in thet bag."

Then Martha, who had been watching the two men beside the fire, was astounded to be confronted by a dark form that appeared to rise out of the earth. It belonged to a third man who evidently had been invisible against the background of the bridge.

"Hyar, sonny, what you totin' there?" he queried, in brisk good humor.

Martha Ann, suddenly rendered weak by terror, made an ineffectual attempt to elude the man. He caught her with so violent a jerk that she would have fallen but for his hold. She dropped the small parcel she carried in her hand.

"Oh!—let me—go!" she cried out, fearfully.

The man swung her around to the westering light and peered closely down upon her. Martha got an impression of a hard, coarse face and a pair of wolfish eyes. She tried to wrench free from the iron grip which was hurting her wrist.

"Hey, fellars, it ain't no boy. It's a girl. Purtier'n a pitcher," called the man to his associates.

"Haw! Haw! Wal, Bill, you know your weakness. But throw us the baggage," came the hoarse reply.

"Come hyar, little one, an' set—"

Martha struggled with what little strength she had left. A kind of paralysis had taken possession of her. It was a new and devastating numbness of will and flesh. All in a flash peril had leaped out of the dusk, and wit, nerve, energy deserted her to be replaced by a horrible sickening faintness.

"Hey, Bill, hyar's a car!" hurriedly called one of the men beside the fire.

Martha Ann heard the puff and then the vibration of a car. Its presence revived her, and she jerked herself free, calling loudly at the same time.

"Let that boy go," came a commanding voice from the car.

Then the occupant stepped out to loom big and wide of shoulder before them. "What's the idea?"

"Aw, nothin'. Jest havin' fun with the kid," returned the tramp surlily, as he backed away.

"Oh—n-no sir," quavered Martha Ann. "He meant to rob—me—and I don't know what—when he saw I was a girl!"

"*Girl!*" The newcomer moved like a swift shadow. Martha heard a sudden crash. The tramp appeared lifted as by a catapult to go tottering against the bank with a sickening impact.

"Beat it, you hoboes, or I'll come down there and mess you up," called Martha's rescuer. Then he turned to her.

"Are you really a girl?"

"Yes, sir. . . . And sometimes I wish—I wasn't," replied Martha, picking up her parcel.

"Of course, you live along here somewhere?"

"No-o. My home's—far away."

"How'd you come to be caught on this lonely road?" he queried.

"I'm hitchhiking out West."

"Hitchhiking?" he exclaimed.

"It's a—a kind of sport. Sometimes I accept lifts—when I can—and hike between."

"Sport! I admire your nerve," he laughed. His voice had a pleasant depth, with an intonation that told Martha that he was quite different from the others she had met on this jaunt. She looked up. There was still light enough for her to discern the features of a young man in his early twenties. His eyes were intently on her face. They appeared to have a mocking look. Martha saw that again she was under suspicion, and the realization almost canceled the sweet warm sensation of gratitude and relief flooding over her.

"Thank you for saving me from I—I don't know what," she murmured, shyly. The strain of her struggle with the tramp, and the manner in which the stranger had accepted her explanation, or perhaps both together, had reacted strangely upon Martha Ann Dixon.

"Girls of today pay a price for the kick they try to get out of everything," he replied, enigmatically. "You look faint. Get in. I'll take you as far as Norfolk."

12

2

Not for many minutes did the effect of panic wear off Martha Ann. It all had been so totally unexpected. She had never before realized what real fright was like. The rickety old car crept slowly along! She relaxed back in the seat, spent and nerveless, scarcely able to hold the packsack upon her lap.

But presently her usual buoyant spirit returned, and Martha Ann became acutely aware of the driver beside her. She realized that she must summon her wits to meet another quizzing. This young man, however, appeared completely oblivious of her presence. His silence condemned her. And before they had gone very far Martha began to find it unendurable.

"You don't live—in these parts?" she began, haltingly.

"How'd you guess that?"

Martha Ann, analyzing her sensations, could not very well tell him that he did not smell of horses, gas stations or harness oil.

"Where are you from?" she substituted.

His hesitation in replying to her question hinted to Martha that he might have considered her query unduly curious.

"I'm a hick from Missouri," he finally replied, with a light laugh tinged with bitterness.

"Yes, you are!" she exclaimed accusingly. "And I suppose your name is Hiram Perkins?"

"My name is Andrew Bonning," he returned, soberly, as if the admission had been forcibly extracted from him.

Martha Ann's best overtures failed to stimulate the conversation and at length she subsided into silence. She peered at him, however, out of the corner of her eye. He wore overalls that had seen very little service. She could make out a clean-cut profile. He was bareheaded and had dark hair, somewhat long and wavy. Martha Ann reluctantly had to admit that this strange rescuer who obviously disapproved of her was good-looking even in the dusk.

"Where are you going?"

"Wyoming."

"Humph. . . . Well, here's your next town," he spoke up, presently. "See the lights?"

"Oh, it must be a pretty big town," said Martha Ann, excitedly.

"You'll get another kick here."

"Kick?" she echoed, doubtfully.

"Yes, kick. Isn't that what you're after? Isn't that what all girls think of nowadays?"

Martha Ann had no reply, for his query edged with bitterness had thrown her back upon introspection. All at once she felt vexed, and because it seemed to be only with herself, she promptly chose to foist her feeling of annoyance upon this disturbing young man. After all, what did she care what he thought about her? Just the same that reflection did not wholly satisfy. The excitement of entering a new and larger town, however, precluded any hope of Martha's to deliver a telling retort. The main street was wide, paved, lined with automobiles, and bright with lights. Martha chose a modest-appearing hotel, and asked to be dropped at its entrance. The fact that he got out first to help her, and to lift out her packsack, struck Martha as significant. He moved with a careless grace which her sensitive observations scarcely associated with overalls.

"Thank you, Mr. Bonning, for—for everything," murmured Martha.

"You're welcome. I wish you better luck on the next lap of your hitchhike. . . . You forgot to tell me your name."

"I didn't forget. I was—"

As he lifted out her packsack he noticed the lettering Martha Ann had so carefully printed in indelible ink on the side of the pack. She had neglected to use punctuation.

"*Mad!*" he exclaimed. Then suddenly he smiled down upon her in a way that made Martha feel like a wayward little girl. Under the electric light she could now see him distinctly, and somehow, someway, that pale handsome face with its sad and piercing eyes seemed incomprehensibly to be her undoing. "Wyoming Mad? It suits you better than any real name. And as you are an unforgettable kid I'll remember you by that. I hope we don't meet again. Good-by."

He got into the car and drove off, leaving Martha Ann standing on the sidewalk, bag in hand, staring up the crowded street. Unforgettable kid? But not because she was pretty or sweet or nice—only because she was mad! Insulted and crestfallen, Martha Ann went into the hotel, engaged a room, and wearily proceeded to unpack and remove the stains of travel.

14

Her left arm pained, and she discovered a bruise where the tramp had gripped her wrist. These were the only tangible proofs of her adventure with the bad men. What if Andrew Bonning had not happened to arrive at such an opportune moment? Martha Ann shivered. They might have murdered her and cast her into the dark stream. Then what of mother! Martha's spirit quailed for a little and her heart warmed again toward her rescuer. How wide-shouldered and powerful—what a blow he had struck for her! Then the next moment, remembering his veiled distrust of her, his spiteful designation of her as "Wyoming Mad," all of Martha Ann's more charitable feelings were forgotten. They would never meet again and she was gladder of that than he could possibly be.

Next morning bright and early Martha was on her way once more. Yesterday's events lay as far behind her as the distance over which she had come. The yellow road entranced her, ever new, ever offering the unknown adventures that were to come. In the broad daylight, so clear and fresh, between the green fields with their singing birds—how could she feel afraid? She stepped out with eager stride, with glad eyes toward the beckoning miles.

During the day that followed automobiles were plentiful. She could take her pick, and she had lifts aggregating a hundred miles or more before mid-afternoon. She likened this passing from car to car to the reading of a huge book which devoted just so much space to each individual. All rides were fascinating to Martha Ann, whether short or long, but she still preferred walking. During the afternoon there seemed to be a scarcity of cars on the road. She walked until she was glad to hear the hum of another motor.

A Cadillac roadster sped past. The occupant, a young man, looked back at her. As Martha continued walking, presently she saw the big car slow down and stop. When she caught up with it, the driver leaned out to say: "Hello, my beauty, wilt ride on my trusty steed?"

"Is it safe?" she queried.

"Is it safe! Lady, you appall me. I'm the original Sir Galahad. My middle name is Saint. Mothers leave their puling infants with me. Old ladies phone days ahead just to have me escort them to the village—"

"I believe I've read about you," interrupted Martha Ann. "You're too good to be true. I'd better walk."

15

"Aw, have a heart! I've got to drive all the way to Sidonia. Please don't mind my kidding. Really I'm mild under my bold exterior."

"All right," laughed Martha. "I'm only going a short distance and I'll take a chance on you."

"Get in. My name's George Proctor."

"Mine's Martha Ann Dixon."

They rode along in the warm sunshine, just two young people thrown idly together, and George's fluent talk of the lore of the Nebraska countryside found Martha a rapt listener. At length George explained that his business was insurance, and proceeded to quote numerous statistics for Martha's edification and profit.

"Whoever heard of a hitchhiker being killed?" she queried.

"Say, you're only one of a pioneer game. You might be the very first to get killed."

"If I had known you'd be saying such pessimistic things to me I wouldn't have accepted this ride."

"Hold everything, Beautiful. I'll make this an enjoyable ride for you."

"Well, speaking of hazards, if you're tired driving let me try."

"Do you drive? Great! I'm sure fed up with driving. It's all I ever do."

Whereupon Martha changed her seat for the one behind the wheel, and drove on, evidently to young Proctor's pleasure. It did not take long for Martha Ann to decide that his intentions were strictly honorable, and since Sidonia was on her way she would continue that far with him. At six o'clock they were within sight of Sidonia.

"My uncle runs the hotel here," said George. "I'll introduce you. And—would you think me awfully cheeky if I ask you to have dinner with us?"

"N-no-o. . . . But I've just one dress—and it'll be fearfully wrinkled."

"Pshaw! Nobody dresses up for dinner in Sidonia."

It so happened that Martha did not think to relinquish the wheel, and as she drove up to an unpretentious hotel she was astounded to recognize a bystander as Andrew Bonning. Yielding to a swift warm impulse she was about to nod gaily when a look in the young man's keen dark eyes sent a hot blush coursing over her cheeks. He inclined his head in recognition, a courtesy Martha did not answer, and which young

16

Proctor did not see. He took her baggage and helped her out, talking gaily all the while. Anyone would have noticed his rapture, which all of a sudden seemed to incense Martha Ann. She knew for a certainty that Bonning had seen Proctor escort her into the hotel, where she confusedly prayed that the uncle-proprietor would be in charge. But he was out. George got her a room, carried her baggage up, and said at the door: "Doll up now, Beautiful, and knock Uncle's eye out at dinner!"

This young fellow was certainly courteous and wholesome. But something had cast a shadow over Martha Ann's spirit. She locked the door and slammed things around, taking out her vague feeling of uncertainty upon a completely innocent bystander.

"Andrew Bonning!" she soliloquized, wrathfully. "Didn't want to meet me again? . . . Doesn't approve of me? . . . What does he think I am, anyway?"

Her wrath and her pride, however, in no wise soothed the little ache this second unexpected meeting had engendered. Martha Ann bathed, pressed her one dress, and gazing in the mirror at the proud amber eyes and the golden hair, knew that she need not be ashamed of her looks. Would Bonning see her? Was he staying at this hotel? She went downstairs all a-quiver and still furious with herself. George met her, to introduce a kindly old man, whose twinkling blue eyes made much of Martha Ann. She knew at once that George had told him about her hitchhiking.

"Wal, Miss Marthy, young George tells me you're goin' to stop over with us for a night."

"Yes, I am."

"We'll take good care of you tonight, but you're liable to be scalped by Indians when you get to the Black Hills."

"Oh dear! Those dreadful Black Hills again!"

"Wal, mabbe you'll slip through. But you oughtn't to walk it. . . . Go right in to dinner, George. I'll be along pronto."

Fate was against Martha Ann. As they entered the dining room with George hanging on to her arm, whom should Martha see but Bonning at one of the tables. He wore the same rough garb, but it did not make him look like a laborer. As they passed he glanced up, and Martha knew as well as if he had spoken it that he thought she had flirted with this young Nebraskan and was getting her kick out of it. Martha

17

Ann could have boxed his ears. She determined that she would make him notice her.

"Howdy, Hiram Perkins," she drawled, as she passed him. "Hope you heered from Mizzourie."

"Good evening, Wyoming Mad," he replied, rising with a bow.

Young Proctor wheeled in surprise, but did not speak until he had placed Martha Ann at a table and found a seat for himself.

"You spoke to that fellow. He called you 'Wyoming' something!"

"Yes. We met back at Norfolk. Just a little camaraderie of the road."

"Oh, I see. Gosh, it sort of took the starch out of me. . . . Well, I can sure recommend our fried chicken."

Martha Ann sat where she faced Bonning and had to meet his eyes. Suddenly the hot blood stole along her veins. If she did not read disappointment, as well as scorn in his dark gaze, then her reckoning was all wrong. At any rate, it had the same unaccountable effect that his first look had had upon her. Martha deigned not to notice him again and audaciously plied young Proctor with all the feminine wiles she could muster. She was actually flirting with eyes, lips, smiles and arch words when Bonning suddenly left his table and went out. The entrance of George's uncle saved Martha Ann at that blank juncture.

Nevertheless, she enjoyed her dinner, and later, when the old Nebraskan began to tell stories of his life on the frontier, Martha forgot all about Bonning. Once again in her room, however, packing the pretty dress, she remembered him, and she found herself thinking of that evening when a young man's strength had stood between her and a terrible fate. She divined that she would meet him tomorrow, or sometime on the road west, and the thought was both bitter and sweet. Before she went to sleep she had almost forgotten the young man's obvious disapproval in the anticipation of meeting him again on the open road.

At six next morning she bade good-by to the Proctors and started out again on her way northward. If her heart beat faster whenever she heard the hum of approaching cars she did not permit herself to turn around to identify the driver. But as car after car caught up with her and passed she confessed to herself that she had hoped Andrew Bonning might

18

be driving one of them, and would give her another lift. Could he pass her by?

The freshness and fragrance of pastures, the green folds of the lonely hills, the lure of the road, and the warming sun—all seemed to have lost some of their delight for the runaway. Martha Ann marveled at this and wondered why the beautiful morning had not the zest of other days. She walked steadily along until nine o'clock. As the sun rose higher and higher she found the road narrowing and the farmhouses growing more scattered.

She heard the sounds of wagon wheels and hoof beats behind her. As they drew nearer Martha looked back and observed an ancient wagon with a man perched on a high seat, and five small boys leaning over the side of the wagon box.

"Wal, sis, kin we give you a lift?" called the driver, as he halted the vehicle beside her.

"You surely can," replied Martha, gladly.

"Scramble up. Boys, make room thar for sis. . . . Air you goin' fur?"

"Wyoming."

"Ain't thinkin' of walkin' all thet way?"

"No indeed, not when I can meet such accommodating people as you."

"Wal, this ain't no gas wagon, but you're welcome. Hep yourself to some apples an' make yourself comfortable for three miles."

Munching juicy red apples and talking to these five lively farm boys was the most enjoyable experience Martha Ann had had so far on her journey. But it ended all too soon. Once more she was reduced to shank's mare.

In the ensuing hour only one car caught up with her. It was full and did not stop. The sun was beating down now with tropical intensity and her clothes were soaked with perspiration. She had not seen a farmhouse for hours. Worry followed soon upon fatigue and she began to wonder about how far it was to the next town. Fields after fields! They must run on forever. But after a time the fields gave way to rocky wasteland harboring only tall weeds.

Four o'clock found Martha Ann still trudging along the highway. A lump seemed fixed in her throat and often the landscape was blurred by the tears in her weary eyes. She kept saying that she did not mind the walk, endless though it seemed. Before she had started this wild-goose venture she

19

had realized that there would be many, many miles of walking. It was the uncertainty of where she might find shelter and the approach of night that weighed her down with anxiety.

Martha Ann stumbled on over the mud-caked road and more than once came near falling. Both her heart and her feet seemed leaden. Suddenly the sound of a laboring motor caught her ear. She stood still and listened. She heard the sound again —the straining clatter of a car traversing the uncertain road. Soon it came in sight. Should she flag it? How could she stay on the road all night? Coyotes, snakes—probably more tramps! She waved frantically. The car halted, and Martha, running hurriedly to meet it, called out: "Please can you take me to the next town?"

The occupants, a man and a woman, were Negroes. Martha swallowed her surprise. They evidently were as surprised as she. Martha studied the couple with penetrating eyes, but they looked honest and kind.

"Missy, if you-all don't mind ridin' with us yo's sho welcome," replied the woman, in a soft drawl.

"Thank you. I'm glad to come with you," said Martha, as she climbed in. "I didn't know it was so far to the next town."

"We are lost, too. I nevah did see so much land in all mah life with nuthin' on it."

"I didn't either," agreed Martha.

While the man drove his buxom spouse talked. They were from St. Louis, on the way west to find work and a home. Sundown found them still on the road, but by seven o'clock they had reached the outskirts of a town. At the town square Martha got out and thanked them, and bade them good luck and good-by. She stopped at a small restaurant for a light supper, and was directed to the only hotel in the valley. She went immediately to bed. To be tired out was the usual thing, but this night she felt forlorn and homesick for the first time. She could no longer keep home and mother out of her consciousness, because she had not sent either telegrams or letter, and she absolutely must not delay another day.

In the morning she was so stiff and sore that she could hardly get up. What would this new day bring forth? Always this was her waking thought. But this morning her sense of humor and the call of adventure did not come to the rescue of her drooping spirits. For the first time she was experiencing the pangs of the guilty conscience of a runaway.

Therefore the first thing she did upon going downstairs was

to begin a letter to her mother. She discovered that the decision to write was one thing. What to write was something else again. In the end she found that she would have to continue with the falsehood with which she had started her journey. She wrote with tears blotting the page that when she and Alice McGinnis had arrived in Omaha, Alice's uncle had invited them to drive to the Black Hills with them. Of course she and Alice were wild to go. "And you know, Mother darling, how I've always yearned to see the West, so don't scold—and forgive me for disobeying."

Posting that letter was a relief, yet it did not still her accusing conscience. How could she ever make amends for this untruth to her family, especially her mother? Her first innocent falsehood had enmeshed her in a situation which would require more and more lies and deception. Where would it all end?

Martha Ann had not been on the road ten minutes that morning before a touring car bearing an Illinois license plate passed with two middle-aged men in the front seat. They slowed down, smiled an invitation, then waved and went on. Soon after that a truck ground up a grade behind Martha and stopped at the crest of the hill.

"Whoa," sang out a deep booming voice. A little boy on the seat beside the driver reached down and with tiny hands made what Martha thought was a pretense of helping to stop the car.

"Hey, traveler, want a ride with my pardner an' me?" called the same deep voice.

Martha glanced up at a strange pair—the man in a blue shirt open at a bronzed throat, with ruddy frank face and his left arm off at the elbow—the lad in diminutive overalls, looking like a wistful little elf.

"I'd like to ride very much if I won't crowd you," replied Martha.

"Plenty room," he boomed.

She hopped up onto the high seat beside the boy. He smiled at her and she smiled back. Then for a while they rattled along the road in silence. Martha thought of a hundred questions she wanted to ask.

After some time the driver started to talk. He came originally from Detroit and had lost his arm in the war. Upon arriving home from France he had learned from the doctors that he had lung trouble and would not live long unless he went west. He had come to Nebraska and in eight months he was a well man. Then he had gone in for farming and had been successful. Much of this good fortune, he said, was owing to the wonderful wife he had found out west.

"I've an older boy, too," he concluded with pardonable pride. "But I just couldn't get along without this young fellow here. He's my left-hand man."

At this sally both father and son laughed happily. Martha at last had run across one returned and disabled veteran of the war who had found himself. This broad open land seemed hospitable to strangers. Martha added to her growing list another reason to love the West.

They drove along chattering gaily until they let her off at a road that branched off to the south. Martha waved farewell to a gallant soldier and a lovable youngster.

"Well," soliloquized Martha Ann, "there's nothing to this hitchhiking but walking and riding, and meeting a lot of people I like . . . and a few I don't."

She thought of Andrew Bonning. He seemed to be fading into the past, the truth of which she recognized with a pang. How could she ever forget his gallant service in her behalf? But he had taken her for a common flirt. "Oh! It's just as well if I never meet him again," she sighed.

The country was growing more rugged. It swept away in series of desolate ridges where signs of civilization were becoming scarce. The trees were now taller and more numerous; the air had a finer, keener edge. It was invigorating. Martha Ann felt that she could walk on forever. Gradually with the exercise she found her stiffness was wearing away. She hoped to reach the next town late in the afternoon. If these towns were only not so far apart she would not have to be so much afraid of not getting a ride. As she swung along, her mind skipping from one thought to another, from home to the imagined ranch of her uncle, a Ford coupé came rolling up behind her and with a screeching of brakes stopped a few feet beyond her.

"How's chances, baby?" queried a young fellow from the driver's seat. He was alone and he had a sunburned, impudent face.

"Not so good," replied Martha Ann, shortly. He kept his car moving alongside of her as she walked.

"Long way to Barton," he said significantly, and stopped the Ford.

Nothing else in the way of words could have made such an impression on the weary wayfarer. She had found very little traffic on this road and she wanted so very much to get along with her journey. She stopped. He smiled at her in a knowing way, as if he were accustomed to being indulgent to a willful girl who was bound to capitulate in the end. When he opened the door her old confidence reasserted itself and she stepped in. She had done so despite an instant instinctive dislike for this overconfident young man. Perhaps her feeling derived mostly from the way he called her "baby." He started the car with one hand and passed his cigarette case with the other.

"Have one?"

"No, thanks."

"Don't you really smoke or are you being snooty?" His eyes were a little too close together and emitted curious glints as they ran over her slim person.

"I really don't like cigarettes. . . . How far are you going on this road?"

"A few miles more. Have to turn off to see a farmer. . . . Where are you bound for, babe?"

"Wyoming," she returned, curtly, hating the epithet he used so freely. She began to fear that she had made a blunder in accepting this young man's lift.

"Gee! That's too far for a dame to be going alone. Not in a hurry, are you, babe?"

"Indeed I am. In a very big hurry," declared Martha Ann sharply. Whether or not her reply penetrated his mind Martha could not tell. Certainly he seemed not to resent it.

"Ever been to an Indian pow-wow?"

"No-o."

"We're having a pow-wow and dance in Lagrange tonight. Why doncha come on and go with me? You'll have a swell time."

"I've relatives expecting me at Barton tonight."

"Tell that to your grandmother," he retorted with a grin. "You're one of these hitchhikers. They're all sports. I know."

"Well, this one isn't."

"C'mon, babe. Be a sport. You can phone from Lagrange. Say you got in late. I'll give you a real time."

"I'm sorry, but I couldn't think of it," rejoined Martha. She felt his eyes on her, as she watched the speedometer mounting higher.

" 'Smatter, babe? Afraid to speed a little?"

"I'm not afraid," she said scornfully. "I was just wondering if you were driving to a fire."

He laughed and laid a freckled hand upon Martha's knee. "Maybe you're afraid of me, babe?"

"Humph! Hardly," she returned. Then decisively, and very deliberately and firmly she removed his hand.

"You know, baby, I could go for you in a big way," he said, persuasively.

"I dare say. But it's not necessary. If you'll slow down I'll get out and walk."

"Aw, don't be like that. You just came. Am I such a bad guy?"

"Skip it!" ejaculated Martha Ann, in disgust. "I'm not your type."

"You're just trying to high-hat me."

"Stop this car and let me out!"

"But, gee whiz, girlie, we're nearly there."

By this time the Ford was careening along the road at the rate of a mile a minute. Martha grew frightened with the speed of the car, if not with the lout who was driving it. To be killed in a wreck—what a futile and tragic end to her dream! Why had she ever yielded to this mad escapade? She called sharply to be let out.

He lifted his foot from the accelerator and made a quick turn to the right down a grassy lane lined with trees that brushed against the car. The swerve of the car had thrown Martha off her balance and over against the driver. He let go of the wheel with one hand and seized her around the waist. Then he slowed down the car so that he would not drive off the rough lane into the brush. He tried to pull the girl to him.

"How dare you! Let me go—you rowdy!" cried Martha Ann, drawing back with all her might.

"Too late, babe!" He had the car barely moving now. "C'mon. Be nice to me. What're you afraid of?"

"Not a thing! Least of all—you!" panted Martha, struggling. "Let me go—let me out of this car—or I'll have you arrested."

"Say, cutie, where do you think you are? There's no sheriff near here."

"I have—relatives near enough—to see that plenty is done to you. . . Let me out!"

He gave a derisive laugh. "Say, listen, dame, you're so far from a sheriff, or anybody, that it isn't even funny. No one will hear you if you do scream. But have a heart. Cut the up-stage stuff. Am I as bad as all that?"

"Our tastes differ. I just don't happen to care for your type."

"Hell you say! I'll just have to change your mind. Anyway, I like my women wild."

With that he let go of the wheel and caught her to him. Martha had succeeded in wrenching almost free. For an instant she was fascinated by his small, scalloped, tobacco-stained teeth. She recognized for the first time in her life contact with a raw, bold elemental force. Then his thick mouth was moving toward her. All the other features faded before this animal ugliness. A terrible rage flashed hot and overpowering through her. What a miserable rotten bully! She sensed that there was no use to scream. She had better save her breath. She was utterly dependent upon her own resourcefulness and strength. The car bumped against a stump, and lurched along the bank side of the lane. She feared for a moment that it might overturn. He had been trying to get farther and farther off the main road. Martha knew that she could not afford to get any farther away from the highway.

With one arm tight and contracting around her shoulder he suddenly pressed his other grimy hand over Martha's breast. She kicked out with all her might. One of her heavy hiking boots struck him on the shin. He let out a yell of pain, but continued to hold her tighter than ever with one arm while again he endeavored to steer with the other. He wanted to get her far along this lonely lane, out of sight and sound of the highway.

The savage kick Martha had administered to the driver of the Ford awakened her to her one chance. She knew her greatest strength was in her legs, so she lashed out again with both feet. At length she kicked herself free, and then doubling up, she shot both boots into the pit of his stomach. Yelling hoarsely he let go of the wheel. Swiftly Martha reached down, locked the ignition, and flung the key out far into the tall grass.

"You damn she-devil!" he screamed, his face contorted by anger and pain.

Then Martha's rage knew no bounds. If she had felt any fear before, it now vanished. With her back braced in the corner of the coupé and her feet up she continued to batter him—all over the front of his body—with swift, hard, savage kicks from her heavy boot. Twice he seized her flying feet, but could not hold them. He was not strong enough—Martha saw, savagely exultant. He could not force her. She could whip him any day. And she kicked him with a hard left to the stomach and a harder right in the nose. Blood spattered the interior of the car. But that only augmented her determination to maim him and even to kill him.

"Let up—you infernal wildcat," he bawled.

Martha Ann dropped her boots with a thump, and sat up to snatch at her bag. Then, opening the door, she plunged out. He had his hands to his nose. Blood was pouring through his fingers down his wrists, staining his shirt sleeves.

"Next time you—get fresh—" she panted, "pick some girl —your class and size—you big bully!"

She marched breathlessly back down the lane to the road— an outraged but a triumphant young woman. This elation lasted only for a few moments; then a reaction set in, and she began to tremble violently and to sob. She could no longer stand up. Staggering against a culvert she sat down, trying to dip her handkerchief into the water to wipe her face and hands with it. A car hummed close by. Could that bully be after her again? Oh, God, she could not find the strength for another battle. But the hum did not come from down the lane. A car hove in sight. She recognized it as the Illinois Buick that had passed her with the two pleasant-faced men. They bore down upon the culvert, and seeing her, halted.

"Hello—you again," called one.

"What's wrong, little girl?" queried the other quickly and got out.

The sound of a kindly voice in that terrible loneliness upset Martha still more. Her sobs increased. She could not answer the queries they put to her. They got a canteen and offered her water. At length she recovered enough to be coherent. "I accepted a lift—from a young man—in a Ford. . . . He drove— over sixty. . . . Turned off down—that lane there and attacked me. . . . Oh, he was beastly! . . . But I fought him off—left him there."

"Damned scoundrel!" rasped one of them men. "Biston, you look after her while I find this fellow."

He strode off and was gone for some time, during which the other gentleman tried to calm Martha, and to assure her that he and his companion, Mr. Madison, would be glad to have her ride with them to the next town.

Martha was in the car, in the back seat, and somewhat composed when Mr. Madison came striding back.

"Well, Miss—," he began cheerfully.

"Dixon," Martha supplied.

"I found your assailant and from his appearance I'm inclined to believe that the question Biston and I were pondering a while back—can that kid take care of herself—is very amply answered. But I gave him a little more punishment just for good measure."

3

ANDREW BONNING decided that there must be something amiss when James, the butler, disturbed his leisurely perusal of the Sunday *New York Times,* and informed him that his father wished to see him in the library.

"Well, it can't come any too soon for me," muttered Andrew, sensing a long-threatened ultimatum, no doubt brought to a climax by his brother Raymond's latest escapade. Thoughtfully he descended the stairway to the second floor, feeling the oppressive atmosphere of that house as never before.

As he expected, Raymond was already there, standing with the elegant nonchalance his handsome person never failed to radiate. His blond head was bent slightly as he scrutinized a bit of paper he held before him. Mr. Bonning sat at his desk, looking up with a cool air of finality.

"That's the last, Raymond," he was saying. "You are on your own now."

"Okay, Pater," replied Raymond, looking up from the check. "Thanks, of course. It's more than I'd hoped for. . . . And I'm to clear out."

"Your sister and I will take an apartment—where there will not be any room for you boys."

"Morning, Andy," said Raymond. "We're in for a ride. . . . So long to both of you." He strode out fluttering the check in a white hand.

"Dad, I guess I don't need to ask what you want," spoke up Andrew, with a short laugh.

"Will you sit down?" queried his father, courteously.

"No, thanks. And please make it short and sweet."

"It can't be anything else," rejoined the senior Bonning. "You doubtless are aware of how hard the latest Wall Street crash has hit me. I hoped to retrieve. But . . . well, I need not go into details. . . . Here is a check for you."

Andrew received it without glancing at the figures it bore. "Dad, I'm sorry," he said, haltingly. "At your age—it's tough. . . . With neither of us boys any help—and Gloria—"

"Your sister has her income," interrupted Mr. Bonning. "Fortunately she has not squandered the principal of the money your mother left her. And she will marry well. I can take care of myself in a modest way. But Raymond and you must now fare for yourselves."

"I gathered as much, Dad," returned Andrew, thoughtfully. He was still fond of his father, which fact seemed suddenly to erase all the misunderstandings and aloofness of the past few years.

"Andrew, I didn't trouble to bore Raymond with my opinions," went on Mr. Bonning, "but if you will permit me, I'd like to express my bitter disappointment in you."

"Dad, I've been under the impression that you had expressed that—more than once," rejoined Andrew, sadly. "But if it will relieve you—go ahead."

"You quit college before you were half through your sophomore year."

"Why not? I wasn't learning a damn thing," said Andrew impatiently.

"You couldn't make good even in football—where you had every requirement except guts," replied his father contemptuously. "Big, heavy, fast on your feet—you could have made a name for yourself!"

"Yeah! Like hell I could," retorted Andrew hotly. "Didn't I go out for the freshman team and scrub team for two years and rip the varsity line to ribbons? The coaches were hot for me, but Captain Higgins and the athletic directors played their favorites. I lost heart and finally lay down on the job."

"Yes, you sure did. But if you had stuck it out!"

"Dad, would it surprise you to learn that I regarded college as too much football, too many fast cars and too much money, instead of a place to study?"

"No, that wouldn't surprise me. You're adept at excuses. . . . The fact is you failed to get a college training. Either physical or cultural. And lastly, you have failed in business."

"Dad, that last I admit," replied Andrew regretfully. "I've been a flop at each job you've got me. I tried hard. Honest to

28

God, I tried! It wasn't that I'm exactly a dumbbell. I'm poor at figures. I can't stand a desk. Confinement strangles me somehow. . . . And, Dad, to come clean—I hate modern business methods."

"Thank you for being frank, at last," declared Mr. Bonning. "You might have saved us both considerable friction, not to say grief."

Andrew slowly tore the check in two pieces and laid them before his father.

"Dad, you need have no further concern about me."

"What!—you won't take it?"

"No."

"Why not?"

"Because you'll need it more than I. . . . And you've awakened me—to my shame. All the same I don't feel wholly to blame for my failure. The world is out of joint or maybe I just don't fit in. I haven't found anything I want to and can do. That's all. . . . Good-by, father."

Andrew stalked out of the library with head erect and resolute step, deaf to Mr. Bonning's call. On the landing above he encountered his sister Gloria, leaning over the rail. She wore a blue dressing gown.

"Andy!"

"Morning, Gloria! Why so intense and dramatic? You always were a tragedienne, but just now you've got Duse tied to the mast. . . . Say, what an idea! Why don't you go into the movies, Gloria? What'd be better than—"

"I heard," she whispered, and drawing him into her room, closed the door. Then she asked gravely: "Dad has refused you the parental roof any longer?"

"It amounts to that, Sis, though I gathered this particular parental roof was lost to all of us."

"Andy, I'm not a damn bit sorry," she said fervently. "Ray is a rotter. And this break will make a man of you."

"Thanks, old thing. You give me hope. In fact, Gloria, you've been the only one who ever held out the slightest hope for me. I'll not forget that. Even Constance always thought me a flop."

"Yes, and she'll give you the gate when she hears this," declared Gloria significantly. "Andy, it gets my goat the way she strings you along."

"We're not engaged, Sis—and honestly, I don't think I care

29

any more about her than she does about me. We've just been together since before I went to college."

"What'll you do, Andy?" she queried, her dark eyes studying him.

"Beat it!" he burst out, as if a sudden thought had possessed him.

"Where?"

"I don't know. Far away, though . . . where there's room —great open spaces—no business."

"West?" she flashed.

"Darling, you can't imagine me going abroad!"

"Andy, you should have taken Dad's check."

"Not me!"

"I'll stake you to five grand."

"You will not! . . . Thanks, old girl. I've still about twelve thousand of what mother left me. It's more than enough."

"Far West," mused the sister, with wondering eyes. "I've been to Yellowstone, Andy. Oh, Wyoming was marvelous! Go there. . . . Andy, you know I have queer inspirations at long intervals."

"Okay. It's Wyoming," replied Andrew, relieved that something had been decided for him.

"It'll be the making of you," she went on. "Somehow, Andy, you never could have made the grade here. New York has lost its kick for you."

"Kick! I hate that word," he declared irritably. "It seems to be the sole aim of everybody nowadays."

"It is—for all of us anyway," she replied, somberly. "I suppose we can't escape the present. It simply is. . . . I've tried every last thing under the sun—except marriage—and I'd try that if I believed it'd be interesting enough."

Andrew bit his lip to restrain a sharp retort. Whatever Gloria's shortcomings, in his opinion she was a thoroughbred and she had been loyal to him, and loyalty loomed big in this hour.

"Draw the line somewhere, darling," he said lightly. "Marrying Ellerton, or even Blackstone, for their money might not give you much of a kick, but it would be safe."

"Andy, you're old-fashioned. And that's where you are wrong. The idea of a twentieth-century girl marrying to be safe—settled—taken care of! Bunk! Who wants to be safe?"

"Sis, I think *you* can take care of yourself at that," rejoined Andrew with a laugh. "Well, I'll go pack up a few things before I change my mind."

"Do. If you weaken now you're sunk forever. Only don't beat it without saying good-by to me."

Andrew plodded on upstairs to his room, obsessed with the resolve he had impulsively made, conscious of sensations he had not experienced since boyhood. He was twenty-four years old. And the thought that struck him so forcibly at the moment was—why had this idea never come to him before? He flung himself down on his bed to face the realization that the turning point in his life had arrived. He had reached an indifferent stage in a futile existence where he imagined nothing worthwhile could happen to him. But he realized now this was because he had not made anything happen. Until the last six months he had accepted his inability to do so with good nature and resignation. He was just a misfit. Later had come discontent and chafing, leading to his present genuine unhappiness. A few words from his sophisticated yet wise sister had changed all this in a twinkling—had shaken him out of his doldrums. He found himself suddenly facing a future that offered a chance and a challenge.

Yet in his heart he realized that he had not given the old life a fair break. The great modern city was all right, for young people who had kept pace with the time. Andrew was not speed-mad, drink-mad, pleasure-mad, money-mad, but there was something lacking. He had not been willing to give the old life what it took to make the grade.

"But I can raise wheat," he replied to his accusations, "or be a garage mechanic, or a forest ranger . . . or something, by golly!"

What should be his first move? A definite, irrevocable one! First he'd telephone Constance. Sure of her reaction, and eager to have it over, he called her number. And while he waited he visualized her blonde head on her white pillow.

"Hello," came the answer presently, in the sleepy, rich, contented voice he knew so well.

"Good morning, Connie. This is Andy," he replied.

"Oh, it's you, big boy? What's the idea—calling me at this ungodly hour?" she pouted.

"News, Connie," he plunged in. "Dad has shot the works. I've been disinherited—turned out—on my own!"

"*Andy!* Don't be so dramatic! Are you kidding me?"

He assured her solemnly that it was only too true and that

somehow he felt strangely glad. "You know, Connie, I've been a total loss in this burg."

Then followed a silence so long that Andrew had to restrain himself not to break it.

"Oh, Andy—what a rotten break! I'm so sorry, dear," she said finally, and that reply gave him the relief he sought.

"Sure you're sorry, Connie. But your heart isn't going to break?"

"My heart break? Andy, be yourself!"

"Darling, I'm being myself. . . . What I mean is that if you—if you considered our—our friendship . . . Oh, hang it, Connie, if you want to hold me—"

"Dear old Andy! What a child you are!" came the answer accompanied by Constance's mellow laugh. "Listen. I never would have married you, and I thought you knew it. We were just good pals."

"I think I remember your telling me that before. But I wanted to play the game straight."

"Andy, darling, you're too fine, too simple, too square for this crazy town. . . . What will you do?"

"Beat it out West."

"Where?"

"Wild and woolly Wyoming."

"Wyoming? For the love of Mike! Wouldn't St. Louis be far enough?"

"Nix on the madding crowd, Connie."

"Darling, you're being a little mad yourself. That's what I always liked about you."

"Me for the tall timbers and the open range!"

"How you do rave! . . . At least you'll get a kick out of it. I'm envious!"

"Can that stuff, will you?" retorted Andrew. "And just get this straight. It's something Gloria sprung on me a moment ago." And Andrew told her exactly what Gloria had said. He heard Connie's low lazy laugh. Then she added: "Tell Gloria it's not so hot."

"Okay, I'll tell her. . . . Well, Connie, old dear, good-by."

"Good-by, Andy—and good luck!"

Slowly Andrew hung up the receiver, conscious of immeasurable relief and at the same time a vague sadness. His thoughts turned back to the many gay times he and Connie and Gloria had had together. He was turning his back upon those irresponsible times, but there would be no feeling of irreparable loss.

Andrew stood at the window for a moment, in a pensive mood. The street was empty, with that stillness which always meant the Sabbath. Beyond the corner house he could see Central Park, with the maples, the beeches and oaks beginning to show freshly green. Spring had come again. And suddenly the realization that soon he would be out where he could breathe, where he could see the sky and face the free wind, and feel the hot sun on his back and smell the earth, rushed over him with almost a suffocating necessity. By that fleeting sensation Andrew knew for almost the first time that what he was about to do was right for him.

Packing was the last act of severance, difficult and a little sad because he had to choose little out of abundance. He packed two large grips and a traveling bag. Only his favorite possessions were included. And to his amazement, when all the selections had been made and the job finished, that Sabbath day had almost come to an end. He changed to a light traveling suit and, calling a taxi, left the house without seeing his father or Gloria again. He would have said farewell to her if she had not been out.

Andrew went to the Manhattan Hotel, took a room, had dinner, and then crossed to Grand Central Station to engage a berth on the Twentieth-Century Limited for Monday morning. That done, he swung down Forty-second Street toward the theater district, conscious of a deep tranquil excitement in his breast. It was done. And he chose a Western movie as his swan song to life in New York.

The picture was a thriller, full of color and action, raucous with sound, and melodramatic in plot. The hero turned his profile too often to the camera and the heroine heaved her obvious breast too consciously. Andrew could not piece together any thread of story. Yet he sat there in the dark, reveling in the sweep of rangeland, the white-tipped peaks, and the racing of horses, the gun-throwing cowboys, the lean Indian riders. He had always experienced a secret pleasure in such pictures, and had kept his habit of going to see them to himself. Now he reveled in it. It happened that the location of this motion picture was near the Tetons of Wyoming. Andrew remained for the second showing of it, and left the theater as keen as any boy who had ever read of Deadwood Dick and Calamity Jane. Such pictures were made for his kind. Strutting actors had to be endured and the pretty stars tolerated because they had youth and charm, but their great undeniable fascination was in the picture quality, the action of horses and the violence of man, thrown upon a wild and picturesque background.

The next morning Andrew Bonning transferred his securities into cash, nine-tenths in bills of large denomination, which he placed in a little leather sack to wear under his shirt. That money had to go a long way. His ticket read second tourist to Omaha, Nebraska. He, who had never considered the value of a dollar before, now meant to make the most of a dime.

"See here, bozo. Thirty-five bucks is highway robbery for this antediluvian Ford," declared Bonning, as he shook the rattling old car with one powerful grasp of his hand.

The scene was a vacant lot far from the business center of Omaha. Andrew Bonning felt that he had put on a new character with the outfit of blue jeans he had purchased. Certainly it must have had some powerful transforming power, for never before that he could remember had he haggled over the price of any commodity.

"Cheapest Ford here, boss," replied the open-lot car distributor. "What you lookin' fer?"

"I want an old car that nobody can run. Something to tinker with," replied Andrew.

"I'll be doggoned!" ejaculated the garage man with a grin. "Reckon we ain't comin' to a deal. All my cars run slick as a whistle."

"Let's hear this Ford purr."

The eager salesman jumped in with alacrity, turned on the ignition and tried to start the car. But nothing happened. He rasped and pumped and pulled to no purpose. Red in the face he looked down at Andrew somewhat sheepishly.

"Stranger, did you jimmy the works?"

"How could I? You haven't turned your back on me. . . . Can't you start it?"

" 'Pears not. Cold, I reckon. But I'll make her shoot in a minute."

Several minutes elapsed and the salesman had lost much of his confidence. In the dealer's chagrin Andrew recognized the psychological moment.

"If you throw in that old lap robe there I'll buy this pile of junk."

34

"How much?" queried the car owner, resignedly.

"Fifteen dollars."

"Take it," snorted the other, throwing up his hands. "But you're worse than Jesse James."

Andrew found himself in possession of a car. Leisurely he set about determining what was wrong with the engine. He had a knack for machinery. In less than ten minutes he discovered that the carburetor intake tube was choked with dirt.

"Hey, I found out what ailed her," he called to the car merchant.

"Ahuh? An' what was thet?"

"The locomotive ingredient failed to coincide with the perihelion," replied Andrew cheerfully.

"Aw, go-wan, you can't kid me," returned the other. "Bet you don't belong in them overalls."

"Nope. And you belong in Wall Street. Funny old world! . . . So long!"

On the way to the lodginghouse where Andrew had left his bags he stopped at a grocery store to buy some fruit and provisions. Soon he was on his way out of Omaha, his last stop being at a filling station on the outskirts of the city. Here he procured gas, oil and road maps. Then driving north on the highway, he realized that his new life had begun at last.

Something like a gray curtain had dropped in his consciousness to hide all of his past failures. He was alone, perfectly free, speeding along an open road into an unknown country. Fields, grazing cows, apple trees in bloom, flights of blackbirds, long strings of swallows on the telegraph wires were realities with which he came in close contact for the first time. Rush-lined ponds by the wayside where ducks paddled, wandering willow-bordered brooks, groves of oaks and elms, with other trees unfamiliar to him, met his eager eyes and brought back long-past summer visits in New England, and vague memories of an even remoter period.

Andrew's mood was one of quiet exultation. As he did not rush at the miles, neither did he inquire too avidly into this unfamiliar mood. He felt, however, as he visualized the ranges of the West, that he was undergoing a transformation. It was a transformation which he welcomed. He had pulled his stakes from the East and must transplant them somewhere in the West. But just how the change would take place did not concern Andrew greatly at this time: he was fascinated none the less by the initiation into the process through which he would be made over.

Toward noon he passed through a village that boasted flaring signs of gas stations at both entrance and exit. Somewhere, Andrew promised himself with satisfaction, he would be traveling beyond the smell of gasoline.

Andrew drove along at about twenty-five miles an hour. This snail's pace caused him to be hooted to the side of the road by other cars impatient to pass. One big flashy touring car honked at him impatiently, and as it got by a florid-faced driver in shirt sleeves, evidently a tourist, yelled something about junking a tin can.

"Drive on, mister," said Andrew, aloud. "You represent what I have turned my back on—speed, luxury, restlessness, idleness, high blood pressure—fleshpots of Egypt."

The hours passed by all too quickly for Andrew Bonning. Sunset caught him at the top of a hill, where he stopped to admire the scene. He drove on, presently, coasting down a winding hilly road, and at the bottom turned a curve under a wooded bank that accentuated the twilight.

Andrew caught sight of a camp fire, whose blaze disclosed two slouchy dark forms moving about it. His lights were not working so he moved slowly along the soft road. When about opposite the fire Andrew's sharp ears heard a cry. Then against the evening sky he saw a man and a boy silhouetted in violent action. Andrew stopped the car. He had come upon his first adventure.

"Let that boy go," shouted Andrew and jumped out of his car. Advancing upon the two he asked what the idea was. The man retreated, with a reply about only having fun.

"Oh—n-no sir," cried the youngster, in a voice that startled Andrew. "He meant to rob—me—and I don't know what—when he saw I was a girl!"

Andrew's exclamation of amazement was followed by a swift leap, a lunge and a blow, the power of which he had not calculated. Like a flung sack the man went over the bank out of sight. Andrew yelled for the tramp's comrades to make themselves scarce.

"Are you really a girl?" he queried, turning to the little figure in the middle of the road. Indeed, after peering down into a white oval face and great staring dark eyes he found that he need not have asked that question.

The girl admitted it and said she sometimes wished she

were not. Andrew asked her a couple of pertinent questions, to learn that she did not belong thereabouts, and that she was a hitchhiker. As she stood there, looking up at him, Andrew Bonning found himself divided between two impressions—one of admiration and solicitation for a pretty slip of a girl who had been caught in a perilous predicament; the other a sudden bitter reminder of modern woman's wiles and the fact that even on a lovely Nebraska road at night he might expect to meet a girl who was only looking for a thrill. The second impression won out over the former. Andrew offered the girl a lift as far as Norfolk, and helping her in, resumed his seat at the wheel and went on.

He could see her dimly in the paling afterglow without appearing to notice her, and it was not easy to subdue his curiosity. She had slim brown hands, beautifully shaped, that clung nervously to the pack she held on her lap. He could feel that she wanted to speak to him, and finally she did, hazarding a remark that he evidently did not live in this section. Then, in the short interchange of conversation that followed, which he did not encourage because he resented his interest in a girl hiker, he was led to reveal his name. But she did not give hers, an omission Andrew added to her discredit. At last they arrived at Norfolk. He called her attention to the fact and remarked her enthusiasm over the bright lights.

"You'll get another kick here," he replied, slowing down preparatory to a stop.

"Kick?" she echoed, turning those strange, luminous eyes upon him in doubt, not of the word, but of his intimation. Andrew could have sworn not only to her innocence, but to the fact that in the bright light he was gazing at the very prettiest girl he had ever seen in his life.

"Yes, kick," he replied curtly, annoyed with himself. Then he laughed. "Isn't that what you're after? Isn't that about all girls think of nowadays?"

She did not reply and seemed to have been affronted by his accusation.

"Please let me out here," she requested, pointing toward a modest-looking hotel.

They stopped, and he stepped out to assist her. Then she said, hesitatingly: "Thank you, Mr. Bonning, for—for everything."

He replied that she was welcome and that he hoped she

would have better luck on the next lap of her hike. . . . "You forgot to tell me your name."

"I didn't forget. I was—"

No doubt her faltering was due to Andrew's exposure of the letters M A D on the pack he lifted from the car, and at which he stared.

"Mad!" he spelled out, "Wyoming Mad?" with a laugh. "It suits you better than any name. And as you are an unforgettable kid I'll remember you by that. . . . I hope we don't meet again. Good-by."

She stood there at the curb, holding her bag, her sweet face uplifted, puzzled, shy, slowly awakening to his rudeness. Andrew flung himself into the car and drove away, conscious of several conflicting feelings. He halted on the next corner at a gas station to fill up. Then he continued on to another hotel further down the street, where he put up for the night.

Andrew ate a dinner less frugal than had been his intention. But he gave very little thought to his plan of travel. He was in a curious state of mind. After dinner he walked twice past the hotel where the hiking girl had stopped, and nearly succumbed to a desire to go in to inquire for her. Then he went to a motion picture theater and stood in front of it for a while hoping like a fool that she might come along. He went in but soon left. After that he walked to and fro in the town's little park, and at length returned to his hotel and room.

"Well, my first adventure is a puzzler," soliloquized Andrew while he undressed. He had to own up to having received a thrill from his rescue of the little hiker with the big eyes. He had been shocked to meet a girl, hardly sixteen years old, he calculated, alone on a country road after dark, confessedly engaged upon what he considered to be a mad prank. He had been alienated by a recurrent bitterness which fostered the thought that she could not be anything else but a wayward girl, on adventure bent. It was this thought that had accounted for his sudden rudeness.

"Unforgettable kid? Nuts!" he concluded, turning out the light. "The world was full of alluring, seductive, irresistible females. What chance had a man? Wyoming Mad? . . . If this isn't the queerest deal I ever had. Suppose I meet that girl again? It'll be funny. Ha! Ha! . . . I don't think! . . . That kid's just no good!" Then Andrew was amazed to hear an inward voice damn him for a sophisticated, suspicious and embittered Easterner who could not recognize innocence when he met it.

38

"My God!" muttered Andrew aghast. "What would Connie or Gloria say to that? That I'm 'Wyoming Mad' myself." But his derision was not convincing. In this new voice there appeared to be the nucleus of a revolt.

At daylight Andrew was behind the wheel of his Ford, and he started with a speed which indicated that he wanted to leave something far behind. Twenty-five or thirty miles an hour, however, was about the limit his old battered car could produce and soon cars began to pass him. To save his life he could not resist trying to get a look at their occupants. But that was seldom possible, unless he deliberately stared as the cars sped by. All day long, he reflected, a trim little figure, between lifts, was probably hiking along that road. Her eyes haunted him, not because of their size, he imagined, or their strange glow, or their color—because he had no idea of their color—but because of the wistful look they held. Had he misjudged her? Had he placed her in a class with all the neckers, flirts and thrill seekers, just because he had found her on a lonely road, waylaid by tramps? It did seem unjust, he had to admit. There was some unquenchable chivalry in Andrew Bonning which had often been the jest of his sportive acquaintances.

Andrew made no stop that day, except at a crossroad refueling station. Toward evening he had dinner at a little wayside hamlet, and then he drove on a few miles to camp in his car. All the next day engine trouble occupied his attention, and gave him enough tinkering to satisfy a long-felt want. It halted him, too, at Sidonia for a minor repair.

He was standing in front of the one hotel, watching the traffic and awaiting the dinner hour, when a car gingerly approached the curb.

The driver was the girl who had been causing him so much speculation. Her companion appeared to be a young local chap to whom this was an auspicious occasion. As Andrew recognized the hitchhiker, she simultaneously looked up to meet his gaze. Then a sudden light, a half-break of a smile, was blotted out in a crimson blush.

Andrew strode into the hotel, somehow glad that she had had the grace to blush. Caught with the goods, he thought scornfully! She had picked up this country bumpkin on the road and had ended a short or long, probably long, ride by driving his car, no doubt to allow him freer use of his arms. It made Andrew slightly sick, because that queer streak of chivalry in him had almost won a battle in her behalf. He wished she would appear in the dining room before he left. He wanted just one more look at her.

Andrew, however, had given up hope and had almost finished his meal when she did come in, escorted by the young fellow who was very overceremonious and obviously self-conscious. Andrew, considerably surprised at her appearance, could only stare.

She had changed the masculine hiking garb for a pretty blue dress that was exceedingly feminine. She had trim shapely legs and little feet on which were patent-leather slippers. Her dainty head, carried high, was bare. The wavy, golden hair caught and held the light. All this Andrew saw in a glance before her face transfixed him. Its opal hue, just hinting of tan, took on a little warmth and color. As she passed she spoke, impudently he thought.

"Howdy, Hiram Perkins. Hope you heered from Mizzourie."

"Good evening, Wyoming Mad," he returned, rising and bowing.

Her escort seated her at a nearby table, and evidently was concerned by the exchange of greetings between her and Andrew. She made some casual explanation, with a deprecatory motion of her hand that seemed to satisfy her escort.

"Knows her stuff," muttered Andrew to himself, and then, drawing a deep breath, as a man about to undergo an ordeal, he looked deliberately at her. It was to find that she was already gazing fixedly at him. For a long moment their eyes held their gaze. Andrew had an odd thought—if those wonderful eyes had expressed the least softness, the least hint of yielding, he would not have been accountable for himself. All Andrew could detect, however, was pride and disdain. And he caught these impressions only as she averted her face.

Then he had his opportunity, and he made the most of it. Pretty? Beautiful? Such terms did not do her justice. She was lovely. Engrossed with his scrutiny Andrew had not at once grasped one dismaying fact. She was flirting outrageously with her escort. She never deigned to give Andrew another glance. Again his vision of her became distorted, though her actions were merely those of a gay young girl having an enjoyable dinner with a newly made acquaintance. Andrew knew that, but his biased mind would not accept it. He imagined them in the shadowy park—nay—riding along a country road in the moonlight to some lonesome spot. He shook his head angrily. Suddenly Andrew found himself hating the girl.

Abruptly he arose, leaving his dessert untasted, and stalked out. "One born every minute!" he muttered, and then in bitter conflict with his skepticism: "Connie, old girl, I guess you ruined the makings of a square fellow!"

He got his car, and after driving half the night, he stopped to watch the moon go down over the western horizon.

4

A WEEK LATER Andrew Bonning made camp outside a little Wyoming town called Split Rock. This was on the Old Oregon Trail which he had followed all the way from Torrington, on the Nebraska line.

Many places along the famous old trail of the trappers, explorers, Indian fighters and pioneers had interested him and almost persuaded him to stop for a spell. But satisfying as had been the rolling sagebrush prairie, Andrew had continued on his way in answer to a call he could not define. On clear mornings he could see the mountains white-toothed in the blue. And they lured him. The Platte River saw three of his camps before he left it at Alcova. He passed over the Rattlesnake Range, and as he drove into Split Rock one golden sunset he saw the Granite Mountains on his right and the Green Mountains on his left. And westward, a hundred miles more or less, stood the Continental Divide, dim yet rosy-white in the sunset, the great wall of the Rockies.

Andrew left his car in a thicket not far off the road, deciding to walk the half mile into Split Rock for the exercise. Satisfying himself that it could not readily be detected by passersby he proceeded into the town to make some much needed purchases.

By this time Andrew had become accustomed to the Wyoming villages along the trail. Casper had been a fairly large place. The other towns from central to western Wyoming held little of interest for the wayfarer. Some of them appeared to be no more than the old wide-streeted, board-fronted frontier towns modernized principally by the gasoline stations of the present. He found that Split Rock leaned a little more toward the past.

Indeed, his observing eyes detected more cowboys than truck drivers or garage attendants. He listened to snatches of their conversation satisfying for the hundredth time his avid pleasure in things western. Deciding to make inquiries on the morrow about the range country hereabouts he returned to his car.

By this time it was quite dark. A wonderful light still glowed in the west, whence came a cold breeze, keen and penetrating, sweet with a tang of the mountain and the range. Andrew breathed deeply of it, and reveled in the lonesomeness of his surroundings. Every camp of late had been visited by coyotes to his growing delight. These wild prairie dogs could not bark and yelp and mourn and ki-yi too much for him. He even threw scraps of his meals to the stealthy prowlers.

He had collected a bundle of dry sticks and bits of sage-brush when a clip-clop of hoofs drew his attention. A rider was passing on the road. He halted opposite Andrew, lighted a cigarette, then rode on a little further, only to come back. It was evident that he was waiting for someone. Andrew had no mind to disclose his hiding place, so he sat down to watch and listen.

The rider appeared to be impatient. Andrew heard his spurs clinking. Evidently he smoked his cigarette half through, then lit another. His spirited horse would not stand still. And the night was so still, the air so clear that this rider's voice carried to Andrew's vibrant ears.

"You dawggone ornery hawse—cain't you stand on yore fo' feet?" drawled the rider. After another cigarette he appeared to start, to crouch and then to stare up the road toward town. Andrew heard rapid footsteps approaching from that direction.

"Thet you, McCall?" queried the rider, in a sharp tone which carried far.

"Yes, it's me," came the answer.

"Git off the road over heah," commanded the rider, heading his horse toward the thicket that screened Andrew's car.

Rider and pedestrian met half way and continued as far as a large rock scarcely thirty feet from where Andrew crouched behind a clump of low sagebrush. There the two halted, and the unmounted one hunched himself up on the rock.

"Tex, I been lookin' fer you at my ranch," he said. "Jest happened to be in town today an' got your word."

"Wal, I shore would have rid down on you pronto, if you

42

hadn't showed up tonight," retorted the rider, curtly. "Mac, I want some money."

"Hyar's all I got," returned the other hastily, and passed his hand up to the horseman. "You'll have to wait till I ship some more cattle."

"Ahuh! Always waitin'," growled the younger man. "I cain't see. How much you got heah?"

"Two-hundred-odd."

"Wal, I'll let you off on thet. But only fer a while. I reckon I'm not long fer this range. I got to pull oot, Mac, an' it's mostly yore cattle deals thet's chasin' me."

"Aw, Texas, thet ain't so. You was talked of before you ever forked a hoss fer me."

"Shore I was. But fer makin' love an' throwin' a gun—not fer burnin' yore brand on calves," snapped the cowboy, in a voice so cold and strange to Andrew that it sent shivers up his spine.

"Have it your own way, Tex. I don't want to argue with you. But I heered Sheriff Slade hang suspicion on you. Right before half a dozen cattlemen, one of which was Jeff Little, who you rode fer once."

"Ahuh. An' what did Jeff say?"

"He got a little het up at Slade. Said you was a wild one all right, but straight as a string, an' thet Slade hadn't savvied thet you was from the old Texas breed."

"Damn thet four-flush of a sheriff!" cursed the cowboy. "He's not so above a slick deal himself. I know. . . . Reckon I'm liable to take a shot at him one of these heah nights."

"Tex, you'll kill somebody yet," declared McCall, anxiously.

"Shouldn't wonder. All you gotta do, Mac, is to make damn good an' shore it ain't you. . . . When do I git the rest of the dough?"

"Reckon pronto. . . . Tex, I got a new deal on."

"Ahuh. Wal, spring it on me."

"There's an old geezer named Nick Bligh just drove in a thousand head of cows, a sprinklin' of yearlings, an' a lot of calves. Hails from Randall, somewhere near the Montana line. This rancher hasn't no outfit at all—jest a middle-aged man to help him handle thet stock. Why, before the snow flies there'll be a couple hundred unbranded calves bawlin' around."

"Humph. How come this Nick Bligh hasn't got no punchers?"

"There can be only one reason fer thet, if he's a Westerner. No money."

"Wal, thet's no reason why a cowboy worth a damn wouldn't ride fer him. I've done it. All depends on the rancher."

"Tex, thet gives me an idee. Suppose you go ride fer this Bligh—"

"Ump-umm, Mac. I don't mind brandin' a few mavericks. Thet's legitimate. An' even when a cattleman knows the mavericks ain't his—he brands them anyhow. All ranchers have done thet—gettin' their start. But what you propose would be stealin'."

"If you're set on splittin' hairs over it—hell, yes!" replied McCall, testily.

"I'll go in on the deal—burnin' your brand on stray calves."

"But, Tex, there ain't much money in thet for me or you," continued the other persuasively. "On the other hand, two hundred calves would fetch between forty an' fifty dollars a head next year."

"Mac, thet's most like old-time rustlin'," expostulated the cowboy.

"Look hyar, puncher. You oughta know thet there's plenty of rustlin' goin' on on Wyomin' ranges right now."

"Shore. But what's a few haid of stock to a cattleman who owns ten thousand? Mac, safety lies in small numbers. You aim to hire me to be crooked. An' I'll be damned if I'll fall for it."

Silence ensued after the puncher's forceful speech. Andrew scarcely breathed in the intensity of his interest and the peril he risked in being discovered. The cowboy struck a match for his cigarette. By its light Andrew saw a youthful reckless face, singularly handsome, almost as red as his flaming hair.

"Tex, I don't trust Smoky Reed over much," at length replied McCall.

"Wal, Smoky is on the level. If you want him to snake oot all the calves thet poor devil owns he'll do it. Smoky told me he'd lost out with the K-Bar ootfit an' was goin' to ride fer the Three Flags. I reckon he won't last much longer heah, no more'n me."

"Will you make Smoky an offer fer me?"

"Wal, I'll carry any word you say. But get this, McCall, I won't have nothin' to do with Smoky's work."

"Thet's all right, Tex. Don't get het up."

"This Bligh deal ain't so good. I'm advisin' you, Mac. If you go whale bang at it you may lose oot. Shore, I've got you figgered. If it come to a showdown you'd lay it on to a couple range-marked punchers."

"Tex, I wouldn't give no one away."

"Aw, the hell's fire you wouldn't," retorted the cowboy shortly. "To save yore own skin you'd do thet an' more. But so far as I'm concerned I can look oot fer myself. I was thinkin' of Smoky."

"Safest way," continued McCall as if he had not heard Texas, "is to drive cow an' calf into rough brush or timber, or a rocky draw—kill the cow, then brand the calf an' fetch it out. Coyotes an' buzzards would make short work of the carcass. An' there ain't one chance in a thousand of Bligh missin' his cows until the job's all done."

"Aw, it's safe enough, but it just sticks in my craw, McCall," rejoined the cowboy in disgust.

"Thet ain't the point. Will you put Smoky wise to this deal?"

"Shore, I'll do thet. An' I'll do my part. But before you bust into this, Mac, listen to me. I never heahed of this Nick Bligh. Most likely he's a pore cattleman, drove west, an' makin' a stand. But s'pose this all happened. S'pose aboot the time you got yore deal half done, say, thet a pardner with money enough to buy more stock an' hire some real cowboys —s'pose he'd show up?"

"Ha! Tex, miracles like thet don't happen in these cattle times."

"Hell they don't! Anythin' can happen, man. Where's yore sense? I ain't carin' a damn, 'cept for the old geezer Bligh. But I'm just tellin' you."

"Reckon you're losin' your nerve, Tex, or figgerin' over-careful."

"Shore, if thet's the way you get me. . . . Where's this Bligh feller located?"

"Down across the Sweetwater River," replied McCall eagerly. "He's bought or leased the old Boseman ranch, on the south bank of the river, halfway between the Antelope Hills an' the Green Mountains. Damn fine range, when the grass is good. An' this spring it's comin' strong."

"Ahuh. I know thet ranch," mused Texas. "Looked at it with a longin' eye myself, more'n once. But it'd take some dough to make good there."

45

"Thet's not our concern. For your an' Smoky's information put this under your hat. There are three outfits on thet big range south of the Sweetwater. The Cross Bar, owned by Cheney Brothers, the Triangle X, run by Hale Smith, an' the Wyomin' Cattle Association, runnin' the W.C. They all work up into the foothills of the Green Mountains, an' anyone ridin' in there must have sharp eyes. Savvy?"

"Shore, I savvy. Slade is in thet Wyomin' Cattle Association," returned Texas, thoughtfully.

"Yes, but not very deep. Slade's in more'n one deal jest for a blind." McCall slid down off the rock. "Reckon thet's about all fer tonight."

"Wal, it'll last me a spell, Mac," drawled the cowboy. "Don't overlook my hunch. So long."

With a wave of his hand the cowboy loped his horse over to the road, and taking the direction away from town, soon disappeared in the darkness. McCall watched him out of sight and stood listening to the dying clip-clop of hoofs.

"By Gawd, thet Texas puncher will spill the beans fer me yet—if I don't fix him," he muttered, and then with a snap of his fingers strode away toward the town.

When he, too, had gone Andrew arose to stretch his cramped legs. His face was wet with sweat and his heart was thumping. He had to laugh at his first introduction to a western drama that was not in any sense fictitious.

"Well, Andy, what do you know about this?" he asked himself. "By golly, I like that redheaded cowpuncher. I'll bet he's the goods. But McCall is that same little old proposition one meets the world around, I guess. And Bligh, just the old fall guy who's to be fleeced. Now I wonder where do I come in?"

Andrew almost forgot that he was cold and hungry. After some deliberation he built a fire, deciding that if the cowboy or McCall should happen back there—which was wholly unlikely—he could allay suspicion by claiming he had just arrived. To be thrown upon his own resources had become an increasing joy to Andrew, but so far he did not exactly shine as a cook. He burned both the ham and the potatoes, and let the coffee boil over. Nevertheless he ate what he had cooked with a relish.

This night he decided not to sleep in the car. He had added a couple of blankets to the old lap robe, and he made his bed on the ground beside the fire. Then he gathered all the available firewood in the near vicinity, and removing only his shoes he prepared to make a night of it.

All the same, slumber soon gripped Andrew and held him tight for half the night. Awakening stiff with cold, he got up to renew the fire. Despite his discomfort, the traveler decided that life in the open had its good points. Andrew had known camp life, but only in a luxurious way. As he sat beside the little fire warming his hands and feet, he knew that he had become a part of this land of the purple sage.

The sky was a deep dark blue, studded with innumerable stars. Black rocks stood up bold and sharp above the brush. There was not a sound except the faint rustling of leaves in the night wind.

On and off, he was up like this during the remainder of the night, until the blackness yielded to gray, when he fell soundly asleep for a couple of hours. He drove into town with the sunrise. While eating breakfast at a lunch counter frequented by dusty-booted men, refueling his car at the service station, stocking a goodly supply of food at a grocery, buying a very fine secondhand cowboy outfit at a merchandise store, Andrew asked the cheerful and casual questions of the tenderfoot. Having thus acquired a lot of general information, he was about to leave town when he happened to think that he had not inquired the way to the Sweetwater River and Nick Bligh's ranch.

He leaned out of his car to accost a Westerner who happened along at that moment. He was a man of about sixty years of age, gray and weather-beaten. His boots and garb gave ample evidence of considerable contact with the soil.

"Excuse me, sir," said Andrew. "Can you direct me to the Sweetwater River?"

"Good morning, young man," the Westerner replied, as he halted. "Straight ahead about thirty miles out."

"Thanks. And how to get to Nick Bligh's ranch?"

Andrew became aware of keen blue eyes fixed upon him. "You know Nick?"

"Sorry to say I don't, but I'd like to," replied Andrew heartily.

"Selling hardware, life insurance, lightning rods—or bootleg whiskey?" queried the old man dryly.

"No. Just trying to sell myself."

"Job, eh?"

"Yes, I want a job."

"Who told you to hit Nick Bligh?"

"I happened to hear that he'd lately come to this range with cattle and no cowboys. So I thought he might want one."

"Wal, son, I happen to know Nick wants cowboys. But he's hard up at present. Looking for big wages?"

"I'll work for my board," declared Andrew eagerly.

"Where you from?"

"East."

"Reckoned that. But East means anywhere from the Missouri to the Atlantic."

"All right, call it Missouri. I don't want to advertise I'm a dude."

"I reckon Nick will be glad to talk to you. . . . Don't cross the river. Take the road left and drive onto his place. You can't miss it, as there's only one. If Nick's not home, wait."

"Much obliged. I'll do that," rejoined Andrew heartily.

The Westerner turned to resume his walk, almost bumping into a tall man wearing a wide sombrero.

"Morning, Slade," he said shortly and passed on.

"Howdy, Nick," drawled the other. Then he approached Andrew and gave him a searching look from keen yellow eyes. Andrew was quick to see the glint of a silver shield half concealed under the man's vest. He was without a coat. His face was sallow and he wore a long drooping mustache. Andrew's pulse quickened a few beats when he realized that he was facing Sheriff Slade.

"Stranger hereabouts?" he queried.

"You bet I am," responded Andrew pleasantly enough.

"Salesman?"

"Nope. Just a tin-Lizzie tramp looking for a job."

"Was that what you was askin' Nick Bligh?"

"Who?"

"Wal, the man you was jest talkin' to," returned the sheriff tersely.

"Oh—him! Was *that* Nick Bligh?"

"Air you shore you didn't know thet?"

"Say, mister, I just arrived here this A.M. I was merely asking the gentleman about work on ranches."

"I see you're loaded up with a cowpuncher's junk. Wonder what you got hid under all this. . . . Get out!"

"Sheriff, eh?" rejoined Andrew lightly as he slid out of the seat. "Delighted to meet you."

Slade searched the car thoroughly, during which perform- ance a little crowd collected. Andrew pretended a show of resentment.

"I'm a stranger, out of work, driving west—and get held up for doing nothing," he complained to the bystanders resentfully.

Slade continued his search in silence. Finally he closed the car door and spoke: *"Quien sabe?"* You can never tell who's packin' liquor."

"No offense," returned Andrew cheerily. "I appreciate what the West is up against. . . . Why, Officer Slade, even *you* might be a bootlegger!" And Andrew gave the sheriff a cool stare, mitigated by a smile.

"Don't get fresh, young feller," replied Slade gruffly, an- noyed by the laughter among the bystanders. "Be on your way an' keep goin'."

Andrew got back into his car. "Most western towns welcome travelers and prospective settlers. What's the matter with this burg?"

"Wal, we Wyomin' folks air partic'lar about our brands," drawled the sheriff.

"But not so particular about whose calf you slap them on," retorted Andrew, and stepped on the throttle. "Gosh!" he ejaculated. "This will never do. I must learn to keep my mouth shut and my temper down. But wouldn't I have liked to sock that yellow-eyed hypocrite!"

Once out of town he slowed to the speed he liked best, which was in fact merely crawling along. All the way across Wyoming he had feasted his eyes upon the increasingly fas- cinating vistas. What he could not get enough of was the far- flung leagues of open rangeland. Along here, however, he was shut in by low mountains to the north, and some few miles to the south by a higher, rougher range.

For the time being Andrew shelved some of the aspects of his latest adventure, content to return to them again after he had reached the ranch on the Sweetwater. Why, he won- dered, had Nick Bligh not revealed his identity?

At the end of two hours of somewhat rough going, he passed the limits of the Granite Range. From there the rolling plains to the north appeared endless. He saw a winding line of trees which probably marked the river course. Cattle in consider- able number in the aggregate, but scattered so far and wide over the rangeland that they seemed very few could be seen grazing. Once he spied a lone horseman topping a ridge, and the sight gave Andrew an inexplicable thrill.

The black patches on the green, so few and far between, he had come to recognize as ranch houses. By his uncertain calculation a dozen miles or more separated the closest of the ranches. And gradually these distances widened, as the ranches decreased in number, until the hour came when he could not see a single house.

At length he approached the river on a long, gradual downgrade. When he arrived at the point where the highway crossed a bridge, and an apology for a road branched to the south, it was the big moment in that day's drive.

The Sweetwater River was a delight to the eyes, as it must have been a boon to the immense range that it traversed. It wound away between wooded banks, now flowing in shallow ripples over gravel bars, and now in long deep reaches, and again spread into several channels around willow-bordered islands. Coyotes stood on the opposite bank to watch Andrew; jack rabbits abounded, and wild ducks skittered off the shoals to wing in rapid flight up the river.

Andrew's view to the south was obstructed owing to the foothills of the Green Mountains which encroached upon the river bottom lands.

After gazing long at the superb view, the traveler turned into the branch road, with the feeling that he was leaving his bridges behind him, if not burning them. The road kept to the river bank, and was of such a nature that he had to attend to careful driving instead of indulging his desire for enjoying the scenery. In due time he arrived at the point where the foothills trooped down to the stream. He drove along their base until he had passed the last one. Here two scenic spots met his delighted gaze—the first, a grove of cottonwoods just bursting into bright green, and the other, a high, isolated knoll from which he was certain one could get a commanding view of the country. Andrew did not make any choice. He would possess them both; and he drove down into the grove of cottonwoods.

A wide-spreading giant of a tree invited rest. Grassy plots and sandy places alternated through the grove down to the high weeds and yellow daisies, and the wall of willows.

"Immense!" ejaculated Andrew with a tremendous sigh. He did not know exactly what he meant by immense, but the feeling was profound. Lifting out the boxes of food, Andrew selected crackers and sardines and a can of peaches for his lunch. This was faring sumptuously. He had a canteen full of fresh water, but he decided to go down to the river. Finding a cattle track he followed it out of the grove, through the breast-high sunflowers and the willows, down to where the river murmured and gurgled over a gravelly bar. Andrew waded in, and scooped up water with his cupped hands. It was sweet and cold. He wondered where it came from and tried to picture its rocky source.

He retraced his steps, stripping leaves and a few of the yellow daisies on the way. Andrew put the boxes back in the car and then headed for the knoll.

As he had been deceived before by distance and elevation, so he was again in this instance. The knoll proved not very close to the road and considerably higher than he had imagined it to be. As he climbed, the necessity for taking the easiest way worked him round to the north slope, so that when he surmounted the knoll he faced the range keenly expectant but completely unprepared for what greeted his view.

"My Lord!" he gasped, amazed at the vivid coloring and infinite grandeur of the view.

The vast panorama spreading fan-shaped before him, with the green-bordered shining river turning to the right, and the rugged slopes of the mountain range on the left, formed a gateway to what appeared to be a purple abyss, and leading to a blue-based, white-peaked barrier in the far distance.

"Aw, have a heart, Wyoming!" cried Andrew. "What are you giving me? . . . Are you real—or is this just one of my dreams?"

He stood there gazing his fill. This was his first unlimited view. The sweep of prairie land, hills and valleys, mountain ranges in the distance—these had become scenes of growing frequency and increasing impressiveness during the last few days of travel. But the scene unfolding before him here dwarfed anything that he had yet seen.

"No, this is no mirage. This is real. . . . And oh, boy, this is the one spot in all the world I've been looking for," he exclaimed.

Westward he followed the black and green river bottom and the shining water to the north of a low range of symmetrical knolls, marked Antelope Hills on his map. Then miles or more beyond he sighted the ranch that must be Nick Bligh's. Indeed, there was no other ranch visible south of the Sweetwater. Its location seemed all satisfying to the traveler. The river went on and on, growing dimmer, becoming a mere thread, to vanish in a blue haze out of which the Rocky Mountains rose, first obscure and like low masses of clouds, and then clear blue, to rise up and up in magnificent reaches to pierce the sky with their snow-white peaks. That was the Continental Divide, the backbone of the West, the end of the Great Plains, the wall of iron, set so formidably on the earth with its jagged teeth in the heavens.

The Antelope Hills blocked the center of the gateway to the south. They shone white and gray and pink in the sunlight. Some were crowned with a fringe of black; others showed black clefts deep down between the domes; still others appeared craggy and rough, with belts of timber at their bases.

But it was the spreading of the fanlike range southward that drew and held Andrew Bonning's gaze. He felt dwarfed. How cramped he had been all his life! New York City would hardly have been a visible dot down in the center of that purple immensity. Poor, struggling, plodding, suffocating millions of men—of toilers—if they could only have found themselves there! Andrew felt a singular uplift of spirits. His instinct had been true. Its source and its meaning still remained inscrutable, but he realized that in following it he had found an unknown heritage.

So engrossed had Andrew been that he had forgotten the field glasses he had carried up the hill with him. These he now remembered and focused upon that mysterious gulf of purple.

What had been wavy lines and pale spots and dim shadows and blank reaches, veiled in differing degrees of the purple hue of distance, resolved themselves into endless rolling ridges like atolls in a smooth sea, and vast areas of flat land, bare and desolate, and wide green valleys, with here and there the tiny dots of ranches leagues apart.

The Easterner descended the knoll with giant strides. He had never, that he could remember, heard the singing of his heart as at that moment. Whatever had brought about the accident of his arrival here, he would bless all his life long. His failures now seemed like successive steps to a new life. He divined that any labors he undertook on this range would be labors of love, and they could not fail. He was profoundly grateful now to his own past inability to fit into an office or to sell bonds or to play the market; to the criticism, the misunderstanding, the bitter defeats and his father's financial fall that had sent him to Wyoming.

Andrew Bonning drove up to Bligh's ranch in this almost reverent mood, which perhaps cast a sort of glamour over the low-walled, mud-roofed rambling cabin, and especially to a large structure on the river bank—a cabin, deserted, with gaping windows, bleached gray logs and crumbling, yellow chimney. He had no time for more than this first glance because the old man whom he had interviewed in town suddenly appeared from behind the nearer cabin.

"You beat me here, Mr. Bligh," said Andrew smilingly.

"Yes, I saw your car as I passed the cottonwoods. How'd you know me?" His blue eyes were twinkling and kindly. Andrew read in them liking for his fellow man. Yet the bronzed thin face, wrinkled like withered parchment, attested to a life of struggle and trial.

"I heard that Sheriff Slade call your name. . . . What do you know? He held me up, searched my car for contraband —the yellow-eyed goofer! I didn't take much to him, Mr. Bligh."

"Did he find any?" inquired the rancher. Andrew saw more in the penetrating eyes than the casual query testified.

"He did not. It made me sore—that digging into my gear. And I made a crack that I'm afraid was pretty foolish. It made the crowd laugh, anyway."

"Yeah? What'd you say to Slade?"

"I told him he might be a bootlegger himself, for all *I* knew."

"Wal! You said that to Slade? Young man, you should bridle your tongue. . . . But get down and come in."

"Say, that's a new one on me," declared Andrew. " 'Get down and come in!' Range greeting, eh?"

"Yes. Motors will never take the place of horses on the range."

"Thanks, Mr. Bligh. But before I get out—or down—please give me some hope that I can land a job with you. I climbed a hill back there to get a look at the country. I'm just plain crazy about it. I'll simply have to get a job here. I can do any kind of work. . . . And, well, Mr. Bligh, I'm the man you need."

"I like your enthusiasm. What's your name?"

"Andrew Bonning."

53

"Where from?"

"I told you—the East. Some day I'll tell you more about myself. It ought to be enough now to say I come to you clean and straight." And Andrew met the keen scrutiny of those usually mild blue eyes with a level open glance.

"Bonning, we cattlemen often hire men without names or homes or pasts. What counts here is, what you *are*—what you can *do*."

"Well, in that case all a fellow can do is to ask for a chance to prove himself."

"It amounts to that."

"Will you give me a chance, Mr. Bligh?"

"I reckon I will, on conditions."

"What are they?"

"You offered to work for your keep, didn't you?"

"Yes, sir. I'll be glad to. You see, I bought a secondhand cowboy outfit."

"No cattleman could miss seein' all them trappin's, son. . . . My condition is this—that you work for your board until I can afford to pay you real wages—provided we get along together."

"Okay. Suits me and I'm much obliged. I'll do my level best to please you—and I'm darned sure I can help you."

"Can you ride?"

"Yes."

"Throw a rope?"

"No."

"Or a gun?"

"No, but I'm a good rifle shot."

"Cook?"

"No, I thought I could. But eating my own cooking for two weeks has changed my mind."

"Good at figures?"

"Lord, no! I couldn't add up a column of figures ten times and get less than ten different sums."

"Neither can I. But we won't have much figuring to do. . . . Bonning, I like your looks and I like your talk. One more question and it's a deal."

"Okay. Spring that one on me."

"Have you got guts?"

"Guts!" echoed Andrew.

"Nerve, in an Easterner's way of puttin' it. I got robbed of most of my cattle up north. Had a ranch on the Belle

54

Fourche River, near Aladdin. Made up my mind to pull up stakes an' try a new range. Like this one fine. But today I learned there's some cattle stealing here, same as everywhere on the Wyomin' ranges."

"Who told you, Mr. Bligh?"

"Cattleman named McCall. Agreeable chap. Went out of his way to scrape acquaintance with me. An' I verified that news. Got laughed at for my pains. One old rancher said to me, 'Rustlin'? Hell, yes, enough left to make the cattle business healthy. When rustlin' peters out in Wyomin' thet'll be the end of the cattleman!' "

"Well, that's a point of view to make one think!"

"Wal, it needn't worry you. But when I put it up to you I'm makin' it plain. If you're white-livered or softhearted, not to say yellow, you just won't do. I've only one man on the ranch. Happened to run across him on the Belle Fourche. He's from Arizona, has seen a lot of range life, crippled—which is why he finds it hard to get jobs—but he's a real man. Married, by the way, to a nice little woman who sure can keep house. I never had a woman about my ranch before. An' eatin' my own sourdough biscuits nearly killed me. . . Wal, his name is Jim Fenner, an' if you make a good runnin' mate for him, I reckon my stock will increase."

"I'm only a tenderfoot," replied Andrew, discouraged in spite of his ardor. Bligh had a set, hard look around his mouth.

"I don't need to be told that. In a way it's in your favor. The thing is—will you learn this hard game of the range—fight for my interests—an' stick to me? It might lead to your good fortune. An' I'm puttin' it strong because I want you to declare yourself strong."

"I do, Mr. Bligh," replied Andrew ringingly, as he took the proffered hand. "I see it as tough, steady work—and no lark. It's a chance that will make a man of me. I'll do my damnedest!"

5

●

MARTHA ANN responded quickly to the cheery and kindly interest of the two travelers who had come upon her in the road, just after the ugly episode with the bully in the Ford. They were on a fishing trip to northern Nebraska.

They did not again refer to the distressing incident, and their keen sense of humor and lively knack of relating their own experiences soon restored Martha Ann to her old self.

They drove at a steady pace all the rest of the day, stopping only for a light supper, and at half past eight they arrived at the small town of Colfax. The men were camping along the way, so they left Martha at the inn, promising to call for her in the morning.

Soon after daylight the three were off again. At Benton, where they arrived in time for lunch, the gentlemen had to take a branch road, leading north. They were sorry that Martha Ann could not proceed further with them. She bade them good-by regretfully, promising to send them a post card when she had safely reached her destination.

Martha Ann faced the road alone once more, on foot, and somewhat forlornly. It seemed a long time since she had hiked even a short distance. All the old apprehensions trooped back into her mind. But when she saw great dark ridges rising above the horizon, and apparently not so very far away, she began to recapture her old adventurous spirit. These were the Black Hills. They thrilled her and also frightened her. Had she not been warned that she would never get through these lonesome hills alive?

A man and woman in a Packard stopped alongside the runaway girl, and the latter asked her if she would like a ride. Martha Ann smiled gratefully, and as the driver reached back and opened the door, she got into the back seat. They introduced themselves as Mr. and Mrs. Corbett of Chicago. In replying Martha gave her name, but neglected to add her address.

"Bet you are headed for Hollywood," chuckled Mr. Corbett.

When she told them that Wyoming, not Hollywood, was her destination, the man said: "If I really thought you were a movie-struck kid, I'd turn you over to the authorities and have you sent home."

Martha Ann realized that this very thing could easily be done. She could not prove that she was over eighteen. She earnestly explained that she was on her way to visit an uncle in Wyoming, and that she was hiking for the fun of it and to save money.

"All right, young lady, I'll take your word for it," replied Mr. Corbett. I'm in the show business myself, but I am glad you're not another girl who wants to be a star."

They reached the next town in time for an early dinner, and then Martha accompanied them to a movie. It featured Tom Mix and his horse, Tony, in a Western. It was a romantic story which left the Chicago girl a trifle sad. How utterly impossible for anything like this picture to happen to her! The only romance so far on this long, long journey had been Andrew Bonning's rescue of her from the clutches of a tramp. The memory of that occasion still warmed her heart. But his rude relegation of her to the ranks of a type of girl she despised had removed any possibility of romance from the episode. Where could he be now? Long ago he had passed by her on the road, perhaps too indifferent even to offer her a lift.

Since the Corbetts were remaining in this town to have extensive repairs made on the car, Martha left next morning on foot.

The air was cold, with a decided sharpness which the young traveler attributed to the altitude. Before noon she had received three uneventful rides, which brought her up into the wooded hills. Passing the beautiful hotel of the Springs, Martha Ann longed to spend a few days there. The tourists lounging around on the verandas seemed so carefree and happy. She wondered if any of them had to work for a living or had ever worried about anything in life.

She walked on to a roadside inn, where she had lunch, and then took again to the white ribbon of road through the black forest of firs. The fragrance of these trees made her short of breath and lightheaded with exhilaration. Except for an occasional car, the road was deserted. No hikers! No campers! Suddenly Martha heard a rustling in the brush, and saw a deer walk into an open glade to stand with long ears erect and watch her warily. How wild and beautiful appeared this creature of the forests—the only one she had ever seen in her whole life. She had a great desire to wander off the road, to mount up the steep slope where the tall dark fir trees shot up straight and spear pointed. She sat down on a rock to watch the trout in a clear pool. Shafts of golden sunlight pierced through the foliage, and a breeze sighed through the trees above her head. As she sat there in the sweet silence the hum of a motor broke in upon her meditations. She heard it almost with regret. And as she rose to resume her hike she determined that some day, far out in the wilds of Wyoming, she would find perfect loneliness where neither motor nor man would interrupt her thoughts.

A huge touring car caught up with her and stopped. She heard a terrier dog barking furiously and childish voices crying out: "Ride with us. Daddy says to ask you."

Martha turned to face a welcoming family, father and mother in the front seat, and a boy, a girl and a dog in the back.

They were so friendly, so eager to have her join them, that Martha could not refuse. When she got in between the children, however, she found them suddenly shy.

"How do you like the Black Hills?" inquired the smiling lady in front.

"Oh, I love them!" exclaimed Martha. "And I had been so scared. People back along the road predicted all sorts of terrible things."

"Nonsense! There's no one to hurt you. We come here often. . . . Tell us, where are you from and where are you going? We arrived at the inn just as you were leaving. A girl hitchhiker! We are dying of curiosity."

"My name is Martha Ann Dixon. I live in Chicago, and am on my way to Wyoming to visit an uncle."

"What part of Wyoming?"

"Randall."

"Don't know it. Must be far. . . . Have you hiked all this way from Chicago?"

"Oh, no. I took a train to Omaha."

"I see. Why didn't you hike all the way?"

"Guess I didn't want to meet anyone who might know me!"

"Naughty child!" interposed the lady. "Do you go to school?"

"Yes, to the university."

"Wonder what your professors would say—to see their star student wandering through the Black Hills?" queried the man, with a smile to his wife, as if they both were familiar with the college and its teachers.

The car climbed higher. The air grew thin and cold. Martha experienced a faint giddiness. When she caught sight of patches of snow along the road, she found herself agreeing with the children when they clamored to get out of the car. They climbed still higher, until they could look out and down over the green slopes to the variegated mosaic of farmlands far below. The driver halted the car by the side of a huge snowdrift, announcing that the radiator was boiling and that they had better stop to let it cool.

Martha marveled at the lovely white snow bank on one side of the road and on the other, wild flowers and green things growing down to a wall of fir trees. From where she sat the eye was led down to the gray and green earth far below.

"No wonder you come here often," sighed Martha.

Shortly afterward the family had to go off the road to a camp where their children were going later in the summer. They told Martha to proceed up to the lodge, where they advised her to take the bus to Rapid City.

She walked the all too short mile up to the lodge, which she expected to find on a mountaintop, but it stood near the edge of a beautiful little lake, under a lofty tower of gray, snow-patched rock. After a short wait on the cool porch of the lodge she found the bus was ready to start. By the time the bus had reached Rapid City night had fallen, and Martha was glad to find a comfortable hotel where she had supper and went promptly to bed.

Before starting out the next morning, she went into the office of the Chamber of Commerce, and of the three smiling occupants she asked collectively: "What is the best and quickest way to get to Belle Fourche?"

"Straight from here to Deadwood and then to Spearfish," replied one of the attendants, spreading a map on the counter. "Where you hail from?"

"Chicago."

Many questions followed which Martha answered good-naturedly and frankly. And when they learned that she actually was on her way to Wyoming, they had several sound suggestions to offer.

"Young lady," said one of the men, "let me fix your pack-sack so it will be easier for you. I am an old-timer with pack-sacks. And yours is on wrong."

"I'll be eternally grateful," replied Martha slipping off her pack.

He went into an adjoining room and returned with straps, buckles and tools. Then he proceeded to alter the straps on the packsack, and to add more. The other two men kept offering suggestions, and between them all they managed to get it to suit them, whereupon they tried it on their visitor.

"I'll choke. Straps all too high," protested Martha.

"No, you just imagine that. Doesn't it feel easier—lighter?"

"I believe it does, at that."

"Are you going to try to make Deadwood tonight?"

"I'll try, you can bet. I'm falling behind my schedule."

"Perhaps I can help you out. There's a gentleman I know, and will vouch for, who intends driving to Deadwood today. May I call him up?"

Martha consented gratefully, and was promised her lift over the phone. She sat down to wait, thinking how many kind and nice people there really were. Presently two men came in, and Martha recognized them as people she had seen up at the lodge the day before. They greeted her in the manner friendly which she had come to expect as typical of the West. After being introduced one of the strangers said, "Well, Miss, let's go." They carried Martha's baggage out, and making her comfortable in the back seat, alone, they drove off.

"I'd like to ask a couple of questions, Miss," said the one who was not driving.

"A couple? That'll be easy. I usually have to answer a hundred. And I have a lot of stock answers."

"Did your parents give you permission to take this long trip alone?"

"No, indeed," Martha confessed.

"You don't need to answer this one: Have you a gun with you?"

"Oh, n-no."

"Or any kind of weapon?"

"I guess I haven't anything you could call a weapon. Except my little embroidery scissors."

Martha's questioner gave his companion a dig in the ribs. "Hear that, Jim Dawson?"

"Sure, I heard. . . . We're a couple of daffy brave firemen, believe you me."

Then they both laughed loud and long. Finally the first speaker turned to Martha again: "Miss, this probably doesn't seem funny to you. But it struck *us* as funny. We're on a little trip in the hills. We bought two shotguns, a revolver, a hatchet, a billy, and two ferocious butcher knives. Each of us weighs around one hundred and eighty pounds. . . . And here we meet up with a wisp of a girl, pretty enough to be a movie queen, hiking the highways alone, her only weapon of defense a pair of embroidery scissors! . . . Can you beat it?"

"Oh, I forgot to mention my hiking boots," said Martha demurely.

The general laugh made them all good friends and that ride seemed to Martha to be one of the best of the whole trip. At Deadwood they insisted on taking her to dinner and letting the hotel people see that she had friends. Moreover next morning early they sent up word to her room that they had engaged a ride for her with a nice old couple driving on into Wyoming. The welcome news expedited Martha's ablutions and dressing. The farther west she got, the more she was beginning to dread the lonely hikes.

In the lobby she was approached by an elderly couple, plain, substantial people whom she trusted on sight. The man might have been a retired country merchant, and his wife appeared to be a motherly soul. She had, Martha thought, rather a sad, sweet face.

They explained that they had been instructed to introduce themselves and offer her a ride as far as Randall.

"It's just lovely of you both," replied Martha feelingly. "I'm a lucky girl."

Not a word about hitchhiking, parents, running away! They had breakfast together and while Mr. Jones went to the garage to get his car Martha helped his wife get together a lunch for the day.

Soon they were off in the bright keen morning, with the dark hills of Wyoming looming on the horizon. That ride almost spoiled Martha Ann forever for hiking. The car was comfortable, the old man drove leisurely and his wife appeared to consider it her duty to entertain their guest. That night when they stopped at an auto camp, Mrs. Jones hardly let Martha out of her sight. She even came into Martha's cottage and tucked her in bed, something that both embarrassed and touched the young hitchhiker deeply.

"You must have a young girl of your own," suggested Martha shyly.

"We were never blessed with a child, my dear."

Before they left the camp next morning Martha came upon her friends in earnest conversation. Her presence ended it so abruptly that she surmised that she must have been the subject of it. And again at noon, when they had lunch along the roadside and Martha stretched her legs by walking to and fro, the earnest talk between the man and his wife appeared to be resumed. She became sure of it when that night at Aladdin, where they stopped, Martha heard Mr. Jones agree to something his wife evidently had been urging most earnestly. "But don't ask her till mornin'," she heard him warn.

All this greatly excited Martha Ann's curiosity. She wondered if she had better get up very early and leave for Randall without bidding these people good-by. She could not understand what urged her to do such a thing, but she refused to consider it as ungrateful. At breakfast next morning, after Mr. Jones had gone out to look after the car, Martha realized that the moment had come.

"My dear, I want to talk seriously to you," said Mrs. Jones, placing a gentle hand on Martha's. "Please listen and don't be offended. I am a childless old woman, but I have known hundreds of girls. I have been a teacher, a worker in our church. John and I did not believe the story your last two traveling companions told us. I know that this hitchhike of yours is more than a lark. You are running away from home. Some misunderstanding has driven you from your relatives. You are a spirited, wild little thing, but I am sure that you are innocent. And you are singularly lovable. Everyone you meet will be drawn to you. But this very attractiveness, this independence of spirit only add to your very great danger on this reckless adventure of yours. Now John has consented to let me ask you this: Will you come with us? We are visiting relatives on a ranch, and then will go on west, stopping where and when we like, on the way to California. Come with us, Martha. And if you ever can learn to love us as we love you, and if it can be arranged with your relatives, then we will adopt you as our own."

Martha Ann's surprising reaction to this proposition was to burst into sudden tears. "Oh, I-I'm such a big b-baby," cried Martha, fighting to recover her composure. "It makes me—so —so angry that people take me for a g-good girl, when I'm really such a bad . . . I lied to Mother! And she's the dearest mother in all—the world. She'll never forgive me. . . . But how can I ever thank you and Mr. Jones for your kindness to me? You have paid me a beautiful compliment, Mrs. Jones. I wish I could be your daughter, too. I know I'd love you. . . . But I've got to go on with this foolish adventure—and God only knows what will become of me."

Martha was in Randall at last! In the excitement of reaching her destination she forgot everything else, even to thank the farmer who helped her on the last lap.

It was about eleven o'clock in the morning. Having breakfasted very early Martha elected to eat lunch. After eating, she sallied forth to ask a few questions. The first person she interrogated was not acquainted with Nick Bligh. Martha reflected that a garage man or store keeper would be certain to know of her uncle. A boy at the service station told her to ask at Toller's store where every rancher for miles around the country dealt. A moment later, Martha Ann stepped into the emporium and asked for Mr. Toller. She was directed to a little, lean, gray man at the back of the store.

"Mr. Toller, do you know Nicholas Bligh?" she asked.

"Wal, I reckon I do, Miss," returned the merchant, eyeing the strange girl up and down with friendly interest.

"I'm his niece—Martha Ann Dixon—from Chicago. And I've come to visit him. I want to be directed to his ranch."

"Wal, wal, if thet jest ain't too bad!" ejaculated Mr. Toller. "Nick never knowed you was comin', thet I'll swear."

"No. I-I wanted to surprise him," faltered Martha Ann, her heart sinking like a leaden weight in her breast.

"Wal, Miss Dixon, your uncle left his ranch on the Belle Fourche several months ago. Jest as soon as the snow thawed. Drove his cattle south an' west to a new range!"

"Gone! Oh, why did he leave his ranch?" cried Martha Ann on the verge of tears.

"Wal, bad luck one way an' t' other. Nick was no hand to keep cowboys an' his stock got lost, mired in quicksand, an' stole till he got mad an' pulled up stakes. Reckon it was a good move."

"Where did he go?" asked Martha Ann.

"Down on the Sweetwater—the best damn range in Wyomin'," replied Mr. Toller. "He left his address. Split Rock is the Post Office."

"How—far?"

"Matter of three hundred odd miles, I reckon, Miss."

"So far!" Martha almost wailed. To travel three hundred miles in this rough country had taken her days, since she had had to hike part of the way. It was too discouraging! Martha had been having such good fortune of late that she was unprepared for such a blow as this.

"Yes, pretty far, an' roundabout. But outside of a couple of short runs, like from here to Beulah, travel is all on state highways. Can be drove in a day—if you want to hire a car."

"I've been hiking—and getting rides—when I could."

"Miss, you can't hike any more. Not safe. You'd be caught out all night."

"But I'll have to walk. I've no money—to hire a car," faltered Martha, tears of disappointment trembling in her eyes.

"Then you'll have to beg a ride, Miss Dixon. Perhaps I—"

"Thank you," mumbled Martha, and fearful of breaking down before Mr. Toller and the clerks, she hastily left the store. What in the world could she do? Of course she could only go on as she had come thus far, but the distance was so great and her disappointment so keen that for the moment she simply could not face the problem. Blinded by tears Martha made slow progress to a bench at a filling station, and there she sat down, feeling very sorry for herself. She had just about decided to go back to Toller's store when a young man came running up to her.

"Miss Dixon, Mr. Toller sent me," he explained. "He's got a ride for you clear through to Split Rock. You're pretty lucky, ma'am. Hurry, and let me take your pack."

Martha, murmuring incoherently, slipped the straps of her pack, and trotted after the boy. He led her back to Toller's store in front of which stood a long, low car, covered with dust and mud. It was a powerful car, and the engine was running smoothly.

"This Bligh's niece?" inquired a tanned individual, in the driver's seat, of Mr. Toller who stood near.

"Yes. Miss Dixon, we've found you a ride. Meet Mr. Lee Todd. He'll land you in Split Rock tonight by ten or eleven."

"Oh, Mr. Toller—Mr. Todd—" But Martha could say no more than that. The girl's hesitation was taken by both men as speechless gratitude.

"Glad to meet you, Miss. I know Nick Bligh. Salt of the earth. . . . Do you mind travelin' fast?"

Martha shook her head.

"I've got to be in Lauder by mornin'. Glad to take you— if you've got nerve."

"That's my—middle name," cried Martha huskily.

"Get in beside me. Put her bags in back. . . . So long, Sol. See you next week."

The car roared and lurched, drowning Mr. Toller's goodby. Martha waved to him and the sympathetic youngster.

64

Then the stores, the service station, flashed by and Martha Ann realized that she was in for the ride of her life.

"Never talk while I'm drivin'!" said Mr. Todd, shouting to make himself heard above the roar of his car.

Martha sank back in the seat and closed her eyes. She did not care how fast he drove. The faster the better! She had been a silly child to give way to her disappointment and homesickness. All the way, everything always had ended well. More than good fortune had watched over her. Prayers that she had never been too weary or discouraged to remember had been answered. Martha just laid her head back and rested for a long while.

At length, when her weakness had passed, she opened her eyes to see the landscape speeding past. The gray road split the rolling plain for miles and miles ahead. But there were hills in the distance, and beyond them low dark ranges of mountains. There were few green fields and the patches of trees and farmhouses appeared even scarcer than in Nebraska. Before Martha had realized it they were beyond Beulah, out on the Custer Battlefield Highway. Sundance, Carlisle, Moorcroft were passed in succession, so quickly that Martha imagined the towns to be close together. At Moorcroft the driver crossed the Belle Fourche River and struck off the main highway for Newcastle. He drove too fast for Martha to see either country or towns with any satisfaction. At Newcastle Mr. Todd stopped at a gas station.

"Gas, oil, water," he ordered, as he stepped out. "We'll have a couple of minutes here, Miss Dixon. Get out an' stretch. I'll fetch some sandwiches an' pie."

Martha Ann took advantage of the stop to get a little exercise. She wanted to ask questions, as well as walk, but as she could not do both she chose the latter. Mr. Todd soon returned carrying two paper bags which he deposited in the front seat. Martha hurried back to the car.

"How are you ridin'?" he grinned.

"Fine. You're the most satisfactory man who has given me a lift on the whole trip west."

"Thanks. Here's some grub, an' milk, too. Pile in, an' we'll hit the pike. Lusk is our next stop. About seventy-odd miles. We'll do it in an hour or so. At Lusk we'll hit the Yellowstone Highway, an' then we will really step on her."

"Seems to me you've been doing fairly well," laughed Martha. "I can't see the scenery."

"Wal, you'll not miss much along here. Too wide an' bare. But it gets pretty out along the Sweetwater."

"What will you have for lunch?" asked Martha peeping into the bags.

"I had a little bite an' a big drink. I'll smoke if you don't object."

"No, indeed. I don't mind!"

"Wal, I kinda took you to be one who didn't smoke," he replied, offering his box of cigarettes.

"I don't."

"Good. There's a few old-fashioned girls left. Say good-by to Newcastle."

Martha found it quite a novelty to eat lunch flying along at a mile a minute. She did not know anything about racing cars or drivers, but she had confidence in this bronzed Westerner. She had liked Mr. Toller, too. Uncle Nick had been thirty years and more in the West, and surely he would have become genuinely western. Musing thus Martha slowly ate her lunch. They passed through Clifton, through which Todd drove slowly enough for her to see the post office. After Clifton came Mule Creek, Hatcreek and then Lusk.

From Lusk the towns on the highway became more numerous, and prosperous looking. And at Douglas they crossed the North Platte River, one of the famous streams of the West, according to Todd. Martha had glimpses of it here and there, as they raced on west, and the wide reaches of sand, the grazing cattle, the green bottom lands of willow and cottonwood, delighted her eyes.

Sweeps of country beyond the river caused Martha more than once to exclaim with rapture. They seemed to promise mysterious and marvelous things to come. Perhaps her uncle's new range land lay in that direction.

At dusk they rolled into Casper, which the city girl found to her surprise to be quite a large place. A wide street, bright with electric lights was crowded with cars, and the sidewalks were thronged with evening shoppers. She kept her seat in the car and ate the remainder of the lunch while Mr. Todd attended to his affairs.

She had more than her reward. A slim wide-sombreroed young man, with mischief written all over his smooth dark face, clinked up to the car and addressed her:

"Howdy, kid, how'd you like to step out tonight?" he inquired with a smile.

"I'd love it," replied Martha, rising to the occasion. It would take a good deal to affront her on this wonderful day.

"Was thet broad-shouldered driver your pop?"

"He was, and he is never so happy as when he is beating up cowboys."

"By glory, he looked it," rejoined the youth sheepishly. "Then we're up agin it, sweetheart. Unless you can give him the slip. What say?"

"Can't be done, Lancelot. I've tried that all too often."

"Lancelot? Who's thet guy?" inquired the cowboy doubtfully.

"Lancelot was a swell guy in the Middle Ages. Wonderful lover, according to history."

"Say, are you razzin' me?"

Martha laughed merrily. "Run along, cowboy. I'm afraid you're no Lochinvar. And here comes pop."

Mr. Todd arrived just in time to witness the rather precipitate departure of the cowboy.

"What was that puncher hangin' around you for?"

"I think he wanted to take me out. Called me 'sweetheart.' I don't think our eastern boys have anything on your Westerners for being fast workers. I told that boy you were my pop and made a specialty of beating up cowboys. It worked splendidly."

The rancher appeared to enjoy Martha's joke. "Doggone me! I wish I *was* your pop. . . . Wal, we'll let 'em eat our dust from here on."

"What road do we take out of Casper?"

"The Old Oregon Trail—one of the first an' greatest roads thet opened up the West. Sorry it's night."

"When will we get to Split Rock?" asked Martha eagerly.

"Wal, if we don't chuck a shoe or somethin' I'd say about ten o'clock."

They were off, beyond the red and white lights into the black open. The night air was cold. Martha's jacket afforded but slight protection—at least on her windward shoulder. The car droned like a giant wasp. The runaway slid down a little way in the seat and fell asleep. She awoke with a start, out of a dream in which she had been struggling with tramps. Mr. Todd was shaking her arm.

"Wal, you was dead to the world," he said. "You shore had a fine nap. We made it in good time. This is your town an' here's your lodgin' house. I've stopped here. Nice woman runs it, good grub an' clean beds. The automobile has sure changed the West."

He carried her bags in, engaged her room, and told the proprietress who she was and directed her to take good care of Martha.

"Remember me to your uncle, Miss. An' now good luck an' good-by."

"Mr. Todd, it was the swiftest—and happiest—ride I ever had! I just can't thank you enough. Good-by."

6

●

MARTHA ANN was awakened the following morning by a bold baritone voice singing "La Paloma." Evidently the singer was below in the yard at the back of the inn. The sun was already high in the sky. Surprised that she had slept so late, she hopped out of bed, quickly, to find that the air was cold. It was quiet except for the slightly nasal rendition of "La Paloma" in the yard below.

"Smoky, you shore cain't sing," drawled a very slow accusing voice, rich with a southern twang. "No more'n you can make love."

"Ahuh. I reckon all I'm good for is to fork a hoss an' hawg-tie a steer," replied another voice, of quite different timber.

"Wal, you play a pretty good game of draw, among some strange punchers."

"All right, Texas Jack. You win. I shore got—"

"Hey, you lean, hungry lookin' *hombres*," interrupted a high-pitched feminine voice. "Maw says to come an' get it."

Rapid footsteps, accompanied by a clinking sound, attested to the importance of this call to breakfast. Martha was at a loss, for a moment, to name the musical, metallic clink. "Spurs, of course," she said, presently. "Cowboys! Golly, this is Wyoming!" Then she gave a tiny squeal as she dipped her hands into the basin of cold Wyoming water.

Martha became conscious of a tendency to delay going downstairs. This was the first time she could remember ever being tardy for breakfast. Notwithstanding her joy and eagerness, and her curiosity, she would just as lief not meet those cowboys, especially the one with the drawl, who evidently considered himself a Lothario.

At length, however, she was packed and ready, without any further excuse to linger. Picking up her pack, she proceeded down the stairs. There was no one in the front room, which appeared to be the office. Martha deposited her luggage in a chair and walked down the hall to the dining room, the location of which was not hard to place. As she entered the room she almost tripped over the foot of someone whom she had not seen.

"Look where you're goin', kid," complained a hard voice. "I got a bunion."

"You've got more, sir—and that is—a pair of enormous feet," retorted Martha, looking up from the huge dusty boots into the lean sharp face of a blond cowboy. He froze with sudden amazement.

"Smoky, you shore air clumsy," drawled a voice Martha recognized. "Let the lady pass."

A long arm shot out and dragged the stunned Smoky from in front of the door. Then Martha saw the second cowboy, and if sight of him did not petrify her in her tracks it was not because he was not the wildest and most magnificent human she had ever seen.

"Good mornin', Miss Dixon," said Mrs. Glemm, the proprietress, and she rescued Martha and led her to a small table near a window. "Hope you rested right well."

"I slept like a log. Don't believe I'd ever have awakened but for some terrible singing in the garden."

The dining room was small and Martha's high young voice carried well. From the hall came a sound of stamping boots and then a "Haw! Haw! Haw!"

"Meet my daughter, Nellie," continued Mrs. Glemm, as a buxom pleasant-faced girl entered the room. "This is Miss Dixon, daughter, who's come out West to visit an uncle. . . . Now, Miss, Nellie will get you a nice breakfast, an' I'm at your service."

"Can you hire someone to drive me out to my Uncle's—Nicholas Bligh?" asked Martha Ann eagerly.

"Yes, indeedie. We'll have a car all ready."

Martha enjoyed a western breakfast, as well as a chat with the Glemm girl. She had nice brown eyes and rosy cheeks. The city girl asked casual questions about the weather, the town, the cattle business, the movies, what kind of social life they had in Split Rock, to all of which she received very full and cheerful answers. Evidently Split Rock was an up-and-coming place.

After finishing breakfast and paying her bill, Martha Ann was informed that her car and driver were waiting. Mrs. Glemm carried her packsack out to a dilapidated Ford, the driver of which, a nice young boy, jumped out to assist.

"Sim, did you find out where Mr. Bligh's ranch is?"

"No, ma'am. He's new hereabouts. But Sam Johnson will know."

"Don't forget to have Sam fill up. . . . Good-by, Miss. Hope you stay long an' have a fine visit. But you never will go back —east—not with them eyes of your'n."

The boy drove down a wide street, where red signs and garish fronts were conspicuous by their absence. Horses, vehicles, cars, dust and men were everywhere in evidence. Martha saw that Split Rock was a small place, but exciting. A halt was made at a service station.

"Sam, fill this bus up, an' tell me where to find Nicholas Bligh," said the young driver.

"Don't know, Sim, but I do know who does. Rustle down to Jed Price. He'll tell you."

No sooner had the boy left than from the little glass-windowed office stepped a lithe, tall young man. The instant Martha espied him she recognized him, and realized that he had been waiting there to waylay her. Her second glance, as he leisurely approached the car, appraised him more closely. His shapely feet were encased in high-top, decorated boots, much the worse for wear, and his spurs dragged in the gravel. He wore jeans, also stained and old, and above his narrow hips was a belt shiny with brass shells. A yellow scarf hung full and loose from his neck. He had a red face, clean as a baby's, eyes of intense, vivid blue, and hair as red as a flame. It stood up like a mane. In his hand he carried a huge old sombrero of a tan color.

"Mawnin', Miss Dixon," he drawled, with a smile that no girl, much less a western-struck maiden like Martha, could have found anything but agreeable.

"Good morning," she replied, a little coolly. It would never do to encourage this cowboy. But Martha wanted to.

"I shore hope thet clumsy cowpuncher didn't hurt you when he kicked you over heah at Glemm's."

"No, I guess I'm the one who did the kicking."

He leaned in at the window on the driver's side, and ringed the brim of his sombrero with strong brown fingers. His piercing eyes took Martha in from head to boots, and back again. But she liked his look, though it verged upon the audacious.

"Hitchhiker, I reckon, an' all alone. Doggone, but I like a girl who ain't afraid."

"What's there to be afraid of in Wyoming?"

"Wal, a lot, Miss. Tough lot of cowpunchers aboot heah."

"Indeed! I've only seen—two that I know of."

He never blinked one of those speculative eyes of his. "You shore need an escort, wherever you're goin'."

"Isn't this young man trustworthy?"

"Aw, Sim is fine. But he's only a kid. You need a man."

"Yes? I'm afraid I'll have to take the risk. I've no money to waste."

"Shore, I wouldn't take no money from a lady."

"You are very kind, indeed. But I think I'll dispense with an escort. What *can* there be to be afraid of?"

"Wal, ootside of tough punchers, there's Injuns, hawse thieves, bootleggers, hijackers, a big stiff of a sheriff who thinks he's a lady killer—to name a few reasons why you shouldn't go alone."

"Oh, what a formidable list! How can I tell, Mr. Texas, that you don't belong to one of those classifications?"

"My Gawd, lady, do I look it?" he protested.

"No. You look very innocuous—not to say innocent."

"What's thet inno-yus?" he inquired, with his dazzling smile. "An' how'd you know I'm Texas Haynes?"

"I didn't. I only heard the prefix. You, of course, read *my* name on the ledger in the hotel?"

"Shore did, Miss Martha. Hope you ain't offended. You see only once in a life-time does a girl like you roll into this town."

"Is that a compliment?" asked Martha, archly.

"Wal, if you want it straight, no girl so purty ever did—"

"That'll do, thanks. It's a compliment."

He stared at her coolly.

"You don't get me. I'll bet you've been scared, bothered, insulted on yore long hitchhike? Haven't you?"

"Yes, I'm sorry to say."

"But by no Texan. . . . Miss Martha, the cowboy from

71

Texas who'd insult a girl ain't been born yet," he drawled with a slow, almost passionate, pride.

"That's something splendid to know. But aren't cowboys from Wyoming just as—as chivalrous?"

"I'll leave thet for you to find oot. An' you're liable to pronto if you don't let me go along with you."

"I'll risk it."

"Where air you haided for?"

"I don't know exactly. My uncle lives on the Sweetwater. The driver has gone to find out."

"Miss Dixon, if you don't reckon me too nosy, what's yore uncle's name?" queried Haynes. His flashing blue eyes seemed shadowed with his swift change of thought.

"It is Nicholas Bligh."

"*Bligh!*" echoed the cowboy. He stepped back from the car to make her a gallant bow. "I've heahed of Nick Bligh, a new cattleman in these parts. Sorry I cain't tell you I've rode for him. . . . Good day, Miss Dixon."

He put on his huge sombrero and strode across the street, a superb figure, and graceful save for the slightly bowed legs. He did not look back. Martha Ann, watching him, pondered over the sudden slight change in his demeanor and expression upon hearing her uncle's name.

Then the young man delegated to drive Martha came running back and jumped into the car. "Found out, Miss. Aw, easy! An' not so fur. Take us mebbe three hours. We turn off at Sweetwater bridge. Only ranch down river, so we can't miss it."

"That's fine news. Is it safe?"

"Safe? You mean this Ford?"

"No, the road. That redheaded cowboy scared me."

"Tex Haynes? The son of a gun! What'd he tell you?"

Martha repeated in full the dire list of calamities which Haynes had vowed would imperil her.

"I'll bet he wanted to drive you."

"Not exactly. He wanted to go along."

"Ahuh. Thet *hombre* will be hittin' yore uncle for a job. I'll give you a hunch, Miss, but you mustn't squeal on me. Tell yore uncle not to hire Tex."

"Thank you. And why?"

"Aw, Tex is gittin' a bad name. He's crippled a couple of cowboys. Been in jail for fightin'. But it's not thet. There are hints out about him. I don't know what they are. Darn shame, too. Tex is a wonderful puncher. Wins all the rodeos at Cheyenne. An' you can't help likin' him."

Martha feared that all her driver had succeeded in doing was to increase her interest in Texas Haynes. Her insurgent mind always veered to the underdog. Moreover, he had not looked down upon her scornfully because she was a hitchhiker.

"Who is Smoky?" asked the Chicago girl, as they drove out of town.

"Smoky Reed? He's a sure 'nough bad egg of a cowpuncher. Sweet on Nell Glemm. An' Nell is loony over Tex. Smoky lost his job, I heerd. An' Tex ain't had a job for ages. He could get one, though. Any cattleman would be glad to have Tex."

"Tell me all about this country. Range, you Westerners call it. Oh, I can't see a thing but these scaly hills."

"Sorta shet in here, for a spell, Miss. But you jest wait till we come to the Sweetwater."

"I'm waiting. . . . You didn't tell me your name."

"Sim Glemm. Sim is nickname for Simpson. I'm Mrs. Glemm's nephew."

Martha Ann loosed the battery of her inquisitive mind, and as there was nothing pretty or unusual to look at in the scenery, she plied her loquacious driver with question after question. Driving the two hours required to reach a point where they could see the river she came into possession of a vast store of Wyoming lore, concerning the history, people and gossip, some of which she accepted with a grain of salt. Sim had the kind of narrative mind that always tried and usually succeeded in amplifying the truth.

But when they drove around a curve that brought them out from the shelter of a drab range which like a wall had hidden the view to the south and west, Martha Ann sat up with eyes wide open.

"Here's the river," pointed the lad. "Shines like a ribbon, don't it? Good fishin' along here, too. An' see the green willows winding down from thet blue range. It ain't the sky you're lookin' at, Miss, but Wyomin' range land. See them round pink an' red things standin' up? Row of little mountains called the Antelope Hills. Yore uncle's ranch is right under them. An' shore you're missin' them white saw teeth way yonder. . . . Way high, Miss. Them's the snow-tipped Rockies. . . . *Now* what do you say about Wyomin'?"

"Wonderful!" cried Martha.

"I'll tell the world," sang out the western youth proudly.

During the descent toward the river and bridge Martha Ann soon lost the far-flung view which had made her imagine that she was looking through colored glasses that magnified and glorified everything she saw. Across the Sweetwater, however, she had an unobstructed vision for leagues and leagues. There was nothing over there—nothing but endless land of many hues dominated by a hazy purple, countless acres of level land, rolling ridges, dark valleys, on and on to the shimmering horizon. She felt that to understand this amazing country, to appreciate it, she must begin with separate parts, first those that lay close at hand and intimate, and by studying them, graduate one day to some semblance of grasp of the vast infinitude that lay beyond.

The river came first. It was indeed a bright ribbon, and in places, several ribbons, flowing between islands of sand and green cottonwoods. But it struck her that there was very little water for so wide a river bottom. From bank to bank the bed was wide. In times of flood the Sweetwater must be truly awe inspiring. The verdant banks and islands, the sparkling white and amber water, presented a vivid contrast to the somber range of grass and sage. Martha Ann gave this lonely river its proper place in the scene as the life and vitality of that magnificent range.

"But I don't see a single living creature!" she burst out.

"Say, Miss Tenderfoot, you oughta fetched a spyglass," replied the driver. "See them tiny little specks yonder?"

"Ye-es, I guess so."

"Cattle," he said, with finality. Cattle were the aim and end of this vast country.

Sim turned off the road to the left just before reaching the bridge, and Martha Ann soon lost sight of all the open country. The bumpy road necessitated slow driving along the river bank. Groves of cottonwoods and patches of willow filled the river bottom.

"See thet tree down thar?" queried her guide, pointing to a huge round-foliaged cottonwood, with wide-spreading branches. "My dad has helped hang rustlers on thet tree."

"Oh, how dreadful! . . . What are rustlers?"

"Fellers who rustle cattle."

"How do they rustle them? Make noises to frighten them?"

"Whoopee!" roared Sim, and then gave way to mirth.

74

"I dare say I'm very much a tenderfoot. But how can I learn if I am not told?"

"You're gonna be a circus for the cowpunchers. But come to think of it you'll have the best of them right off pronto."

"That's good news, anyway. How will I?"

" 'Cause you're so durn pretty thet they won't dare—not even Tex Haynes—to torment you an' play tricks."

"I fail to see why my—why that will protect me?"

"Shucks! You jest wait."

"I'll wait patiently, young man. But tell me, what does 'rustle' really mean?"

"Rustle means to rustle off with cattle. To *steal* them. Calves, sows, yearlin's, two-year-olds, all kinds of cattle. An' there are rustlers workin' yet on this range. Only two-bit stuff, sure. But my dad says there always has been rustlers in Wyomin' an' always will be."

" 'Two-bit stuff.' What's that?"

"Two bits is twenty-five cents."

A long stretch of better road put a different face on the last lap of the approach to Bligh's Ranch. The land to the left began to slope gradually upward toward the beautiful bare colored hills. And suddenly Martha Ann became conscious of a nearer view of the grand panorama which had so enraptured her more than twenty miles back. Here it was clearer, closer, more eye-filling and breath-taking. But the near approach to the ranch drew and held the young girl's gaze. She saw a long low squat building without a vestige of green about it, and beyond it stood sheds and pens and fences, all sadly in need of repair. And then as the car advanced farther she caught view of a gray old log cabin, picturesque in its isolation and ruin, situated on the river bank, facing the west.

Martha's mounting excitement left her with a sudden constriction of her throat. She swallowed hard and found breathing oppressive. If she had been mad with yearning for Wyoming, with the sacrifices this trip had cost, she now realized how true her instinct had been. The solitude of the scene drew her, the wildness of the view called to something deep and instinctive within her, the beauty made her soul ache with sadness.

But she must not give way to her emotions now that she was here, or present herself to Uncle Nick as a maudlin, sentimental girl. The driver was babbling on, but Martha could not attend to him. She saw a colt sticking a curious lean head

75

over a fence, she saw two busy little puppies that could scarcely waddle, then a big yellow-haired, fierce-eyed dog. Suddenly she realized that the car had come to a stop.

"Hi! Anybody home?" yelled the driver, with the lusty voice of youth.

"Don't shout. I-I'll go in."

"Nix. Not with thet yaller dawg eyein' us."

Trepidation vied in Martha's breast with a bursting joyous expectancy as she espied a man, little and lean and gray, fit habitant for that dwelling, come ambling around a corner of the house. When he aimed a gentle kick at the yellow dog she saw that he was bowlegged. But all Westerners had legs more or less bowed. Already she had the door of the car open, and now she leaped out to run up to the little man.

"Uncle Nick—I'm—your niece—come to—" she cried, and failing of voice threw her arms around him and quickly kissed his cheek.

"For the land's sakes!" he ejaculated mildly, as he gently released himself. "Lass, I'm plumb sorry, but I jest don't happen to be yore Uncle Nick."

"Oh-h! . . . Ex-cuse me. You must think I'm crazy. . . . But I never saw him," burst out the fair visitor, adding confusion to her agitation.

"Hey Nick, come a-runnin'," yelled the little man.

The door opened to reveal a tall man, gray-haired, weather-beaten of face standing in the doorway. The instant his astonished blue eyes saw the girl he ejaculated: "Martha Dixon!"

"Yes," cried Martha, running to him. "Martha Ann. . . . Your niece."

A swift change from amazement to unmistakable gladness, and the quick embrace, relieved the girl, not only of her strength, but of the overwhelming dread that had consumed her. Uncle Nick resembled her grandmother. He had kind keen blue eyes that were filling with tears.

"My niece? Bless your heart! Child, I'm plumb buffaloed. . . . Who's with you? How'd you come? What—"

"I'm alone. Walked a lot of the way. Begged rides—to save my money. . . . And here I am—to stay."

"Martha, did you run away from home?"

"So did you, Uncle Nick. . . . I—I wanted to help you."

He held her in his arms a little closer and bent his lined face close to hers.

"I never expected to see any of my kin again," he said, with

76

a voice that trembled. "Much less havin' Martha Dixon's daughter run away from home on my account."

"It wasn't, Uncle—all on your account. I was crazy to see the West."

"You must have been. Never heard of such a thing. Trampin' alone an' stealin' rides! Jim, what do you think of thet?"

"Wal, Nick, I reckon I'm loco," grinned the little man.

"Come in, Martha. You can tell us all about it," said her uncle. "Jim, fetch in her packs."

"Oh, I mustn't forget to pay Sim," cried Martha, running back to the car.

"I'm tellin' you, Miss. It won't be very long till you're gettin' all the free rides you want," said Sim, pocketing his fee.

Martha's uncle led her into the house, apologizing for his humble abode, which he had not expected to be graced by such a fair guest. Martha's quick survey was much at variance with her preconceived idea of the interior of this rude house. She saw a fairly large room, consisting of roughly plastered walls covered with skins and Indian ornaments, guns lying across the horns of a deer head over the open fireplace, a wooden floor, bare except for a couple of Indian rugs, table and oil lamp, an old rocker and a couch. There was only one window, which was large enough to let in the western light.

"Come in, Mrs. Fenner. See who's here," called Bligh through an open door.

"I been lookin'," replied a feminine voice, and a little woman hopped in like a bird. She had the brightest of dark eyes shining out from a small face, pleasant despite the havoc wrought by a hard, lonely life.

"Mrs. Fenner, this is my niece, Martha Ann Dixon," said Bligh proudly. "Martha, meet Jim's wife."

Greetings had scarcely been exchanged before Martha had taken a liking for this little western woman. Then Jim came in with Martha's bags.

"Set down, Martha, an' make yourself to home," invited Bligh, as he placed the rocker for her. "Mrs. Fenner, I reckon this room will have to be Martha's."

"Oh, I couldn't take your living room," protested the girl.

"Wal, you'll have to, 'cause it's our only one. It's got to be fixed up, too. What'll we need, Mrs. Fenner?"

"Washstand, mirror, bureau, some pegs to hang clothes on,

some more rugs on the floor an' a curtain for the window," replied Mrs. Fenner practically.

"Reckon we can find all but the bureau. We'll get thet in town. We'll rustle things pronto. . . . Martha, tell us how in the world you ever got here, alone, an' in them togs."

Whereupon Martha, inspired as well as excited by her glad-eyed, wondering audience, related the pleasantest part of her hitchhiking experience.

"An' nothin' else happened?" ejaculated her uncle.

"Not much. Tramps tried to rob me and a couple of young men got fresh. But altogether my trip was uneventful."

"Nick, it was them eyes," spoke up Jim Fenner solemnly.

"No—the good Lord!" added Mrs. Fenner.

"Wal, she's here, an' I say the day of miracles isn't past. . . . Come, we'll rustle what we can find to make her comfortable."

"But, Uncle, the driver told me that to rustle means to steal," remonstrated Martha. "Please don't rustle all those things for me."

They laughed and departed in great excitement, plainly bewildered by her unexpected arrival, but undoubtedly happy over it. And that was what made Martha's heart sing. She began to unpack her luggage, but the unpacking, owing to frequent interruptions, took a long time. At last between the four of them they had the living room most satisfactorily furnished.

"Wal, thet's fine," declared Bligh, viewing the result of their labors. "I'll send Jim or Andrew into town tomorrow for what else we can think of. . . . Mrs. Fenner, will you fix some lunch for us? Are you hungry, lass?"

"I'll say I am!" cried Martha.

"Wal, it does my eyes good to see you," replied her uncle, taking her hand. "You look so much like your mother that at first I thought she had come. . . . Child, I don't know what to say to you."

"Don't scold, Uncle," she pleaded. "I just had to come."

"You ran off?"

"Yes. I lied to Mother. That hurts terribly. It seems so much worse now."

"Have you written her?"

"Once. I told her I was with a girl friend, whose uncle wanted to take us to the Black Hills."

"Your mother will have to know."

"Yes—but—but there's no hurry. . . . Oh, what can I say to her?"

78

"Martha, is this a visit you are paying me?"

"A long one—perhaps forever," replied Martha Ann, as she looked away.

"What has hurt you, lass?"

"Oh, everything."

"An unhappy love affair?" he asked, with a grave smile.

"No. I'm sick of boys and men who keep pestering me. . . . Then I grew to hate the city—the noise, dirt, rush—and being poor. I worked while I went to college—paid my own way— saved a little to come west. . . . Uncle, I didn't realize till I got to the Black Hills what it was I really wanted and needed. It was change, freedom, loneliness. To be thrown on my own!"

"How old are you, Martha?"

"Nineteen last February."

"You look younger. . . . Now, my dear, I'm curious to know how a slip of a college girl aims to help a poor old cattleman?"

"Uncle Nick, wait till you get acquainted with this modern college girl! I shall help you in a thousand ways. . . . Tell me, Uncle, just how are you situated?"

"Wal, I've picked up considerable in health out here. It's higher country. As for worldly wealth, lass, I have mighty little. Got here with the last thousand head of cattle I saved back at Belle Fourche. I should tell you thet before I left there I corresponded with a cattleman whose range is on the Sweetwater. An' he induced me to come in on a deal with him— which I'm sorry to say Jim Fenner doesn't like."

"What kind of deal?" queried Martha Ann.

"I was to furnish stock an' he would run them with his, savin' me the expense of an outfit."

"On what basis?"

"Equal shares. But when I got out here he bucked. I expected an equal share of his stock, but he claims I was only to get a share of my own thet he'd raise an' market."

"How much stock has this man?"

"Wal, some less than mine."

"I think he drove a sharp bargain."

"So do I. Anyway, he now refuses to reconsider the deal. Says he has my agreement in black an' white. An' if I don't agree he'll take the deal to court."

"What's his name?"

"McCall. What's more, he claims thet he has a lien on this homestead. A homesteader named Boseman settled here, but never proved up on his claim. Abandoned the farm, which was homesteaded by other cowmen, who in turn never got a patent on it."

"Did you lay out any more for it?"

"Only on improvements."

"How much?"

"I don't know. Not much yet."

"Then if you have to get off you won't stand to lose much?"

"No. But I've taken a shine to the place. Spring water has some mineral quality. Good for me. I'd like to stay."

"Then you bet we'll stay," declared Martha Ann.

Uncle Nick clapped his hands. "Once in a long while I have a hunch. . . . I just had one."

"What is it, Uncle?" asked Martha smilingly.

"You've changed my luck."

"Why, of course. What do you think I hitchhiked out here for?"

"I reckon the Lord sent you. Come to think of it, Martha, I believe he's rememberin' my years of toil an' defeat on the ranges. He has sent me help. This man Jim Fenner is an Arizonian. He threw in with me, not in hope of profit, but because he an' his wife liked me. They've had a hard time since Jim got crippled an' couldn't do a regular cowboy's work. Then a handy man came along—works for his board. Now you come with a modern college girl's ideas on cattle raisin'!"

"Uncle, I'm going to run outdoors where I can yell!"

Martha Ann did run. She ran so fast that she could scarcely see where she was going. Pell-mell she ran around a corner of the barn only to bump so violently into a man that she sat down with a thud. Her hat fell off and her hair cascaded down over her eyes. She put both hands flat on the ground in order to raise herself when the person with whom she had collided uttered a strange exclamation.

"Do you occupy all the land on this range?" inquired Martha flippantly.

She shook the hair out of her eyes to see a tall, wide-shouldered young man in blue jeans. His face was familiar. She saw a sudden cloud of red tinge his brown cheek. His gray gaze seemed to bore right through her.

"*You!*" he burst out.

"Who else did you think I am?"

"Wyoming Mad!" And he threw up his hands.

Then Martha Ann recognized him. He was changed somehow, thinner, sun blistered yet he was the one real hero of her hitchhike, the rescuer who had so rudely disapproved of her, and whom she could never forget—Andrew Bonning.

"You!" she exclaimed weakly, and she would have crawled into a hole had there been one near to hide her blush.

"Howdy, little kick hunter. . . . Who else do you think I am?"

"Here—in Wyoming—on Uncle Nick's ranch?"

"Sure. Don't you see me?"

"You're the new hired man—the handy man—who works for his board?"

"The very same, Wyoming Mad," returned Bonning, with a bow.

Martha Ann leaped in front of him. "Then—you're fired!" she cried.

7

ANDREW BONNING leaned back against the corral gate a victim of emotions that were compounded of surprise, annoyance, amusement and reluctant admiration. So this independent young hitchhiker who had haunted him for the past few weeks had turned up again under even more complex and bewildering circumstances. He might have expected her to bob up any day.

"Yeah? So I'm fired?" he queried slowly.

"You bet you are," she snapped.

"Who's firing me?"

"I am."

Andrew studied the girl. She was certainly angry, as well as surprised. Her face was pale and her eyes were blazing. She had the strangest, most beautiful eyes he had ever seen in a woman, and though he remembered them, this nearer view under the bright sun seemed to render null his former impression. They flared upon him with a clear amber light. She had red lips, just now set determinedly.

"Who are you?" asked Andrew.

"I'm Martha Ann Dixon. Mr. Bligh is my uncle. And I've come west to help him run his ranch."

A laugh interrupted Andrew's gravity. "Miss Martha Ann Dixon," he said. "That accounts for the M A D. . . . Well, we seem fated to meet each other. I'm sorry. . . . Do you mean to run Bligh's ranch, or to run off the hired men who don't fall for you at the drop of a hat?"

"Mr. Bonning, all I mean is that I wouldn't have you on this ranch," she blazed.

"I see. Well, if I were to consider only myself, I wouldn't want to stay. But it just happens that Mr. Bligh needs me."

"No more than any other hand, I'm sure."

"Indeed he does—more than *any* man you might find."

"Oh. You certainly have a poor opinion of yourself."

"If I had, it evidently could not be as poor as yours of me. May I inquire why my presence on this ranch is so obnoxious to you?"

"If you were on the level you wouldn't ask."

"That's the last thing I'm not, Miss Dixon," he returned, coldly. "And if you're not throwing a bluff with your pretty pride, your outraged dignity, you'll explain why you say I'm not on the level."

"You're not—because you—you insulted me."

"I did nothing of the sort," declared Andrew flatly.

"You did! I was terribly indebted to you when you rescued me from those tramps. But you spoiled it by—by taking me for a common—for something I'm not."

"Miss Dixon, that wild stunt of yours, hiking the roads alone, hunting for kicks, ready and willing to be picked up by anyone, laid you open to—"

"I wasn't hunting for kicks," she interrupted almost in tears. "I wasn't ready and willing to be picked up by anybody—"

"Now *you're* not being on the level," he returned, with obvious sarcasm in his voice. His anger was struggled with a deeper emotion.

"I *am* on the level, but I don't care to prove it to you," she retorted, her face flaming red. "I simply don't care what you think. I did, but not any more. . . . For all I know you might be a confidence man, a rustler—anything but a Missouri farm hand."

"I might be, but I'm not. It doesn't matter in the least to you, or to anyone out here, what or who I am. I'm honest, and I chose to offer my services free to your uncle because I needed a home and he needed an honest hired man. That's all. And you're sore at me because I saw through you."

"You didn't see through me."

"Wyoming Mad, you'll understand me better if I say that you're not very convincing."

She grew white even to her bright red lips.

"Andrew Bonning, you thought me a wild, wayward girl, didn't you?" she queried furiously.

"What else *could* I think?" he retorted.

"You called me 'an unforgettable kid,' didn't you?"

"I'm afraid you are."

"*Why* am I?"

"You are rather pretty and distinctly original," he answered in a way that made what he said sound almost uncomplimentary.

"But sailing under false colors?"

"I certainly wouldn't call you true blue. You strike me as the chameleon type, Miss Dixon. You change your color—or your line—to suit the individual you want to impress."

"You think I flirted with that boy who took me to dinner?"

"I saw you. And you impressed me as a fast little worker—especially with hicks like him."

"You think—I'm even—worse?" she faltered, in a suffocated little voice.

"I'm ashamed to confess that I did. I let my imagination run riot—and pictured you with him in the park, or in his car."

"Oh, you're like all the rest of the beastly men," she cried, with renewed fury. "You've a one-track mind when it comes to women. What kind of sister could you have, or girl friends? . . . Isn't there *any* man who can understand a girl's longings to be free—to have adventures—to find herself—to be let alone? Oh, what a rotten world! I thought I'd escape from all *that*—way out here in Wyoming."

"So did I, Miss Dixon," he returned, stung to a bitterness that overcame his surprise.

"Well, you can go to blazes!" she concluded, with finality, as she turned away.

"Thank you. After firing me you consign me to blazes. You certainly have a nice, gentle, sweet disposition," he replied, following her around the barn. "Here's your uncle now. I'll tell him."

It was evident that Miss Dixon wanted to escape this encounter.

"Hello, here you are," called out Bligh, intercepting them. "Have you scraped an acquaintance? . . . Martha, this is Andrew—"

"Uncle, we've met before, to my sorrow," interposed the girl icily.

"Eh? What? Wal now?"

"Mr. Bligh, we have met, back in Nebraska somewhere," said Andrew hurriedly. "I did her some trifling service. But I offended her because I disapproved of a young girl hiking alone along the highway—picking up men to ride with. I'm sorry. But I think it's a pretty reckless stunt even for these modern days. I had no right to criticize her. And for that I apologize. The harm is done, however . . . and in fact she won't have me on the ranch."

"Uncle, I fired him," cried Martha. "I hope you agree with me!"

"Fired him! . . . Why, lass, what're you talkin' about? Of course I wouldn't keep any man—but be reasonable. I agree with Andrew that your hike out here was a pretty wild thing to do. The Lord must have watched over you, Martha. . . . An' as for Andrew's leavin'—I'd hate to see him go. Cowboys are hard customers for me to handle, Martha. They drink an' leave the ranch. Now Andrew is steady. He's different, lass. He'll fit in here. Jim Fenner particularly likes him. Can't we fix up your quarrel somehow?"

"No, Uncle. But if Mr. Bonning is so valuable to you I withdraw my objection," replied the girl, and walked away with her head proudly erect.

"Wal, Andrew, this day is one of surprises," said the rancher. "Strange you two should meet on the road an' then meet again out here. She seems a mighty fiery little lass. . . . Which of you is to blame for this?"

"I am," replied Andrew, emphatically. "I reproved her pretty harshly for this hiking stunt. It was none of my business."

"Reckon you've been pretty hard on the lass. She's only a spirited filly. Like her mother and grandmother before her. . . . Fine old family—the Campbells. Poor now, an' perhaps thet's one reason why Martha ran off. I ran off thirty years ago. . . . How about you?"

"Well, I ran off from something, that's sure. Probably my own morbid self."

"It will all come right. But not soon. The Campbells don't forgive easily. . . Thet was funny about her firin' you. Wal, she withdrew her objections. I hope thet'll be the end of it."

Andrew had his doubts about that. As he walked away

84

toward his quarters he found that his unreasonable temper had cooled, and that he was now in a state close to self-reproach. He had answered the girl's pertinent queries coolly and to her discredit. Any young woman with a grain of spirit would have resented what he had said and would have defended herself. She had done more. Then remembering what she had declaimed so passionately, he felt deeply ashamed, and suddenly he was horrified by the thought that it was quite possible that he had completely misjudged her. How scathingly she had denounced all men! It made him feel decidedly uncomfortable. She was perfectly right. But what else could she expect from men? It seemed to Andrew that she had almost invited approach. Of all the escapades that had ever come under his notice, of all the crazy stunts that he could conceive, this hiking alone by a stunningly pretty girl through the West was the most audacious and questionable. She seemed clever, intelligent, refined. Bligh vouched for her good blood. All the more reason to suspect her! This twentieth-century restlessness, this boldness so typical of the age, this urge for thrills she could not satisfy at home, this wanderlust of the past combined with this modern obsession to meet and captivate strange men —these all must be at the bottom of Martha Ann Dixon's flight from a good home. It was a pity. Old Bligh would never be able to see through this clever little minx.

"But she can't fool me," he reassured himself. "Not a chance! She knows her stuff. She has my sister and Connie tied to the mast. For they played the game openly and aboveboard."

Having delivered this ultimatum to his smarting conscience, Andrew stamped into the old cabin where he had elected to make his abode. It was getting to mean a great deal to him— this ancient abandoned cabin. The initials cut on the logs and the charcoal drawing of brands on the stone fireplace, the accumulation of years of range dust on the rafters, the friendly mice and squirrels that had at first regarded his presence as an intrusion, the bleached antlers over the mantle, the old couch of boughs in one corner, the black smoke stains on the chimney, the holes in the roof that he had not yet mended— these things and everything about the big room held for him the atmosphere of bygone frontier days.

Andrew worked at odd times on making the cabin more habitable. Before the snow came he would have it snug and dry and comfortable. Just now there was nothing but his blankets and his bags and saddle. He pictured himself during the winter, on dark nights when the blizzard was howling, sitting beside an open fire, watching the red embers, and reveling in his solitude. His favorite place during this summer weather was out on the porch that faced the river and the magnificent reach of purple and gold stretching to the Rockies.

This porch spoke as eloquently as the big room of what had happened there. It certainly needed a good many repairs. Andrew decided, however, that the bullet holes in the posts and cabin wall, made during a rustler-cowboy war in early days, should not be removed for any repairs. The slope of the land toward the river caused the floor of the porch to stand high off the ground. The wide steps leading down had rotted away until they were now unsafe.

Andrew flung himself into one of the old crude chairs, and threw his sombrero aside. His brow and hair were moist. No matter how hot it was in the sun, the shade was always cool. Bligh's cattle grazed along the river banks and down in the bottom lands. Soon they would work up into the draws of the hills; and then the real riding for Andrew would begin. There were horses out on the grassy slope.

All at once it struck Andrew that a rift had come into his new and pleasant way of life. He did not need to puzzle it out. That amber-eyed girl! He thought he had dismissed her and the disturbing thoughts she had aroused with a scornful finality. And here she was back!

"What a sweet, pretty kid!" he mused regretfully. "She will put this range on the blink. . . . Damn it, I like her! Maybe she didn't hand it to me! Eyes and lips! Never will I forget those eyes. . . . If that girl was only straight I'd—I'd—fall for her like a ton of bricks."

Andrew admitted this startling possibility. He realized, too, that he was in a strangely receptive and unusual condition of mind. He had severed old ties. He had traveled far and every league, it seemed, had eased his pain and bitterness. This great open range land had expanded his soul. Now this new self seemed in conflict with the old.

While Andrew was in the midst of these introspective self-confessions, the little Arizonian, Jim Fenner, limped into the cabin.

"Where are you, Andrew?"

"Come out here, Jim."

"Bligh wants some goods trucked from town. Will you drive

me in? I'm leery of thet truck. She bucked on me last time."

"Jim, I can make her run if anybody can."

"Wal, I'd like to see you take to hosses thet way. But we haven't a decent nag in the outfit."

"What'd a good horse cost, Jim?"

"Around fifty. An' thet reminds me. I heerd the little cyclone who just blew in askin' about hosses. Andrew, we haven't one thet's safe for her. An' Bligh can't afford to buy one."

"Is he pretty hard up, Jim?" queried Andrew thoughtfully.

"Hard up ain't tellin' it. But I'm glad this niece came. She'll put new life in us, Andrew."

"Life? If that were only all!"

"Say, I was in the barn when you an' Martha had thet set-to," confided the Arizonian.

"Yeah? . . . Then you heard me get fired?"

"Wal, I reckon, an' told to go to blazes. . . . Andrew, you an' me took to each other right off. We're goin' to get along. Mebbe thet doesn't give me license to be too curious. All the same I'll risk it. . . . Wasn't you an' Martha kinda gone on each other—before you landed out west?"

"No. I never met her until one night on the road. I came on her in the hands of a tramp, so I slugged him. We met once after that."

"An' what happened then?"

"Nothing. We had very few words until this meeting. Then we had plenty, believe me."

"I savvied thet you had sort of a pore opinion of her an' it riled her."

"Yes."

"How pore an opinion, Bonnin'?"

Andrew shook his head as if reluctant to interrogate himself. "Pretty poor, I'm afraid, Jim."

"Wal, you know these eastern youngsters. An' I reckon they're a wild outfit these days. It shore was a turrible thing for thet kid to run off from home an' come out here alone."

Andrew nodded gloomily.

"But she's honest, Andrew."

"Honest?" echoed Andrew, quickly.

"Straight, I mean. No matter how wild thet kid's been she is decent. *Sabe, Señor?*"

The curt assertion of the Arizonian annoyed Andrew as much as the hint of his own lack of chivalry.

"Jim, I'm sure I didn't think—"

"Wal, I'm glad you didn't," interrupted Jim bluntly. "My hunch came from my wife, Sue. She never made a mistake about figgerin' a girl. She cottoned pronto to this pore little runaway. An' so did I. An' Bligh, why she'll make a new man out of him. I'm tellin' you, Andrew, 'cause I want you on our side of the fence."

"Thanks, Jim. . . . Lordy, I'm not such a poor fish. . . . And see here, old-timer, I've got something to tell you. It has weighed on my mind."

"Wal, go ahaid an' shoot," replied the Arizonian, leaning back against a post to fix Andrew with his penetrating eyes.

"Listen. The night I reached town I camped out in the brush," began Andrew swiftly. "Walked in to buy some grub. It was dark when I got back to camp. You couldn't see my car from the road. I was about to make a fire when a horseman came along from the open country. Then a man on foot from town. They met—came off the road—near where I had crouched down. Briefly, the rider was a cowboy called Texas something. The other was a cattleman. He owed the cowboy money for branding calves with his brand. The man's name was McCall. He told Texas about Bligh's recent arrival on the range—that Bligh had driven in so much stock, an' he wanted Texas to begin what I grasped to be wholesale stealing. Texas refused. He agreed to brand calves as before. Also to carry a message for McCall to another cowboy, named Smoky Reed, who was to clean out Bligh. . . . I heard all the conversation distinctly. When Texas rode away McCall made a crack that showed he feared the cowboy."

"Wal, you don't say?" mused Jim thoughtfully.

"I forgot to include some pertinent remarks about Sheriff Slade. He must get a rake-off from bootleggers and Texas knows it. Next morning when I was about to start out here that sheriff searched my car. Quite a crowd collected, and I told Slade to his face that for all I knew he might be a bootlegger himself."

"Andy, you'll do," returned Jim dryly. And Andrew gathered that a compliment greater than he could estimate had been paid him. "Wal, I oughta have a smoke. . . . Say, why didn't you tell Bligh about this deal?"

"I meant to. But he seemed already to be bearing a pretty heavy burden. I didn't want to add to it."

"You figgered correct. It'd never do to tell the boss right now. You an' me have got to handle this deal."

"Jim, that tickles me," responded Andrew eagerly. "Do you know I had a fool notion I'd like to work it out alone. Absurd, of course, but it sure got into me."

"Wal, you an' me together can handle it at present. I don't know about later."

"How'd you suggest we handle it, Jim?"

"We'll ketch those cowpunchers red-handed."

"Then what?"

"I reckon beatin' the rustlin' out of them would be a good idee. Of course we used to string up rustlers in the old days. Jail is about all they get now, an' thet not for long."

"Humph! That Texas cowboy wouldn't take a beating. He'd shoot, Jim. Struck me as a tough proposition."

"Wal, if it comes to shootin' you'd be in serious."

"I'm okay with a rifle."

"Good, so long as you ain't in close quarters."

"You'll have to coach me, Jim. . . . What'd you mean when you said you didn't know how to handle the deal later?"

"Wal, Andy, if Bligh loses a lot of his cattle or if McCall gyps him, an' I reckon both is liable to happen, it'll take a long time to build up again. I'd hate to fail on this range. So I'd persuade Bligh to keep on. He's gettin' along in years an' a crownin' disappointment would go hard."

"But Jim, how can disaster be averted?"

"It cain't. Thet's the hell of this cattle business. Good grass, good water at times are no better than a bad drought. Because all the calves will be stole. It's not easy to trace stolen calves. You jest can't unless you ketch the brander with his runnin' iron."

"You believe there's a paying ranch business to be developed here?"

"Payin'? Hell, there's twenty per cent at least."

"How'd you go about developing this ranch to clear such a big percentage of profit?"

"Wal, son, you gotta have some coin. Cattle are way down now. You can buy cheap. If Bligh could restock, say with a mixed herd of two thousand haid, an' get some Arizona punchers to ride this range, why he'd double his money when prices went up."

"That's the rub, then? Bligh is without means to restock. . . . Couldn't he borrow?"

"The banks jest ain't lendin' money without big securities."

"Why hire Arizona cowboys?"

"Wal, to be shore, they ain't any better than Wyomin' punchers. But they'd be on the prod. They'd be like a pack of hounds. Playin' one outfit agin a rival one used to be an old trick of mine. I've been foreman on some great ranches. Bucked the Hash Knife outfit once. An' I still carry some of their lead."

"What was the Hash Knife outfit?"

"Hardest ridin', drinkin', shootin', an' sometimes hardest stealin' outfit in Arizona."

"You'll have to tell me all about it some day. . . . Well, Jim, then it's lack of capital that handicaps our boss—and that stands between us and a swell job?"

"It is, Andy. But what's the use to smoke our pipes? We're all broke, an' the best we can hope for is to make a bare livin' for Bligh an' ourselves. Andy, we wouldn't have any jobs at all if we asked wages."

"Jim! Are you working for your board, the same as I am?"

"Shore am, an' satisfied, too. I tell you, son, I don't mind for myself, but it sticks in my craw thet I can't give Sue the pretty things women like."

"Jim, wait a minute," said Andrew, acting upon an impulse. He ran inside to return with his wallet which he got out of his grip. "I've got a little money—and I'm going to lend you some, Jim."

"Hell, no!"

"Yes, I am. It worries me, all this dough. There—two hundred bucks. I'd lose it in town. I've got a little left, Jim. I want to buy some lumber and tools and odd things to fix up my place here."

The Arizonian fingered the crisp bills while his eyes shed a warm light on Andrew.

"Son, you don't know me."

"I'll gamble on you, anyhow."

Jim folded the greenbacks and stowed them carefully in an inside vest pocket.

"Wal, all my life I've found two kinds of men. One kind makes you want to keep on fightin' an hopin'. . . . Let's go in to dinner. I heerd the bell."

"I'll wait and get mine in town," replied Andrew hastily. "When will you be ready?"

"Pronto. You see if you can start thet truck."

"Okay."

Half an hour later Andrew drove the truck over in front

of the house and honked the horn. Jim and his wife came out beaming, to be followed by Bligh and his niece. Andrew had only to see her again to realize why he had shirked dinner when he was hungry. Martha had changed her gray blouse to a white shirt, and she had done something to her hair. It was fluffy and shone like spun gold.

"All aboard," sang out Andrew. "Mrs. Fenner, hadn't you better come with Jim? I won't guarantee his sobriety."

"Wal, I will," declared Jim, as he climbed in.

Whereupon Andrew reacted to a sudden impulse. "Miss Dixon, there's room for you. Won't you come? You'll get a kick out of my driving."

"I'd do anything under the sun for a kick, Mr. Bonning, as you know—except ride with you," she replied coldly.

"Wal, Sue, you'd better wait up for us," said Jim.

"I haven't done thet for years, but I shall tonight," returned his wife, with an air of happy mystery.

"Mr. Bligh, what can I fetch you?" inquired Andrew casually.

"Jim has the list."

"Don't you dare forget *mine*," spoke up Martha saucily. "Go to a dry-goods store and ask the price of what I want. It's all carefully written out. If the price comes to more than fifteen dollars cut out the articles checked off. Can you remember all those instructions?"

"Andrew, you heerd them, so you can jar my memory."

"If we forget or lose the list we'll buy lollipops, gum, candy, some movie magazines and a Victrola with a dozen jazz records," replied Andrew facetiously.

Martha Dixon did not join in the laugh that followed, but fixed Andrew with unfathomable eyes. She might either have hated or loved him, to judge by the look she gave him.

"Mr. Bonning will be surprised to see that I can make my own clothes," said the girl.

Andrew spent a strenuous and absorbing afternoon in town. What with Jim's supplies and the bulky nature of his own purchases, they had a good load by the time they were ready to start back. Leaving after supper, they gave several hours to the return drive, but Jim made the trip seem short by the resumption of his coaching of the tenderfoot. Andrew let all the Arizonian told him sink in. If there were any range subjects Jim did not touch upon Andrew could not imagine them.

"I shore liked both the hosses you bought," Jim said on one occasion. "Thet bay has good points, an' the pinto is a purty dogie. I reckon he'll make trouble for you at the ranch, an' I ain't sayin' how. . . . Hosses are most important on the range. Now when you're ridin' to an' fro practice with your rope. You don't do so bad. But practice. Rope everythin'. An' shoot at every jack rabbit an' coyote you see. Learn to see trails an' tracks on the ground. By studyin' your own hoss tracks an' others at the ranch, fresh or old, you can judge other tracks out on the range. For instance, you see your fresh track. You study it. An' then one made earlier. You see what has happened to it—a little dust blown in or water, or mebbe another track over it. You know just when they was made, an' if you make pictures of them in your mind soon you'll get the hang of a tracker. Don't miss nothin', Andrew. Use yore eyes. You've got field glasses. Use them when you're undecided or too far away from somethin'. When you're lookin' for strange riders keep out of sight. In the brush or timber, behind ridges an' back from canyon rims. If you're ridin' in the open do it bold, as if you saw nothin'. When the cattle get up in the foothills—an' thet'll be any day soon—you can ride out at daybreak, find a hidin' place an' watch. I'll be with you part of the time, an' I'll tell you how to look an' what you see. But shore you'll be alone a good deal. An' it'll happen when you're alone. These two-bit rustlers of McCall's will be slick an' keep to cover. But often they'll drive a cow an' calf from the open into rough goin'. You listen for a gun shot an' look for smoke. An' when you sneak up on one of them, draw down on him with your rifle. Order him to throw up his hands an' turn his back. Then disarm him an' march him to the boss."

Andrew was up with the dawn. How many years had he slept away the beautiful hours from the break of day to the burst of the sunrise! The soft mist above the river, the winging of ducks across the bars, the obscurity of the range yielding to a sudden magic brightness, the ghosts of mountains growing clear—these new facets of the morning held him absorbed. Then came the change from gray to rose and at last the glory of the lord of day.

He unloaded the truck and packed his purchases inside the old cabin. He discovered a fondness for tools, as well as hands unskilled in their use except when it came to tinkering with automobiles.

Mornings and evenings thereafter he labored at the pleasant task of rendering his new abode dry and warm and less bare to his gaze. But he had made no luxurious purchases. A hard, primitive simplicity seemed to be Andrew's goal.

As he ate with Jim in the kitchen and was absent from the house except at meal hours, he saw little of Martha Ann Dixon. Nevertheless she seemed omnipresent. She filled the lives of her uncle and this Arizona couple. They had suddenly awakened to something joyous. Andrew watched her from afar and sometimes, to his discomfiture, he was caught in the act. Yet he wondered how she could have caught him had she not also been taking cognizance of him. He had to listen to Jim's talk of her interest in horses, in the ranch, in everything and everyone but Andrew Bonning. On Sunday more visitors called on Bligh than during the entire preceding time since he had arrived on the Sweetwater. Some of these were cowboys, spick-and-span in their Sunday best, with boots as shiny as their hair. Andrew regarded them with a vague uneasiness.

Late one afternoon Andrew was riding in from the range, and coming to a wide shallow valley he espied a saddled but riderless horse galloping up the opposite slope toward the ranch. The distance was too great for him to recognize the horse, which disappeared before he could bring his field glasses into use.

Andrew rode rapidly down into the draw, and had not proceeded far along one of the banks when he saw a bright object on the sand. Urging on his horse, he plunged down into the dry stream bed to verify his fears. He came upon Martha Dixon sitting on the sand, her face white and drawn with pain, her hands trembling endeavoring to unlace one of her boots. Andrew leaped off his mount to rush to her side.

"Miss Dixon, you've had a spill?" he queried anxiously.

"Yeah," she replied, without looking up.

"I saw your horse galloping home. . . . Did he buck you off?"

"The old bag of bones tripped in the sand."

"I hope you're not badly hurt," continued Andrew solicitously. "There's blood on your cheek."

"That's rouge. . . . I hate to ask you, Mr. Bonning—but please ride to the house and send Jim or Uncle."

"Nonsense. Take all that time while you're suffering? Let

93

me see. You appear to have sprained an ankle." Andrew knelt down to place his hands gently on the boot she had half unlaced.

"Thank you—never mind," she said, pulling her foot away. "I can get it off. You go for help."

"But I can help you, Miss Dixon," he said, looking up into a frowning face lighted by pain darkened eyes.

"I don't want you to."

"But it's only common courtesy."

"I'd lie here and die before I'd let you help me," she said, turning her face away. He could not help noticing, before she did so, that her lips were trembling.

"So I see. All the same I shall not allow you to sacrifice yourself. . . . Take your hands away." He pulled them free and unlaced the rest of her boot and despite his care in removing it, he hurt her.

"Oh-h! You brute. . . . Great, big, strong, he-man stuff, eh?"

"Your ankle is swollen. I advise you not to try to walk on it."

"Mr. Bonning, you seem to know all about the shape of people's ankles—"

"I have been in college athletics," he replied stiffly.

Struggling to her feet she tried to take a step with the injured member, but faltered. With a moan she sank to the sandy floor of the draw.

"You stubborn little fool. I told you," he burst out, sorry for her, but angrier still.

"Go get—somebody," she said faintly.

"I'll do nothing of the kind. I'm going to pack you up to the house."

"You will not!"

"Watch me!" Whereupon he led his horse beside a low bank from which he could easily step astride the saddle. Then he returned to the girl.

"Don't you dare touch me," she flared.

"Martha Dixon, you ought to get a real kick out of this," he replied with a grim laugh.

"You really are a brute, aren't you?"

In spite of her struggles, he picked her up bodily. She kicked out with her feet, but suddenly subsided with a scream.

"Serves you right. Lie still!" And he shook her slightly. "Anyone would think you imagine I *want* to take you in my arms. Well, let me set your silly little mind at ease. I don't."

94

"You don't because you imagine I'd want you to—that I planned all this," she retorted.

"I never allow my imagination to run riot," he replied coldly, and approaching his horse, cautioned him with stern words, then stepped astride. "I forgot your boot. Oh well, I can come back for that later. There. Are you comfortable?"

"I have never been so wretched—in a man's arms," she answered, avoiding his eyes.

"You don't need to remind me that it is no uncommon experience."

He held her in front of him with his left arm around her and her head against his shoulder. He had his right arm under her knees, and managed also with his right hand to hold the bridle. He gazed down at the pale face against his arm, aware of its loveliness and its danger. She was watching him with a look no man could have interpreted. But it was a look that made him tremble. Her eyes were the clearest amber, large, luminous, the color of a tawny pansy or a topaz. But it was the look in them rather than their beauty that moved Andrew. In times past he had found himself susceptible to feminine charms. He recognized the symptoms now, in magnified form and he determined that he would not permit it to happen again.

"I hate—you," she panted.

"That's all too obvious," he replied, inclining his head. "And it puzzles me. It seems to be my misfortune to keep receiving you—and getting no thanks for my pains. If you ran true to form you would be employing the moment—to your peculiar satisfaction."

"You are simply horrid."

"Why? Because I tell you the truth? Martha Dixon, you certainly are the prettiest creature the sun ever shone on. And it infuriates me that one so sweet, so fresh, so young, so intelligent, so much of a joy to people like your uncle, and Jim and Sue, should be such a cheat to them—and to everyone."

"I'm not—a cheat," she cried.

"Yes, you are, if not a brazen little hussy. Didn't I see you come down the street driving that boy's car? Didn't I see you at dinner, all dolled up, flirting shamelessly with him?"

"Yes, you—did. But I did it because you expected it of me. If you were half as smart as you think you are—you'd have known why I was doing it. You had hurt my feelings. I was mad. . . . I played up to your opinion of me . . . and I was just fool enough to want to make you jealous."

"Good Lord! You switch your line to suit the occasion. Martha, you have no finesse. You just trust everything to your looks. Well, you've cause. But you can't get me with such sugar."

"I don't want you," she cried struggling to pull herself erect.

"I meant string me, darling," he rejoined mockingly.

"Miss Dixon to you, if you don't mind."

"And what were you to the young fellow at the hotel?"

"Just a 'sweetie,' of course, if it's any of your business."

"Bah! You're as bad as Connie—worse, for she was only a gold digger. You run away from home—from a nice mother. You want to get out where no one will know who you are or care what you do. And you pick up a saphead like that—drive his car so he can put his arms round you—doll up for him, a mere stranger—eat with him—go out with him—let him kiss you—let him—"

"That's enough of that," she commanded hotly. "No one can talk to me like that! Whoever your Connie was I'll bet she handed you exactly what you deserved."

"Plumb center," he returned. "I'm sorry that I spoke that way. I have no right to ask you, but . . . did you go out with him that night?"

"No!"

"Did you let him kiss you?"

"No!"

"Martha, I think you're a little liar," he said softly. "Just to prove it, I'll bet even *I* can kiss you and get away with it."

Fired by a sudden rash impulse he bent his face close over hers. He had not really meant to carry out his threat. But once under the spell of her dilating eyes, and the sweet red lips so close to his he found it impossible to refrain. He pressed his lips to hers in a kiss that started in defiance of her and scorn of himself, but which lingered in ecstasy. Sharply he drew erect, astonished by his act, ashamed of having given way to his real feelings when he had meant only scorn.

"I'll kill—you!" she whispered huskily.

" 'Hell hath no fury . . .' Martha, that was coming to you. But don't get me wrong. . . . Well, here we are in sight of the house. Your uncle sees us. And there's your horse tied to the fence."

"Jim! Sue! Rustle out here," shouted Bligh, as Andrew halted. "My Gawd, boy, don't say she's bad hurt."

"She had a spill. Sprained her ankle. But she'll go to the dance next week. . . . Here. Easy now. She's a pretty hefty little armful."

As Andrew handed her down to eager arms he had a last look at her white stained face and great eyes, dark with emotion, as she turned her eyes away from his. They haunted him all the way back to the draw where he returned to fetch her boot.

8

TRAINING for college football had been mild compared to the strenuous exactions of Andrew's ranch work.

Digging post holes, building fences, repairing barns and corrals, piping water down from the hills, and innumerable odd jobs fell to Andrew's lot aside from the work on his cabin. There were hours in the saddle and an occasional trip to town in the truck or car. His labors began at dawn and ended long after dark.

For the past few years his portion had been blistered hands, sunburned face and aching muscles. He thinned down to one hundred and seventy pounds, which was considerably less than the weight his football coaches had allowed him. Steady hard toil with his hands was something entirely new to Andrew. In the first stages sheer physical discomfort, then actual pain and fatigue that dragged him to bed heavy as a log, could not be denied. In spite of the unaccustomed toil he remained cheerful and to all outward appearances indifferent to the hardships.

But it was the actual range-riding, all day and every day under the hot sun, or facing dust or hail or rain, that put him to the crucial test. A stock saddle was a new contrivance to him; and to keep on riding when he wanted to rest was surely the hardest physical ordeal that he had ever met. When hot midsummer arrived Andrew had to hunt the cattle up in the foothills. Sometimes Jim rode with him, and they would lie out over night in the cedars, or out under the stars. That first week of torture in the saddle sweated and bled all the softness and the indolence, and most of the morbidity, out of Andrew

Bonning. He had welcomed the trial; never for a single moment had he quit. From the very first he had sensed something vastly healing in this elemental contact, in this driving of spirit and flesh. He just kept on without thinking much about it, realizing that some distant day he would be made over.

In due time Andrew grew hard and strong and enduring. The day came when he awoke to the fact that joy in action and labor had imperceptibly come to him. Happiness still held aloof; often a strange melancholy lay on his spirit like a mantle; and sometimes his old bitter, mocking self returned, though less and less often. Martha Dixon could still rouse that almost forgotten self in many baffling and humiliating ways. When he was out on the range, where he could not see her as she puttered around, planting flowers, feeding the stock that she had adopted as pets, riding the horses, doing everything imaginable—even to standing like a statue to watch the sunset—then he seemed free of his old somber self. Also it had no place in a man's mind while out in the open. There were the elemental things for man to combat, the inherited instinct for action without introspection. Martha Dixon did not belong in the West any more than he, and he doubted her complete assimilation. Yet she appeared the gayest, happiest girl he had ever seen. On Sundays the cowboys rode in, more and more each Sabbath. Andrew had to admit that she had handled the situation in a different fashion than he had anticipated.

Andrew knew the West had claimed him. Still he had not faced that realization yet. It was too good to be true. He had expected to find work, to wander from place to place until he was settled, but to fit in as he had, to love the open, the solitude, and particularly the man's game of wrenching home and competence from wild nature—this had been a revelation to him. And in it he was going to become completely absorbed.

This range had once supported millions of buffalo. It could never be cultivated, except along the waterways and around the spring holes. It would support cattle and horses, in which he calculated man would always find use and profit. There would never be any radical change in the level reaches, in the rolling ridges, the black and gray foothills, the vast purple hollow of sage and grass, in the white-tipped barrier of the mountains. What inexplicable comfort he derived from this assurance!

"Andy, where was you ridin' yestiddy?" queried the Arizonian one morning.

"South. Along the foothills to Stone Tank."

"No wonder I didn't run acrost you. Reckon you seen some of our stock?"

"Yes, a good many. Branded three calves. Cows getting wild. Saw a lot of Triangle X and Cross Bar stock."

"See any riders?"

"No, and I didn't pick up any tracks."

"Wal, I had better luck, or wuss, accordin' to how we take it. I rode west along the river, haided the creek thet runs in about ten miles down, an' then struck for the west end of the Antelope Hills. Must have rid nigh unto thirty miles. Rough and brushy in the draws. Lots of water an' grass. Reckon I seen two thousand haid of cattle. Located three daid cows by watchin' the buzzards. Thet's our best bet, Andy. You gotta have sharp eyes, though."

"Dead cows?" repeated Andrew. "Dead from what?"

"Lead slugs, son. What'd you expect? I cut one bullet out. Forty-five, I reckon. Gave it to the boss. He hit the roof. He's touchy these days, with McCall pressin' him."

"Jim, then—it's begun?"

"Begun! Why, cowboy, it's been goin' on for weeks. I'll bet we've lost a hundred calves. An' thet means the same number of cows."

"Two hundred head!" cried Andrew, shocked by the Arizonian's estimate.

"Wal, it's a hell of a big country. Our stock is scattered all over, same as thet of the other outfits. We couldn't keep track of them if we had a dozen riders. I found where some slick *hombre* had buried the ashes of his brandin' fire. Trailed him half a mile, then lost the tracks. I've a hunch he tied up those calves in the brush an' drove them away after dark."

"Where would he drive them?"

"Ask me an easy one. Across the river, mebbe, or around in some canyon where there were cows wearin' the brand he was burnin' or possibly to some far part of the range. We're helpless unless we can ketch him at it. An' then if there's more'n one rustler operatin' . . . Aw, hell, it ain't no cinch, as I heerd Martha say."

"Jim, locate me out there. Give me a landmark," said Andrew eagerly.

"Wal, jest make for the west end of the Antelope Hills.

Anywhere up them draws. I reckon on the south side we'll have our eyes opened. But thet's purty far. You'll have to lay out all night."

"I'll be glad to! Will you come?"

"Cain't today. Mebbe I'll meet you out there tomorrow. Keep yore eyes peeled, Bonnin'. You want to see these *hombres* first an' hold 'em up. Otherwise—wal, you mightn't come back. Two cowpunchers was shot last spring, an' one's still missin'. Blamed on bandits. But I'm doubtful of thet. You look sharp. I hadn't ought to let you go alone, but the boss needs me here."

"Don't worry, Jim, I'll be careful," replied Andrew, and turning toward the kitchen he saw Martha Dixon standing in the doorway. Something about her eyes told him she had heard what Jim had said. It pleased Andrew. Her wonderful eyes had fooled him often, but he felt certain that he saw in them now a fleeting look of apprehension.

"Morning. Is Mrs. Sue here? I could use a little grub," said Andrew, briskly, as he moved closer to the girl.

"She's house-cleaning."

Andrew noted then that Martha's sleeves were rolled high over slender round arms. Her hands were white with flour. She wore a colored gingham apron which did not entirely conceal her shapeliness. A golden tan had now replaced the sunburn of her face. Her golden hair waved rebelliously. He could not look at her saucy mouth without remembering the kiss he had stolen, and which had left him ashamed and troubled.

"What are you doing?" he queried brusquely.

"Mixing dough."

"Dough tell?" he said with a grin.

"Can't you ever come near me without saying something mean?"

"Martha Dixon, you get me wrong. You always do. . . . I was surprised, of course, to see flour on your hands. But I didn't mean to be mean. I was even trying to be funny. It flashed over me what a distractingly pretty little wife you'll make some cowboy—*maybe*."

"Indeed!" she retorted mockingly. But a blush mantled her neck and cheek.

"Would you be good enough to fix me up some sand-wiches?" he asked.

"Certainly," she answered, and went into the kitchen.

Andrew stepped inside and sat down. Martha paid no attention to him, and he watched her in silence, sure of only one thing—that she was decidedly pleasing to look at. He made up his mind then and there never to say another mean thing to her. Presently she turned to hand him a small package wrapped in brown paper.

"Thank you," he said, rising, and made as if to go. But he did not. "How's your ankle?"

"Most well."

"Well enough to dance—at the rodeo?"

"Oh, yes." She seemed detached, and the absence of her usual spirit and excitement impressed Andrew acutely. Yet he admitted his inconsistency. It was certainly ridiculous of him to disapprove of her, doubt her, insult her, and then feel peevish because she did not act as though she enjoyed being in his presence.

"If I go, will you dance with me?" he found himself asking, outwardly cool and nonchalant, but inwardly uncertain and fearful.

"Do you dance?" she inquired, as though in great surprise.

"Of course I do."

"I rather imagined that you would think dancing immoral."

"Do you take me for a prissy reformer?"

"I take you for a Mid-Victorian."

"Well, that's better than being a modern lounge lizard. . . . You haven't said you would dance with me?"

"No."

"Oh, all right. . . . I asked you—anyhow," he replied lamely, and went out. His unpremeditated friendly overture had been rebuffed. It made him smart. Still for some occult reason beyond his ken he was glad that he had unbent as far as he had. When he came out of the corral with his horse a few minutes later he glanced back at the house and felt that he saw her peeping from behind the window curtain. That was a queer thing for her to do when she despised him so cordially. He ruminated over it. Perhaps she was just curious about his trip—from which he might not return! That prompted him to shout to Jim, who had come out with Bligh.

"Hey, Jim, I'll be back tomorrow night sure—unless something unexpected happens."

At the moment he had a juvenile impulse to stay out another night, just to frighten Martha Dixon. However, he doubted that she would even notice that he was away. He mounted and rode away toward the west.

He took the river trail, a hard-packed cattle thoroughfare that wound through the cottonwoods and out into the open. Andrew had long since learned to know his horse, and like him better every day. He was a bay with white spots and bars. Andrew changed the cowboy name of Slats to Zebra. It had required a little time for him to find out that Zebra was fast, tireless, spirited yet tractable under a gentle hand, and that he was what the former owner had called a single-footer.

As he rode along, thoughts of the girl, and her strange attraction for him, gradually gave place to more tangible things—his horse, the river, the fragrance of sage, the long swelling slope up to the Antelope Hills, and the vigilant search for moving objects. Rabbits, coyotes, deer crossed his vision. For Andrew, in a ride like this, the absorbing fascination of it and his intense eagerness to practice what he had learned from the Arizonian, seemed to make the hours fly. Always the sense of bigness, of openness came first, then the tremendous force of the range as a thing to be conquered. This horse, this range, this wildness was a job; and always before he had been a failure. Now he was on his mettle, and he must win.

By mid-afternoon Andrew had reached the foothills at the west end of the range. Down between them, opening wide and choked with rocks and cedars, ran draws that were almost as deep as canyons. They were dry as dust and hot, despite the breeze from the heights. Far up these draws water remained in pockets in the rocky stream beds. Cattle trails threaded the maze of narrow deer trails zig-zagging through the brush up the slopes. White bleached grass stood knee high in the aisles and glades, while under the shade of the trees, the grass was still green. The air was fragrant, a tangy mixture of dry sage, dry cedars and the hot earth.

Andrew penetrated to a grassy glade where a thin ribbon of water ran down a shallow gully, forming shallow pools here and there. He unsaddled and hobbled his horse, hung his canteen and food on a branch and, rifle in hand, took to the trails.

It occurred to him that he was proceeding with almost ridiculous caution. But since that was the order he had given himself he kept to it, peering, listening, smelling, sensing—using all of the faculties he had learned to use. Whenever he came to a patch of sand or bare earth, or a dusty length of trail, he searched for tracks. And old tracks, which he had learned to know on sight, did not interest him. Fresh signs of cattle did, however, and soon he heard rustlings in the brush, the bawling of calves and the lowing of cows. As the afternoon was very quiet he sat down often to listen, rifle in hand. The several horse tracks he found were old and had been made by unshod animals.

From time to time he arose to steal on up the draw, which became wilder and rougher as he progressed. It surprised him to find how wild the cattle were. He would come upon a group standing on guard like listening deer, and as soon as they espied him they would gallop off, crashing through the brush. And presently it occurred to him that if there were any cattle thieves working this canyon they surely would be forewarned and be able to slip away. A better plan might be to hide at the entrance to one of these wide draws and wait.

Zebra was quietly grazing, yet scented or heard him. For he threw up his fine head to look. Andrew approached him with keen appreciation of what a horse could be to a man in the open. He ought to have a dog, too. Twilight was stealing into the glade and the air was turning cold. An abundance of firewood, however, assured him that he could make a comfortable night of it. First he cut some armloads of cedar boughs for a bed; then he collected a store of dead wood and started a fire. By this time darkness had set in. With his rifle at hand, and his saddle blankets for a seat, he sat down and opened the package of food Martha Dixon had put up for him. He had tied it up in his slicker. Opening it, he was more than surprised to discover its generous contents. Where had his eyes been while that girl had packed this food for him? Where? He shook his head dubiously: "I'm skating on thin ice. Character in a woman has nothing to do with what a man falls for," he muttered. "Well! I'll be jiggered!"

Evidently Martha had taken him for a dude tourist. He had asked for sandwiches. In addition, she had supplied cake, pie, cheese and lastly, wrapped in a small packet which he nearly missed, a single lump of sugar. Sugar! She might as well have included apple sauce or caviar. Sweets to the sweet!

This discovery, however, did not keep Andrew from enjoying his supper. When he had finished eating he drew his saddle up for a back rest, and made himself comfortable before the fire.

As he sat there, watching the glow of the embers and the

last ruddy flames, it was hard for him to realize that only a few months ago, all of this would have been impossible. The night was black, the sky overcast, the silence oppressive. After a while the wild ki-yiing of a coyote accentuated the loneliness of the wilderness. This little scene of a lone rider and his horse, a campfire in the hills had been enacted there many, many times for years on end. The Indian, the padre, the *courrier des bois*, the trapper, the explorer, the gold digger, the frontiersman, the soldier, the hunter, the pioneer, the cattleman, the cowboy, the rustler and bandit and outlaw—all of these alone, and with their kind, had sat by a campfire in the wilderness. That lonely scene had been epochal in the history of the West.

As he sat there watching the embers, he knew that he had never been meant for the crowd, for work in an office, for gambling in business deals with men. Peace hovered somewhere near him.

He lay down to sleep with one blanket underneath, the other over him, his feet to the replenished fire, and his head pillowed on his saddle. He lay down expecting to stay awake for hours only to find his eyelids grow heavy, his body grow still, his thoughts fade. When he awakened, chilled to the marrow, the fire was dead. He rebuilt it, warmed his hands and feet and his back, then went to sleep again. Gray cold dawn saw him stirring.

Leading his horse, he walked down to the open slope and then kept to the edge of the cedars along the base of the hills. He passed several draws where cattle were grazing.

Sunrise was lost to Andrew because he had gotten around to the western side of the hills. But the glory and color now were spreading across the vast prairie leading to the mountains. Something to be conquered—this range land! That was how it affected Andrew. To endure it, to fight it, to live by it—what a man's game!

Coming to another canyon with rugged slopes, he entered it far enough to hide his horse in a thicket, and then continue on foot. First he spent hours high up on a bank watching the gray slope down to the river. During this vigil he counted more than a hundred cattle, near and far. Then he went down to explore the canyon. The sight of lowing cows with full milk bags, dripping udders, and no calves filled him with deep anger. Manifestly here was the work of Smoky Reed or one of his henchmen. When Andrew came upon the remains of a little branding fire, he felt of the ashes, but they were cold. Between this point and the head of the draw he found three more such signs. Allowing for the very small amount of the actual acreage he could cover, he estimated that the brander of calves had done well there. But what he did with the calves was a question. Ranchers had spring and fall roundups when each collected all stock wearing his brand. The game puzzled Andrew and roused him thoroughly. He saw but few of Bligh's cattle, and did not find a single dead cow nor a horse track.

The day passed swiftly. Night overtook him before he got back to where he had left his horse. He made camp and relished what was left of his dry sandwiches, leaving one for the next day. What would Jim Fenner and Bligh think of his absence? They would be worried. What would Martha Dixon think? Andrew regretted his impulse, in so far as she had been the cause of it. He slept more warmly that night.

At break of day he rode into the wide entrance of the largest draw he had yet encountered. It actually was the opening of a valley leading up into the hills. Cattle dotted the landscape.

Andrew decided that he ought to watch that gateway during the early morning hours. Returning to a patch of cedars half a mile back along the way he had come, he halted Zebra in a well-screened shady spot. Then he took his field glasses and rifle and set out on foot.

By the time he had reached the wide draw again the slopes, the range land and mountains had lost their gray mantle to take the color of the sunrise. For his hiding place he selected an outcropping of rocks on the slope nearest his house, and taking up his position there he swept with his glasses the ten miles of sage slope between the hills and the river. Halfway down the slope he picked up two moving objects.

"Horsemen, by Judas!" he muttered excitedly.

With his naked eye Andrew could scarcely discern the riders. But through the field glasses he watched them approaching at a brisk trot. It was to be expected that he would see cowboys at any time or anywhere on that range. Most of them would be going about their work honestly, which meant that any one of them was innocent until proved guilty. Branding of calves went on daily. And he could not assume that all the calves belonged to Bligh. Not a tenth of them! McCall's hired rustlers, however, were concentrating on Bligh's stock simply because there was little risk for them. He had to come upon one of them branding a calf the mother of which wore the N.B. brand. It was a ticklish job, and he revolved slowly in his mind all of Jim's words of advice.

Meanwhile the riders came on, making straight for the wide canyon entrance. Since both rode horses that camouflaged well against the sage brush, he could not make certain that he would be able to recognize them.

As he watched them through the glasses, he saw the horsemen halt at the edge of the scattered thickets and carefully survey the range between the hills and the river, and on to the north. One of them removed his sombrero, revealing a brightly shining head of flaming red hair and a red face, which could belong only to the cowboy Texas. The other rider wore a black sombrero which hid his face. All that could be noted as distinctive about him was a striped gray and black shirt, plainly visible through the glasses.

After a brief discussion they separated, the rider in the striped shirt taking the left side of the valley, and Texas proceeding to the right. He was the last to disappear. Andrew could hear the cracking of dead branches and the ring of metal on stone. Presently all was quiet again.

"Well, they're here," said Andrew to himself, feeling his pulse beating high. "Smoky Reed's the one in the striped shirt, I'll gamble. It's not likely that Texas would take up with another cowboy. . . . They're both crooked. And now what?"

He answered his own query with immediate action, gaining a higher level without risk of being seen. He slung the field glasses over his shoulder, and moved on, ears alert and eyes roving. Presently he came to the place where the nearest rider had entered the canyon. He quickly picked up the fresh hoof tracks, and started to trail them, conscious of a thrill he had never before felt in his life. He was on the track of a crooked cowboy whom he meant to brand as an outlaw on that range.

He followed the tracks for half an hour before he realized that he was moving too slowly. Becoming bolder he quickened his pace. Before long he heard a distant crash of brush, and the bellow of a cow. But he could not locate either sound. Cattle trooped down the draw but they were mostly steers and yearlings. Andrew crouched behind some brush while they passed. Then he went on. The valley was no longer silent, and that emboldened him. Nevertheless he did not advance without being sure of cover. This needful caution grew more difficult to act upon as he advanced. The open places increased, and the cedars and thickets correspondingly afforded less protection. From before came the sound of water splashing somewhere near over stones.

Suddenly the whip-like crack of a gun rang out. The surprise of it shocked Andrew. Cold sweat exuded from his face. Then he realized that he should have expected it. Reed's method was to drive the mother of a calf into a thicket or rocky recess, kill her, and then brand the calf.

Andrew stole forward as noiselessly as he could, soon learning that stiff cowboy's boots were poor adjuncts for a stalk of this nature. Presently across an open patch of grass and beyond some cedars there rose a thin column of blue smoke. Andrew knew that he must hurry if he were going to catch that rustler redhanded, yet he doubted the wisdom of crossing that open place. So he made a detour and then could no longer locate the smoke. He listened. Far across the canyon he could see dust rising, and could hear faint thudding sounds. Texas must be busy over there. On this side there was now comparative silence. The movement of excited cattle did not mean much to Andrew at the moment. But his nostrils were assailed by a pungent odor of burning hair.

He came to a clump of cedars and scrub oaks. All at once against the background of barred light he caught sight of something moving. It was crossing a small sunlit aperture in the foliage. A patch of striped gray and black! At the sight Andrew's nerves grew tense. He felt that he had been heard, but he had no idea if he had yet been seen. An impulse to shoot flashed over him, difficult to restrain in the heat of that moment.

The next instant dead cedar branches close to his head exploded to scatter their fragments almost in his face. The heavy report of a gun followed. Andrew gasped, and actually ducked when he realized that he had been shot at and narrowly missed by a bullet. Angrily he leveled his Winchester and fired into the midst of the cedar brush where he had seen the gray and black object. The high-powered projectile crashed through the branches and ricocheted off some rocks. The thump of hoofs, the plunging of a horse, either tied or under a strong hand, gave Andrew another location for a target. He sent a bullet spatting through the thicket, and working the lever of the rifle as fast as he could, he shot three more times. Sound of the bullets hitting and glancing afforded him considerable satisfaction. Then he waited with rifle cocked.

Rustlings and crashings, apparently both close at hand and far away, stealthy footsteps and heavy hoof beats—these all confused Andrew, and added to his rage. His determination to close with the man who had tried to kill him caused him to make a precipitate move from behind the tree that had screened him.

He felt something like the snap of a whip above his temple, then a tearing pain, followed by a stunning blow that knocked him against the tree. He sank to his knees. Realizing that he had been hit and aware of hot blood pouring down his cheek, he still knew that he was conscious, that he had the will and the strength to kill his assailant. He waited for him to appear. But the wall of gray-green thicket did not split to emit a man. Instead a rapid crunch of boots, a clink of spur on iron stirrup, a crash in the brush and the pounding clip clop of hoofs, told Andrew that the cowboy he had been stalking was on his way out of there.

"Thinks he—got me," grunted Andrew, sinking to a seat. "Maybe he has. Look at the damn blood!"

He took off his sombrero to find that the bullet had gone through the band. It took courage for Andrew to run his forefinger into the wound from which the blood was streaming. For a moment he thought it was all up with Andrew Bonning. Then he found the shallow groove above his ear.

"Close shave, but I'm still kicking," he muttered grimly. "Smoky Reed, if I ever get my hands on you—good night!"

He folded his scarf and bound the wound tightly. While he was attending to his wound he heard another horse rapidly passing his position over to the right. That would be Texas making himself scarce. Listening until the sounds had ceased, Andrew got up to wipe his bloody hands on the cedar foliage. Then he pushed through the thicket to the open patch of ground from which the rustler had shot at him. A little fire of dead cedar sticks still was burning brightly. A running-iron, still smoking and smelling of scorched hair, lay on the ground. But the calf had disappeared. Andrew's search beyond the opening in the thicket was rewarded by finding a dead cow with the brand N.B. on her flank.

"Well, I can prove Bligh's cow was killed, his calf branded, and that I was shot . . . but no more. . . . I'll have to look Smoky Reed up and see if I can make him give himself away."

Andrew went back for the branding iron, and after cooling it in a pool of water, he hurried down the canyon. At the entrance his search with the field glasses for riders proved unavailing. Soon thereafter he returned to the spot where he had tied Zebra, mounted his horse and headed ranchward. The sick giddiness had left him, and except for a dull throbbing pain, he did not seem to suffer any great inconvenience from his recent experience. As he rode slowly along, the determination to discover his would-be murderer vied in Andrew's mind with more speculative fancies about how he would be received at home. He had to laugh at his own boyishness. It was the first time he could remember desiring to dramatize himself. But he did remember what he had promised Bligh, and he smiled in anticipation of old Jim's droll humor over his first experience with a bullet, and he could hardly wait to have Martha Dixon see him ride in all covered with blood.

A hard downhill trail and a horse eager to get home argued well for a quick return to the ranch. But the way was long, the sun hot, and Andrew did not bear up under both as well as he had expected. Evidently he had lost considerable blood. When after three hours of riding he arrived at the ranch he felt that it was not any too soon. He did not stop at the barn, because he knew he was going to fall off, and he wanted to be near the house where he would be seen.

Jim was on the porch, however, and with a call that fetched his wife, Bligh and Martha, he came running out.

"Wal, if you're not a bloody mess," he said coolly, striding quickly to the side of Andrew's horse.

"Andrew! What happened to you?" shouted Bligh, in consternation.

"Somebody took a pot shot at me," replied Andrew, trying to be nonchalant, but the words were very faint. All sensation seemed to be leaving him from his legs up. As he reeled in the saddle his fading sight registered Martha's great staring eyes dark with alarm, and as he toppled over he heard her cry as from far off: "Oh. . . . How awful!"

Andrew lost his equilibrium but did not quite lose consciousness. He felt in a dull way that he was being upheld and then laid down on the cool grass. Someone supported his head while cold water was slapped in his face. Then he recovered to hear what was being said, but did not open his eyes.

"Jest a bullet crease," Jim was saying with evident satisfaction. "Wash it clean an' tie it up. Reckon he bled a lot, an' the long ride . . ."

"Let me drive to town for a doctor," pleaded Martha Dixon. It was she who was holding his head.

"Wal, thet's unnecessary trouble an' expense," replied the Arizonian. "His hurt ain't nothin'. He'll be around tomorrow as usual."

"I'll bandage it, Sue," cried Martha. "First aid is old stuff to me."

Andrew remained quiet until his wound had been dressed— a procedure both painful and pleasurable—after which he opened his eyes and sat up. Martha and Sue were on their knees beside him, and the men stood by watching. Jim had his rifle out of the saddle sheath, examining it. "Much obliged, folks," said Andrew. "Guess I went down and out for a little. I'm okay now. . . . Say you got blood on your hands!"

Martha gazed down at them. "Why, so I have," she said simply, and rose with averted face to go into the kitchen.

"Andy, you been firin' this rifle," said Jim.

"Yes. Three or four times," replied Andrew, and rose to his feet.

"What at?" queried the other sharply.

"Well, the fellow who shot at me."

"After he hit you?"

"No. He missed the first time. I saw him move. He was hidden behind brush," replied Andrew, and briefly related his experience. He kept his suspicions and deductions to himself.

"Wal, thet opens the brawl," said Jim, dryly, as his eyes narrowed.

"Andrew, you were careless," interposed Bligh.

"I'm afraid I was, boss. Overanxious. Believe me, I've learned a lesson."

"Jim, things are goin' from bad to worse," declared the rancher, gloomily.

"Wal, it's a way things have."

"What'll we do about this?"

"Leave it to Andy an' me, boss. But stavin' off McCall— thet's another matter."

"What new has come up since I left?" queried Andrew.

"McCall sent word that he wanted his outfit to drive my stock across the Sweetwater to mix with his, as I agreed. I don't see anythin' else but to comply with this demand. He has my letter, which is equivalent to a contract."

110

"Letter hell! We ain't goin' to let McCall have nothin'," growled Jim.

"If he hales me into court—"

"It would be most damn disastrous for him, Mr. Bligh," interposed Andrew quickly. "Let's rely on Jim's judgment in this matter. . . . There's something fishy about McCall."

"Jim, do you agree with thet?"

"Shore. Somethin' rotten—fishy."

"I had a hunch, myself."

"Boss, you're goin' to take Martha to the rodeo. McCall will be there. Call his bluff. Tell him the deal doesn't look good to you no more an' you won't go through with it."

"But man, I can't go into court now," protested Bligh.

"You won't never have to go to court."

"McCall says he has hired a new outfit, built a cabin over on Willow Creek, trucked lumber an' supplies in. He has a comeback at me."

"Wal, we have one on him, an' a hell of a good one."

"Then we'll take the bull by the horns."

Soon after that Andrew was called to supper. Since his departure two days before the dining table had been moved out onto the back porch, where all Bligh's household were to eat together. During supper Andrew began to feel that his status with Martha Dixon had changed somewhat. She was a disturbing presence at any time, but now that she seemed no longer angry with him, he could see complications ahead.

After supper Jim found him on the front porch of his cabin.

"What's on your mind, son?"

"Martha Ann Dixon," replied Andrew, truthfully.

"Wal, thet's fine an' shore sarves you right. But I mean about this deal you had in the hills. You didn't tell Bligh an' me all of it."

"No. I thought I'd better not. But I'll tell you, Jim." And Andrew recounted the entire adventure in detail, and ended the account with his own deductions.

"Wal, whoever thet cowpuncher was, he shore figgered he'd done for you. An' if you can face him sudden-like, surprise him, he'll give himself away, if he recognizes you."

"Jim, that is my angle. I *know* it's Smoky Reed."

"Ahuh. But no proof except the striped shirt. There might be two cowboys wearin' thet brand. Anyway, it's a good clue,

111

thet an' the brandin' iron. What you goin' to do if you identify him?"

"Old-timer, I'll incapacitate that cowboy for some time to come."

"Sounds good—thet word, but I don't savvy it. . . . Andy, whoever this *hombre* is, he'll be with his outfit. They'll be mean. They'll kid the pants off you. Razz you in front of the girls. Cowboys are death on tenderfeet. You'll have to take a crack at ridin' somethin' in the rodeo. An' thet'll give them a chance to humiliate you still more. But it'll give you a chance, too—to get sore."

"Don't need it, Jim. I'm sore now—at any outfit that Mr. Striped Shirt rides for."

"You'll have to fight them all."

"Okay."

"Andy, was you skeered out there in the hills—when you heerd the bullet?"

"I'll say I was. Scared stiff," declared Andrew, with a short laugh.

"Are you goin' to be thet way when you meet this outfit at the rodeo?" asked Jim curiously.

"Will they be packing guns?"

"No. Thet ain't allowed at rodeos."

"Then I'll simply be delighted."

"Humph! I don't figger you, son. It shore ain't no cinch to buck up agin an outfit of mean cowpunchers."

"Jim, out here on the range, on a horse, or alone in the hills I'm not of much account," returned Andrew. "But flat on my feet—facing a bunch of unarmed men—well, that's different. I may say I've often held my own in a husky crowd. Ha!"

"Ahuh. You have? Wal, I ain't never seen a puncher yet who could pitch a hundred pound sack of oats around like you can. I'm gonna be there when you meet up with thet outfit. I'll get a man to take my place here for a couple of days. But don't tell the boss."

On the following day Andrew felt very little the worse for his creased skull, and ten days later he dispensed with the bandage over his temple. If anyone had been particularly interested in the young man's movements these several days, they would have discovered something unusual for a ranch. He had filled a small burlap bag with sand and had hung it up about face high from a rafter in the barn. Then he put on his buckskin riding gloves and proceeded to punch that bag. When he hit the bag it gave forth a sodden sound.

"Not so bad!" he muttered, at the end of his last workout, which was on the morning Bligh asked him to drive the car to town.

Martha was the last to come out of the house. That was one of her failings, Andrew had long ago observed. She just could not be on time. But when she appeared she looked bewitching in a trim blue dress she had made herself. Her shapely legs were bare, except for socks rolled down over flat-heeled shoes. She had apparently given up wearing hats. Andrew turned away his eyes. This young lady was getting surprisingly on his nerves.

"Please, may I drive?" she asked, leaning over the car door on Andrew's side. He might have refused the spoken solicitation, but the man did not live who could have denied the appealing look in those amber eyes.

"Why—er—certainly," stammered Andrew, hastily sliding over to the right side of the front seat.

Martha threw her little bag upon the seat and got in, and as she manipulated the gears with deft hands, her eyes on the dashboard, she said in a most casual way: "When I ride with a handsome young man I always like to drive."

"Yeah, so I've noticed," Andrew retorted, and looked across the range to the hills. Her remark hinted at the old enmity. But the look in her eyes when she had asked permission to drive remained with him. He pondered over the lovely expression in those amber eyes. Had it been nothing but youthful, thrilling eagerness to drive the car? Any expression in them was bewildering. They were dangerous eyes because they appeared to any poor, asinine, masculine clod to say infinitely more than she obviously meant. Their exquisite light, their strange color, their indescribable loveliness were simply facts of nature, and therefore false. He had seen them blaze with scorn and that had been something to remember. They had been true then. But how much of their play and change and charm had been intended, for instance, that evening when she flirted so outrageously with the callow youth at the hotel? The recollection of that occasion seemed crude and raw to him. As Jim would say, "it stuck in his craw." But nature could make a woman a flirt when she was absolutely innocent and unconscious of it. Then he groaned inwardly at the reali-

113

zation that he was developing an excuse like this for everything that Martha Ann Dixon had done. All the same the idea persisted, and another formed, haunting and ruthless—an attempt to imagine how perfectly glorious her marvelous eyes would be if motivated by real, unselfish love.

Martha drove all the way to Split Rock without exchanging another word with Andrew. In town, the moment they stopped, the Glemm girls and their friends claimed her and drove off with her in their car to the rodeo. Andrew felt relieved. If it were not for the serious business he had in mind he would have gone back to the ranch. Bligh learned that McCall had gone to Casper. A few minutes later they took to the road again with Andrew at the wheel.

The run from the ranch to Split Rock had been short, but this one to Casper seemed endless, although he gave the old engine all it could stand. They arrived about dark. Andrew did not remember very much about Casper. It appeared to be a big town and the main street blazoned a welcome to visitors. They went to two hotels before they could find lodgings. The town was full of visitors, tourists, cowboys, ranchers, with two girls to every man.

The hotel to which Bligh had taken Sue and Andrew appeared to be a second-class place, full of noisy cowboys. That suited the Easterner, and immediately he was on the *qui vive*. Bligh took Sue in to supper while Bonning changed his rough garb. When he came downstairs the lobby and lunchroom were crowded with a noisy, jostling smoking, haranguing lot of cowboys. All were youthful and some had been drinking, though Andrew could not help liking them.

After supper he sat down beside a plain, weather-beaten little cattleman and made himself agreeable.

"Stranger hereabouts?" queried the cattleman casually.

"Yes, I suppose I am, though I've been west a while."

"Easterner, I see."

"I was. My name is Bonning."

"I'm Jeff Little. Reckon you're here for the rodeo, same as everybody."

"Sure am. Never saw one before. Just what is a rodeo, anyhow?"

"Cowboy circus. Thet's about all. Casper puts on a good show. But nothin' compared to Cheyenne or Kalispel. Some professionals here, though."

"What are professionals?"

"Cowboys an' girls who make their livin' out of rodeos. Trick riders. There's some home talent here, though, thet can make any riders go some. I've a couple in my own outfit."

"Interesting. Where's your range, Mr. Little?"

"Down on the Platte River, south of the Pathfinder Reservation. I run the Double X."

"How is the cattle business right now?"

"Perkin' up. I'm runnin' about forty thousand head, an' am not sellin' this year. Thet's a hunch."

"Forty thousand. You must employ many cowboys?"

"Only two outfits now, but they're good. I don't keep poor riders. Reckon one time or another I've hired every puncher in middle Wyomin'."

"Ever hire a redheaded cowboy called Texas something?"

"Shore have, an' ain't likely to forget him. Likable lad, finest of horsemen, wonder with a rope, but unreliable, if you know what I mean. Proud, wild, Texas breed. Never heard his last name. He's here, by the way. Saw him today. Great fellow for the girls."

"Aren't they all pretty much the same?" inquired Andrew with a laugh. "Let's see. There's another cowboy I heard mentioned over at Split Rock. Smoky—something."

"Reed. I know him. He rode for me once—about a day," returned the cattleman, with a brevity that was significant to Andrew.

"Thanks. I think I'll go out and look them over," said Bonning, rising.

"So you like Wyomin'?"

"Crazy about it!"

"Any idea of ranchin'?" queried the older man shrewdly.

"Well, the idea has occurred to me."

"Buy cattle before fall then. In a year you'll double your money."

Andrew strolled thoughtfully out into the street. He was revolving in his mind the fact that out here in the West everything gravitated to him. Back east they had passed him by. If he were going to get into the cattle business this appeared to be the time. He walked down his side of the gaily thronged street and up on the other. One busy place halted him and that was a brilliantly lighted corner store where ice cream, sodas and other refreshments were served. It was being patronized so briskly by young people that he could not get waited on. Then he went into a moving-picture theater where there was standing room only. Tiring of the picture, he left and went back to the hotel to bed. He was honest enough with himself to admit that he felt disappointed at not having seen Martha Dixon. A melancholy and absurd regret was plaguing his spirit, though he knew that if he had not been a fed-up and morbid Easterner, he might have been having a jolly time with that girl.

In the morning Andrew donned his cowboy duds, except the chaps, and sallied forth to what he had a feeling would be a memorable day. He devoted a few hours to listening and watching on the street and in the stores and hotels. More than one bantering cowboy made his ears tingle, not by some tart or crude words of ridicule, but because he seemed unable to hide the tenderfoot in him. This, however, was more than compensated for by the decidedly roguish and flattering glances which he received from several pretty girls. The town was full of them. In all the store windows were placards advertising the rodeo dance. Andrew kept a keen eye open for three persons—Martha Dixon, Texas and Smoky Reed.

On the street, in the hotel lobby or at the lunch counter, everywhere that he encountered cowboys he met with the prevailing good-natured western raillery, offensive only in a few instances. He started early for the fair grounds, where the rodeo was to be held.

A short time afterward, he found himself inside the high fence, free of the noisy crowd and gibing cowboys, holding in his hand a ticket that permitted him to enter any or all contests. The preliminaries were being run off before a half-filled grandstand, and Andrew thought he would get the agony over quickly. At a window to which some one directed him, he made application and presently found himself outside the circular fence bounding the race track. Things were happening right then, but he was told to do this and that, and before he realized it he was climbing into a little pen. To his horror the beast therein was not a horse but a ferocious-looking long-horned steer of a species unfamiliar to Andrew. There was a rope around its body, evidently for the rider to clutch.

"Get set, cowboy," called the guard curtly. "Fork him!"

Andrew dropped down to straddle the steer, grasped the rope with his hands, squeezed the huge body with his legs and held on desperately. The door slid back, the wild buffalo, or whatever the beast was, bawled and plunged out.

116

A tremendous force broke Andrew's leg hold and flung his feet high in the air. But he held on to the rope to descend with a sickening thud upon the back of the animal. Up he was flung again, like a feather. The spectators roared with glee, and Andrew was sure that they were looking at him. Down and up, down and up, while the infuriated beast ran faster than any horse Andrew had ever ridden. It bounded like a monstrous jack rabbit, all the way down the oval enclosure, to wheel and plunge back again, at every leap flinging Andrew aloft. He long had ceased to come down astride the steer. At last Andrew's tenacious hold broke and he soared aloft for the last time and then crashed to the turf. The fall jarred his teeth to the roots, but he did not appear to be killed or maimed. To his astonishment the audience gave him unstinted applause. Bonning limped off vowing that his ambitions to be a rodeo star had been completely squelched. At the gate he encountered Jim, who drew him inside.

"How'd you like thet?" queried the Arizonian mildly.

"Man alive! Never again!" panted Andrew, feeling to see if any of his bones were whole.

"Bust anythin'?"

"I guess not."

"Wal, you needn't look so flustered. You rode thet steer better'n any puncher I ever seen. Fact! An' the crowd cheered you."

"Quit your kidding, Jim."

"Honest. It was funny—the way you rode in, standin' on your haid. But it ain't the way you ride thet counts. It's stickin' on. I'll bet you win a prize."

"No!"

"Wal, anyway, Martha Ann is up in the grandstand with a bunch of girls. You should have heerd them squeal."

"Okay, Jim. You're an encouraging chap," declared Andrew, plainly pleased. "I'd like to take another whack at something."

"Wal, we'll see. Come along here, Andy. I've located a striped shirt an' it's on Smoky Reed."

He felt his arm swell tight under his companion's guiding hand. "Yeah," he said, glancing at the dark, impassive profile of the Arizonian.

"Lot of punchers over here, waitin' for their turns an' watchin'," explained Jim. "Some of them been lookin' on red likker too. I reckon you won't have no trouble gettin' a rise out of Reed, unless he recognizes you. In thet case you'll know him, an' you can brace him pronto. But if he doesn't know you, then you'll have to get a rise out of him. . . . There he is. Tall puncher, freckled, towhaided, wearin' the striped shirt. Strut up an' down before him an' the outfit he's with. I'll hang back an' watch."

Andrew saw a long shed, open in front, facing the arena and directly next to the circular fence. Horses and cowboys were much in evidence, to men standing mostly in little groups, smoking, talking, laughing. There was a fairly wide aisle between the benches and the fence.

When he got a close view of the four cowboys Jim had pointed out, Andrew strode toward them. As he did so he felt for his buckskin gloves, to find that he had not removed them from his hands. There was no redheaded cowboy in the quartet. The nearest to him was a mature man, stocky in build, with a round paunch protruding above his belt. The next two were lean, hard-faced youths, and the fourth was the cowboy Jim had described. He appeared to be muscular, but not heavy. His eyes were blue and bold of expression, gleaming from under bushy brows. He had a sallow freckled face somewhat flushed from drink. When Andrew saw the striped gray and black shirt his heart leaped, and he was certain that he recognized it. But recalling Jim's instructions, he got himself well in hand, and walked past the four men, looking squarely at them. Then he wheeled and came back, this time giving Reed the benefit of a searching glance.

The cowboy stared at him, but did not wink an eye. If he had associated Andrew in the slightest with the man he had deliberately tried to kill and had left for dead or wounded, he would not have been able to conceal some slight start that would have given him away.

Nevertheless Andrew felt doggedly sure that he had his man cornered. He was absolutely certain of McCall's offer, of Texas' promise to arrange the rustling deal, and of the fact that the two had ridden into the canyon out in the Antelope Hills.

"Hey, puncher, was you the *hombre* who jest forked thet steer?" called one of the four.

"Yes, if it's any of your damned business," retorted Andrew. "Trying to kid me, huh?"

"Not at all. You did fine—fer a Yankee tenderfoot."

Andrew glared at the speaker, who was the short stout one

118

of the four. His retort focused the attention of the others upon Andrew, and evidently they at once discovered the aptness of their comrade's epithet. Bonning proceeded to strut and swagger up and down before them. And they began to make remarks. The tenderfoot pretended to take no heed, but his sharp ears took in everything. Meanwhile, with his object nearly attained, he used his eyes to further good advantage. There was an open space between the grandstand and the shed where the men were standing. Spectators could look right down upon it. To the right stood a refreshment booth before which a crowd was lined up. People were straggling in through the gates. Jim, within ear shot, leaned over the fence watching the preliminary exercises on the rodeo track.

"Shore he's a Yankee," drawled the spokesman of the quartet.

"Pretty snooty," said another.

"Lady killer, I'd say. Swell Stetson, fancy-top boots, buckskin gloves, an' all."

"Swelled-up tenderfoot," snorted Reed, loud enough for cowboys of other groups to hear. Laughs were immediately forthcoming. Plenty of fun seemed imminent. Only Andrew knew just how much fun there was going to be. Perhaps Jim, standing now back to the fence, had an inkling. A flood of range banter eddied around Andrew's ears. He gave no sign that he heard, and went on strutting to and fro.

"Look at that mail-order cowboy!"

"Ump-umm. He's a dude-ranch tourist."

"Where'd he git thet outfit?"

"Hey, pretty boy, stop obstructin' the landscape," called Reed derisively. "Reckon you're thet dude tenderfoot who drives the little hitchhikin' queen around."

"Are your remarks addressed to me?" Andrew queried, wheeling. He did not raise his voice, but there was a note in it that stopped the conversation and directed everyone's attention upon him. A moment of surprised silence ensued. The tenderfoot's sudden change of front gave the cowboys pause.

"Shore they was," replied the older man cheerily. "We was jest pokin' fun."

"Fun, hell! If you didn't insult me, you sure insulted a lady!"

"Aw wal, take it thet way if you like," returned the other, plainly nettled.

"That's how I do take it," snapped Andrew. "Certainly I'm

a tenderfoot. An Easterner new to the range. I'm not used to cowboy humor. But I know the difference between fun and insult. And I demand an apology!"

"Haw! Haw!"

"Say, dude, shet your loud mouth."

Andrew poked a finger in the face of the eldest of the four. "One at a time, will you?" he cried. "You seem to be half human. Answer me this. If an eastern tenderfoot called an outfit of Westerners like you—called them some choice names and invited them to swallow it or fight—what would happen?"

"Wal, I'm afeared the tenderfoot would git mauled jest to beat hell, an' swallow a lot of dust in the process."

"All right, then, listen. You're a bunch of dirty pack rats! Four lousy cowpunchers! Coyotes, skunks, and all the rest of the range vermin put together. And probably rustlers besides."

"Stranger, we're shore gittin' an earful," retorted the eldest, sharply, red as a beet in the face.

"Do the three of you know the company you keep?" demanded Andrew, scornfully indicating the astounded Smoky Reed, whose slow mind seemed to be assimilating a startling thought.

"Keepin' company at rodeos doesn't mean ridin' pards, stranger," parried the other harshly, as the blood left his face.

"Then the three of you are only vermin, but this striped-shirt *hombre* is a coward in the bargain. Now you gentlemen of the range are invited to step out, one at a time. Let me see the western stuff you're made of."

"Wal, it'll only take one of us, you rantin' dude," yelped the stout man, and he lunged out.

Andrew swung a savage right uppercut to the pit of that prominent abdomen. A deep bass sound rumbled out. The victim doubled up and his round face grew distorted, with eyes bulging, and mouth open sucking at air that would not go in. He sank down to his knees convulsively clutching his paunch.

Swiftly Bonning leaped forward to swing a snakelike left to the gaping mouth of the next cowboy and a right to the breadbasket of the third. Down like tenpins they crashed.

"Step out, Smoky, you polecat, and get yours," shouted Andrew, and snatching at the striped shirt, he gave the cowboy a powerful pull which propelled him out from under the shed into the open space below the grandstand. Excited yells drew the spectators on that side of the grandstand to the rail.

"Lay off me, you bruiser! I'm on to you," harshly rasped out Reed.

Bonning threw his sombrero aside, and pointed to the angry red bullet mark over his temple.

"See that, Reed! You did that! *You* shot me! From behind a bush like the coward you are!"

The cowboy turned livid and snatched at a gun that was not on him.

"You dirty low-down calf rustler!" yelled Andrew, in a voice he meant to carry into the stand. "This is no gun-slinging scrap." Then he charged the cowboy, beat down his defense, slugged him with lefts and rights, knocked him down and dragged him up, and then backing him against the fence landed terrific blows on the already bloody face, and would soon have knocked him out completely but for the interference of some shocked bystanders.

"Hyar, let up!" roared a rough voice, and its owner seized the angry Easterner by the shoulders. Like a top he spun round to strike the man before he could see him clearly. The would-be peacemaker fell his length in the dust.

"Did you sock me?" he bawled, in strident rage, as he labored to his feet, one hand at his bleeding nose.

"No—but I will if you lay hands on me again," panted Andrew.

"You're thet tenderfoot puncher of Bligh's. You're arrested. Assault an' battery . . . resistin' an officer!"

Then Andrew recognized the man as Sheriff Slade.

"Okay. Suits me fine, provided you arrest Reed too."

"Who?"

"Smoky Reed, the cowboy I was punishing when you interrupted me."

That battered cowboy manifestly had taken advantage of the moment to slink away into the crowd. Slade, however, did not make any apparent attempt to locate him.

"Stick out your hands," ordered Slade, producing handcuffs.

"I'll go with you," replied Andrew quickly, as the crowd surged closer.

"Stick 'em out, I tell you."

"No!"

Jim Fenner interposed his person on the scene, confronting the sheriff with cold narrowed eyes and hard lips.

"Slade, cut the grandstand play," said the Arizonian sharply. "I'll be responsible for this lad."

"Who the hell air you?" demanded Slade.

"I left my cyard at the gate," rejoined Jim, significantly. "If you're keen about seein' it, we'll stop as we go out."

"By Gawd, you strangers air gittin' altogether too cussed fresh. . . . Come on."

Between them they led Andrew out of the press of spectators. As he passed the grandstand he looked up to see a line of girls leaning over the rail, and in the center stood Martha Dixon, white as a flower, with telltale eyes upon him.

9

Two INCIDENTS, the bold overtures of a cowboy named Reed and the arrest of Andrew Bonning, spoiled what would have been a perfectly marvelous day for Martha Ann.

That very morning on the way to the rodeo Martha had received a letter from her mother, not only fogiving her for the mad escapade to which she had confessed, but also enclosing a check to defray her expenses home. Martha had arrived in Casper with her new friends, excited and happy. The crude overture of a cowboy whom the Glemm girls knew had disturbed her, because the man had evidently heard of her hitchhiking, and had assumed that to be sufficient license to make an advance which had to be squelched in no uncertain words. Then Andrew's spectacular riding of the steer, ludicrous as it was, had won her unwilling admiration. These had been forgotten, however, in the excitement of the rodeo, the magnificent horses and the daring trick riders, until Andrew's fight and arrest had broken up the show for Martha Ann.

It chanced that she had been a witness to both. Nellie Glemm, leaving her seat to meet some friends coming up the steps, had halted with them to look over the rail. Something evidently had happened below. People were leaving their seats. At the moment there was nothing going on on the track. Suddenly Nellie had turned to beckon her sister, Martha and the two other girls.

"There's Smoky Reed now," said the Glemm girl, pointing. "Cal Brice, and the Hazelett boys. . . . Making fun of the

122

young man who drove you to town. Bligh's hired hand, isn't he?"

"Yes. That's Andrew. . . . His name is Andrew Bonning," returned Martha Ann.

"I've seen him before," said one of the girls.

"Handsome fellow," added Nellie.

"Say, look at him parade! That Brice outfit won't do a thing to him."

"Girls. He's just showing off—for their benefit," Martha had hastily interposed. "Andrew isn't the least conceited."

"This is going to be fun," replied Nellie. "I'll say he has his nerve with him. That's a bad outfit."

The ensuing harangue and fight, the interception by the sheriff and Andrew's arrest had quite robbed Martha Ann of any further enjoyment in the rodeo.

"Looks like your big boy picked a fight with Smoky's outfit," declared Nellie Glemm, meaningfully, after they had returned to town to their hotel.

"He's not mine," replied Martha Ann, hastily feeling her cheeks grow hot.

"Well, he sure made hash out of Smoky. And wasn't it rich when he hit Cal Brice in the breadbasket?"

"Will they keep him—in jail?" queried Martha nervously.

"They sure will, if he can't pay his fine."

"Jim Fenner went with him. I hope they have enough money."

Martha Ann felt on pins and needles. She was at a loss how to escape from these spirited Western girls, all so friendly and eager for her enjoyment, without giving them further reason to think that she was interested in Andrew. Still she simply had to find out if he had been released. The idea of his being kept in jail over night was intolerable. The terrific beating she had seen him administer to Reed had made her forget completely the latter's insulting words. She could not explain her swift championship of Andrew, her unholy delight at the sight of the vulgar cowboy bully standing helpless before Andrew's amazing onslaught, and lastly her unreasonable alarm over his arrest. These varying emotions left her heart in something of a fluster. For long she had accused herself in the comforting darkness of her room of thinking too much about Andrew Bonning, a confession she had easily scorned in the light of day.

The entrance of Mr. Bligh, with Jim and Sue, delivered Martha Ann from the turmoil of her thoughts.

"Howdy, niece, we been huntin' you," said her uncle. "Have you had a nice day? You sure looked excited."

"Oh Uncle Nick! . . . Yes, I-I've had a nice day—pretty nice," cried Martha, and checked her impulsiveness.

"You girls stayin' here?"

"Yes. We have rooms all in a row. . . . The girls are taking me to the rodeo dance tonight. Uncle, you've heard of course about Andrew?"

"Yes. We just come from the jail."

"Isn't he—out?" faltered Martha.

"Lass, thet bloomin' Slade locked Andy up an' slapped a fine of a hundred dollars on him," declared Jim, without his usual dry humor. "Andy said he had the money, but couldn't get at it. Don' knew what he meant. So I rustled out to find the boss."

"Martha, think of it!" exclaimed Bligh, mournfully. "Jim an' Sue an' I altogether can't dig up enough to get Andrew out."

"I can," retorted Martha gladly, tearing open her handbag. "Came this morning from Mother. Can you cash it?"

"Sure, right here. You endorse the check," he said, and led Martha to the desk. Jim and Sue followed.

Martha Ann found herself writing in a scribble that bore little resemblance to her usual neat, firm handwriting.

"Damned outrage!" ejaculated her uncle as he received the check. "Hundred-dollar fine for nothin' but a fist fight."

"Wal, Andy socked Sheriff Slade," interposed Jim. "It's all over town. Casper don't 'pear to like Slade much."

"Never mind, Uncle. It was worth a hundred dollars—even if the money was sent to fetch me home. Now I can't ever go!"

"Andy will pay it back. But if you'll be leavin' us, I hope he doesn't pay you for a long time."

"I'm not leaving you, Uncle," replied Martha warmly.

"Lass, did you see thet scrap?" queried Jim, curiously.

"Indeed I did. Lordy! I was scared at first—and then tickled pink."

"Andy had somethin' up his sleeve, didn't he?"

"He did, Jim. It looked as if he deliberately picked a fight with those cowboys. The fellow he beat so terribly was Smoky

124

Reed. The Glemm girls know him. He was introduced to me right after we got here. And he got fresh immediately."

The Arizonian studied Martha Ann with shrewd penetrating eyes that seemed to read her thoughts.

"Wal, I reckon thet was what Andrew was so het-up about," he drawled.

Something suddenly struck Martha Ann that seemed surprise and pain and bliss all together. "Jim—d-did Andrew know?"

"I reckon so, lass."

"He beat that lout—for my sake?"

"Shore. What else?"

"But how'd he find out?"

"I heard Reed speak light of you to Andy."

Bligh returned with the cash, which he forced into Jim's hands. "Rustle an' get Andrew out."

"Jim, don't tell Andrew—" called Martha, but Jim already had got out of hearing.

"Lass, are you havin' supper with us?" asked Bligh.

"I'm not hungry," replied Martha, trying to appear composed. "Besides I've got to fix my dress for the dance."

"Tell me, how'd this Smoky Reed insult you?" demanded Bligh.

"It was at the Glemm's. He boards there. I met him and several other cowboys. Reed had had a drink or two. He followed me out to the car, hanging on to my arm. 'Baby,' he said, 'you're such a swell little hiker, suppose you step out with me tonight?' I declined and got into the car. He didn't take the hint. 'I'm the neckin'est *hombre* on this range. Don't you want some of my brand?' Here Nellie Glemm broke in. 'Shut up, Smoky. You're half lit. If you haven't any manners, at least try to be decent.' Reed drew back on the curb and said: 'Aw hell, she's lookin' for it, ain't she?' "

"Martha, I'd hoped that hikin' stunt of yours wouldn't become common gossip," returned Bligh regretfully.

"Uncle, I'm afraid it was a mistake," replied Martha Ann, her lip trembling. "But I had to come. And there was no other way. . . . I don't care what vile-minded people think."

"Don't be distressed, child. Jim says Andrew's takin' it up so fierce will end cowboy talk, anyway."

Martha Ann made some excuse to the girls and fled to her room. When she had locked the door against intrusion, she went to the mirror and stood there gazing at her face. And as she looked, she felt that a false shell fell away from her. That afternoon the blazing stunning truth had burst upon Martha with Jim Fenner's revelation. Until now she had been pretending to be in love with Andrew Bonning. Now she realized that she was hopelessly, terribly, passionately in love with him.

"In love with *him?* . . . With Andrew Bonning? With a man who thinks me a flirt, a loose woman, a hussy! . . . My God, if this isn't the limit!" Her eyes filled with rebellious tears. She began walking up and down in the tiny room, beating her fist into the palm of her other hand. There came a knock on the door which shocked her into an appreciation of the time and place.

"Who's there?"

"Just me," called Nellie Glemm gayly. "You've got one hour to dress. Doll up for us, Martha. You'll drive Wyoming mad tonight."

"Do my—damnedest," replied Martha Ann, trying to sound gay, too. Wyoming mad! The words stung her to battle. Quickly she undressed and washed and tried to brush her hair into staid waves. Then she put on her stockings and blue slippers, and at last the flimsy blue gown with its simple relief of color.

It was a new and demure Martha Ann Dixon whose amber eyes met her gaze in the mirror. Where had vanished all her golden tan? Her face was the hue of marble. But rouge changed that, so far as lips and cheeks were concerned. Only what to do with her eyes! It seemed to Martha that all the old mischievous and deceiving lights had gone. What she saw now no pride could hide. Now her eyes were transparent windows of amber through which love shone, unashamed. And she suddenly realized with a kind of wonder that never in her life had she looked so well. Would Andrew come to the dance? Would he see her and think her pretty? And chide herself as she might, it made no difference; she gloried in the thought.

That thought might have been short-lived, to judge from warning memory, had not happy voices in the hall and the pounding of impatient hands upon the door, given Martha Ann the glad assurance that she would not be alone any more till the dance was over.

She opened the door, to be swooped down upon and swept away downstairs, lighthearted once more as her natural response to the gaiety and the bright colors and movement of young people reasserted itself with vivid pleasure. The lobby of the hotel was filled with many young men and girls, with all of whom the Glemm girls desired to make Martha acquainted. They were all wholesome red-cheeked girls, and clean-cut tanned boys, none of the latter appearing to have the earmarks of cowboys. They escorted Martha a couple of blocks down the main street, and up a wide stairway of a large building to the top floor. Here they had to run a gauntlet to get into the hall.

It was a big bare place, decorated with bunting and every manner of rodeo paraphernalia that Martha had seen this eventful day. The shiny floor was vacant at the moment, except along the sides where young people sat or stood in gay conversation. At the far end of the hall there was a wide stage on which the musicians sat tuning their instruments. Arched doorways on one side led out upon a porch. Martha's quick eyes took in all these details, also the obvious fact that the young men far outnumbered the girls.

Once inside, Martha met many more young people including some cowboys. She did not catch many names. These Westerners were a democratic, free and easy people, not all strong on formality. She liked their simplicity and sincerity. She had to admit, too, that she had been stared at more at a university formal than here. She had quickened to the promise of an enjoyable evening—until she suddenly found herself gazing about the hall, searching for someone who was not there.

"Martha, here's Texas," whispered Nellie Glemm. "You remember the cowboy who wanted to drive you out to the ranch? Well, it's he. Such a handsome boy! He's a gentleman, too! Too bad he's so wild."

Martha looked up easily recognizing the red-haired cowboy.

"Howdy, Nell. I shore am glad to see you-all," he drawled.

"Howdy, yourself," replied the Glemm girl pleasantly, and turned to Martha. "Let me introduce one of our real cowboys, Texas Haynes. . . . Tex, meet Miss Martha Ann Dixon."

Texas made her a graceful bow and his flashing blue eyes took her in admiringly.

"Evenin', Miss. We've met before but not reg'lar," he drawled.

"Good evening, Mr. Texas Haynes," returned Martha Ann smiling. "I seem to remember something about you."

"Wal, my red hair, I reckon. Doggone it, I don't see why I cain't be towhaided, or somethin' else."

"No. I was not alluding to your hair."

"Did you ever dance with a cowboy?" he asked.

"Not yet."

"Will you let me be the first?"

"Certainly, if you ask me!"

"Thank you. I'm askin' you for the openin' dance, an' if I don't step all over yore feet, mebbe I'll make bold to ask for another."

"I don't know about two dances," replied Martha, dubiously. "I'll ask Nellie. Your last name is Haynes, isn't it?"

"Wal, I don't use it very often," replied Texas with a smile. "Fact is, Miss Martha, I kinda forget it myself."

"Oh, I see."

"I don't care much aboot Tex fer a handle, but I'd like you to call me Jack."

"You do things rather quickly in Wyoming, don't you?"

"Shore, an' I gotta be quick now. Let's dance before them other buckaroos horn in heah."

He led her out and somewhat diffidently put his arm around her. Martha needed only that and his touch to decide that he was quite all right, and that she need not have been on her guard against this cowboy. He held her lightly and at a distance. He took his dancing very seriously and did almost no talking. According to Martha's standard he was a very poor dancer. At the conclusion of this first number he led her back to her party. There was something quaint and charming and deferential about him.

"Gosh, thet was the swellest dance I ever had," he said gratefully, as his dark blue eyes gazed admiringly down on her. "Last summer I was up at Cody where the dude ranches are. An' I met an eastern girl who rode an' danced with me —when she couldn't get nobody else. I shore fell for her powerful hard. But I'm tellin' you, ma'am, as a looker an' as a dancer she wasn't in the same corral with you."

"I see you have kissed the Blarney Stone, Mr. Jack," returned Martha with a laugh.

"Nope. I'm no kissin' bug. Don't brand me with these other punchers, Miss Dixon," he said curtly. "I was jest tryin' to tell you how proud an' happy you made me by dancin' with me."

"Thank you. That is a lovely compliment," she replied,

quick to sense a fiery pride in him. "It will be something to remember my first cowboy dance by."

"Wal, thet makes me bold—"

"Hello, you two. How'd you get along?" interposed Nellie Glemm, with her frank eyes upon them.

"Powerful swell for me, Nell. I'm hankerin' turrible to ask—"

"For another dance? The nerve of you, Tex."

"Nellie, I'd be glad to give him another if you say it's all right," interposed Martha hastily. From what she had seen of couples on the floor, Texas Jack would be more than acceptable as a dance partner.

"You lucky cowboy! All right, let's see. As for me, I'm dolin' out these treats pretty stingily, believe me," replied Nellie, consulting a card. "You can have the sixth from this."

"*Gracias, señorita,* I shore will dance at yore weddin',"* he drawled, with the bow that became him so well. "Don't forget, Miss," he said turning to Martha. "I'll do better next time."

He made way for other aspirants to Martha's hand. From then on she met and danced with five young Westerners, all of whom were more accustomed to dancing, and four of whom added to her growing pleasure of the evening. The fifth, however, a tall, dark-faced young man, reminded her that all dances could not be so innocently enjoyed.

"You are holding me too tight," she said, the instant she took to the floor with the tall stranger. He laughed and eased the clasp of his arm, and during the round of the hall he acquainted her with the fact that he had run over from Cody to see the rodeo.

"You did not strike me as being western," replied Martha, and presently when she again felt a slight tightening of his arm she said she was tired and wanted to stop.

"Have a heart, honey," he remonstrated. "What's this line you're giving me?"

Martha left him standing at the entrance to the dressing room. She had recourse to her vanity case, and only when the music ceased did she return to the hall. Nellie's party was not in sight at the moment. And before Martha had gone very far, she was intercepted by Texas Jack.

"Wal, heah I am," he said, happily. "I watched you dance with thet last *hombre* an' I cain't say I liked it."

129

"Neither can I, Mr. Texas. But I got rid of him as quickly as I could," she replied, smiling up at him.

"I seen he tried to hug you an' you shied," he said tersely. "He jest don't belong heah, Miss Martha. An' if he tried to get fresh. . . . Did he?"

"He didn't try. He just did."

"Wal, I'll look him up after I dance this one with you."

"What for?" asked Martha quickly, suddenly alive to his cool drawl and the blue threat in his eyes.

"Where I come from, Miss Martha, thet sort of thing ain't imposed on girls."

"That would be Texas, of course. And why is Texas so different from the forty-seven other states?"

They were stopped in the middle of their promenade by someone.

"Pardon me," said a pleasant deep voice Martha recognized with a start. She looked up into the face of Andrew Bonning. He wore a dark suit which detracted from his muscular build and gave him an air of distinction. It clarified something that had often puzzled Martha. She quickly looked down, anxious that her eyes should not give away her love for him. "Good evening, Miss Dixon. I was detained. I hope I am not too late for a dance."

"I—I'm afraid you are," replied Martha, in evident confusion.

Bonning shifted his dark gaze to her escort.

"Hello, Texas," he said familiarly.

"Stranger, you got the best of me," replied the cowboy.

"I have, at that. But I hope you'll give me this dance without my having to explain."

"Explainin' what?" queried Texas, bluntly.

"How I've got the best of you."

"Say who'n—who air you?"

"Andrew Bonning. I ride for Bligh."

"Ahuh. I heahed yore handle somewheres," drawled the cowboy, his expression changing almost imperceptibly. "Air you the fellar who pulled the sluggin' trick oot heah at the rodeo?"

"Yes."

"Wal, thet ain't givin' you any the best of me. I'm no pard of Cal Brice or Smoky Reed."

"No, but if I were to remind you of the night you met McCall some weeks ago?"

"McCall!" repeated the cowboy, turning slightly pale.

"Yes, McCall. Do you recollect?"

"I cain't say that I do, Bonnin'," rejoined Texas guardedly, feeling his way. Martha Ann sensed something in him that made her shiver. Andrew, too, was strangely quite another person, cold, sarcastic of speech, piercing of eye.

"Texas, you don't strike me as a liar."

"Air you callin' me one?"

"Not yet. I'm just reminding you."

"What of?"

"The night you rode nearly into Split Rock. And met a man on foot. McCall. Does that help you to remember?"

"Wal, I reckon it does."

"Then you'll be sport enough to let me have your dance with Miss Dixon?"

"Bonnin', I don't know aboot bein' a sport. But I'll oblige you jest 'cause I don't want to call yore bluff heah—an' embarrass this lady any more. Savvy?"

"Good. You can call it some other time and place."

Texas turned to Martha with a somber and troubled look on his face.

"Miss Dixon, I shore hate to give up this dance."

"Then why should you?" asked Martha, finding her voice. "*I'm* sure I don't want you to."

"Wal, yore N.B. rider has insinuated somethin' agin my good name, an' I don't want to call him heah before you. . . . *Adios.*"

He stalked away, his red head held high, and left the hall. Martha Ann watched him depart, as if his going had spoiled some of the happiness of the evening.

"Martha, that was the only way I could stop it."

"Stop—what?" He seemed laboring under a strain, his brow clouded, his eyes bent sternly upon her. It was what he so obviously was thinking that liberated her. In another moment she could again be flippant, but right now he was too close to her, too overpoweringly the man who had captured her heart whether she liked it or not.

"Your carrying on with him."

"Yes? Please explain what you mean by carrying on, will you?"

"I just won't allow you to flirt with *that* cowboy, anyway."

"*You won't?*" she queried with deadly sweetness, while her

131

spirit leaped at his assumption of authority. "I'll flirt and carry on, and—and . . . with anyone I like, Andrew Bonning."

"Smoky Reed was the cowboy who shot me. And Texas Jack was with him at the time."

"*Oh!*" cried Martha, suddenly weak with all the blood rushing back to her heart. "Smoky Reed! . . . But Texas said he wasn't a friend of . . . Andrew, you don't mean to say—you don't think that he was a partner to that attempt on your life."

"I don't claim so much. But he was with Reed. I saw him."

"That nice, soft-spoken, old-fashioned boy! . . . Andrew, I simply don't believe you. It was just a mean trick to get his dance."

"Good heavens! I didn't want to dance with you. But I suppose I'll have to for appearances' sake. That Glemm outfit is watching us."

"You needn't trouble yourself. What do I care about appearances?"

"Come," he said as the music rose seductively, and he whirled her away.

She felt as stiff in body as she was pliable of mind. He would take for granted that she—she hated him for what he was thinking. But she suddenly realized that he was the most wonderful dancer she had ever known. The surprise of it dwarfed her other feelings, and it drew from her a mechanical response. Her uncle's hired man! With her mind suddenly averted from herself, from her shame and humiliation, Martha Ann had not glided half round the hall with him before she was sure she had penetrated his masquerade. Missouri farm hand, indeed! The strong yet light clasp with which he held her, the perfect timing of his steps and their intricacy, the flying grace of the swing he gave her on the reverse—these told the well-schooled Martha Ann that he was to the manner born. It explained so many of the acts that sat rather incongruously upon a rough-clad, heavy-booted cowboy. He was no cowboy, no garage mechanic, nothing that he pretended to be. Tonight he had the grace and cut of a college athlete.

"Put one over on us, didn't you, Mr. Andrew Bonning?" she said, unable to keep silent longer.

"Yes—and I'm reaping the whirlwind," he replied bitterly.

"Ne'er-do-well, blasé society man, wanderlusting realist, swell fugitive from the law—or what?" she queried mockingly.

"Outcast, Martha Ann."

She quivered in his arms and left off that tack. She gave up to the sheer sensual joy of the dance, and if it had lasted longer she knew she would have swooned. But before she had betrayed her true feelings the music ended.

"Let's get a breath of fresh air," he said, and led her out through one of the arches to the porch. The moon was shining brightly. Couples were leaning over the wooden railing.

"May I smoke?" he asked, without offering her his cigarettes, an omission which she noted.

"Yes."

"Found these among my store clothes—relic of my past."

Martha Ann tried to be her old audacious self, the hitch-hiker whom no road or man could daunt. What she wanted to appear to Andrew was what she really believed herself at heart to be. But wit, flippancy, flirtation would not come, any more than the play of eyes and smiles which she once had lavished upon the country youth back there on the journey west.

"You dance beautifully. With whom did you study ballet?"

"I've had ten thousand teachers."

"Starry Eyes, I have been kidded by experts. Actresses, heiresses, adventuresses. You didn't learn to dance like that in the night clubs."

"Nor did you—in Missouri," she retorted.

He laughed as he flicked the ash from his cigarette. He seemed entirely natural tonight. There was nothing forced, moody, or brooding about him.

"I wonder what Connie would say to that."

"Who is Connie?"

"A girl I once thought I loved—but didn't."

"Did she love you?"

"Martha Ann, I have not thanked you for getting me out of jail," he said, ignoring her query. "It was good of you. I'd have had to stay in that dirty hole all night."

"Now all of us are broke."

"No, not quite. I have a little left and will pay you when we get home."

"I have something to thank you for too," she replied softly, her face downcast. "But I can't understand why you did it."

"What?"

"Beat up that cowboy Reed."

"I had it in for him anyhow, Martha Ann. But I could

have killed him for the crack he made about you. Just as well brother Slade dragged me off him."

"Did Jim tell you Reed insulted me this morning, at the Glemms'?"

"No, he didn't."

"Funny—these western folk."

"Aren't they? When I told the magistrate that I'd been shot at by a rustler—no other than the cowboy Smoky Reed, he wanted to know if I'd caught him with the goods on. I admitted that I had not. Then he said I'd better be careful how I shot off my chin about rustling around here. And the sheriff searched me again for bootleg whiskey."

"We're Easterners—tenderfeet."

Then they fell silent. Martha Ann chafed under the fallaciousness of her position. Why did he not do one of two things—make some advance that accorded with his shallow conception of her—or tell her what a damned idiot he had been to judge her from appearances? How she would have reveled in an affront! But he was too much of a gentleman to respond to what he imagined she was inviting; and too stupid to see that a girl could defy certain conventions, could long for her own freedom to court adventure, and still be a decent person. She turned from the rail as the music started up again. He threw his cigarette away.

"It's a pity, isn't it, Martha Ann?" he asked, his somber eyes on her face.

"Yes. . . . I wonder if you can possibly mean what I mean?"

"Not a chance. Come, my dear, I have monopolized you long enough."

They went in. The dancers were whirling out from all sides. Martha Ann hoped that Andrew would take her again into their midst, and betrayed her wishes with a shy, uplifted glance.

"Martha Ann, you are too lovely a girl and too wonderful a dancer to waste yourself on me," he said.

"Fiddlesticks! You don't think me lovely or wonderful or— or anything but—" She could not conclude the passionate speech, but she showed him very plainly the silent wrath in her eyes.

"Don't deceive yourself about that. The genus homo is a queer duck. In this judgment of Paris I hand you—"

"A lemon," she interrupted with a wild little laugh. How cheerfully he could cut her to the quick! How miserably she longed for his respect! They were strangers—as far apart as the poles—he a Mid-Victorian and she a waif of the highway. "I would suggest that you don't interfere the next time you see me with Tex. . . . So long!"

If she expected a protest, it was not forthcoming. He conducted her to the little group waiting for her, and with an easy courtesy that made Martha feel almost like a rowdy he thanked her for the dance and bade her good night. Nellie Glemm's face expressed a curiosity which she did not voice. But it was easy to see that she and her friends would have liked to meet Andrew Bonning.

The rest of the dance was a nightmare to Martha Ann. She did not know or care with whom she danced. She would have welcomed Texas Jack or even Smoky Reed, if dancing with either of them could have brought Andrew back. She railed at herself for having played up to his idea of her. There it was; the evening had been spoiled. All seemed tasteless dust and bitter ashes in her mouth.

In the wee small hours she returned to the hotel and crept into bed, her feet dead and her heart numb and her brain the abode of conflicting tides of thought, and proceeded to cry herself to sleep.

10

●

ONE LATE AFTERNOON, a week after the rodeo, Martha Ann caught sight of Jim Fenner approaching her favorite seat under a shady tree on the river bank. It had been a painful period of suspense for Martha, first on account of her own uncertain and baffling state of mind, and secondly owing to her uncle's increasing troubles.

Jim limped across the road and, favoring his crippled leg, placed himself beside her on the grass. The August day had been hot. His lean face, like a bronzed mask, gave no indication of his feelings, but there was a shadow in his hazel-flecked eyes.

"Lookin' fer Andy?" he asked, as he swept the purple slope toward the hills.

"Jim, I like you very much," she replied. "But if you don't leave off this Andy stuff I'm off you for life. How many times have I told you that I come here because of the view, so open and beautiful, because I can see the river wind away, and all the range and the mountains beyond?"

"Wal, shore. It's a grand view. Most as fine as some in Arizony. But no scenery is worth much without some life to go with it."

"I see horses, cattle, sometimes a rider, rabbits, wild ducks, eagles, and once I saw an airplane. What more do you want?"

"Wal, I kinda hoped you might be watchin' for Andy," replied the Arizonian simply. "You see it's this way, Martha. The comin' of you two young folks bucked us all up. Bligh was failin' in more than stock raisin'. An' me an' Sue, never havin' had a youngster, an' always yearnin' for one, sort of got a new lease on life. Natural-like, we're powerful interested in you. Both of you so young an' live an' full of fire. Don't hold it against us, lass. We're growin' old an' all alone."

"Forgive me, Jim. I'm sorry," replied Martha, a little hand going impulsively to his. "I am a cross, spiteful, ungrateful cat. I don't deserve your interest and kindness. . . . But you don't seem old to me, Jim."

"Wal, I'm ten years older'n Bligh, an' he's nigh on to sixty."

"I wouldn't have believed it," replied Martha Ann, with a sigh. "Have you got bad news, Jim?"

"I reckon so, lass. We went to town, hopin' to fix up the deal with McCall. But he's a mean *hombre*. Appealin' to the Wyomin' Cattlemen's Association didn't get us nowhere. An' Cheney Brothers wouldn't lend us two bits. Money is still tight an' stock has jest begun to move. McCall insisted on stickin' to the original deal, which we know now ain't to be thought of. I started to tell him thet in Arizony his deals would look mighty shady, but your uncle shet me up. Jest as wal, fer McCall got redheaded. We laid the deal before a magistrate. An' it's up to Bligh to decide to go in with McCall or stand trial."

"What did you advise, Jim?"

"I'd stand trial. This feller McCall ain't a big cattleman. An' he ain't any too wal thought of. In the meantime we might get somethin' on him."

"But if we don't?"

"Wal, we lose, thet's all."

"Does it mean ruin for uncle?"

"Yes, so far as runnin' cattle is concerned. I doubt thet he could ever get another start, at his age, an' without capital. It's a good farm, though, an' we can live off it."

136

"That's a grain of comfort. Oh, let's hope it is not as bad as you fear."

"Martha, what air you goin' to do?"

"Me?" queried Martha, with a start.

"Yes. Air you goin' to stick by yore uncle? Me an' Sue have wondered a lot about you. Pretty, smart girl like you—thet could do most anythin'—an' shore marry a million if you was thet sort—comin' to this lonesome range. But you've seemed so happy—till jest lately—layin' yore hands to all kinds of work. An' so crazy about horses an' the outdoors. We jest kinda figgered thet this sort of life was intended for you. What do you suppose brought the pioneers out West? It was thet, Martha—thet spread of prairie an' valley an' hill an' mountain all open an' free to the eye. Wal, thet pioneer stuff is in you if you only knew it."

"Oh, Jim, do you really think so?" murmured the girl, deeply moved.

"Shore I do. Lemme see them little hands of yores."

Martha Ann stretched forth the small brown members for his inspection, smiling at his earnestness as he stroked them and turned them palms upward.

"Prettier to me than when they was so white an' soft. . . . Wal, work is good for anybody. All the same, lass, I wouldn't like to see you chop wood, plow the field, an' clean out the stable. Andy said thet same thing one day."

"Goodness gracious! How kind of him! . . . Neither would I. But honest, Jim, I like to bake, to sew, to milk the cows, although I hated housework at home."

"Wal, you gotta do some tall figger'n', my lass. It's only fair to tell you thet we may go from bad to wuss here. Sue an' me will stay by yore uncle. I put thet up to Andy an' he cussed me proper fer hintin' thet he might want to quit jest 'cause the goin' has got hard."

"He did? . . . That was good of him," she murmured.

"Andy can't see the bad side of it," continued Jim. "He says we'll lick hell out of McCall an' his range riders. Somethin' will turn up. Wal, Bonnin' is young an' full of hope—an' shore in love."

"In love? I don't believe it. He's too—too—" protested Martha.

"These boys air all crazy about you."

"I hadn't noticed it, Jim. . . . Are you sure you haven't

been eating some of that Arizona loco weed you told me about?"

"Hosses an' cattle eat loco, my child. I may be smokin' my pipe at thet. But I reckon Andrew Bonnin' is as deep in love with you, lass, as a man ever falls."

"Jim!"

"Wal, you needn't bark at me like thet. . . . An' go red—an' then white—as you air now. You know it, don't you?"

"No," whispered Martha, averting her face.

"Haven't boys an' men, too, been fallin' in love with you, ever since you put on long dresses?"

"No."

"Ain't thet Texas Jack cowboy who ride out here Sunday—ain't *he* in love with you?"

"Cowboy-taffy," replied Martha Ann tremulously, striving against the rising tide within her breast.

"Ridic'lous, lass. Thet's yore own word. I've heered it often. Ridic'lous! . . . I don't know about you, girl. You're a deep youngster. You're honest as daylight, mostly. But I can't figger you, in this partic'lar. I'm afraid you're—"

"Jim Fenner, if *you* side with my parents, my relatives—and a lot of old fogies—and An-Andrew Bonning—I-I'll never speak to you again," cried Martha Ann, the tears coming into her eyes.

"All right. Thet settles thet," said Fenner placatingly. "From now on I'm takin' you on yore word. I'm on yore side, Martha. An' thet means Sue, too. If we two old Westerners can't understand, we shore can trust an' sympathize an' love. I reckon it ain't been so easy fer you back home, or anywheres. You ought to have been a boy. An' instead you're the sweetest girl thet ever was born to vex men. It's tough, honey. When a girl can't lift her eyes or smile without some fool thinkin' she wants him to grab her—wal, thet's shore tough."

"It's just exactly what happens, Jim," she replied brokenly. "It was that way at home. . . . And it's almost as bad here."

"Martha, did Andrew do thet?"

"No, not he."

"Wal, thet's somethin' to his credit. I can't see Andrew makin' game of a girl."

"Bah! He'd be no different from any of them—if he believed he was the *only* one."

"Are you shore, lass?"

"Well, no. But I've met boys like that. Boys who want a

138

girl all to themselves—and hate her if she looks at someone else. I was fed up on all of them."

"Listen, Martha. You've got Andy figgered wrong," continued Jim earnestly. "He's ain't what he lets on to be. An' at thet I don't savvy what he is pretendin'. Sue says she always feels funny when he sets a chair fer her, or stands up when she comes in—things like thet thet women notice. But he *is* somebody."

"At the rodeo they called him a prize fighter," said Martha with a queer little laugh.

"Wal, he shore was a whirlwind. I ain't got over tinglin' over thet fight yet. . . . No, Andrew Bonnin' ain't no common sort. Whatever druv *him* out here it wasn't anythin' crooked. All my life I've dealt with men who have things to hide. Andy hasn't anythin'. But he's awful sad an' quiet."

"Some woman," ventured Martha Ann, with a twinge of jealousy.

"Some girl! . . . Martha, when you first come here Andy was pretty hard on you. I called him fer it, an' he's never mentioned it again. I reckon he still thinks the same about your hikin' out here alone. I didn't use to think myself thet that was the foolest stunt any girl ever tried. But I see it different now. The rest of us air wrong. Thet idee was natural an' innocent, 'cause it was *you*."

Martha Ann laid her head against Jim's shoulder. "Jim, you'd have made a swell Daddy," she sighed.

"Not too late yet, by jingo! . . . But don't upset me, lass. I'm in turrible earnest. I feel like—like one of them wise fellars who settles the fates of nations. . . . No matter how Andy disapproved of you—or what he thought you was—it still didn't keep him from fallin' in love with you. An' grow wuss an' wuss as times go on."

"What makes—you think—he—he—?"

"Wal, Sue seen it first. An' believe me, Martha, thet woman never is wrong. . . . An' after I was put wise I watched Andy an' I've seen a hundred proofs of it."

"Give me just one, I dare you," said the girl, color mounting in her cheeks.

"Wal, let me see. It's darn hard to pick jest one out. . . . Do you remember the day yore hoss piled you up on the sand down here?"

"Yes."

"I didn't know what it all was about till afterward. But

when Andrew went back for your boot I happened to be ridin' along the bank an' I seen him get off an' pick somethin' up, an' set down on the sand to hold the thing in his hand, an' look mighty fond at it. I swear it looked thet way to me. Course it was most dusk an' I'm a sentimental old cuss. But he sat there like a Navajo watchin' the sunset. Somethin' pathetic an' lonely about the way he looked off over the range. So I didn't call. Later I asked him where he'd been, an' then he told me about goin' after yore lost boot. . . . Now, lass, is thet convincin'?"

"Not at all! You certainly have an imagination, Jim. . . . Tell me something else."

"Wal, the way he beat up Smoky Reed," ventured Fenner.

"No. He meant to do that anyhow."

"The rodeo dance, then. He never seen any other girl but you—let alone dance with one. An' the girls was certainly layin' fer him. A blind man could have seen thet."

"It might be taken as testimony," she replied ponderingly. "But it would never convince me. You lose, Jim, unless you have a better one—out of those hundred proofs." And she drew back from his shoulder to regard him demurely.

"Wal, he shore watches fer you all the time, an' you couldn't pop yore head up anywhere on this blasted range but he'd see it."

"Masculine curiosity and his obsession to boss some woman. No more," proclaimed Martha.

"Sue says it's somethin' she can *feel* in Andy, whenever you come near."

"But *I* don't feel it."

"Then you're jest not flesh an' blood. . . . Martha, I tell you I know he's fallen for you. An' I shore feel low-down to double cross him this way. But I gotta do it. 'Cause you might up an' do somethin' jest fer spite. So I'll tell you. Andy carries a little round picture of you in a frame. I seen him lookin' at somethin', an' when I come into camp he slipped it back pronto in his breast pocket. After supper he went to washin' in the creek, an' I sneaked to his clothes an' fished thet picture out of his shirt pocket. It shore was a sweet picture."

"Oh! the—the. . . . I missed that picture on the day we went to the rodeo. I drove. . . . He had my bag in his lap. It dropped out or he sneaked it."

"Wal, is that any proof?"

"Jim, that's very strange indeed—*if* he took it and kept it and looked at it—just to see what a bad girl looks like. . . . Still I couldn't be sure."

"Do you want to be shore?" he demanded suddenly, as if he now had her at his mercy.

"Jim! . . . You—I—Oh, yes!" She cried, and her composure seemed about to leave her.

"I seen him kiss thet little picture," cried Jim triumphantly.

"You're lying, Jim Fenner! . . . He didn't—he couldn't. Not Andrew."

"I swear to Gawd I seen him."

"You're cruel, Jim. You've tormented me for weeks. But today you're a positive fiend."

"Ain't you glad I told you?" he asked chuckling.

"Go away!"

"Shore, I'll mosey along," he replied, getting up stiffly. "But you haven't tole me yet if you'll stay here with yore uncle an' see it through."

"I shall see it through, Jim," she replied simply.

"Wal, if thet ain't fine. I reckoned you would. You can go home on a visit some day—or have yore folks visit you. It'll all turn out right in the end."

"Go away!" cried Martha Ann. "Or I'll—I'll kiss you!"

"Wal, as I don't want thet big gazabo to lambaste me one I reckon I'd better make tracks."

Martha Ann leaned back against the tree. She would stay and see it through! Both sadness and rapture pervaded her soul. By what strange steps had she finally found her niche in life. Tomorrow she would ride and ride, far away and up the purple slope, to some lonely spot where only the wilderness could witness her joy.

The sun was sinking gold and red behind the Rockies. The river traced its winding, green-bordered course out to fade in the ruddy haze of the range. Great clouds of rose and pearl piled to the zenith, stately and serene. Like a sea, the sagebrush rolled and heaved as far as the scalloped hills.

No living creature crossed Martha Ann's vision. How lonely were the vast spaces! They had been like that forever or, remembering her geology, for the millions of years since the icecap of the north had receded. What was there here so restful to her soul, so like some place she had known before she was even born? The peace that was in her heart had something to do, too, with what Jim had told her about a man's strange behavior with a misplaced locket.

At that moment a lone horseman appeared, far out in the sage, a black spot becoming gradually perceptible of movement. He gave life to the scene. All it needed! But it gave infinitely more to Martha Ann, who pressed her hands tightly to her bosom, and watched and watched with slowly dimming eyes.

It was toward noon of the following day, and for hours Martha Ann had been alternately trotting and walking her horse up the endless purple slope. She had never before dared to ride so far alone. But this day she knew that she had to find solitude. How easy to think things out in the saddle, riding alone over the range, with the wind whipping in her face, the sun bright and warm, the loneliness calling!

She was heading for the Antelope Hills and they now loomed close. She would wait, she would hold herself in, she would postpone this battle between her two selves until she had found an ideal spot where no other woman creature had ever poured out her innermost heart before.

Soon she was riding among a grove of trees. It was dry and sweet here among these scattered trees where the sage mingled with silver grass and golden flowers. When she looked back down the long slope she was thrilled by the splendor of the descent, sloping to the distant thread of the river and the dot that was the ranch.

At last she felt that she could ride no longer. She had come upon a kind of bowl of silver grass, surrounded by straggling trees, a lonely, isolated glade, hidden from all eyes except those of the eagles, and shining there, peaceful and tranquil, an altar for her abnegation. For she would never rise from this lonely vigil the same wild, intolerant, proud and selfish girl.

Martha tied her horse in the fringe of trees, and chose a low-spreading one under which to rest. A thick fragrant brown carpet of tiny needles covered the ground. Her tree was some species of pine. She gathered a lapful of the little spears, and let them run through her cupped hands.

She found herself loath to give up feeling, seeing, smelling this lonesome covert for the thoughts that she knew she had to straighten out. She had her first intimation of how wonderful it would be never to think at all. Only to use her senses!

Perhaps it was that inherited instinct that had lured her to Wyoming. Who could understand who had never felt that enchantment?

And presently Martha Ann lay back on the bed of pine needles and let her thoughts roam. "So he stole my picture! . . . Darling!—Oh, if you *do* love me—how terribly I shall make you suffer before I prove that I'm not what you believe I am. . . . And if you *don't* I shall—be what you believe I . . . Oh, no! no!—I shall only die!"

A sudden sound interrupted the girl's bittersweet reverie. It was a sound which at first she could not define. Alarmed, Martha sat up trembling. The thumping sound grew louder. Hoofs! Her horse had broken away. No, the pounding came from the opposite side of the little amphitheater. Crashings among the trees preceded the shrill bawl of a calf. A cow stumbled through an opening between the trees and behind it galloped a calf. Then something yellow and snaky shot from behind the green, to loop round the calf and jerk it off its feet. It the next instant a horse appeared whose rider was bending low to escape the branches. He pulled his horse back on its haunches and leaped off, to throw the calf down and kneel upon it.

Martha Ann crouched there, her terror of the unknown changing to the terror of an act whose significance she vaguely guessed. When the rider arose to toss his sombrero aside and wipe his sweaty face, he exposed a flaming mop of red hair. But Martha had recognized the lithe form of Texas Jack even before he revealed the telltale hair.

"Bawl an' be damned, you ornery little cuss. You're a maverick now. An' you git oot of heah." He picked up a rock to fling it at the cow. She lowered her head and threatened him, but another rock, well directed, struck her with a resounding thump. Martha Ann's wide eyes glimpsed the N.B. brand on the flank of the cow. The distracted beast went as far as the edge of the open and continued to bawl.

Texas broke some dead branches off the nearest tree. These he placed on the ground near the calf. He struck a match and started a fire. Picking up his sombrero he fanned the fire until it roared. Then he slipped something from under the flap of his saddle—a thin curved tool. Martha had seen it like— a running iron, Jim had called it—a thing to burn brands on stock. Texas placed an end of the iron in the fire and began

143

to fan the flames with his hat. They roared as if blown by a bellows.

Suddenly he bent down, and seizing the iron he ran to the calf, and knelt to apply it to its trembling red flank. The calf bawled lustily. Martha heard a sizzle, another and another. She saw smoke arise, and then she smelled burning hair. The smell of it sickened her.

But nausea, fright, and all her other feelings yielded precedence to righteous wrath. Texas Jack was branding her uncle's calf. He was a thief—a rustler. She had caught him red-handed in the very act.

Quickly Martha Ann rose to brush aside the branches that had screened her and to step into the open.

Texas heard her step and his flaming head shot up like that of a frightened deer. Suddenly he wheeled and whipped out a gun in one single action. At any other time, Martha might have recoiled from his fierce face, but now she kept right on, indifferent to his menacing posture, and to the gun held low and level.

"Wal, fer Gawd's sake!" he burst out, astounded and visibly relieved.

Martha Ann kept on until the bound calf lay at her feet. On its flank had been branded a double X, the lines of which shone raw and bright in its hide.

"McCall's brand!" she ejaculated in amazement, and then she faced the cowboy. "Texas Jack, you have burned McCall's brand on one of my uncle's calves."

"Caught with the goods," replied Texas, and flipping up his gun he caught it by the butt, to return it to his belt. He seemed cool, laconic, devil-may-care, but the paleness that had not disappeared, and the quivering pinpoints in his blue eyes, told Martha that he was not altogether invulnerable.

"You calf thief, you paid rustler, you low-down thieving cowboy," she blazed, with eyes before which he quailed. "You ride for one man and steal for another. You come to my uncle's house. You eat and drink there, accepting his hospitality, and my friendship. . . . Oh, you despicable vermin. You coward, liar, cheat! . . . You brag of being a Texan—you wouldn't insult a girl—bah! You're worse than Smoky Reed. At least he doesn't sail under false colors."

"Martha, doggone it, I'm not so low-down as all thet," he expostulated, his face now scarlet, his eyes shamed and appealing. "You're a tenderfoot. You jest cain't savvy the West.

144

All cattlemen brand mavericks, when they happen on them. It ain't exactly stealin'."

"A maverick is a calf without a mother," flashed Martha. "There's this calf's mother. And she's got an N.B. brand on her."

"Wal, if you split hairs over it—I reckon I'm a rustler," he said, and kneeling beside the calf he released it. Then, when it had scrambled up to bawl and run he sat down in the grass. He took out a little tobacco pouch, and rolled himself a cigarette with steady fingers.

"Texas, I'm simply shocked. I'm terribly disappointed. Only last Sunday you told me you loved me."

"Wal, I did an' I do. What's thet got to do with this job? I swear to Gawd it was my last—this deal with McCall. But I was in it before I ever seen you. He owes me money. He even threatens to give me away. I had to go on with it, thet's all."

"But, Texas, if you're a rustler you just can't make honest love to a decent girl," declared Martha.

"Shore it was honest love, I was goin' to ask you to marry me."

"Oh! To think I—liked you—and I might even have fallen in love with you!"

"Wal, you didn't act much like it," growled Texas, and took a long pull on his cigarette. "An' don't roast me no more. I can't stand it from you."

"Have you no shame? Can you sit there and make excuses for this piece of crooked work? Deliberately ruining my uncle, who's old and poor! Oh, you're a fine Texan."

"Say, my little spitfire, I'll clap a hand over yore pretty trap in a minnit, if you don't shet it. If I wasn't a gentleman an' a Texan, I'd do what Smoky would do, or any other free-lance rider on this range."

"And what is that?"

"I'd pack you off in the hills an' keep you there," he replied with sullen passion.

"Texas, you couldn't do a cowardly thing like that!" she returned hurriedly, not so sure as she pretended to be. The cowboy looked like a man at bay.

"No, I couldn't do that. An' you can bet yore sweet little self that it's only because I am a Texan. An' what'n hell air you doin' way oot heah? Suppose it'd been Smoky, or half a dozen *hombres* I could name, you damn little fool! Haven't you got no sense at all? You gallivant oot west alone in a pair of short pants an' now you come ridin' into the foothills all by yoreself."

"I'm not afraid."

"No, I seen thet. But you're too brainless—too damned innocent an' trustin'. If you keep this heah sort of thing up, Martha Dixon, you'll meet with outrage from someone who'll think you're askin' fer it!"

She gazed at him with mute lips, surprised by his passion.

"That's all. Somebody had to tell you. Why didn't yore friend Bonnin' tell you?"

"Why should he?"

"Wal, why doesn't he make you stay home? If he's so doggone stuck on you as the girls say?"

"He's not. . . . And he couldn't make me do anything."

"It's too damned bad somebody cain't. You oughta fall for some lucky dawg an' stop this heartbreakin' game. . . . Wal, you caught me with the goods. Now what're you gonna do about it?"

"Texas, what'll you do if I tell?" she asked earnestly.

"Wal, I'll try to collect some money from McCall, an' vamoose oot of the country onless someone tries to stop me, which wouldn't be so healthy for him!"

"If I promise not to betray you will you promise never to steal again?"

Texas rose to his feet, with the blood of shame again flooding his face. It receded, leaving him pale. His eyes held a piercing blue intensity.

"Martha, thet's a big order, as you see it," he said. "I reckon I never appreciated jest what kind of a girl you air. I'm askin' you to overlook my love-makin' which wasn't so honest as I swore it was. But I'd never laid a hand on you. . . . If you don't squeal on me I'll promise to go straight."

"It's a bargain, Texas. Here's my hand," she returned gravely, and held it out to him.

"Wal, I had a close shave," he drawled with his old smile, as he pressed her hand. "Come, find yore hawse. Smoky Reed is workin' round in the next draw, an' if he seen us I'd have to kill him."

"Perhaps you had better ride home with me, or part way," she suggested, nervously.

"Go ahaid. I'll trail along an' keep you in sight."

146

Breathless and exultant Martha Ann ran to untie her horse, and after tightening the cinches she mounted and rode down the slope.

For once in her life she had done something worth while. One good deed, at least, might result from her mad Wyoming adventure. Martha placed reforming a wild cowboy above saving some of her uncle's stock. And somehow she felt certain that this footloose and reckless Texan would keep his word. If he did not keep it from any innate reversion to what was right, he would because of that queer honor held by Texans in regard to women. Martha Ann was proud of herself. She could confide in Jim Fenner, at least. But she would not tell her uncle. And as for Andrew Bonning, he would not believe it even if she did confess. The thought galled her. At the same time she knew it was true—she had caught Texas Jack red-handed and she had brought the perplexing and dangerous situation to a clever and happy close.

Looking back over her shoulder she saw Texas half a mile behind, sitting sidewise in his saddle, a figure of a rider that fitted the wild environment. After she had traveled several miles further, to drop into the trail, the exuberance of her feeling wore away, and she came down out of the clouds. It astonished her a little to realize that the revelation that Texas Jack was a rustler had not destroyed her liking for him. He still seemed to be a thoroughly likable chap. She did not see any reason why she should not loiter on the trail until Texas caught up with her. Accordingly, she held her horse to a walk, which he did not like on the homeward trip; and was presently chagrined to observe that Texas also had slowed his gait to accommodate hers. He was showing consideration on her behalf, and suddenly Martha realized just what Texas meant by his holding back, when it certainly would have been so much more interesting for them to proceed down the trail together. Texas was keeping her in sight as a matter of protection, and avoiding the ride with her, because in the event that his status as a cowboy might be revealed, such association would reflect upon her good name.

"Amazing! I can't escape that even out on this uninhabited desert," exclaimed Martha Ann disgustedly, all her old antagonism welling up. She felt here, as in everything, that she knew her own motives, her integrity, the truth about herself; and for anything else that could be thought by curious narrow people she did not concern herself in the least.

She halted her horse, and while waiting for Texas Jack to catch up, she gazed down upon the ranch. Those gray houses appeared lost in an immensity of green. It was a lonely place. She tried to picture it with snow everywhere, white and desolate. But the thought pleased rather than otherwise. Winter would be a time to read and study and sew and learn to cook; and perhaps go home some Christmas time. Across the white-barred, green-bordered river the range spread far as the eye could see, endlessly rolling, unrelieved by a break of any kind.

A clatter of hoofs distracted the girl's thoughts as Texas came loping up to come to a stop beside her.

"Wal, what's it all aboot?" he asked, eyeing her keenly.

"I got tired loafing along alone," she replied with a smile. "Let's have a little run down this wide stretch."

"Martha, I reckon you oughta be moseyin' on by yoreself," he drawled.

"Don't you want to ride with me?" she demanded.

"Doggone! Girls air queer. . . . I reckon I'll ride as far as the creek with you."

Martha urged her horse into a canter, but when Texas' bay lined up beside her that gait did not suit either horses or riders. They broke into a gallop and then into a run. Martha awoke to something she had heretofore never experienced—the thrill of riding at breakneck speed, the sting of the wind in her face, the blur of sage whirling past, the unexcelled joy of violent action.

The race was won by Martha, a victory no less delightful because she knew Texas had let her win, and she sat her horse breathless and tingling, with smarting skin and flying hair.

"Oh, that was glorious! I never—dared go—so fast before," she panted.

"Wal, you don't fork thet hawse so porely at that," drawled the cowboy. "Shore you cain't help lookin' beautiful, but I'm not figgerin' looks. Reckon you got strong laigs an' thet's what it takes to ride. You set a little too stiff. You wanta be easy in the saddle. Ketch the swing of yore hawse with yore body. An' squeeze with yore knees. . . . It wouldn't take long fer me to make a rodeo rider oot of you."

"Please—please do," pleaded Martha Ann.

Texas sat up with a start and his expression of genuine

pleasure vanished. "Wal, I reckon thet'll be aboot all," he said. "Look who's comin'."

Martha whirled in her saddle, all her delight suddenly ended. Halfway across the sandy draw she saw a black horse trotting toward her. The rider was Andrew.

"It might be a good idee fer me to vamoose," suggested Texas.

"Why?"

"Wal, if my eyes ain't pore, Bonnin' is seein' red. I can always tell the way a fellar sets his saddle."

"Suppose he is?"

"Shore it was fer yore sake, Martha," he replied coolly. "The man doesn't live who can scare me."

"Stay then. Andrew Bonning has no claim on me. I can ride with whom I choose."

Andrew blocked the narrow trail, so that they had to halt their horses or turn aside into bad going. They were at the place in the dry creek bottom where Martha had once been thrown.

"Hello, Andrew," called Martha gaily. But her spontaneity did not ring sincere. How white his face was! And his eyes gazed upon her with a dark, scornful look of passionate conviction.

"Howdy, Bonnin'! Fine day fer ridin'," drawled Texas, nonchalantly, as he leisurely rolled a cigarette.

Andrew did not give the cowboy so much as a glance or a nod. He fixed eyes upon Martha that suddenly she felt to be filled with accusation and with terrible disappointment. They were desperately hard to meet.

"So you've done it," he spoke coldly, bitterly.

"Done what?" she demanded, a hot blush burning her cheek. His look, his query aroused the red flag of her ready anger. But there was some quality in his tone, of disillusionment, or pain, or bitter conviction, that enraged Martha more than his interference.

"You met this cowboy out on the range."

"Certainly I did. Anyone could see that."

"You had a date with him."

"No, I didn't. It was purely accident. I . . . But see here, Andrew, this is none of your business. I'm free, white and over eighteen. I can meet whom I want to. You have no claim on me. I told Texas that."

"You would," he replied, darkly. "No, indeed, I haven't

any claim on you. But I happen to be the only one who dares oppose you, Martha Dixon. You ran away from your mother, father, brother—if you have them. You can easily fool these two doting old men back home—who worship you. There's no one left but me to try to save you from making a complete fool of yourself."

"Oh, fiddlesticks! The old stuff! Andrew Bonning, I'm *not* making a fool of myself!" she cried hotly.

"I hope I'm not too late," he retorted, with a look that made Martha quail inwardly.

"Maybe you are. But it's none of your damned business," she burst out.

"I've made it my business," he said deliberately.

"Is that so? Well, try to remember where I told you to go once before."

"Girl, if you are absolutely shameless yourself, can't you have some regard for your uncle?"

"Regard? You know that I love him dearly. What do you mean—regard?"

"An old-fashioned virtue in disrepute with modern girls. Honor. Something due Bligh because he has given you a home. He is a newcomer here on this range. He needs to make friends. It will not do him any good to have his niece gossiped about. To have open scandal about her rendezvous in the hills with a dissolute cowboy."

"Andrew, you don't know what you are talking about," replied Martha Ann, beginning to feel her spirits flag.

"Nothing to you! Good Lord! What a cold-blooded, self-centered, kick-hunting little proposition you are!"

"I've done—nothing that I'm ashamed of," faltered Martha Ann.

"Could you ever feel shame?"

"Yes, I could."

"About what? For what?"

"That a supposedly decent man like you—could make me out the—the rotten little hussy—"

"I didn't make you out rotten," he interrupted, a dark flush spreading over his stern, pale face. "Some other time I'll tell you what I think about you. Suffice it now to say that you are a reckless girl who isn't helping an uncle who is very much in need of help—as this cowboy knows!"

"Oh! And you have constituted yourself the valiant knight to rescue me?" she exclaimed satirically.

"Only today Jim Fenner said you'd make bad blood out here—and spill it, too, if you were not stopped."

"Jim! Did Jim—say that?" gasped Martha, stung to the quick.

"Yes. And it was Jim who sent me out to look for you. I, like an idiot, thought you were riding the ranch trails."

"I rode too far, perhaps, this time—to—to— Oh, never mind," cried Martha tragically. "You couldn't understand. Let me pass. I want to go home."

"Very well, go on home. I'll settle this with your friend here," rejoined Andrew grimly, and dismounted to lead his horse out of the trail.

"Texas will come with me," spoke up Martha hurriedly. She did not like Andrew's look or the cowboy's cool silence. She dared not leave them alone.

"Wal, Bonnin', a lady's word is law with me," drawled Texas.

"Just the same you don't go," snapped Bonning, and seized the cowboy's bridle.

"I'm liable to run you down. Let go them reins. Don't you know any better than to grab—"

"Stop, Andrew," cried Martha Ann fearfully, as the cowboy's horse reared. "Texas will stay. So will I. . . . But have a heart—and get it over with."

"Texas, pile off and face me like a man, if you're not too much of a coward," commanded Andrew.

"Say, tenderfoot, I wouldn't be scared of a million Easterners," drawled Texas with a smile, and he leisurely slipped out of his saddle.

"Listen then. This reckless girl is not on the level. Do you get me? She doesn't care a rap for you or me or for anybody. All she thinks of is getting kicks out of everything. She will vamp some poor sucker just to watch him wriggle. And believe me, cowboy, it doesn't make a damn bit of difference *how far* she has gone with you. Do you understand?"

"I'm listen' powerful hard, Bonnin', an' I'm gettin' mighty riled," replied the cowboy.

"All the better. I intend to rile you, one way or another. . . . You're supposed to be a square shooter, Texas, at least, so they say. Everybody likes you, especially the girls. I like you myself. You're a clean, fine good-looking cowboy. I'd sure want you for a partner, if that were possible. Well, considering all this, do you think you're living up to your reputation—do you

151

think it honorable for you—and *fair* to this girl—to meet her way out on the lonely range?"

"No, doggone it, I don't," declared the Texan, as if moved by Andrew's eloquence.

"You made love to Martha last Sunday, and before that. I saw you."

"Bonnin', I ask you, what in hell would any cowboy do? Or any man?"

"Dubious flattery, cowboy, if you get what I mean," snapped Andrew. "I see that you have made quite some headway with the little lady."

"Bonnin,' you talk too fast an' too deep fer me," declared Texas angrily. "Let's get down to callin' cyards."

"I told Martha that you were with Smoky Reed when he shot me."

"Hell you say! Who else did you tell?"

"I didn't repeat that about you. But I told Sheriff Slade and the magistrate at Casper who shot me. They wanted to know if I could prove it. Well, I couldn't. And they advised me not to make cracks about Westerners, unless I could prove them. I'm going on my own after this."

"Ahuh. An' what's all this heah talk got to do with me?"

"You were with Reed. I saw you—recognized you through my field glasses. You separated, and you took the far side of the canyon. Do you imagine I thought you were hunting birds' nests?"

The same fierce wolfish look that Texas had exhibited to Martha when he had wheeled upon her with his gun now settled on his lean face. Blue flames from his eyes.

"Not on your life," went on Andrew accusingly. "You were up there for precisely the same reason as Smoky Reed."

"Naw, I wasn't."

"You lie, Texas. I *know*, I tell you, I heard you make the deal with McCall. You refused to kill cows—like Reed is doing—and you stuck to your idea of maverick branding. But that is the bunk, Texas. You know it is. You stick to your method, because in case you are held up on suspicion you can use that maverick alibi."

"Bonnin' cut yore talk mighty short. You'll say somethin' in a minnit."

"You're damn right I will," cried Andrew. "You're a rustler!"

Out leaped Texas' blue six-shooter, to be thrust almost against Andrew's abdomen. Martha screamed.

"You can't call me thet," rasped the cowboy. "Girl, mind yore hawse, an' keep oot of this!"

"The hell I can't. I do call you rustler, damn you! What do I care for your gun? You can't murder me in cold blood before the eyes of this girl. But I'd call you even if she weren't here. And that's what I mean. If you made a date with Martha Dixon—all the time when you knew that it couldn't be honorable love-making because you *are* a rustler—well, you're a disgrace to the Texas you seem so proud of, you're a low-down yellow thief whose aim is to ruin this girl's old uncle."

"Bonnin', if it wasn't fer her I'd shoot yore laig off."

"I don't doubt it. And that would simply prove what you are. Why, you poor ignorant cowhand, if you had any real manhood in you you'd fight for her, instead of betraying her and her family."

"I been comin' to thet. But you gab so much I can't get a word in. Now gimme a chance. You hot-haided tenderfoot! You're wuss'n a Mexican fer bein' jealous. All because you ketch Martha with me! How the hell do you know what came off? As a matter of fact we had no date. She ketched me red-handed brandin' the Double X on a calf. An' she shore called me proper. Then she made me swear I'd never rustle another calf. An' by Gawd, I'll keep thet promise if it's the last thing I ever do. . . . Now you come along, like a baby cyclone, to insult as good an' sweet an' innocent a girl as ever breathed. Too innocent an' fun-lovin' fer you fed-up eastern high-brows. She had to run out west to get understood. An' thet to me makes it wuss for you than my bein' a rustler."

"Rot! You do it well, Texas. But too late," snarled Andrew, his face blanched. "Drop your gun, if you're not too much of a coward. But if you are, then I'll fight you your own way. I've a gun on my saddle."

"Fairest thing you've said yet," replied the cowboy. Then he unbuckled his gun belt and hung it over the pommel of his saddle.

Martha Ann came out of her trance and got off her horse, almost falling, to run between the belligerents, who were now glaring at each other.

"Andrew . . . Texas!" she cried imploringly. "Don't fight.

It's so—so silly of both of you. All for nothing. Please, for my sake—Andy—"

He put her firmly aside. "Get out of my way, Wyoming Mad," he said with his bitter smile. "This is where your kick-hunting has led to. Now watch and see what I do to your cute cowboy."

"Oh, Texas—you give in. *He* is hopeless. Oh, I beg of you!"

"Hell, lady, what am I up agin?" shouted Texas furiously. "Between the two of you I'm aboot nutty. I cain't stand around an' let him pound me the way he did Smoky."

He, too, thrust Martha to one side, not too gently, and when she recovered her balance they had plunged at each other like two infuriated bulls. Their first onset took them completely off the trail. The distracted girl stood riveted to the spot. If she had not been tongue-tied she would have screamed for Texas to whip Andrew within an inch of his life. But she knew that he could not do it. What she dreaded was the possibility of a fight with guns after this one with fists was settled. Andrew would punish the cowboy terribly and that portended a disastrous end for the duel.

It developed that Texas was a far tougher proposition than Smoky Reed. He was as tall as Andrew, as agile and supple, almost as heavy, and what he lacked in skill he made up in ferocity. He resembled a redheaded whirlwind, swinging, striking, feinting. Many vicious blows were struck. It appeared that Andrew received almost as many as he gave. Blood flowed down both furious faces. In the midst of a lunge Andrew tripped in the sand. Texas, swinging hard, struck him alongside the head, a blow that sent Andrew flat on his back. Like a cat he leaped up just as Texas reached him, meaning to throw himself down upon him. Bonning met the charge by knocking Texas down. Nimbly the cowboy was up and at it again, bleeding, snorting, cursing. They fought all over the place, plowing up the sand.

In the end, the battle went against Texas. He could not cope with his antagonist, who appeared to release more vigor as the fight progressed. Again the cowboy went down. When he got to his feet, more slowly this time warily countering and backing away, Andrew yelled: "Stand up and fight, you range Romeo!"

"Wal, I ain't—no dancin' tenderfoot!" panted Texas, and suddenly he dove to catch Andrew by the legs and trip him up.

They rolled over and over in the sand. Then Martha saw

where the cowboy had made a blunder. Andrew made no effort to rise again. With marvelous ease and swiftness he moved over the ground, breaking Texas' hold, but never letting him go, battering him on head and body. Texas evidently saw his mistake and endeavored to get up, but it was too late. He was being made a toy in the hands of a giant. Martha understood it when she saw Andrew tackle the half-rising cowboy, almost to bury him in the sand. A little more of these football tactics, a few more thumping blows, and Texas lay still, while Andrew got up to brush his clothes, and wipe his bleeding face with a handkerchief.

"Come—take a look—at your rustler friend," called Andrew gruffly.

Martha Ann left the trail, gathering strength as she went, until she reached Texas, who lay, a battered spectacle such as she had never seen.

"Help—me—sit up," he asked faintly.

Martha Ann assisted him to gain a sitting posture, and half supported him.

"Oh, Texas, he has hurt you—terribly," cried Martha, distressed at the sight of the sagging head. Texas' hair and face appeared a mass of sand and blood.

"I—reckon," whispered the cowboy.

"Fetch some water, Andrew," commanded Martha.

"Doggone! What kinda—avalanche struck—around heah?"

"Never mind, Texas. I'll never—never forgive him," sobbed Martha.

Andrew fetched a canteen and, unscrewing the top, poured water on his scarf, which he handed to Martha.

"Tex, you were okay—while you stayed on your feet," said Andrew, breathing heavily. "But you shouldn't have mixed it with me on the ground!"

Martha Ann gave him a fleeting hateful look. "You big bully!" She wiped the blood and sand off the cowboy's face, and her action disclosed sundry bruises and a bleeding nose.

"Wal, I feel kinda shaky, but I can hold a gun. Come on. Bonnin'. Mebbe this won't be—so easy fer you."

Martha fell on her knees beside him. "Don't—don't fight with guns! That would be awful. Texas! He whipped you—but he didn't get off easy." Then she turned to clasp Andrew's knees.

"Let go. Don't do that," cried Andrew harshly.

But she would not let go. She clung to him. "Andrew—An-

155

drew—don't make it any worse! . . . I was to blame. I—I must be just—no good. But I hated you so—for being—so—so wrong about me. . . . For God's sake—give in!"

Andrew gazed down upon her, his face working.

"Bonnin'," spoke up Texas, reaching for Andrew. "If you don't show yellow—I will."

"That's for me to do. I apologize. . . . Texas, you're a good sport. I must be the mad one. . . . Martha, get up," said Andrew huskily, and stooped to help her to her feet.

11

SEPTEMBER CAME with its frosty mornings, its hot hazy days and cool nights, painting the gold and scarlet hues of autumn on the Sweetwater Range.

The willows and cottonwoods along the river stood in colorful contrast with the dark-pooled, white-rippled wandering watercourse. And tiny bits of scarlet shone like fires amid the purple monotony of the plain. Flocks of wild ducks, flying from the north, heralding an early winter, alighted on the wide, still reaches.

Since Andrew's encounter with the rustling cowboy out in the hills, Bligh had refused to allow him to ride alone. Accordingly, Fenner accompanied Andrew on his scouting trips, of which they made several each week, sometimes camping out over night. It did not take long for the old Arizonian to size up the situation. They never got within miles of any cowboys who were not minding their own business. As far as the Antelope Hills were concerned, the Cross Bar, Triangle X, and the Wyoming Cattlemen's Association had set a date in early October for the fall roundup. The smaller outfits, of which Bligh's was the smallest, necessarily had to wait for that event. McCall's Double-X cattle had ranged, or been driven two days' ride around on the south side of the hills.

But Jim and Andrew came upon an increasing number of branding fires, many of which must have been built by perfectly honest cowmen in the pursuit of their work. It was impossible to tell anything about them. On a few occasions, however, they had happened upon cowboys burning brands. These men had complaints of their own. They were losing cows and calves, as they had always lost them, but not in numbers that warranted any procedure such as Bligh's men were engaged in. This was the feature that made the case all but hopeless. What could two riders, one of them crippled and the other inexperienced, do in a big country where they could not find half the N.B. cattle in a month of searching? Nevertheless, up in the canyons, in the rough thickets and rocky fastnesses which they did get into, they came upon enough dead cows to make them sick and furious. These days the sky was black with buzzards and there was no choice of canyons over which the birds of prey hovered.

"Too slick fer us," said Jim one day, as he and Andrew rode the homeward trail. "They must have a lookout with a pair of glasses. He spots us long before we get near the canyons. He tips them off an' they ride somewhere else."

"How much are we losing, Jim?" queried Andrew, gloomily. He used the plural pronoun unconsciously, identifying himself with Bligh and his old stockman.

"Wal, thet's impossible to say. I hate to figger on it. But at least a few calves an' cows a day. Cows daid an' calves branded. Say two hundred dollars' loss every day. An' thet's low."

Andrew cursed through clenched teeth. Between McCall and these rustlers, Bligh would be ruined before the snow fell. There did not appear to be any redress. It was ridiculous to call on the law when Bligh's two riders could not prove anything except the presence of dead cows.

"What's to be done?" queried Andrew.

"Wal, if the worst comes, we'll go to farmin'," replied Fenner, with a sigh.

"Will you tell Bligh?"

"Let's hold off a while yet, Andy. We might ketch this *hombre* Reed, an' if we do we'll make it so damned hot for him thet he'll quit. An' he's runnin' this two-bit rustlin'."

"Will we hale him into court?"

"Hell, no! Thet'd do no good an' jest cost the boss more money. We'll try some old time Arizony medicine on thet *hombre*."

"Jim, let's camp out for a week, hiding all the time. Leave the ranch after dark, so they can't spot us on the way up."

"Not a bad idee. I'll figger it over."

When they rode up out of the river bottom, to pass the corrals and the barn, Jim who was ahead, reined in his mount.

"Look there, Andy," he said, pointing toward Andrew's cabin on the bank. "You shore ain't makin' any hay with Martha Ann these days!"

Andrew did not need to look, but he did. It was Sunday afternoon, and he knew what to expect. One reason why he rode on Sundays as well as on week days was to avoid seeing Martha with her admirers. On this occasion, she was evidently playing tag around his cabin with several boys. Three cars were parked in front of the ranch house. Andrew heard a shriek of gay laughter.

"Andy, damn if I wouldn't do somethin'," said the old Arizonian, doggedly.

"What about, Jim?"

"Wal, if I was you, I'd either fall in with this outfit of youngsters an' play their game, or I'd bust it up."

Andrew dismounted without a reply, and set to unsaddling his horse. For the day, at least, he had been free of the state of mind engendered by Martha Ann Dixon. It came back now. He walked slowly toward his cabin, to find the spacious front porch occupied by Martha and her friends, among whom were Nellie Glemm and her brother Tom, a girl named Bradshaw, whom he had met before, two young fellows whose faces were familiar, and Texas Jack Haynes.

"Hello, Andrew," called Martha, waving. "We've been dancing and picnicking on your front porch. Hope you don't mind!"

"Evening, Martha, and everybody. You're quite welcome, if you don't mind my ablutions."

"Andrew, you're gettin' to be the ridin'est cowpuncher," said Nellie Glemm. "Any old day and Sunday, too. You're missin' a lot, Mister."

"I dare say I am," replied Andrew slowly. He was dog tired, and the bewitching, excited face of Martha, the glad light in her amber eyes, and the smile that she seemed to have for everybody but him kept smoldering in him, a jealousy against which he was powerless. He removed the grime of his long hot ride, and went inside to change his shirt, while the young people kept on with their games.

Presently Martha Ann called through the doorway: "Are you presentable, cowboy? May I come in?"

"I'd hardly shock *you*. Come along," he replied.

She stood framed in the doorway, a perfect picture of joyous youth and beauty. Slowly she entered, and as she did so

158

it seemed to Andrew that she lost something of her radiance.

"Andrew, please don't mind my taking possession of your cabin," she said. "There are some nice old people calling on Uncle. We were being rather noisy, so I brought my company over here."

"Why should I mind, Martha?" he asked.

"I thought—because Texas is here," she replied hurriedly. "Nellie brought him out. I've seen him, of course, since—since . . . He seems to want to be friendly, Andrew. Will you meet him halfway?"

"For your sake?" asked Andrew quickly.

"Be yourself," she retorted, flushing. "Not for mine—or yours. But for *his*."

"Oh, I see. Still on the reform job?"

"Andrew, you'd make an angel curse," she answered, glaring at him. "Forget it. Go out and break some more of his ribs."

"Gosh! Did I mess him up that bad? I'm sorry."

But Martha was hurrying out the front door, evidently on her way to the ranch house. Andrew presented himself on the porch and made himself agreeable. They were pleasant, wholesome young people, and excepting Texas, a little shy in his presence, yet obviously eager to know him better. When the supper bell rang they ran pellmell for the house, leaving him and Texas to follow.

"Jack, I hope you didn't come out to hold me to my word," said Andrew with a smile.

"What aboot?"

"That gun fight we damned near had."

"Aw, I thought better of thet, Bonnin'," drawled Texas. "It'd been oot an' oot murder. I'd had to beat it, leavin' Martha with a wuss name than she's already got."

"Very considerate of you, cowboy," replied Andrew coldly.

"Not at all. An' don't git sore. These range folks have nothin' to do but talk aboot each other. An' the women don't savvy Martha. Why, I heahed they reckoned she was thick with Smoky Reed, an' thet was why you licked him."

"It wasn't. But that's just as well," said Andrew curtly.

"Wal, I don't know. If this panther-eyed kid would behave herself I reckon thet turrible beatin' you gave Smoky would keep other fellars kinda shy. But Martha does the damnedest things anyone ever heahed of."

"What has she done now?" asked Andrew with a groan.

"Wal, it do beat hell. What do you call them night duds girls wear nowadays? Paji-bers, or somethin' like."

"Pajamas. Eastern girls wear them during the day now. They're all the rage for the seashore or for lounging about. Bright colors, very pretty, and modest, too, believe me, compared to former styles."

"Ahuh. Wal, I don't give a damn aboot thet. This heah is Wyomin'. An' when Martha rode Jem Hart's pinto down Main Street the other day when it was crowded—in them flimsy paja-mas—wal, no circus would have beat thet."

"Good Lord!" gasped Andrew.

"She didn't even know Jem. Piled on to his hawse in front of the Glemms', an' jest rode off. She damn near got throwed, too. Thet was what jarred me. I gave Martha fits aboot it, called her good an' plenty. She swore she meant to ride oot of town, instead of down Main Street. You know Glemms' is at the end of town. But the blasted pinto ran off with her."

"How on earth did she come to wear pajamas?" asked Andrew, helplessly.

"Wal, the Glemms had a party an' Martha stayed there all night. They slept late next mawnin' an' when the girls got up, then it happened. The wust of it, for Martha anyhow, was when Jem Hart reckoned thet stunt entitled him to get free with Martha."

"Get free? My God!—What the devil did she do?"

"I didn't see it, wuss luck. But the girls told me thet she slapped Jem so hard he lost his hat. Later I called Jem all I could think of, which was wrong of me, seein' we was in a crowded drug store. 'Cause he yelped murder. He'd had a couple of sodas with a kick in them. 'Ahuh, I'm on to you, Tex. Want to hawg all the pettin' to yorself!' . . . Wal, course I socked him one. He busted a showcase, which cost me fifty bucks. An' now Jem, same as Smoky, is hell-rattlin' agin me an' Martha."

"It can't be helped," said Andrew, as if to himself.

"Nope. I reckon it cain't till some *hombre* kidnaps thet kid, breaks her an' marries her. An' even then I ain't so damned shore."

"Original idea, to say the least," laughed Andrew. "Speaking of breaking—Martha hinted I'd broken a rib for you, Texas. I hope that isn't true."

"It shore was. Busted two ribs. I was laid up fer a week. Doggone, I don't savvy why I ain't gunnin' fer you, Bonnin'.

160

Thet girl has worked a turrible change in me. I kinda like you, dammit."

"Texas, that girl, as you call her, plays hell with *all* men."

"Shore, but only 'cause she's so infernal sweet. Them eyes! My Gawd, did she ever look at you when she was mad? Thet's wuss fer me than when she's jest full of the old Nick. . . . Bonnin', you oughta know you cain't touch thet kid with a ten-foot pole."

"I don't know about that," replied Bonning shortly. "Texas, I like you, too, in spite of myself. But please don't try to kid me."

Texas threw up his hands. "Wal, they're yellin' fer us to come an' get it," he drawled. "Let's eat even if we air in love."

Something about the cowboy's frank and open friendliness shamed Andrew. His first, almost irresistible impulse had been to rush off, forgo his supper, and as he had done many times before, sulk moodily on his porch or out under the stars. But for once he was able to overcome his moodiness and went in to supper. With Texas' example before him, he drove himself to a gaiety and spontaneity of which he had never believed himself capable. His unusual attitude drew from Martha Ann a look of amazement, and then of grateful and pleased attention. Her obvious pleasure spurred Andrew on. After supper he invited them all over to his cabin, and as the night was cool he started a roaring fire in the big open fireplace, around which the company sat in a circle with no other light save the ruddy blaze. They popped corn, and passed from merry badinage to storytelling.

It may not have added to Andrew's enjoyment that when his turn came he was well aware of Texas' close proximity to Martha Ann, and that the cowboy had his arm round her in the shadow. But so well did Bonning have his emotions under control that he did not even appear to notice.

He told a story of a famous football game, during which in reality he had sat on the side lines, but which he now related as if he had actually participated. The bitterness of the memory of his failure in college coupled with a prescience of a deeper failure here in the West lent his tale a vital and compelling interest which held his little audience spellbound. Once, at least, he was aware that he was holding the interest of the amber-eyed girl from Chicago.

"Doggone!" ejaculated Texas, the only one to break the

silence. "Now I savvy why Bonnin' is like a mud turtle full of chain lightnin'."

Only Martha failed to join in the laugh that followed Texas' remark, as her thoughtful eyes were fixed upon the narrator.

Another week went by. Andrew rode the range four days, spent one day in town, and the weekend at the ranch. Looking backward on that Sunday night after the young people had gone, it seemed the hardest week of all since his arrival in Wyoming. The longest, fiercest riding had piled evidence upon evidence without the necessary proofs. In town there had been rumors that he was an upstart Easterner bent upon undermining the good name of certain Wyoming cowmen. Might seemed to be right on that range. Bligh could not pay his bills and Andrew was faced with the problem of a definite decision as to his future action.

On this late Sunday night as he sat smoking before the dying embers of his fire, and watched them glow and fade, two indisputable facts stood out from that eventful day and night in town, and the previous unforgettable weekend at the ranch. Both had to do with Martha Ann. The whole world seemed to revolve around her now.

He realized beyond further doubt that he was caught in the toils of her charm for better or worse, surely the latter. He had watched her for hours on end, when she had not even been aware of his presence. She had improved during her sojourn in Wyoming. Her face now had a clear golden glow, her eyes a wondrous luster, her cheeks a wild-rose flush, her lips an alluring sweetness. But her physical loveliness was only a small part of her charm. It was intangible, impossible to define. He thought of her smile, of her whimsical laugh, of her quaint gestures, and the little graces peculiar only to her. He thought of her sincere interest in all her uncle's troubles; and her voice, her words, the touch of her hands. He thought of her friendliness. He could not deny the evidence of his eyes and ears. She liked everybody. People, just as long as they did not oppose or criticize her, were tremendously interesting to her. Martha Ann gave unstintingly of her time, her self, her friendliness, her liking to anybody who happened along. She could not go on an errand in town, to the post office, anywhere, without scraping acquaintance with someone. She was attracted by anything and everybody that she saw.

She was quick to take the side of anyone maligned, especially if that person was not present.

This gracious side of Martha Ann proved itself to Andrew without her knowledge. But when she knew that he was present, then it seemed that she went out of her way to show the other side of her nature. If possible, she added something to the coquetry with which she had subjugated the youth back at the hotel in Nebraska. At the last dance in town she had been the gayest, wildest creature of a madcap group of girls whom she had inspired. She had verged dangerously close upon the immodest. He had been the miserable witness of her gay, roguish, seductive and resisting struggle with Texas, during which, in the end, she had been soundly kissed on cheek and neck. She ran to be pursued. She denied only to be more desired. She played a game, with that side of her nature, which to Andrew could have only one interpretation.

And it was beginning to interfere with Andrew's work, peace of mind, happiness, hope for the future and his waking and sleeping hours. This be confessed to the dying embers of his fire, as the autumn wind moaned under the eaves of his cabin. It did not make any difference what Martha Dixon was, how many good and bad sides she had, what she did—he was lost, his future as well as his past. His failures in the East had only been steppingstones, but a failure here would be the end of Andrew Bonning. And without Martha Ann, life would not be worth living. That was the decision he made during his lonely vigil that cold, windy autumn night.

The next day Jim took Andrew off on a long ride to the headwaters of a creek, where in deep, dark pools under golden-leaved trees they fished for trout. Fishing was a passion with the old Arizonian, all the more so because of the little opportunity to indulge in it. They found few signs of N.B. cattle, but they had a day that gave the younger man a chance to forget his troubles. The streams, the silence of the lonely hills, the hard ride and the hard fare, the contact with nature that had awakened in him an endurance he had never suspected—these all contributed to a peace of mind which he had not felt for days.

On the way home Jim Fenner rode beside Andrew a long while in silence.

"Son, what's most important jest now?" he queried, at last.

"With whom?"

"Wal, with Bligh, me an' Sue, an' you?"

"I hardly know, Jim. The cattle problem, I should say, because it's our living."

"No, it's thet girl."

"Girl!" echoed Andrew in surprise.

"Shore. Martha. She's upset us plumb bad. Thet ain't nothin' agin Martha. She's jest like a young filly, feelin' her oats. I reckon Gawd Almighty is to blame fer it. It gits me, Andy. You know what the Bible says about a woman: 'Turrible as any army approachin' with banners!' . . . Wal, it is plumb so. I can remember the feelin's I had when I courted Sue over forty years ago. She was only eighteen. An' had a flock of beaus. . . . But to get back to Martha—"

"What are you driving at?" demanded Andrew gruffly.

"Wal, I want to give you a hunch."

"Thanks, old-timer. But judging what it might be from your eloquent preamble, I don't believe I want it."

"Son, thet girl really cares fer you," replied Fenner imperturbably.

"What girl?"

"Martha Ann!"

"Nonsense!"

"She does. I'm shore of it."

"You're loco."

"She watches you when you don't know it. I've seen her. Sue's seen her. We've seen her turn away from the window with the wistfulest look in her eyes."

"Yes. She's got the eyes, old-timer," interposed Andrew. "They'd fool any man, even more—er—an old jackass of a romancer like you."

"All right. I ain't tellin' you any more thet I seen. But take my hunch. She cares for you some way or other."

"You're crazy as a hyena. She hates me because I saw through her from the very first. Because I wouldn't fall for her."

"You was an idgit fer not fallin'. You had a chance to win thet girl. You have one yet, if you don't stay bull haided. What do you care how many fellars air after her—or what she's let them do?"

"What do I care?" repeated Andrew thoughtfully.

"She's wuth carin' fer, an' she needs carin' fer," replied Jim. "If you was half the man I thought you was, you'd take the bull by the horns, an' when you get back to the ranch tonight, you'd go right up to her and tell her how you feel."

164

It was dark when they reached the ranch. Andrew built a fire on his hearth before he washed up for supper. Then as a man plunging toward a precipice, he made for the house. Jim was eating alone in the kitchen, waited upon by Sue. Andrew did not do justice to the good supper, and did not respond to Jim's or Sue's efforts at conversation. Just when he was ready to rise from the table, Martha's fresh, young voice could be heard singing in another room, and Jim kicked him in the leg. Andrew got up, stamped out, and going round to Martha's door, he rapped.

"That you, Uncle?" she replied.

"No."

"Jim?"

"No."

"Oh, it's Texas," cried a tantalizing, laughing voice. "Come in."

"It's Andrew."

"Excuse *me*. What do *you* want?"

"You."

"Indeed. How amazing!"

"Come out here," ordered Andrew.

After an interval the door opened, sending a broad beam of lamplight into the darkness, and exposing Martha, dressed in a pair of brightly flowered pajamas.

"Where are you?" she called.

"Shut the door."

She did so, leaving the step in darkness.

"Say, who was your personal slave this time last—"

He cut her short with one of his swift moves. As he caught her up in his arms, she cried out in protest. He set out for his cabin, carrying her as if she were an infant in his arms.

"Oh-h! Andrew! Put me down!"

He gazed down at the disheveled head in the crook of his elbow, at the big staring eyes, black in the starlight.

"Let me go!" she cried, suddenly beginning to struggle frantically. But when he tightened his arms about her she could scarcely move. Suddenly she ceased and relaxed, limp as an empty sack. "Andrew—what do—you mean?" she faltered.

He made no reply and when he looked down at her again her eyelids hid her eyes. He felt her warm body quivering in his arms. The softness of her, the warmth and fragrance, the

165

appalling sweetness of her worked upon him so powerfully that when he entered his cabin, he dropped his burden on his bunk, and breathing heavily, backed away.

She lay there while he went to the grate to kick the smoldering sticks and put on some fresh ones. After a moment he got his breath back. The blaze brightened, lighting up the room. Martha sat up in a daze, her face white, her eyes large and strange in the firelight.

"Andrew! . . . What in the world has got into you? What are you doing with me?"

He stepped over to look down upon her.

"What do you think?" he demanded, leaning down.

"You look so—so terrible. . . . I know I deserve . . . but you wouldn't—"

"No, I wouldn't—whatever it is you fear," he interrupted her. "I suppose you think I might treat you as you deserve. I wish to God I were beast enough to maul you good and plenty. To teach you that at last you had fallen into the hands of one guy who wasn't nothing but wax in your hands! . . . But I'm not. I'm—"

Then he stopped, unable to continue. The sight of her white, frightened face robbed him of his anger; checked him with the sudden thought that he might have completely misjudged this girl. He stepped back to the fire, kicked the sticks again, then paced to and fro with long, nervous strides, until he had recovered the stern purpose which had driven him to fetch her to his cabin.

"Martha, will you marry me?" he asked.

"Marry you?" she repeated incredulously, staring at him as if she were dreaming.

"Yes. That is why I so unceremoniously packed you over here . . . to ask you to be my wife!"

"Your—wife!" She seemed to undergo a sudden transformation. "Why are you asking me to—to—?"

"I don't blame you for asking that question. It does seem absurd, after my attitude toward you . . . but listen, Martha. I have just lately found myself. I think I must have fallen in love with you that very first night on the road, when I rescued you from the tramps. But I didn't know it. All I thought I knew was what a beautiful, unforgettable, wayward child you were. And because I had been hurt back east, by my own people, by life, by a woman I fancied I loved, I was intolerant and suspicious of your hitchhiking. And out here that feeling increased all the time, while I have grown so jealous that I was about ready to commit murder. While you were slaying these cowboys with your eyes—and your wiles—well, I fell too. And I have fallen for good and all, Martha. My rudeness to you, my indifference, have been simply because I was so desperately hurt by your flirtations that I could not be myself. Jealousy is a terrible thing. But it brought me to a realization of what was wrong. I have known for some time, dear, that I loved you. And it has taken such possession of me that I can think of nothing but that I adore you, I know now what a wonderful person you really are, and I want to marry you."

"Andrew Bonning! You love me like that?" she whispered.

"Yes. But words are futile. Won't you marry me, my darling? . . . Let me prove—"

She moved as if to lift her arms up to him. But then something like a sudden shadow chased the glory from her eyes. Andrew felt all love and hope and bliss trembling in the balance. He saw the quickening of intelligence over emotion—the cold reasoning that inhibited her.

"You ask me to marry you, believing me a hitchhiking, wild girl, tramping the roads in order to meet men—to have adventures—to get kicks?" she queried, low and tense, her anger gathering like a sudden summer storm.

"Please don't think of that any more," entreated Andrew hastily, feeling the ground slip from under him. "Forget what I thought. I will forget it, too."

"Never. And if you are on the level, Andrew Bonning, you will tell me the truth. No man could change so completely or so suddenly."

"I would not lie to you," he said.

"You had nothing but contempt for that hitchhiking venture of mine, didn't you?" she demanded passionately.

"Yes."

"You believed I made it only to get out alone—away from home—from parents and friends—out where I could answer to some wild instinct to be free, to meet strange boys and men—who would never see me again and with whom I could be natural—to flirt, to get a kick out of life, and all the rest of the modern stuff you hate so strangely?"

"Yes, I am afraid I did," he replied, huskily.

"You think it still?"

"Martha, there has not been anything to change it."

"You thought I was a liar, a cheat, a rotten little hussy?"

"Not the last, Martha, I swear it. Just a crazy unthinking kid. You don't know yourself. You've two sides, dear."

"Don't hedge, Andrew. . . . I *know* what you thought. You made it perfectly plain to me. But I'm going to make you confess it . . . to face me with it. You believed me just no good, didn't you?"

"On the contrary I believed there was a great deal of good in you," he parried.

"Well, then—a bad girl?"

"Hardly bad. Wayward, perhaps heedless—"

"I know what you thought then, and what you think still," she interrupted, rising with white face from the bunk.

Andrew reached for her hands, but she put them behind her back.

"You're making it damned hard," he said. "Since you force me—I confess that I thought you had been pretty wild—and yet I hoped you hadn't. You'll have to allow for the thoughts of a man who had been an idler and a failure, which I was when you met me first, an Easterner, fresh from the disillusionment of my sister and my fiancée, who have a free and easy view of life. That side of me took you for the necking, lap-sitting type. But deep in me, at variance with all I had known and experienced, there was a conflicting still small voice, weak enough and pitiful, God knows, that tried to convince me that you were the innocent and gallant girl I love."

"Andrew Bonning, I—I wouldn't marry you if you were the last man on earth," she blazed.

"If you really mean that, then you might have said so at once and spared me this."

"Did you ever spare me? Have you ever spared me any of your scorn and contempt?" she demanded, standing closer to him, with white, angry face uplifted to meet his gaze. "Andrew Bonning, I ran away from home to escape the very things of which you have accused me. I had been driven to sheer disgust by young men who wanted me, by marriage or otherwise. And college men like you had fed me up so sickeningly on love—their kind of love. What did they care for my fears, my needs? . . . So I ran away. Do you imagine if I had wanted *that* kind of kick, I would have had to hitchhike the highways with farmer boys, garage mechanics, traveling men, tourists and what not? No, I wanted to get away from all such rottenness, and with one single exception, I did escape it. I liked most all the boys and men who gave me lifts. I liked *you*, first off, until you froze me with your damned superiority. And that night at the hotel I flirted with a perfectly nice boy just to show you, to play up to your idea of me. To satisfy your morbid distrust of modern girls! And out here I have done that—and more—and worse, for the same and identical reason. Do you imagine I had no pride? I would have died before letting you see my shame, my humiliation. I let those boys hold my hand and clasp my waist—I even let Texas Jack kiss me—I endured contacts repugnant to me for no reason but to foster your vile suspicions. Did I get a kick out of *that*? I'll say I did! But you would never have known if you had not proposed to me tonight. Your offer of marriage squares you with me. It is the best any man can do for a woman. I suspect that you hoped, perhaps, to reform me. But there is nothing to reform, as you shall see from now on. I thank you, Andrew, but I must decline the honor."

"Martha! You're being rather hard on me! How could I ... Don't go! Please!"

"No!" she almost screamed, running across the floor.

"You must care a little—or you—"

"No!" she cried from the doorway.

"Darling!" he beseeched.

"No!" came mockingly from the blackness outside. She was gone. Andrew sank down on the bunk she had shortly vacated. The lovely scent of her still was in the room. The wind moaned under the eaves. The dead leaves on the cottonwood rustled on the roof. And the shadows deepened in the cabin. A familiar specter stalked out of the gloom. It was the stark, gaunt, ghost of another failure. Only this time it was life itself that had failed him.

12

WITH THE COMING of morning, after a few hours of sleep, the new savage spirit that had been lately born in Andrew reasserted itself. This spirit was based on pride. He had humbled himself to tell Martha of his love for her. Now he would put that love forever aside and he would give himself wholly to saving the fortunes of Bligh.

In order to forget he had to have ceaseless, exhausting action in the open, privation to undergo and problems to solve, something to fight physically and alone. With horse and meager fare, Andrew took to the hills.

Boldly he rode into cow camps at the eastern end of the hills where no N.B. stock had yet ranged, and made known his errand.

"You ridin' fer this newcomer, Bligh?" asked an old cattleman.

"Yes."

"I don't see no runnin' iron on your saddle."

"We haven't branded a calf this summer."

"How come?"

"My partner is a cripple and I'm a tenderfoot. There are riders who get to our stock first."

"Ahuh. I see you air packin' guns," returned the other, with a speculative glint in his eye, taking Andrew in from head to foot.

"Yes. And if I catch any cowman burning brands on Bligh's cattle, I'm going to use a gun."

"You the feller who licked Cal Brice an' his outfit at the rodeo?"

"I'm that fellow."

"Is it true that you blamed Reed fer shootin' at you an' licked him fer thet?"

"It is. And here's his trademark on my scalp," returned Andrew, exposing the long red welt.

"Close shave, youngster. What makes you think Reed shot you?"

"I don't think it. I know."

"Wal, thet's short an' sweet. Git down an' come in. Grub is aboot cooked."

Half a dozen cowboys stood and sat around the campfire. A chuck wagon stood nearby. Horses grazed along the grassy flat.

"Boys, this hyar is Bligh's one rider—no old-timer as you can see," announced the cattleman. "Wyomin' hasn't done so well by him, an' some of us ought to be ashamed. He's the feller who busted Cal Brice's outfit. Partic'lar sore at Smoky Reed fer shootin' at him. He's lookin' fer Smoky or any other rider who's appropriatin' N.B. cattle."

They were civil, but not friendly. Andrew ate with them, and absorbed considerable from this first contact with a range outfit. The older man evidently was the boss, and owner of the K-Bar stock.

"Thanks. I'll be rolling along," said Andrew, when he had finished his meal.

"Packin' light," said his host. "You're welcome to a bed with us."

"No, thank you. I'll be hittin' the hay out here some place," replied Andrew as he mounted.

"Hope you don't mind me bein' curious?"

"Not at all."

"Is your crippled pardner a cowman?"

"Old-timer from Arizona."

"Wal, he'll learn the ropes hyar pronto. An' what you want to learn, youngster, is not to take this cattle stealin' too much to heart. So long as the range ain't fenced there'll be some stock missin'. All the cattlemen have the same thing to deal with. An' they just don't notice it."

"But in Bligh's case it can't be overlooked. He's a poor man. He had only a small herd to begin with, and because he can't afford enough cowboys to watch the stock these rustlers are taking advantage of it."

"Thet's different. Tell Bligh to throw in with some other cattleman."

"He can't because he made a deal of that nature with McCall. Then he changed his mind, which made McCall sore. He's taking the case to court."

"McCall? Runs the Double X. Wal, if I was Bligh, I'd buy or trade off."

"I'll tell him. So long."

Several of the cowboys waved. When Andrew had ridden a short distance, one of them called after him. "Work the big draws on the south."

That seemed like a reasonable and friendly gesture. Andrew rode on until sunset overtook him. Then he made camp beside a rocky stream. For half the night he was awake, alternately freezing and replenishing his fire. The still cold, the lonely hills, the white, watching stars calmed his spirit, but were not conducive to sleep. Next day, from daylight until dark, he rode the slopes and draws with which he and Jim had become familiar. The third day took him to the south side of the hills where cattle were more numerous. He saw several riders in the distance but did not come up with them. Late in the day while sitting beside his little campfire he heard the thud of hoofs. Soon a horseman rode up. It was Jim Fenner.

"Howdy, Andrew," he said, as he laboriously dismounted. "Been trackin' you since noon."

"Anything wrong at the ranch?" asked Andrew quickly.

"No more'n usual. Bligh jest mopes around. Martha moons on yore porch. An' Sue keeps agoin'. . . . Run across anythin'?"

"I met the K-Bar outfit. The boss was pretty decent," replied Andrew, and related the circumstance of their meeting.

"Wal, he's right. I tell you, Andy, nobody can see our side of it. We're jest too small potatoes."

"So I've gathered lately. Jim, if I'm ever to be a rancher, is this good training?"

"Best in the world, son. But how'n hell you'll ever make a rancher by stickin' to Bligh, I can't see. We're gonna be awful poor pronto."

Andrew bent over the fire to rake the red embers. "Jim, I had it out with Martha. I packed her over to my cabin and asked her to marry me. She gave me the damnedest acing any fellow ever got."

"What fer?"

"For once believing she was no good."

"Wal, you desarved thet," replied the Arizonian bluntly.

"So it appears," rejoined Andrew. "She declined the honor."

"Ahuh. Wal, she's crazy about you jest the same."

"You crazy old fool!" burst out Andrew derisively.

"Shore. I'm old, anyhow. An' I feel it tonight. . . . Say, would you like some dried beef broiled over them coals, some biscuits an' coffee an' a piece of cake?"

"Jim, my spirit cries 'No!' But my flesh is awful weak."

"Wal, it's a way of the flesh. When I seen you hadn't fetched any camp tools I reckoned I'd better hit yore trail."

"How did you find it out?"

"I didn't. Martha did thet. An' she told me."

"Yeah? . . . What'd she say?"

"Wal, she says, 'Andrew has run away empty-handed from home just to get a kick and because he likes to sulk. I hope he starves to death!' "

"Kindly little soul!" said Andrew with a mirthless laugh. Yet his sore heart warmed even to the sarcastic remembrance. She, too, had been terribly hurt.

"But Martha wrapped up the cake. Andy, I've discovered something pretty damned cute about thet kid."

"Only *something*?" scoffed Andrew.

"Her bark is wuss than her bite. . . . Wal, let's eat. Kick up yore fire. An' fetch some water while I open this pack."

A cheery crackling blaze, a hot meal and a companion drove away Andrew's melancholy thoughts. Fenner, however, did not appear to be in a talkative mood, and soon after the chores were finished he spread his blanket in the thick grass and rolled up in it without even removing his boots. Andrew paced to and fro under the stars. He was not ready yet to talk to Jim and Bligh about a new ranching venture, but he had pretty well made up his mind that he would make them a proposition sooner or later.

Clouds drifted over the sky, and an unusual mildness in the night air presaged a change of weather. The range needed rain. Many of the valleys that ran up into the hills were as dry as bone dust. Cattle had begun to work down toward the river, along which they would range during the winter.

A fine misty rain set in, sending Andrew back to camp. He dragged saddle, blankets and slicker under a thick bushy cedar, and made his bed there. The coyotes were unusually noisy. He lay snug in his covert and listened. The damp wind blew under the cedar across his face, and drops of rain filtered through and pattered down on him. The thin, high cadence of the insects seemed to carry a knell of passing autumn. The snow would soon sweep down this draw and winds would howl through the cedars.

Andrew got snatches of slumber during the night, and happened to be asleep when dawn broke. Jim called him. The morning was raw, dull and cloudy, with a light rain still falling.

"Rustle a fire, son, while I fetch in the hosses," said Jim. "You can strip a lot of bark from under the dry side of the cedars. Never hard to build fires in cedar country. I reckon a cedar is the range man's favorite tree, leastways in high country."

They rode out of the protected draw into the teeth of wind and sleet that were disagreeable to face. The range looked dreary and gray. For ten miles along the south slope cattle were few and far between. They worked two draws together, and then coming to a wide valley they separated, Andrew riding across to the east side. This evidently must be one of the big draws the K-Bar cowboy had told him to investigate. It was unfamiliar to him, being farther to the east than he had ridden until this time. Grass was good in patches, water was running down the gulch, and there was a plentiful sprinkling of cattle of various brands. The N.B. mark appeared conspicuous by its absence.

Andrew rode through cedar groves and thickets of oak, across grassy parks and over rocky areas, up to where the valley narrowed to a canyon box, and travel became rough. He turned back presently and took to Jim's side. Farther down he met a considerable movement of cattle that evidently had been run that day. Fringes of thickets alternated with meadows. Andrew saw some steers running, and then he heard a distant shout. He galloped across a flat and worked through a wooded stretch to emerge into a small park. His quick eye spotted riderless horses, and then two men on foot, close together in a proximity that excited his suspicions. A thin column of smoke rising near the men confirmed Andrew's surmise. At last Jim had rounded up Reed or one of his thieving partners.

They were just outside the rocky timbered cape that jutted out from the north slope. Andrew soon reached them and leaped off his horse. Jim was holding a gun on a man who stood with his hands above his head. Near the smoking fire lay a bound calf, still panting desperately. The rustler had evidently been disturbed in the initial part of his branding procedure, for only one mark was visible upon the red hide of the calf.

"Andy, there was two of them," said Jim. "The other was ridin' a calf down when I busted out of the brush. He rode off. . . . Take this feller's gun."

Andrew located the butt of a weapon protruding from under the man's belt. It had been hidden by his coat.

"Cut the calf loose, an' tie this *hombre's* hands behind his back," ordered Jim.

This order Andrew performed under pressure of excitement that made him clumsy, but he got the job done speedily.

"Rustler, walk ahead of me," curtly commanded Fenner. "I'm gonna introduce you to an old-time Arizony way of treatin' cattle thieves."

Andrew followed them, leading his horse, considerably disturbed by Jim's threat. The Arizonian had a flinty look. He kept punching his gun into the back of the rustler who shrank visibly at each thrust. Jim halted under the largest tree along that wall of timber.

"Bonnin', take yore rope off yore saddle, drop the noose

174

over this gent's head, an' toss the other end over thet branch there."

"My God! Are you going to hang him?" cried Andrew incredulously.

"Shore I am. Rustle now."

"But Jim! You can't be serious. . . . Give the poor devil a good hiding, then let him go."

"Ahuh. To go right back stealin' our stock? Not much! There's two daid cows of ours in thet bush. I seen one, an' I heerd two shots. I'm gonna put a stop to this rustlin' once and fer all."

"To *hang* him! . . . Jim, that's taking the law into our own hands! We'd go up for manslaughter, if not murder. But even if we could get away with it—I couldn't be a party to such—such—"

"You blasted tenderfoot!" yelled Fenner, so fiercely that Andrew stood shocked. "Pitch me yore rope."

Andrew made haste to comply. The man turned deathly pale. He was not young. His haggard face had a bluish cast under the paling skin. He had thin, tobacco-stained lips, a beaked nose, and hard, glinting eyes. Jim made him turn his back, and sheathing the gun, in a twinkling he had done what he had ordered Andrew to do. Then he strode round in front of the rustler and picking up the end of the rope he hauled it taut over the branch.

"If you want to talk, do it pronto," shouted Fenner in a threatening voice.

"I'm a poor man," replied the rustler hoarsely. "Been driven to steal. An' my cattle gets stole, too. Stringin' me up fer—"

"Who's backin' you?"

"Backin' me? Nobody. What d'ye mean?"

"You been hired to rustle?"

"No, sir. I won't hide behind thet. I done my—"

"You lyin' *hombre!* Up you go!"

Fenner hauled on the lasso. The man let out a strangled cry. His head stretched with the knot of the noose biting into his leathery neck. When he had been drawn up until his toes just supported his body Fenner held him there a moment, then slowly relaxed the rope. The man sagged back flat-footed, his mouth gaping, his eyes starting from their sockets.

"How'd you like thet?" demanded Jim.

"Fer—Gawd's sake!" gasped the rustler. "Let me—off—"

"Who hired you to do this dirty work?"

"Nobody. I—mean—"

"Wal, mebbe I can help you remember," interrupted the Arizonian, and with a heave he drew the man higher still, until his shaking limbs appeared to stretch. Jim held him in that position until the man's tongue stuck out, his eyes rolled until only the whites showed and his face turned purple.

"Jim, let him down!" yelled Andrew frantically, charging in to snatch the rope from Fenner's hands. Andrew again let Jim's victim down. He fell to the ground, and was choking when Andrew tore the noose free. The hissing intake of his breath assured Andrew that the man still was able to breathe.

"Spoiled my necktie party," growled Fenner.

"You bloodthirsty Arizonian!" cried Andrew, almost beside himself. "I've a mind to bat you a couple."

The rustler sat up, sweating freely, and rubbing his neck with unsteady hands. Color began to creep back into his ghastly face.

"Boss," he said huskily, "you're on the wrong scent. Nobody's hirin' me. I been stealin' a few calves on my own hook. My name's Hall Pickens."

"Where you live?"

"My homestead is about twenty miles east, in Spring Canyon."

"You a homesteader?"

"Yes. Been hyar four years. Jest proved up on my property."

"You married?"

"Sure. An' got two kids. I've had a tough row to hoe."

"You swear nobody hired you?"

"I'm tellin' you honest."

"Who was the rider with you?"

"I ain't tellin'," replied Pickens.

"Happen to know a cowpuncher named Smoky Reed?"

"Don't recall thet name."

"All right. I could put you in jail fer this day's work. But if you'll agree to lay off N.B. stock from now on, I'll let you off."

"I'll agree to anythin'," returned Pickens gratefully.

"My name's Fenner. An' this is Andy Bonnin'. We ride fer Nick Bligh. He runs the N.B. Have you seen many cattle wearin' thet brand?"

"Good many steers, but mighty few cows."

"Have you been wise to another outfit workin' this cow-killin' game?"

"I been suspicious of some fellers from the Platte River country."

"Humph! None from the Sweetwater?"

"No. Course I know the Cross Bar an' the Wyomin' outfits across the Hills."

"Andy, toss his gun out there in the grass. . . . Pickens, you beat it. An' take a hunch from an old-timer. Fer the sake of yore wife an' kids quit the cow-killin' game."

The homesteader hastened to snatch up his gun and run for his horse. He was soon out of sight.

"You didn't really mean to hang him?" queried Andrew.

"No. I wanted to throw a scare into him an' make him confess he was ridin' fer McCall. But we was barkin' up the wrong tree."

"You had me scared stiff."

"Wal, I've seen many a rustler kick at the air, Andy. . . . I felt kinda sorry fer this *hombre*. Pore as Job's turkey. Did you see his feet? Had a boot on one an' a shoe on the other, both full of holes."

"He looked pretty seedy."

"Reckon you an' me will be scarecrows, too, like him, before long. . . . Andy, let's go home."

"Home!" echoed Andrew, startled.

"Shore. It ain't sense fer us to waste no more time hopin' to ketch Smoky Reed in the act. Probably he's quit fer a spell. Anyway they got about all of our young stock, that's a shore bet."

"When will we know for certain what we have left?"

"After the roundup."

"I hate to quit, Jim."

"We ain't quittin'. We're gonna tackle this game from some other angle. An' I'm damned if I can figger what."

"Okay. Back to the ranch," cried Andrew.

In a sense it seemed to him that Jim's ultimatum was a surrendering to evil forces which they were not strong enough to combat. He gave in only to experience and wisdom. After four hard days and nights with little to eat and no shelter, and the long ride in the face of rain and sleet, wet to the skin, Andrew could not help conjuring up supper at Sue's table, and the comfort of his own open fireplace. Taken all together, his labors at the ranch and his rides in the open during these months had pretty well acquainted him with the life of a cowman. The never-finished manual tasks, the sun and wind and dust, the long rides when the saddle burned, the hours of loneliness, the cold nights sleeping out and the sting of sleet in his face—these physical tests had been welcomed by Andrew, and met, he believed, without discredit to himself. He found in them absolute refuge from the complexes that had tormented him back in the East.

When he rode out of the canyon after Jim, with the hard ice-bitten wind at his back, he hugged something glad and strengthening to his heart. He would make good in the West.

The moment Andrew faced ranchward it all flooded back—the love he had determined to forget—only more tumultuous and demanding after these four harsh days of oblivion. If he had been alone he would have thrown back his head to laugh his scorn to the winds. If the mere thought of seeing Martha again could make his blood surge so madly, how desperately he must love the girl! Just at the thought of seeing her! How could he ever put such a love behind him?

Andrew rode for a long time with his head down, insensible to the wet and the cold. And as he rode home he no longer doubted the strength and depth of his love for Martha Ann Dixon. How tragic that the realization had come too late, that she would never be able to forgive or forget his first mistaken estimate of her character. He was paying for that jealousy-inspired conclusion now—and would continue to pay. Yet Andrew was grateful to the fate that had sent him to Wyoming, though he railed at the bitter thought of finding his salvation in exultant, all-satisfying toil of body only to lose it in the scorn of the girl he loved.

Down off the high slopes Andrew and Jim rode into clearing weather. The gray cloud that hung over the hills did not extend to the river bottom. The sun came out to turn the water and the autumn foliage into silver and gold.

"Jim, do you ever take any stock in dreams?" asked Andrew, riding up to a position beside his comrade.

"No, son, I quit dreamin' long ago. Do you still believe in 'em?"

"No, but I can tell you a dream I had."

"Fire away."

"It was about Bligh's ranch. I dreamed we threw in two thousand head of cattle, best of stock, carefully selected for building a big herd and a successful cattle business. A bunch of fine horses from Colorado. You picked out four Arizona cowmen, the best you knew, steady, sober fellows, neither too young nor too old, to handle the stock. You brought in some Mexican farm hands. We built new barns, new corrals, new pens, fenced the pastures, pumped water for irrigation, planted whatever the soil will grow and all the acreage will stand, bought a tractor and truck, a new car—"

"By gorry, when you dream, you shore dream yourself dizzy," declared Jim heartily, as Andrew paused for breath.

"Chickens, pigs—did I include horses? A brace of good hunting dogs, a fine collie or shepherd, shotguns and rifles, saddles, bridles, chaps, spurs—and, oh hell! a lot more stuff!" Out of the corner of his eye Andrew saw the old range man turn to gaze at him, as though he were beginning to doubt his sanity.

"Oh, hell! Shore. An' you forgot a weddin' ring fer Martha." Andrew landed out of the clouds with a jar.

"No, Jim. I sure didn't dream that," he replied soberly.

"Wal, if you had, I'd said thet was somethin' mighty fine. . . . Andy, I hope you ain't goin' dotty."

"Do I talk dotty?"

"Sorta. You started wal, but you've growed kinda wild. Yore face is red, too. I oughtn't have let you out four nights alone. Andrew, have you got a fever?"

"I guess so, come to think of it."

"Wal, you've ketched cold. Thet sudden change from dry to wet is bad. Sue will have to doctor you up a bit."

"Jim, it's not that kind of a fever."

"What kind then?" asked Fenner anxiously. "Is yore haid burnin'?"

"I'm afraid so."

"An' do you ache?"

"Fierce!"

"Hell! You're gonna be sick. Does thet ache ketch you all over?"

"No. Only in one place. . . . But, Jim, tell me, did that pipe dream I had seem far-fetched and impossible to you?"

"Shore, fer us, wuss luck. If we had a little money, though, it wouldn't be, by thunder! Bligh has a thousand acres—wal, he has if McCall doesn't force him off—finest kind of land thet'll raise most anythin'. Andy, we could develop a great ranch, the prettiest one in Wyomin' an' a plumb good money-maker. . . . Aw hell! After all, dreams only make you sad."

"Jim, this one will come true. I know it."

"Huh?" grunted Jim stupidly.

"I have been kidding you, old-timer," cried Andrew joyfully, finding it impossible to react calmly to the thing he had disclosed. "It has been a dream, ever since I got here. And now it's coming true!"

"Andy! You're out of yore haid!"

"No, Jim. I've figured it all out. I've got the cash. I've got enough for all the things I enumerated. And then some left to run things for a couple of years. . . . Lord, I don't see how I kept it from you so long!"

"You got the cash!" yelped Jim.

"Bet your life I have."

"Whar?"

"Under my cabin. Buried deep. Safe."

"Honest, Andy?"

"Absolutely. On my honor, Jim."

"Gawd Almighty! Andy, I always was leery about you. Don't say you're a bank robber or a politician!"

"Not on your life!"

"Whar did you git it?"

"My mother left me an inheritance, Jim."

"An' you're gonna stake Bligh?"

"Bligh and I will be partners."

"An' me?"

"You'll run the ranch. Foreman isn't a good enough job for you. You'll be superintendent!"

Fenner's face worked. He had halted his horse to confront Andrew. The sun had set and dusk was shadowing the trail.

"So thet—was it!" he finally ejaculated weakly, and nodded his lean old head as if to an invisible interrogator.

"What was?"

"All the time—thet was it!"

"Jim, you're the loco one now."

"Andy, somethin' kept me up," replied the Arizonian in a low voice. "I never seen a more hopeless deal than Bligh's. But I never gave up—not since you an' Martha came. I reckoned mebbe it was her sweetness, her gay bossin' me around an' never lettin' me be false to the hope an' youth of her—an' yore comin'—somethin' about you thet I could never figger."

"Whatever it was, I'm glad."

"Andy, the same thing thet called Martha out here called you," averred Fenner solemnly. "An' we old folks have been waitin'. . . . It'll make a new man of Bligh. Sue will be happy

180

an' thet wonderful girl—thet Martha. . . . Aw! she's gonna break her heart now, an' crawl to you on her knees."

"That's where you're wrong," laughed Andrew. "Jim, you're not to tell Bligh or Sue till we have it all worked out. And the whole deal must be kept absolutely secret from Martha."

"Aw! to keep such good news!"

"Tough, yes. But I demand it. Let her be curious when the cattle and horses drift in. You will buy her the swellest pony in Wyoming. And saddle, and bridle to match. Get me, Jim?"

"I git you. An', by thunder! thet Aladdin geezer never had nothin' on you, Andy. . . . I agree. I swear by you. I'll be dumb. But don't expect me to look down in the mouth while I'm doin' it."

"Look any way you like. It'll be all the more mysterious. . . . Well, here we are at the barn," said Andrew, dismounting with cramped and stiff limbs. "I'm damn near frozen. . . . After supper you come over to my cabin. We'll go over all the plans and settle everything."

After unsaddling and looking to his horse Andrew went with Jim to the kitchen. By this time it was dark, and the yellow lights from the windows of the house were shining a cheery welcome. Jim went in and Andrew followed.

"For the land's sake!" exclaimed Sue. "Of all the bedraggled, dirty-faced punchers I ever seen, you two are the worst."

Andrew bent over the hot stove to warm his red cold hands. The light, the warmth, the steaming kettle and coffee pot, the supper table already set, the familiar fragrance and comfort— these struck Andrew with a stunning realization of how little it took to make a man humble and grateful.

"Andy has had an orful drill, Sue. I had to track him. Whar's the boss an' Martha?"

"Bligh is not so well," replied Sue, and then turned to call Martha.

As she opened the door to enter, Andrew felt a lift of his heart. Had only five days elapsed since he had seen her? A glamorous light appeared to surround her lovely face and golden head. Her eyes showed the marks of weeping, but that did not account for the subtle change Andrew felt. She went to Jim, where he sat beside the stove, and put a hand on his shoulder.

"Howdy," she said, including both in the greeting. Then she took cognizance of their grimy state, and laughed. "Have you been mining coal? You look it!"

"Lass, I've tracked gophers an' badgers in my day, but fer a shore-enough ground hawg Andy takes the cake," drawled Jim.

"How come?" she inquired quickly, and her eyes, dark in that light, swept from Jim to Andrew.

"Martha, what have you been crying about?" asked Andrew.

"Uncle Nick," she replied forlornly.

"Is he ill?"

"He has worried himself sick over this McCall deal."

"Anything developed?"

"McCall is going to force Uncle off the ranch."

"Well! That is bad news. Has he gone to court?"

"Not yet, Uncle says."

Andrew filled a lard pail with hot water from the kettle. "I'll run over and clean up. Don't let Jim eat all the grub," he said as he went out. While Andrew strode across to his cabin, and set about starting a fire his thoughts dwelt on the change in Martha Ann's attitude toward him. Her civility came as a surprise. His return could have meant nothing to her. Probably days ago she had relegated him to the long list of the undesired and discarded. Still there had been something—that same old unsatisfied look. He was glowing still with the delight her loveliness had inspired. He made haste to shave and change. The thrill of the new ranch project already had faded. Had he been nursing that dream, and divulged it to Fenner, solely for Martha Dixon?

Soberly Andrew went out into the dark, empty, windy hall of the night. He found himself strangely happy. There was no reason why he should feel at all hopeful as far as Martha was concerned. Had she not passionately scorned him? Had she not declared that she would not marry him if he were the last man on earth? Had he not accepted this decree? Certainly he had not blamed her. Whence, then, this longing to see her, to be in the same room with her? Would she be glad of his return—that he had come back safely? Would she think him brave, strong, courageous to venture forth to run down the rustlers? Jim would lose no time telling that story. Could he ever be a hero in her sight? Had she realized that she had driven him into the wilds where, like a wounded creature, he could hide and lick his wounds? Had she thought of him at all? In that short walk to the kitchen a hundred longing, questioning thoughts besieged him—to see her again, to hear her, to watch the play of her features for that sweet smile, to catch the light of her eyes. And at the very door he hesitated for fear that she would read him as an open page and laugh him to scorn.

Boldly he went in. Martha Ann was alone in the kitchen.

"Oh, I'm sorry to be so late. Where's Jim?"

"He went out to help Sue. I've kept your supper hot."

"Thank you," said Andrew, and sat down, feeling betrayed again. He did not look up while she placed his supper before him. She brushed against his shoulder and once her hand touched him. How easy it would be to jump up from the table and clasp her in his arms. What an idiot a man could be!

"You don't act hungry," she said presently.

"I am, though," he replied hastily, and fell to.

"Jim told us."

"What?" he mumbled.

"About your catching the rustler red-handed, then letting him off because he had a wife and babies. You would!"

"Yeah. But Jim had as much to do with it as I did."

"Andrew, it was very wrong of you to run off alone, without food or bedding," she went on severely. "Uncle was worried. And Sue scolded Jim roundly just now, as if poor Jim were to blame for your wild-goose chase."

"Ha! Wild-goose chase?"

"Yes! You rode off in a huff, like a little boy who hoped to get hurt, perhaps killed, just to make his—mother feel sorry."

"I had suffered a slight—disappointment," returned Andrew, raising his eyes. She stood by the table gazing down upon him with what seemed to be genuine disapproval.

"But suppose you had?" she retorted, flushing. "That is no reason for you to distress Sue, worry Uncle—and—"

"You?"

"Yes, me. . . . I—I suppose I hate you, Andrew. But that didn't keep me from worrying. . . . Once a young fellow shot himself on my account. . . . Oh, it was horrible." There was now a mischievous glint in Martha Ann's eyes.

"What for?" asked Andrew, fully aware that she was improvising as she went.

"Because I—I wouldn't give him a kiss."

"Did he kill himself?"

"No. But that wasn't his fault. And I felt almost as bad as if he had."

"My sympathy is all with him."

"Don't try to make fun of me, Andrew," she rejoined with

183

asperity. "You're no callow youth. You've had real women sweethearts—"

"I had one and she was—all that's modern rolled into one."

"Connie. I'd like to meet her sometime. . . . But, Andrew, just because I—I do not love you—and *do* hate you—and wouldn't marry you—don't do such a foolish thing like this again. You aren't the type for heroics or for dramatizing yourself! Just to make me sorry! You've probably gotten over your—disappointment already!"

"That's what *you* think!"

"Now I ask you, Andrew," she expostulated. "If you go play-acting this way, with ruin staring us all in the face, running off to starve and be shot at—won't life around this ranch simply be impossible?"

"I'll say it will."

"Then please stop taking such risks."

"May I presume to inquire if *you* wish me to avoid risks?" he queried satirically.

"Yes, you may presume," she flared, and the flush on her face decidedly deepened.

"But why? I cannot conceive of a girl with your peculiar tendencies—"

Just then Jim and Sue entered the room to end an exchange that once more was headed for danger.

13

●

ANDREW BONNING had tackled a man's job—sawing wood. He had a notion to recommend to all college football coaches the unlimited possibilities in a bucksaw as an infallible test of an athlete's stamina. The huge pile of driftwood that Andrew had snaked up from the river bottom showed little inroad for all his labors. It seemed to require hours to reduce one hardwood log to firewood.

As an occasional relief from this back-breaking labor, Andrew packed the sawn billets into his cabin. The long room was too big and the north wall did not keep out the wind. So he decided to stack wood solidly all the way across and up to the roof. This would serve a double purpose, first as a wind break, and secondly to furnish an ample supply of firewood for the winter season soon to come. Already he had learned to love a ruddy blaze in the open fireplace. What that would mean on bitter nights, when the gale howled along the eaves, he could well imagine. He must have a comfortable chair, a bright lamp, and plenty to read. He did not choose to spend all of his leisure hours in moodily staring into the embers.

Several times he had caught glimpses of Martha passing to and fro, on errands too obvious to deceive him, and the last time he had discreetly withdrawn into the cabin. When he went out again, he found her tugging at the bucksaw. She was wearing dungarees, top boots and a white blouse, and with her hair flying, she made a most distracting picture. He watched her, surprised to see that she was strong enough to pull the saw through the hardwood log. The extreme effort she had to put forth showed in the clench of her little brown hands, and the strain and bind of the slender figure. As she tired, the saw moved more slowly.

"Damn!" she ejaculated, giving up, quite out of breath.

"Vain oblations, Martha. You will never make a pioneer woman," said Andrew.

"Who are you to talk?" she replied. "You've been at it for two whole days, yet I can't see that you have accomplished very much."

"Take a look inside."

She did so, only to return and say: "Well, I guess you *have* worked. . . . Looks as if you meant to stay all winter."

"All my life, Martha, if I am big enough to deserve it."

She sat down upon a log and watched him for a while. There plainly was something on her mind.

"Andrew, what has got into Uncle Nick and Jim and Sue the last few days?"

He took care not to meet her questioning eyes and kept on sawing. "Well, it must be the contagion of my indomitable spirit. My nature not to give up. My unquenchable hope. My unabatable faith."

"Honest injun, Andy? Are you really like that?" she asked, momentarily deceived.

"I wish to God I were."

"But Uncle is really much better. He's being almost cheerful. And as for Jim and Sue—they're certainly up to something. I hear them whispering, laughing. Sue is packing a grip for Jim. He's going some place. I asked him, but he put on an innocent air of surprise. What's come over them?"

185

"Come to think of it, I have noticed a tendency to cheerfulness," replied Andrew, resting an elbow on his saw.

"Tendency, my hat! They're happy now, and they weren't a week ago. . . . Andrew, this scarcely applies to you; I can see *you* are still feeling your customary grumpy self."

"Me? Oh, sure. I can't be any other way."

"I could forgive Jim and Sue, but never you," she said darkly.

"Forgive? What on earth for?"

"I don't know. But if there was any tiny little hope for us—and *you* knew about it and kept it from me I—I'd hate you even more than I already do."

"There is always hope for good people."

"Good people don't need hope. It's bad people, like me—and you."

Andrew shook his head and went on sawing. Martha would find out sooner or later. He sawed through the log. Martha picked up the blocks and carried them into the cabin. She remained a considerable while. Upon her return she said: "That's really a lovely big room. If you fixed it up, it'd be simply darling."

"I like it the way it is now."

"But it's so bare. You ought to clean it, stain the logs, hang curtains instead of bony old horns, put in some nice solid furniture and rugs. Oh, I could make it cosy and warm and bright."

"I dare say you could—for some girl. But unfortunately for me there is no girl. I'll make out somehow with my pet squirrels."

"You might send for Connie," she said mischievously, but as he ignored her remarks she went on: "Are the squirrels really pets?"

"Yes. They run over my bed."

"Excuse me! I'll bet you have mice and snakes, too. Primitive stuff! You are a kind of a cave man, at that, aren't you Andrew?"

"I believe I reacted to some such instinct once with you. . . . Once was enough."

"Why?"

Andrew declined to answer. The girl was an enigma. Nevertheless, how much better this mood of hers than one of indifference or of hostility! He would not distrust her again, be she as infinitely various as the winds. He was beginning to have another and most disturbing suspicion, and it was that this mood of hers was a sincere one.

"Are you going to work all day?" she asked petulantly.

"Certainly I am."

"But you don't get paid for it. . . . I should think you'd want to loaf a little."

"Work is my one salvation."

"Oh! you confess then to being a sinner? . . . Gives me a kind of sisterly regard for you."

"Martha, I never knew what work really was until I got out West. It's great," he said, and spread out his big, strong, brown hands for her to see.

"What kind of work did you do after leaving college?" she asked curiously.

"I tried office work."

"I'll bet you were no shining success."

"Certainly I was a complete failure."

"I worked in an office for almost two years, and went to the university besides," she said casually.

"Indeed? Tell me about it."

"You'd be interested only in the formals, and the boys who were chasing me for dates between times. And there were hardly enough kicks in that to intrigue you."

"Kicks! I wonder where I heard that expression before?"

"This conversation is getting nowhere fast," she said, getting up. "You just saw wood and say nothing—at least nothing intelligent."

"Martha, why all this preamble?"

"Andrew, will you drive me into town?" she asked.

"Can't you go with Jim and Sue?"

"Uncle is going with them. They'll have the car full. Besides, I can't stand Jim's driving."

"Take my car. I guess it'll hold together for another trip."

"You won't drive me, even when I ask you as a favor?"

"But I have so much work to do. The ranch ought not be left completely alone. And—"

"Please, Andrew?"

"Well, all right, if you insist."

"Thanks," she cried eagerly. "The Earnshaw girls are giving a party tonight and I'd like to go. They're nice. . . . Will you take me, Andrew?"

Taken quite by surprise, he dropped the bucksaw, and while stooping to recover it he asked: "Why do you ask me—

when you've a dozen admirers who would jump at the chance?"

"They've overdone the jumping, Andy," she returned, averting her eyes. "Same as I overdid—my fun. . . . I don't see why you and I can't be friends. Platonic friends, you know."

"There is no such thing as Platonic friendship. . . . Besides you are forgetting that you hate me."

"I—I don't exactly hate you now, Andrew. Of course, I don't love you—but—"

"Listen. Will you please stop harping on that? I *know* you don't love me. You told me. And once was enough."

"All right. All right. But, will you take me?" she pleaded, coming close to him.

"Very well, Martha, I'll be glad to escort you if you really want me to. When do you wish to go into town?"

"Right away," she said, glad-eyed and eager again. "Andrew, you're really awfully nice. You're so dependable. I was rather afraid to ask you. I wish you—you—that you could look on me as a—a sister. Then it'd be so—so nice to have a—a brother to ask favors of, without his wanting to marry me or something for my pains."

"Well, Martha Ann, even though I can't qualify as a brother, I can try to be agreeable."

"Oh, Andy, I'm truly sorry I can't love you the way you want me to," she said, and her voice sounded sad. Then she stopped. "There I go again. I'm the limit! But it's all the fault of you men. You never seem satisfied just to be friends. . . . I'll rustle and get ready while you get out of those overalls. I've a new dress, a lovely blue. Bought the goods and made it myself. Out of the money you paid me back! . . . But I'll have to shop a little today. You can pick me up at the Glemms' before supper. I don't want to stay there. You can take me to that Mexican café where they have such delicious fried chicken. Then we'll go to the movies—there's a Western—and after that I can dress for the party. Is that all right?"

"I am entirely at your disposal," he replied, with an exaggerated bow.

"Still you're not smiling. Won't you get even a little kick out of it, Andy?"

"I suppose I will. Another jealous kick under the slats."

"Andrew Bonning, if you love me—as you swear you do—and if you are *with* me you ought to make an effort to be

188

appy whatever I am, do, feel or say," she announced regally, ith her head held high.

"My back's too stiff, or I'd get down and kiss your feet," e retorted. "I'm sure you're razzing me. . . . The funny thing, artha, is that I shall be glad to be with you—whatever you e, do, feel or say." She saw that he was quite in earnest.

"Funny?" she asked with a doubtful smile, and suddenly ached out and gently touched his arm. "I love it when you're nny." Then she ran toward the house, calling: "Rustle now. et out your old bus."

As it turned out, if either Martha or Andrew had had ex-ectations of anything romantic taking place on the ride into wn, they were disappointed. For the rancher, at the last inute, elected to ride with them, which meant that what was have been a twosome laden with all sorts of possibilities ecame a sedate threesome.

Not improbably this bore upon the young lady's mind, for ter a while she stopped babbling and fell pensive.

"Andrew, let me drive," she begged after they had gone a ort distance. And once seated at the wheel she sped up the cient car until Mr. Bligh first cautioned and then impor-ned her to slow down. As for the vehicle's owner, he did ot care how fast she drove; if they skidded over the bank in- the river or wrapped the machine around a tree, at least he ould be with her. To such a sad pass had love reduced him!

"I'll get out at the Glemms'," said Martha Ann, as they tered town. The car drew up in front of the Glemms' and e gathered up a large parcel, her bag and hat, and received r jacket from Andrew. As she stepped down, she gave him e of those quick nods of her head which were always so sconcerting. "You'll come for me about five?" she asked seriously as if it were of very great importance to her.

"Okay. Unless I get pinched by my friend Slade," replied ndrew.

"If you have to punish another of my admirers, won't you ease wait till tomorrow?" taunted Martha Ann.

"Miss Dixon, if I *have* to lick someone, it will be the first rson wearing pants that I see with you," he retorted.

"Andrew, you and Martha seem to be speaking to each her, at least," remarked Bligh, drily.

"Yes. It's encouraging. . . . Where shall I drop you, boss?"

"Wal, I want to see Jim before I look up anybody, especially McCall. . . . Jim has got me all haywire with his hints and hunches."

"Me, too. Has he given you any facts?"

"No, except that he is goin' to Arizona in the hopes of raisin' money for me. I didn't take him too seriously at first But I can see that he's got somethin' up his sleeve."

"I'll say he has. Trust him, Mr. Bligh. And no matter wha McCall has up *his* sleeve, you discount it. I want to be witl you today when you meet him."

They went up one side of the street and down the other at length locating Fenner on the outskirts of town near th stockyards. He was talking to a Westerner named Stanley whom Andrew knew by sight. Stanley was proprietor of a shady poolroom and rooming quarters for cowboys. He also ran a feed store and livery stable in connection with a larg corral.

"Fenner, I can have the pick of them hosses hyar in ter days," Stanley was saying, as Bonning followed Bligh out o the car.

"Jim, are you hoss-tradin'?" queried Bligh with a laugh "Give me a minute. Then I'll run along an' you can—"

"Hell!" ejaculated Fenner, looking with sharp eyes beyon Bligh. "McCall! An' it's a safe bet he's run you down."

Andrew wheeled to see Sheriff Slade and a short wide shouldered, large-headed man get out of a car. Andrew woul not have recognized in the smug, coarse features the McCa he had spied upon that memorable night of his arrival in thi town.

"Howdy, Bligh. Was on my way out to your ranch whe someone said you had come in," spoke up McCall sharpl

"How'd do," returned the rancher curtly, and nodded t the sheriff. "Just as well, I was on my way to see you."

"Good. We'll settle this dead pronto," said McCall, his ligh steely eyes glinting. "Come into Stan's place here, where w can be alone."

"Right here will do. An' I'm not talkin' any more busines without a witness on my side. Fenner's my foreman, an' thi is Andrew Bonnin'."

"All right," snarled McCall. "Are you goin' to settle?"

"Not on the terms you stated."

"There ain't any other terms."

"Then we're stuck," replied Bligh stubbornly, spreading h hands.

At this juncture Andrew heard a jingling, slow step behind him and felt a slap on the back. Texas Jack had evidently come out of the poolroom to join the group. The cowboy had been drinking, yet he appeared quite sober, but ugly. Face and hair flamed red.

"Howdy, all. I reckon I'll jest have to butt in," he drawled in his cool, slow way. But his usual geniality had given place to a reckless insolence. His piercing, blue eyes fell upon Slade and McCall with unmistakable intent.

"Hyar, puncher, watch yore step or I'll run you in," blusteringly interposed Slade.

"Sheriff, you cain't arrest me for insistin' on my money. Mac owes me plenty an' I'm askin' fer it now. Heah's witnesses."

Andrew could see in a flash that a startling revelation was about to ensue which could mean a change in the fortunes of everyone present. Texas had chosen an opportune moment for himself as well as for Bligh. Fenner's nudge alerted Andrew. McCall eyed the cowboy with exasperation.

"I don't owe you any money, Tex."

"The hell you don't!" shouted the cowboy, moving in a little. He was slow and easy. Slade regarded him uncertainly, but the little rancher manifestly had no doubts about his mastery of the situation.

"Bligh, never mind this drunken puncher. He's looked on redeye till he's red all over. Once more I tax you. Will you settle with me?"

"No. Do your damnedest, McCall," replied Bligh, trembling with anger.

Andrew concluded that it was time to put in his oar, which he imagined might be something of a surprise to the greedy little bargain driver.

"McCall, would you settle for cash?" he interposed calmly.

"I reckon I would. But what's the sense of talkin' cash? Bligh hasn't got two-bits, an' you're only a windy tenderfoot."

Andrew stepped forward and slapped the rancher's face so hard that his head jerked back and his hat fell off.

"Take it slow, McCall," cut in Andrew swiftly. "Don't call names and don't jump to conclusions. I am Bligh's partner."

McCall stepped back, an angry tide of color flooding his face.

"Slade, arrest this feller," he shouted.

"Don't do anything so foolish," cried Andrew in disgust.

"Slade won't arrest me, because I won't stand for it again. He may be your paid henchman, but he's not a complete fool."

The sheriff, who had made a threatening gesture, suddenly checked it when he saw a lightning-swift movement on the part of Andrew. He might have guessed that, before he could get his gun half out, he would be knocked down by a fist whose devastating weight he already had witnessed.

Fenner eased himself into the foreground. "McCall, fer a Westerner, you strike me as shore dumb. You're in a corner."

"You calf-hustlin' Texan!" exploded McCall furiously. "Have you gone an' framed me?"

"Wal, not yet. But I ain't so damned patient, either," drawled the cowboy.

McCall stared at Texas for a moment and then turned to Bonning. "Bonnin', I'll settle with Bligh fer one thousand dollars," he declared.

"You're a highway robber!"

"How much will you pay?" fumed the cattleman.

"Not a plugged dime. What's more, Mister McCall, you won't burn another Double-X brand on one single calf of ours."

That seemed to be like waving a red flag in the face of a bull. Andrew had seen his advantage and meant to push it.

"Mister Easterner, the Double-X outfit is mine. An' thet insinuation comes from this thievin' cowpuncher. To hide his own crooked tracks!"

"You're a liar, McCall," returned Bonning coldly. Several cowboys had collected in front of the poolroom during the altercation. A Mexican and a cattleman had lounged out of the feed store. All these spectators added strength to Bligh's cause. "You know you're a liar. But I can prove it."

"Slade, stop this damned rantin'," cried the irate cattleman.

"Stop it yoreself. It's directed at you," replied the sheriff testily.

"I won't stay hyar an' listen any longer. This Bonnin' has framed somethin' with his low-down redheaded puncher pard.'

McCall waved his arm in passionate finality, and lurched into a stride that would take him away from the scene.

"Mac, better stick it out," warned Stanley.

Andrew leaped to grasp McCall's coat and spin the cattle-

nan around. "Not so fast, McCall. You started this, and
ou'll see it through," he declared firmly.

"Slade, do you hear this fresh tenderfoot threatenin' me?"
houted McCall.

"Sure I'm threatening you. You stand your ground or you'll
neasure your length on it, and damn pronto."

Slade interposed a hand. "I'm advisin' you to hold yore
nosses, Mac," he said hurriedly. "You're on the track of
business, not a fight. An' I'm tellin' you, if this slugger nails
ou one, you'll think a mule had kicked you."

"Lost your nerve, hey, sheriff?" queried McCall in furious
corn. "Bluffed by a redheaded cowpuncher! *He's* the one
ou're 'fraid of. But neither he nor his pard can bluff me. . . .
Now, Bonnin', I'm damn good an' fed up. I'll take a thousand
ollars or take over Bligh's property."

"You'll take a stiff poke in your ugly snoot if you don't
ool off. Who the hell do you think you are? . . . McCall,
ou don't represent this Wyoming community or the law. You
an't scare me. I've got plenty on you."

"So you been hintin'! Wal, spit it out!"

"All right," replied Andrew rapidly, as he glanced around.
Stanley, get this, and you fellows also. . . . McCall, one
ight late in May, you went on foot out of this town. You
net a mounted cowboy on the road, and the two of you left
he road to talk without being seen. But you were seen. You
eaned against a big rock and the cowboy sat his horse close
y you. Somebody saw you, and what's more—heard you."

"Aw, hell! What you givin' me? Some cock an' bull stuff?"
aculated McCall, angrily. But it was noticeable that the red
f his face had faded.

"Somebody heard every damned word you and that cowboy
ttered," continued Andrew. "And *I'm* that somebody. I had
riven my car off the road behind a thicket. I saw you com-
g. There was something sneaky about the way you left the
oad. So I crouched down behind some bushes, not five good
eps from you both and I listened. I heard every word of
at plot. Now how'd you like to have me tell what you and
e cowboy plotted to do in a courtroom?"

"Mistook your man, Bonnin'," replied McCall hoarsely.

"I heard your name. McCall. I saw your face when the
owboy lighted his cigarette. I recognize you now."

"Jest a frame-up to save Bligh," the cattleman muttered.
ut he was looking down.

"No, it's not a frame-up. And if you don't want that story told in court, you lay off Bligh."

"Bonnin', I ain't hankerin' fer lawsuits or gossip no more'n you. I deny thet I was the man you seen. But such talk won't do me no good. I'm willin' to call the deal off."

"Okay, it's off. We'll meet over at the hotel and draw up a little paper to that effect."

"My word is good," growled McCall. He had perceptibly weakened and grown restless toward the end of the interview.

Texas Jack flipped away his cigarette and elbowed Andrew aside to confront the cattleman.

"Mac, yore word ain't wuth a damn!" he drawled. "I been layin' back heah listenin'. An' now I say thet'll be aboot all the fixin' you fellers will do. Yore deal with Bligh is off. But with me you can bet yore sweet life it's on!"

The insolent, cool-voiced cowboy manifestly had the power to infuriate McCall.

"You're responsible for this holdup," he fumed.

"Ump-umm. I ain't responsible fer nothin' nor nobody but myself. Air you gonna fork over my dough?"

"What you aimin' at—blackmail?"

"I ain't above aimin' at you, if you press me, Mac. Come across, you dirty crook!"

"You never rode fer me, Texas Jack. I don't owe you anythin'. You been drinkin'. Your head's muddled."

"Mac, you overlook what kind of a man you're up agin. I'm wise now. You're a hawg, a two-bit greedy cattleman who hires grubline cowpunchers to do his dirty work. . . What're you gonna do aboot all thet Bligh stock we ironed yore Double-X on?"

McCall jerked up as if a galvanized current had coursed up his frame.

"Puncher, I told you I'd have none of your rustlin' deals," he shouted stridently, his thick neck bulging purple. "If you put my brand on Bligh's stock, you did it on your own hook by Gawd!"

"An' you deny you was the man Bonnin' saw meet me the night?" queried the Texan. "You deny he heahed you make *me* thet proposition? I was thet cowboy. I agreed to brand mavericks fer you. I took yore message to a cowboy who'd agree to kill Bligh's cows an' slap yore brand on his calves. . . An' we played yore dirty game. All fer nothin'?"

"You're lyin, Texas. You can't palm your thievin' off on me."

"McCall, you're wuss'n a thief."

"I'll blow your laig off—you lyin' redheaded calf rustler," roared McCall, his right hand going significantly to his hip.

The cowboy's brown hand flashed down and out. Andrew saw the barrel of a gun stuck against McCall's prominent abdomen.

"Don't move!" His voice was cold.

But McCall did move. It might have been mere nervous contraction or a further action to draw. He quivered. His crooked arm straightened. Then came a muffled report. Texas leaped back to cover Slade.

"My—Gawd! He's—bored me!" gasped McCall, his working visage distorting. As his big hands came around to clasp his abdomen, a gun clattered to the ground.

"Gentlemen, I call on you all," said Texas swiftly, "you are witness that he tried to throw his gun on me."

"Yes, we all seen thet, cowboy," replied Jim Fenner.

McCall sagged with blood pouring out between his fat spread fingers. Stanley put an arm around him.

"Help me get him inside. Somebody run for a doctor."

But Stanley had to support the wounded man alone. The other bystanders seemed waiting in horror-stricken immobility for Texas to shoot the sheriff. Certainly that individual seemed to express the same fear himself.

"Slade, thet's exactly what you'll get if you don't lay off me, now an' forever," said Texas, his voice cold and hard. "You represent the law, an' I'd respect thet if you wasn't as low-down as McCall yoreself. You was in with him. Smoky gave you both away. An' you're a bootlegger besides. We can prove it. Figger on thet when you spill yore case agin me."

He backed the sheriff up to the car that McCall had been driving.

"Get in an' make tracks," ordered Texas.

Slade half fell backward into the car, and floundering over the wheel made haste to drive away.

Texas watched him out of sight. "Bligh, pick up thet gun, an' turn it in as evidence," he said, sheathing his own weapon.

"Good God, boy, you've played hob!" ejaculated Andrew, coming out of his trance.

"Wal, it was about time."

Andrew and Fenner followed the cowboy to where he had

his horse haltered. Texas mounted, and began to roll a cigarette. His fingers were steady. The pallor of his face and the magnificent blue of his eyes had not changed.

"You fellers will have better luck now," he said. "Make shore you git them Double-X calves back."

"How many, Tex?" asked Jim huskily.

"Aboot a hundred, mebbe more, I reckon. All on this side of the river, anyway." He gathered up his bridle and looked down upon Andrew with a ghost of his old smile. "Say so long to my lost sweetie fer me!"

Spurring his spirited bay he galloped out beyond the corrals, and headed for the open range.

"Same ole Texas breed," muttered Fenner, as if to himself, wrenching his gaze from the fast disappearing horseman.

"Well," exclaimed Andrew, fighting for a full breath, "how sudden it all was!"

They joined Bligh, and the other shocked spectators of the shooting, in the wide areaway of the feed store. McCall lay on the slanted planking. His pallid, clammy face and closed eyes, his low rattling gasps suggested a speedy, tragic end.

"About gone," said Stanley, rising from his knees. "I reckoned he wouldn't need no doctor."

"What can be done?" queried Bligh.

"Nothin' fer him."

"Isn't there someone to notify?"

"Slade was his only particular friend thet I know of," responded Stanley. "He shore vamoosed quick. Damn close shave for him, I'd say."

"Let's go up town an' see what Slade's figgerin' on," suggested Jim.

They proceeded to the hotel and made inquiries. No one there had heard of the shooting. Nor had it been reported anywhere around town. Finally they went to the sheriff's office.

"Howdy men, has McCall cashed?" Slade queried as they stalked in.

"Reckon so by now. He was goin' fast when we left," replied Fenner.

"Bullheaded fool! I told him not to rile thet cowpuncher. He brought it all on himself."

"Slade, we was witnesses, an' we'd like to know what will be expected of us?"

"Nothin' much thet I can see. Soon as McCall croaks I'll phone the report in to the Casper authorities."

"Ahuh. An' may we ask what yore report will be?"

Slade leaned back in his chair. "As I see it, McCall an' Texas had some dealin's. McCall evidently would not pay money owed. They clashed, an' McCall went fer his gun first. But he was beat to it. Thet's my report, gentlemen. I'll advise against tryin' to catch the cowboy. It couldn't be done. An' I don't see any sense in repeatin' the peculiar circumstances. Do you understand?"

"We shore do, an' agree," replied Fenner. "But here's a stumper. What're we gonna do about them Bligh calves thet Texas an' Smoky Reed stole?"

"It'll be roundup time in two weeks. By then this will be blowed over. I'll probably have to settle up McCall's affairs, as I had dealin's with him. An' I'll see you get all the Double-K stock on this side of the Sweetwater."

Without more ado the three marched out of the sheriff's office. Once around the corner, they halted to face each other.

"What do you know about that?" queried Andrew.

"You could knock me over with a feather," added Bligh.

"Plain as print. Our law-abidin' sheriff is scared stiff," snorted Fenner.

"Jim, our luck has changed. Mr. Bligh, the worst is over," said Andrew feelingly.

"It does seem so. We haven't lost everythin' an' we can begin anew. . . . Jim, you won't need to go off on that mysterious errand."

"Wal, I'm started now, an' I'll jest keep agoin'," replied him cheerfully. "See you both later today. I've gotta talk hosses."

"I forget what I wanted to ask you," said Bligh ponderingly and then as the Arizonian limped away he added: "Never saw Fenner like this before."

"Boss, as soon as I recover from the shock Texas gave us I'll be feeling sort of flighty myself," replied Andrew.

They separated, and Andrew went into a range supply store.

"I want to order a saddle," he said to the proprietor. "It must be a Mexican saddle with silver trimmings, bridle and spurs to match."

"They'll have to come from El Paso. Cost you plenty."

"How long will it take to get them here?"

"Inside of two weeks."

"Okay. I'll pay a deposit. Here are the specifications."

Andrew went out of the store conscious of the strangest emotion—a melancholy gladness following hard on the terrible excitement he had just labored under. He was on his way back to the hotel when he ran into Martha Ann. She was carrying an armful of bundles. Above the armload her flushed face, piquant and sweet, beamed upon him.

"Hello. I've blown my last red cent. . . . Andrew, you're pale! What's happened?"

"Let me pack that truck for you," he replied as he relieved her of most of the load. "Which way are we going?"

"Glemms'. . . . Why do you look so?" she returned very quietly.

"I've had a little shock. It'll be bad for you, too, I fear. Brace yourself a little, Wyoming Mad."

"Uncle!" she cried.

"No. He's okay. It's just—bad news."

"You?"

"Well! If it were? I wouldn't expect you to look like—"

"Andrew, tell me," she insisted.

"Texas Jack shot McCall," replied Andrew. "We met him over here, and during the argument Texas bobbed up from somewhere. To be brief, he took the argument out of our mouths. McCall owed him money. Texas wanted it. They fell into hot talk, believe me. Slade, the sheriff, was with McCall. Then I saw my chance and butted in. I told McCall what I had on him, and that we would not give him a dime. Apparently I scared him, bluffed him. He withdrew his claim on your uncle, and—"

"Oh, Andrew, how perfectly splendid of you!" interrupted Martha Ann. "But this shooting—tell me quick."

"Well, Texas went after McCall again. This time it looked bad. Texas asked McCall what he was going to do about the Bligh calves he had put the Double-X brand on. That precipitated hell. McCall accused Texas of putting up a rustling proposition to him, in fact, tried to lay the guilt on Texas when it was his own. Texas called *him* the thief. McCall, the idiot, tried to draw his gun. Then Texas bored him."

"Is—McCall—dead?"

"By now he is, surely."

"Oh, how dreadful! . . . Did Slade arrest Texas?"

"He did not. I thought for a few moments he'd get it, too. I was so paralyzed I couldn't open my lips to beg Texas not

198

to kill him. But that cowboy was cool and calm as Christmas. He told Slade the plain facts and that he'd get the same if he didn't lay off. Then Texas ordered Slade uptown, and took to his horse and the range."

"He got away?" queried Martha happily.

"I'll say he did. But before he went he gave me a message—"

She turned to catch his arm. Her face was pale and her eyes dilated.

"Andy! You're—implicated? . . . You will be held?" she whispered.

"No, my dear. Don't rush at conclusions," he quickly replied. "It was self-defense. McCall tried to draw. Texas shot him. That's all there was to it. Slade has reasons of his own for not pressing the case. Your uncle is free. He'll get his stock back. It has been a pretty strenuous day for us, but also very rewarding."

"Oh, I—I can well understand. . . . Wait for me—please," she replied, and taking her parcels from him, she hurried into the Glemms' home.

While Andrew waited, he reviewed the girl's reaction to the news. All he succeeded in settling was the absurdity of his own hope. Naturally she would be disturbed for Texas' sake and for her uncle's, but that did not necessarily imply any intimate concern for the cowboy—or for him. Presently Martha came out, still white, with eyes dark with emotion.

"Take me somewhere," she pleaded.

"A ride? No, the movies would be better."

"Yes."

He observed that she clung to the sleeve of his coat and walked close to him, as they headed back to town. For the hundredth time that sense of her simple trust and her wistful youthfulness rushed over Andrew, rousing anew the longing to protect.

"Tell me, Martha. Do you care—very much—for Texas Jack?" he asked earnestly.

"Care? What do you mean?"

"Do you love him?"

"Andrew! Don't be ridiculous. I liked Texas. Who wouldn't like him?"

"Then why do you take this thing so hard?"

"He killed that McCall for our sakes. For mine!"

"Martha, you're being ridiculous now. Please be reasonable. It was an old grudge."

"You be reasonable, too! Texas was a rustler. I caught him in the act. That day, you remember? I promised I'd never betray him if he'd let that be the last time he stole. He gave me his word, and he kept it. I know. . . . One day not long ago I told him how McCall was hounding uncle, and was going to ruin us. . . . Andrew, what do you think that wild Texan said to me?"

"I've no idea, but I'll bet it was something original," replied Andrew.

"He took his cigarette out of his mouth and smiled at me, and in his lazy southern drawl he said: 'Sweetie, look heah. I'm gonna pick a fight with McCall an' shoot the gizzard oot of him!' . . . Those were his exact words. I'll never forget."

"Well! What did you say to that, Martha?"

"I coaxed and scolded. But it was no use. Finally he said: 'Listen, honey. You don't savvy us western *hombres* yet. If you was in love with me, or if there was any hope you ever might be, I'd let McCall off an' go straight. But you don't, darlin'. An' so it's all day with thet graspin' rustler!'"

"Ah! I see through it now," cried Andrew. "Tex could have bluffed McCall. But he forced the issue. Lordy! The crazy loyal, sacrificing idiot! He never thought that his act would make you unhappy. . . . Martha, he sent you a message by me."

"What?"

"'Say so long to my sweetie for me!'"

"'So long'? . . . Good-by forever! That's what he meant. It hurts me a little, Andrew. . . . He was in love with me and I laughed at him." She halted in the center of the sidewalk, to gaze up with tear-wet, tragic eyes at Andrew.

"Come on, dear. Don't cry right here in the middle of the street. Be a good sport, Martha Ann, and try to be on the level, too. You never tried too hard to keep the men from loving you—now did you?"

"I never tried to make but *one* love me," she answered resentfully, turning aside.

"Martha, all women are loved at least once in their lives by one man. Some women are loved by more than one, and some by many. That is your case, Martha. It is because you are beautiful and because you are lovely. You look at a poor sap once—and presto! He is lost. It is nothing you feel or really want."

"Oh, so you have changed your mind about me?" she asked. "I'm not really a flirt, then?"

"I told you before that I had misjudged you."

Inside the theater, after they had found seats in the dimly lighted place, Martha slipped her hand to Andrew's sleeve, and down to touch his wrist with the lightest of fingers, and on and on, until she had her hand in his. It was a cold little hand, and it was trembling. Andrew simply held it and pressed it warmly. If in these childish moods, when she seemed to need father, brother or friend, he would do his best, silently, without making any more blunders. She sat through the whole picture without speaking. When they reached the street, once more the colored lights were blazing along the sidewalk.

"Andrew, I don't want to go to that party tonight," she said.

"I dare say it wouldn't be much fun, considering."

"Please take me to that Mexican café. After supper we'll go home with Sue and Uncle."

The October days came, Indian summer days, hazy, purple, melancholy. A hush lay over the land. Nature seemed quiescent, waiting. Wild ducks lingered over the river; the willow leaves fell yellow and sear, to carpet the ground.

It was Andrew's favorite season. Often during his work he would pause to gaze down the gold-bordered river, out to the gray-bleached range, and on to the white-mantled peaks. And he would realize that the time and place suited him, that loneliness and solitude had claimed him for their own. His range-riding had, for the time being, been abandoned; and his work consisted of the various tasks around the ranch and his cabin that he could lay a hand to.

Andrew missed Jim. The old Arizonian rang true as steel; still in his kindly and persistent mania to throw Andrew and Martha into each other's arms he had kept open a wound that would not heal. A few days after Jim had gone, the long-conceived plan of becoming a rancher and Bligh's partner had begun to lose its zest. All that was left was the satisfaction that the old man had been saved, and therefore that Martha Ann would be happy, too.

The last trip to town had supplied the final revelation that had quieted all his doubts about Martha. He had been wrong about her; and the truth was devastating. Probably Martha Ann had not the slightest idea there had ever been a battle for her soul. But Andrew knew it; and he would have liked to communicate his infinite gladness to this girl's mother. Martha had been deeply involved in her problem to get away, to be free from something like a deadening lichen on her heart, to discover the lure of new places, new faces, to yield to the unsatisfied longing for adventure, to seek and to find she knew not what. But Andrew understood it now, to his sorrow. Without a friend or protector this valiant young woman had set out alone on the highways, trusting in her belief in people, in life, in the future. Freed of her passionate intent to hurt as she had been hurt she had reverted to the gay, wistful, fun-loving, whimsical and curious girl that he in his cynicism and jealousy had failed to understand.

For days after Texas Jack's coup, which had made him an outlaw and had saved Martha's uncle, she was somber-eyed and unhappy, as if she might have been partly responsible for bloodshed and ruin, even though out of that good had come for her. But the spell passed. She was too young to be permanently affected by an act of violence that she had not witnessed. In a short time she was her happy self again. Life was good and she lived it to the full. She had found something she had risked so much to seek. She worked, she played, she sang, she was the life of the ranch. She rode often, but never far from home. She did not go to town, though she was sought and importuned by her friends there. On Sundays the place was overrun by the young people with whom she had become so popular. Her erstwhile severest critic, Andrew, however, could find nothing amiss with her deportment.

As for Andrew, during those pleasant Indian summer days, he found that his old cynicism was gone, and he thanked God for it. It had been love that had burned it to ashes, even though a love that appeared to be unrequited. Nevertheless his gratitude to her was infinite. In the East Andrew's sister and sweetheart had been thorns in his flesh. He had wanted them to be different from their class. They were independent, imperious, demanding, making playthings of men and never to be wholly won. They were victims of the age. But Martha Ann represented another type of womanhood, one that Andrew had not believed existed. There might be—there must be—many, many girls like Martha. He was glad to have found this new American girl, even though, for his own happiness, he had found her too late. Andrew had loved his mother, his sister, many girls, all that was feminine. And though he had lost his one chance of perfect happiness, he had gained the knowledge that girls actually existed who, like Martha, could be free and unspoiled and altogether lovely.

14

"FOR THE LAND'S SAKE!"

Sue's familiar exclamation, that always indicated a real reason for excitement, came trenchantly to Martha Ann's ears.

"Now, Sue, what's come off?" she called.

"Martha, if things don't stop comin' off around here, I'll go plain loco."

"Let me join you in loco land!" cried Martha gleefully, and ran from her room.

Sue had gone out of the kitchen leaving the door open. Martha discovered her in the yard, arms akimbo, gazing spellbound at a boy and a horse. The former did not appear to be anyone so unusual as to cause Sue to react so violently. Martha shifted her gaze to the horse.

"Oh!" she cried out, her eyes lighting up in admiration.

The horse was a mottled buckskin with long black mane and tail, a graceful body, racing limbs and a most beautiful spirited head. There was a halter around his neck which he did not seem to like at all. The boy held it in one hand while with the other he brushed the glossy arched neck.

"Prettiest bit of hossflesh I've seen in ten years," said Sue fervently. "Like the mustangs we used to see in Arizona. Navajo ponies, black as coal, with white manes an' tails. Or Piute pintos with moon eyes! . . . Say, boy, what's the idear fetchin' him heah?"

The lad appeared to be about sixteen, a tanned, ragged youngster whose face was familiar. He smiled at Sue, but did not answer her.

"Whose horse? Why did you bring him here?" cried Martha Ann. "Oh, he's adorable! . . . Whom does he belong to? Where'd he come from?"

"Wind River Valley. Colorado sire. Them Colorado folks breed the bloodinest hosses in the West," replied the lad enthusiastically.

"He's the most beautiful pony in the whole world. Oh, Sue, I never dreamed of such a horse. I'll buy him if I have to pawn all my jewelry. Boy, is he for sale?"

"I reckon not. You see he couldn't have been bought at all 'cept the girl who rode him died, an' her folks couldn't bear to see him around."

"But who owns him now? . . . Sue, I'll have him—if I have to—marry his owner."

"What's his name?" asked the more practical Sue.

"Buckskin."

"Who owns him?" almost shrieked Martha Ann.

"Wal, accordin' to my boss, Stanley, he was bought fer another girl," replied the boy.

"Who? What's he doing out here? Some one of those town girls showing him off—to make me miserable!"

"Name is Martha Ann Dixon."

"Me!" called Martha faintly, and sat down on the kitchen bench.

"For the land's sake! . . . Some of thet Jim Fenner's work. Martha, he was shore actin' queer before he left. . . . Boy, who sent him?"

"My boss, Mr. Stanley."

"An' how come?"

"Wal, all I know is thet Jim Fenner picked Buckskin out of a thousand haid an' sent him by cowboys with some other hosses. Buck arrived yestiddy, an' the saddle this mawnin'. So my boss sent me right out. Buck shore hated bein' led out by an old Ford, but he acted decent. He's shore a dandy pony."

"For—*me?*" gasped Martha, rising with bells ringing in her ears. "Boy, if this is a joke—I'll murder you."

"Fact, Miss. Look heah, yore name's on the tag." He stepped to the car nearby and lifting out a large package wrapped in brown paper he deposited it on the ground before Martha. "There."

"It's my name, all right," cried Martha incredulously. "Oh, dear, I *am* going loco, too. . . . But, Sue, I always believed in fairies. I never stopped playing with dolls. . . . I never grew up. This is a dream and I'm Alice in Wonderland."

"Lass, it 'pears to be true thet Jim sent the mustang an' this package," said Sue. "He's made some kind of a deal or trade. Mebbe gone deep in debt. You was always wantin' a nice hoss so bad. Wal, he's shore done it up brown. . . . Boy, help me open this pack."

Timidly Martha Ann took the halter, and then recalling Jim's advice never to be afraid of a horse she drew closer to Buckskin, her heart in her throat, and put a slow gentle hand on his neck. He threw up his head spiritedly and his fine dark eyes seemed to say: "Well, who are you? And what are you going to do about me?"

He pranced a little, until Martha drew him down, and he trembled under her hands, and finally surrendered to her soft voice and caressing fingers. When at length he rubbed his nose against her, then Martha gave way completely to her rapture. "Oh, you darling horse! Oh, you Buckskin! I adore you!"

"For the land's sake!" ejaculated Sue for the third time. "Martha, look heah! There's been a holdup, or a fire. This is all Mexican stuff, an' the finest ever."

"Oh, Lordy! What is it all?" asked Martha Ann, and gaped helplessly at what appeared to be a pile of shiny black, silver ornamented leather.

"Double-cinch saddle with tapaderos, bridle, spurs. All silver-mounted. An' two Mexican saddle blankets."

"Simply gorgeous! . . . But, Sue—"

"Shore. I'm stumped. Must have cost a lot of money. Finest of Mexican stuff. Been used some, which makes it all the better."

"Where'd he get the money?" faltered Martha Ann.

"Gawd only knows!"

Just then Andrew came striding across the road, his dark eyes alight, a smile on his usually stern face.

"What's doing? . . . Glory! What a pony! . . . And black saddle, bridle. . . . Martha, have you gone back to one of your old tricks?"

"Andrew, don't make fun of me *now*," she wailed. "Is it true? Do you see what I see?"

"Well, I see a wonderful little mustang and the swellest saddle and trappings I ever laid my eyes on."

"Where did Jim get them?"

"Let's look . . . Saddle marked Yaeger, El Paso. Yaeger? He's the most famous saddle maker in the West. . . . So Jim sent these? Well, I'll say that's fine. Martha, I'm tickled for you." His dark eyes shed a warm light upon her and his voice was rich with pleasure.

205

She tried to transfix him with accusing eyes, though at that moment she would have forgiven her worst enemy. "Andrew, did you lend Jim the money?"

"Me! . . . Absolutely not, child! . . . But don't distress yourself with where Jim got these gifts. Be happy with them."

"Happy, when we are so hard up!"

"Martha, to me this seems like a sign of better days to come. Let's take it that way. . . . Go change to your riding togs. I'll saddle the mustang for you."

Martha rushed to her room in a state bordering between tears and rapture. "He was *glad!*" she whispered, as her hands flung things about. "I have never seen him look so glad." And the hot blood flooded her cheeks.

When she emerged from the house presently, Buckskin stood there saddled and bridled, with a bit of the bright saddle blanket showing. For anyone who loved a horse he was perfect.

"Don't stand staring. A horse is for riding," cried Andrew. "I wonder if he'll give you the flying mount. . . . Well, I'm a son of a gun! Martha, he's kneeling for you."

To Martha's amazement and glee, Buckskin bent a knee and let her step into the saddle.

"A horse that'll do that will never pitch. Put him through his paces, Martha."

She rode off into the grassy open pasture. The rest was pure enchantment.

That night, as usual, after dark Martha Ann slipped out of her room, careful not to let Sue or her uncle hear her. A cold wind blew off the range, and she needed her warm coat. The stars were all out, though there was no moon. Keen-eyed and vigilant she crossed the open to the river bank, and glided along the rim in the shadow of the trees. A pale gleam of water shone out of the darkness. The few remaining dead leaves whispered. Wild dogs of the range, as she called the coyotes, were making the welkin ring. For several nights she had been keeping this stealthy vigil, but tonight there seemed a subtle difference, and it must have to do with the happiness Jim Fenner's gift had given her. That glorious ride had left her spent, rapturous. She was too happy, too strangely happy. For days and days Andrew had slowly drawn away, aloof, stern of lip, sad of eye, a lonely young man, a victim of his own pride, and of his firm decision, that if there were to be any change in the impasse between them, she would have to make the first move.

Martha stole like a stalking Indian under the tree whose branches brushed Andrew's cabin. Unseen, making no more sound than a cat, she glided to the wall and felt for the little peephole she had poked through a chink between the logs. The peephole had been made in the tenant's absence. Martha's heart always beat high during this act, her blood raced and her mind whirled between fear and delight. But before undertaking this nightly spying, she had been careful to ascertain just about when she might expect him to be sitting before his fire. So far she had succumbed to this temptation without suffering any embarrassment for her temerity. But trepidation always attended the moment that she glued her eyes to the little peephole. More than once she had doubted the propriety of what she was doing, but—as she certainly meant to marry Andrew eventually it would not matter so terribly—. But that was always as far as she got and she always was hard put to it to stifle a giggle.

Andrew on this occasion sat in his accustomed place, in the light of the fire, his head bowed, his somber, piercing eyes upon the fire. How handsome, how chastened he looked! That bitter cynical line had left his lips. He was greatly mellowed. His face in this unguarded moment seemed infinitely sad. Martha Ann was jealous of the fire. What did he see in those flickering flames? Did the face of that vile Connie shine there, or the fair faces of other women he had known? But Andrew's eyes did not see the fire or the past. Had she but known, it was her own lovely face that he was seeing in those flames.

Martha tore herself away and silently walked through the frosty grass, back to the line of trees, and so across the open to the house and her room. She did not light either her fire or her lamp this night. She did not want to see her face. She knew that she was caught in her own toils. Undressing, she murmured her prayers and hastily got into bed to lie there with wide open eyes. And over again she repeated the same nightly refrain.

Andrew loved her. He was breaking his heart over her. The wrong he had done her in his judgment long had been atoned for. She knew beyond any passionate denial, any scornful needs of her pride and vanity, that he now knew her to be true. He had wanted to marry her believing her untrue to what he held the best in womanhood. And she had hated him for it. She had told him the truth, and from that very moment had recognized her real self.

The shame, the smart, the indignation he had caused her had eased away, as night after night she had witnessed his silently endured pain. But still she had been satisfied. She wanted proof, proof of his misery, of his yearning, of his love. It had been unutterably sweet, this nightly vigil, this intimacy with him in his unguarded hours. The thing had taken a terrible hold on her. She had reproached herself, fought with her conscience, only to go back the next night to watch him brood over his lonely fire.

Martha Ann this last night was certain that she was being a spiteful, revengeful little cat. But she would have her due. And a voice whispered to her conscience, the greater his reward must be. That thought recurring oftener in these days, always filled Martha Ann with shame. She was lost as deeply as Andrew, though she would not face it. She would not have had his courage. The thing which consumed her now, and always denied the still, small voice, or froze the warm sweet tide, was the needful all-satisfying proof of Andrew's worship of her, of his will to renounce what his heart was not ready to renounce. She had to go on. She must watch him again and again, though she flayed herself, she must see more and more how he wanted her. And when the time came when she saw that he would have reached the end of his endurance —then—then—then.

"Then!" Martha whispered into her pillow. That night, as on every other night since she had begun this last mad prank, obeying this imperious need to look upon the forlorn face of the man she loved, she cried herself to sleep.

About noon on the following day Martha Ann was coming from the corral, which she had already visited three times to feel and pat and talk to Buckskin, when she saw a great cloud of dust up along the river road. She halted, nonplused. It could not be a storm for there was no wind. Then a low thunder of trampling hoofs and the bawling of a herd of cattle smote her ears.

"Of all things! Look what's coming," she cried, and mounted like a squirrel to the top bar of the corral fence. There she perched in the thrilled expectation of her first sight of a great range herd after the fall roundup. "Uncle Nick! Sue! Oh, Andy, where are you?"

208

Bligh heard her and ran out into the road, where he threw up his hands in excitement, and stood for a moment as if transfixed. Martha's shout was drowned in the oncoming up-roar. Bligh ran to take refuge in the doorway of the house. Sue appeared from the kitchen to peer about as one bewildered. When she located the moving wall of dust she turned frantically as if to warn Martha. She ran to Bligh, and he pointed to where Martha was sitting astride the high corral fence.

The forefront of that herd appeared to be a mass of red and white cattle, of legs and horns moving through the rolling dust. It was not a stampede, as Martha had imagined, but the steady drive of a great herd, rendered frightful by the roar and bawl, and the cloud of yellow dust that swept onward with them. Like a cataract the left flank spilled over the river bank, the center came on squarely across the wide space comprising road and pasture, and the right, split by the house, sheered off across the range. Soon all the space between the house and Andrew's cabin was filled with bawling moving cattle. There were hundreds, thousands, Martha thought, steers and cows and yearlings and calves, a great herd on its way to the range.

It enveloped the ranch buildings and swallowed them up in the yellow dust pall, and rolled on past Martha Ann, leaving her excited and a little frightened, and choked and blinded by the dust. She kept her seat on the high fence, coughing, fanning herself with her handkerchief. The herd swept on and began to spread out over the range. The dust cloud blew away.

Then Martha Ann espied an odd, high-boarded wagon, drawn by two teams, and flanking the chuck wagon were five dusty riders on dusty tired horses. They dismounted before the house. The wagon stopped. The five men lined up before Mr. Bligh and shook hands. They talked. Bligh made gestures unusual for him. Sue ran in one door and out the other, wringing her apron, like one completely confused. Then Martha was startled to see four of the men turn to look in her direction, and then stalk toward her.

"Good heavens! What can these cowboys want?" she asked herself. "Where's Andrew? . . . Oh, well, let 'em come!"

Something about their leisurely arrogant bowlegged gait roused Martha's ire. They walked as if they knew that she could not help finding them irresistible. In fact they were, only she did not want them to know how she felt. As they approached she observed that they were older than the cowboys she had been accustomed to, a matured, rough, hardbitten quartet. Moreover, they were dust-grimed from long riding. The one on the left was the tallest cowboy Martha had ever seen. He fairly towered over his companions and his sombrero was so huge that it made him look top-heavy. The one on the right was the shortest and oddest-looking cowboy that had ever come into Martha's view. He was so bowlegged that he never could have stopped a pig in a lane!

The pint-sized cowboy removed his sombrero with a sweep, to disclose a round red face, with black streaks of dust and sweat running down it, and the boldest, merriest, most mischievous eyes Martha Ann had ever looked into.

"Mawnin'," he said. "Air you Miss Martha Ann Dixon?"

"I guess I am," replied Martha dubiously.

"Mister Bligh said fer us to interduce ourselves to you," went on the cowboy pompously. "Thet tall member of us Four Musketeers is Tully Sloane."

The tallest cowboy promptly bared his head which was almost minus hair and shone like a polished nut. His face was thin and weathered, like Cordovan leather. He was so tall that his face was on a level with her knee. Martha liked his smile, but did not trust it. He had very clear, gray eyes that appeared to twinkle as he looked up at her.

"Howdy, Miss. I shore am glad to meet you," he drawled, and stuck out a hand as wide as a board.

"Thank you. I return the compliment," replied Martha, and gave over her hand to have it squeezed until she could have screamed.

"An' this hyar is our lady killer an' sport, Cash Tanner," went on the spokesman. And he indicated a handsome floridfaced man of at least forty years, large of frame, with a huge bow-shaped mustache and big ox-like brown eyes under bushy eyebrows.

"Miss Dixon, how do you do," replied this worthy in a deep, cavernous voice. "Don't pay no attention to Bandy. When you get to know me, wal—"

"An', lady, this heah is Sylvester Hay. He's shy—a gurl dodger from Montana," interrupted the short one, this time indicating a slim, superbly built cowboy, the youngest of the four, fair-haired and blue-eyed, with smooth unlined face just now betraying considerable embarrassment. He appeared to choke over his acknowledgment of the introduction. Martha Ann murmured her pleasure.

"An' I'm Bandy Wheelock," concluded the little man, grandiloquently, transfixing her with his merry, impudent eyes.

"Welcome to the ranch! How'do. And now what am I supposed to do?" said Martha Ann, divided between a desire to glare at him and to shout with mirth.

"Wal, fust off we gotta get acquainted," declared Bandy.

"That will be—lovely," replied Martha.

"Lady, air you free?" inquired the deep-voiced one.

"Free! I hope so. What do you mean?"

"Fancy-free an' unattached. 'Cause if you air—"

"Miss Dixon, I ain't perickler," interposed Tully Sloane. "An' I'm gettin' my bid in pronto fer the dance thet's goin' to be give us soon."

"Thank you. I'll consider your invitation," rejoined Martha gravely.

"Wal, he was correct," said Bandy critically, running his bold gaze over Martha and back to her face. "She's the dog-gonedest, purtiest gurl I ever see."

Martha Ann blushed. This was being a little too sincere.

"May I inquire who has been flattering me?"

"Why, Jim, of course."

"Jim? Jim who?"

"Who else but Jim Fenner? He shore had us all het-up over you, Miss Martha."

"Jim Fenner! Do you know him?" cried Martha.

"Wal, I should sniggle we do."

"Where is he?"

"He come with us. Didn't you see him?"

"Where you from?" she asked weakly.

"Arizony. All of us 'cept Syl used to ride fer Jim, when he was foreman of the Hash Knife. But when thet outfit got shot up we scattered. Shore is a happy reunion fer us old-timers."

"*Arizona!*" gasped Martha. "And this—cattle herd?"

"Wal, lady, we regret to state thet this stock ain't from Arizony. Jim picked 'em up down on the Medicine Bow, meanwhiles sendin' fer us to come pronto. We didn't let no dust collect."

"To come pronto?"

"Shore."

"To meet Jim?"

"Wal, Jim is shore some cow wrastler, but he couldn't drive twenty-two hundred haid of cattle alone."

"You drove them here?"

"Lady, them eyes of yorn don't look as if they could ever miss nothin'."

A light began to dawn in Martha Ann's bewildered brain. But for a moment her vocal powers were not equal to her curiosity. With a hand trying to steady her thumping heart she gazed down upon the four, from Bandy to Tully and back again. They stood at ease, warmly regarding her, already in their opinion personally and intimately known to her and happy because of it. Strong odors of dust and toil emanated from their soiled, shiny-leathered persons. The three older men packed guns in their belts.

"Whose cattle—are these?" Martha asked haltingly.

"Our new boss's, of course."

"*Boss!* Jim, you mean?"

"No. Jim's only foreman."

A loud halloo came from the house. Martha looked up to see Jim, her uncle and Sue, standing near the kitchen door. Jim was waving a gloved hand. Something about him seemed charged with importance. His lean brown face shone and his eyes were flashing.

"Lass, how you like our new ootfit?" he called.

Martha Ann leaped off the corral fence and ran over to the house.

"Jim! . . . Jim! . . ." she squealed, almost beside herself with joy. She hugged and kissed him. "Oh! but I'm—glad to see—you!" she panted. "But, what have you—put over—on me?"

"On us, Martha dear," interposed Bligh with strong feeling. He was pale and somewhat agitated. "All a surprise. I never dreamed this was what Jim left for."

"I told you that old fox had an idee," chimed in Sue. She was crying.

Martha Ann gripped the old Arizonian's vest with tight little hands. She shook him. "You've done it now! You deceiving, adorable wretch! . . . Are you a magician or a rustler? . . . Jim, is this herd ours?"

"Shore is, lass," he replied proudly.

"How did you get it?"

"Bought every darn hoof. Fer cash an' cheap. Shore is a bargain."

"Where did you get the money?"

"Andrew Bonnin'. He's gone in pardnership with yore uncle."

"An—drew?" faltered Martha Ann.

"I reckoned Andy would tell you. He wanted to surprise you. But I figgered he couldn't keep it from you."

"He—did. . . . Jim, where did he—get so much money?"

"Wal, he had it."

"All the time—since he's been here?"

"So he says. Lord knows, he's got me buffaloed. Sue swears he's a millionaire jest masqueradin' oot heah."

"So that's where my Buckskin came from?" whispered Martha Ann. "My Mexican saddle—my—"

"Lass, Andy made me promise not to give him away. But I can't lie to you. . . . There he comes now. Pitch into him, Martha."

Andrew came strolling leisurely from his cabin, his hands in his pockets, apparently quite cool and unconcerned over all the hubbub. Martha Ann knew that her eyes were dim with tears, but that could hardly account for a magnified vision of an Andrew Bonning whom she could not face just then.

"Folks, little Martha Ann'd better fade out of the picture—for a spell," she cried, and fled.

15

●

"DARLING MOTHER," wrote Martha Ann. "Since you have forgiven your naughty child I will be dutiful and truthful and tell you all that has happened to her in these last wonderful days.

"I wrote you about receiving the money, that I wasn't so happy, and couldn't think of coming home yet awhile. I hope I thanked you. Anyway I bought the sweetest dress and underthings with that railroad fare. But first I paid my hero's fine and got him out of jail, and then he paid me back.

"If you still love me and if you want me excruciatingly I will come home for the holidays—and bring *him*. You are all going to go loco—dippy, I mean, over my Andrew, and the girls who used to be so catty to me will be green with jealousy, and my old beaus won't ever again try to kiss me at the foot of the stairs in the hall—not after they see Andrew. To see him is enough. You don't have to be told that he was an end on one of the big college football teams.

"Mother, I'm so happy that I'm crying like a baby right now. And you know I never was the weepy kind. Uncle was just about ruined. What with cattle thieves (Oh, Honey, I caught one of them myself, and I *reformed* him, and he— but that's another story) and in a crazy deal Uncle made with a rancher here, he lost nearly everything. I was ready to die. Uncle was down in the depths, like Father got when the bills used to come in. Then something strange happened. Jim Fenner, our man—he's an old Arizonian—left mysteriously for parts unknown, supposedly to try to raise money to save Uncle. Sue, that's Jim's wife and the dearest soul, suddenly perked up, and so did Uncle. Andrew, however, slowly and surely sank to the depths of despair. That was my doing, and had absolutely nothing to do with the ranch problem.

"I began to think that little Martha Ann had been so blue —so love-sick—yes, *love-sick*, herself that she would never be able to understand what was going on. I began to do a tall lot of cogitating. But for once I was on the wrong track.

"One day a boy came along with the most wonderful pony, and the most gorgeous silver-mounted Mexican saddle, bridle, etc. For *me*. I was dazed, then enraptured, then scared. Jim was fond of me, and I feared the old fellow had turned rustler or bank robber just to get me what I had yearned for so long.

"Then on another day along came a great herd of cattle, almost running over our house. They chased me to the top of the corral fence, where I nearly strangled with dust. When the herd passed, four cowpunchers appeared to face me up on my perch. Mother, they were the most thrilling, the toughest, the fiercest, the most enchanting, the funniest human beings I ever saw. At first they had me buffaloed (that means stampeded), and I'm afraid I was sort of upstage. They turned out to be old cronies of Jim Fenner's, when he rode the wild range in Arizona, and they had come with Jim, and had driven that great herd of cattle here for Uncle Nick.

"I was dumbfounded. I was thunderstruck—I was scared stiff. I couldn't understand it. Then Jim showed up to whoop at me. I tumbled off the fence and rushed to him. It all came out then. Jim had really bought the herd and sent for his cowboys—all for Uncle Nick! Andrew had supplied the money —thousands of dollars—and he and Jim had hatched the deal

214

to surprise Uncle Nick and me. They darn near killed me of heart failure.

"Now, Mother, here's where we dig in, and try to get serious.

"I met Andrew Bonning on the night of May 13th at 7:35 on a lonely road. Some tramps had waylaid your not so dutiful daughter and one of them had collared me. I didn't have time to let out a squawk when up comes a Ford, out jumps Big Boy, and wham! that tramp must be falling yet. Well, it was 7:36 when I looked up at my savior and that moment was curtains for Martha Ann. I fell terribly in love with him right on the spot. But I didn't know it then.

"He gave me a lift. He took me for a wild little jayhawker, crazy to hitchhike the lonely roads to get kicks out of meeting men. Oh, Mother! I was sunk—and so mad that I saw red. He dropped me at the next town, and I know he hoped he'd never see me again. But I was crazy to meet him. Well, I did. Worse luck! I was picked up by a nice kid, was having a perfectly lovely time driving his car into a town, when all of a sudden I saw my rescuer. Oh, Mother! His eyes looked daggers at me. They said as plain as print that I had vamped this callow youth. I had a funny feeling around my heart. We met in the dining room. I don't know why I was so—so flip. But he infuriated me. He looked so disappointed in me. Well, for once in my life I flirted. I sure flirted. I can understand now why girls like that line. But it was the only time I can remember that I ever tried deliberately, and I did it to prove to that big handsome prude that I was exactly what he took me to be. All the same, that night I cried myself to sleep.

"I went on my way. I had a wonderful time during all the rest of my hike, except for one horrible experience out of which I kicked myself—literally kicked myself free—the dirty bully—and which right there taught me the error of my innocent hitchhiking ways, and why Andrew was so absolutely right. This is hard to say, Mother honey, and I say it here for the first time, because I'll have to be on the level and say it to Andrew too. There are some things a girl simply cannot do. Spirit and virtue and religion and training—and *nerve* are not enough to see a girl through situations that she should never have gotten into. All this new woman, modern-century stuff is the bunk. Women cannot be as free as men. A girl is restricted—that is, a good girl—by her sex. She has a responsibility a boy does not have. She is the mother of the race, and if the race is to progress instead of retrogress, she has to hold herself more sacred than men do.

"How's that, Muth, for little Martha?"

"Well, imagine! When I got to Randall at last, I found that Uncle Nick had moved way out into western Wyoming. I forgot to tell you that Andrew nicknamed me Wyoming Mad. I hated it—and very consistently ended by loving it. The blow nearly killed Martha. But I went on, and had the marvelous luck to get to Uncle Nick's ranch on the Sweetwater in less than two days, without hiking a step.

"Now brace yourself, old dear. Listen! I've already told about Uncle Nick and the ranch. But not this. I hadn't been there an hour when I ran around a corner of the barn and plump into—Andrew Bonning. Right into his arms, in fact!

"He had become Uncle's hired man, working for his board. No accident! Not chance! It was fate, Mother, and it sure floored me. From that moment on we were at dagger's points. Then came a day when a horse pitched me off and I sprained my ankle. Andrew found me. He was kind, sorry, worried—insisted on helping me. But I was nasty—I didn't want him to carry me in his arms. But he did, and during that ride he kissed me. . . . Oh, dear! It was then that I found out I loved him madly. And that was where I started to backslide. I didn't want *him* to find out. Things went on happening. I met young people; nice folk, wholesome western girls, and some bad cowboys. They all took to me, especially the bad ones. Andrew came to the first dance I attended. That night I saw that he was no Missouri garage hand, as he had tried to palm himself off. He looked what he really is, and he danced my poor heart right out of my bosom. It has never come back.

"You couldn't expect your child to be anywhere without starting trouble. (Mother, I really ought to be married. I'm a menace to society.) It happened. Andrew caught me riding home with the cowboy cattle thief I told you I reformed. They were like a couple of gamecocks. Did they fight over me? Did they? They did. Andrew gave Texas Jack a terrible whipping. And then I had to go on my knees to Andrew to keep him from fighting the cowboy with guns. Another time at a rodeo (that's a cowboy circus) Andrew beat up four cowboys at one time because one of them had insulted me. Also he punched the sheriff on the beezer. Oh, Sir Galahad never had anything on my darling! This was when Andrew got arrested and I had to pay his fine.

216

"I flirted some more, Mother. I let the boys hold my hand, and once I let Texas Jack kiss me. If I had known then what I know now, I'd have let him hug me, too. All this when Andrew was in sight! To torture him! Because I knew by then how much he cared for me. All the same, Mother, despite my mad temptation to bring that proud boy to his knees, I did not lose my head over the other boys.

"At last my hour came. One night after supper Andrew called me out—and he—well, never mind what, except that he told me in as beautiful and manly and humble a way as any girl could ask, that he loved me, that despite disapproving of me he worshipped me, and he begged me to marry him.

"How I ever kept myself out of his arms, I have no idea. But I was a demon. I made him confess that he had thought me a vamp, a flirt, a necker, a—oh, almost everything that was bad—that he still thought so and would marry me in spite of it. To reform me! I told him honestly what I was and am. Poor Andrew, that was a tough night for him. I thanked him for the honor and said I wouldn't marry him if he were the last man on earth. Like some royal lady I stalked away. But when I got in bed in the dark I thought I would die.

"That ended my play with the young fellows, and it was a relief, believe me. Since Andrew found out his blunder he has gradually gone downhill. I had my revenge. Little-souled as it seems of me it was sweet. Because, oh, how he had hurt me! And oh, how I loved him! I watched him. I gloated over his misery. I saw his heart breaking inch by inch. And all this while I worked, played, sang, made merry—I was a perfect angel. Mother, there is a sadistic streak in all women.

"Then came the unexpected—the thing that devastated me —that makes this letter to you possible—that bends the knees and bows the head of little Martha Ann. Andrew sent me that adorable pony—that magnificent saddle. But I was supposed never to know that they came from him. Only Jim could not keep the secret. Ah! but that old boy is a matchmaker!

"That was sweet of Andrew. But the noble thing, the great deed was for him to save Uncle Nick and back him in a cattle deal that in this country is far from being a sure success. Jim and Sue imagine Andrew is a millionaire in disguise. I don't. I take him to be a boy of fine family, who came west for much the same reason as I. He had told me he had a little money. He never said how much, and of course I never dreamed that it was enough to save us and start us anew. Evidently it was.

"That's my tale, Martha Dixon, as Uncle Nick calls you. The sequel is on the knees of the gods. I have yet to crawl to Andrew, to confess I loved him all the time—that when I swore I hated him I was a liar. Telling him will give me the greatest kick of all my life. This letter is my preparation.

"It would serve me right if he scorned me. I have a cold, sick feeling at the bottom of my heart when I think of it. But he, too, has found himself in this wonderful country. He could not change. He would not hate. He can only love.

"And so I dare to hope. I pray I do not hope in vain. You may be assured, dearest, best, most loving, long-suffering Mother, of your unworthy daughter's happiness—and through that the promise that she will be worthy. I will write again as soon as my fate is decided. But lest you distress yourself anew I give you my word here that I shall come home with Andrew for Christmas.

MARTHA ANN

"P.S. I think I'll steal unawares upon Andrew, when he is brooding before his fire, and slip in quietly and up behind him. Maybe I will plump right down in his lap. (I'll be pretty weak in the knees by then.) Maybe I won't have to, because if he is any good on earth he'll grab me.

M. A."

The night was dark and cool, with stars obscured, and a misty rain beating out of the north. Out there the open range gloomed like a vast windy hall, from whence came the bawling of cattle and the wailing of coyotes.

Martha Ann ran with light feet and lighter heart. Her hour had struck. It had been propelled by the long letter to her mother, and precipitated by Uncle Nick's startling news that Andrew thought he would go to California for a while. Never would Andrew Bonning leave for California without Martha Ann! She meant to make sure of that tonight.

A flickering light shone out of his window upon the bare boughs of the trees.

Martha Ann felt eager, cool, brave, happy to capitulate at last. But when she saw Andrew through the tiny aperture between the logs, all but her love deserted her. He was dozing in his chair, and with the mask off, his face appeared terrifyingly tragic and sorrowful. She had gone too far. Always too little or too much—she knew no happy medium! Was it too late? She must not lose another moment.

She drew back trembling. The cloak dropped from her head. She felt the cool rain drops upon her burning face.

Like a shadow she crept onto the porch and tiptoed to the door. It was slightly ajar. She stood there, fighting for breath, in the grip of a strong sweet happiness that slowly replaced her terror. Her fingers shook when she flipped them inside the door. She opened it a little and glided in. The room was in shadow except for a ruddy circle before the forgotten fire. She smelled the pungent wood smoke. Andrew's dark head showed above the back of his chair. He stirred.

That broke the strain under which Martha Ann had labored. A shuddering gladness engulfed her. She had not lacked courage or strength, but she had not bargained for a failure of her heart, her breath, her thought, her sight.

She crept to the chair, laid a supporting hold upon it. She moved around beside him. Into his half-closed eyes came some change of perception, as if he were dreaming a dream. Martha Ann slid over the arm of the chair upon his lap, and as he started violently, she put an arm around his neck and hid her face from him. She felt him touch her, lightly, then with a hungry convulsive clasp.

"My God! . . . This is no dream," he cried hoarsely.

"No—Andy. . . . You wouldn't think so—if you'd had to do it," she replied quickly.

"*Martha Ann!*"

"Yes. I hope you were not dreaming of Connie."

"What? . . . Oh, you would! . . . Martha, you have come to thank me. Please don't! Don't!" he begged.

"I haven't come for anything of the sort," she retorted.

He plied her with incoherent queries, all the time trying to raise her to the arm of the chair. But Martha Ann clung to him all the tighter.

"Listen, tenderfoot. Don't ask questions."

"Good Heavens! Are you mad? Wyoming Mad! . . . What does this last mad prank mean?"

"What does this—mean?" and she kissed him on the cheek. He sank back. All his rigidity left him. His hands fell limp to the arms of the chair. She felt a vast heave of his broad breast and she heard a thumping there.

"Martha, have you no heart—no conscience? . . . After all, are you only—"

She stopped that question with her lips.

"Andy, every time you try to question me I'll do that. . . . I have anticipated all your questions. I will answer them."

She felt safe now. He could not see her face. She slipped her other arm around his neck.

"First. No, I have not come to torment you. Yes, I am terribly sorry I could not do this long before. No, I would not lie to you to gain the whole world. . . . Did I want a little revenge? I did. To my shame I confess it. I did—"

"For mercy's sake! Martha, do you love—"

"There! . . . I—I warned you," she went on shakily. The fire of his eyes—the response to her kiss had wrought their transformation in her. But she would see it through. "Yes. I do—love you! . . . Since thirty-six minutes after seven, on May thirteenth, I have loved you. First unwittingly. Then hopelessly. Then furiously. Then angrily. Then horribly. . . . And now, deathlessly, with all my heart and soul!"

"Oh, amber-eyes, my darling! . . . Are you just a wraith? Are you just that golden phantom I've been chasing—and trying to clasp—only to fail and fall and weep—"

"Again!" she interrupted, to close her eyes and find his lips. "Oh! . . . I begin to doubt you. . . . All you want are kisses. . . . No, Andy, I am flesh and blood. Yours. . . . Yes, I—I will marry you. And be the happiest, luckiest girl. . . . Yes, I deserved your censure for my hitchhiking madness. It was a wild, desperate, perilous stunt. But I am glad, glad, glad. For it took me to you."

"Wyoming Mad! You *do* love me after all—you *will* marry me?" he cried rapturously.

"Once more! . . . I might just as well keep my lips close to yours!"

"When?" he whispered.

"When what?"

"When will you marry me?"

"Andy, this *is* the last. . . . Oh, but I'm a little liar! How I have yearned to kiss you—to have you hold me like this! Don't imagine that you suffered alone, Andrew Bonning. That Connie dame. . . . When? When will I—oh, tomorrow—or next day—or next week—any day—if you do not put it off too long—and promise to take me home for Christmas—and never misjudge me again for being Wyoming Mad!"